ISBN 978-1-330-69685-9
PIBN 10093658

This book is a reproduction of an important historical work. Forgotten Books uses state-of-the-art technology to digitally reconstruct the work, preserving the original format whilst repairing imperfections present in the aged copy. In rare cases, an imperfection in the original, such as a blemish or missing page, may be replicated in our edition. We do, however, repair the vast majority of imperfections successfully; any imperfections that remain are intentionally left to preserve the state of such historical works.

1 MONTH OF
FREE
READING

at

www.ForgottenBooks.com

By purchasing this book you are eligible for one month membership to ForgottenBooks.com, giving you unlimited access to our entire collection of over 700,000 titles via our web site and mobile apps.

To claim your free month visit:

www.forgottenbooks.com/free93658

English
Français
Deutsche
Italiano
Español
Português

www.forgottenbooks.com

Mythology Photography **Fiction**
Fishing Christianity **Art** Cooking
Essays Buddhism Freemasonry
Medicine **Biology** Music **Ancient**
Egypt Evolution Carpentry Physics
Dance Geology **Mathematics** Fitness
Shakespeare **Folklore** Yoga Marketing
Confidence Immortality Biographies
Poetry **Psychology** Witchcraft
Electronics Chemistry History **Law**
Accounting **Philosophy** Anthropology
Alchemy Drama Quantum Mechanics
Atheism Sexual Health **Ancient History**
Entrepreneurship Languages Sport
Paleontology Needlework Islam
Metaphysics Investment Archaeology
Parenting Statistics Criminology
Motivational

Édition de Luxe

BEY..NE

BY

CHARLES DICKENS

VOL. II.

WITH ILLUSTRATIONS BY H. K. BROWNE.

BOSTON:
ESTES & LAU...
1890.

TYPOGRAPHY AND ELECTROTYPING BY C. J. PETERS & SON. PRINTED AT THE ESTES PRESS, BY BERWICK & SMITH, BOSTON, U.S.A.

CONTENTS.

VOL. II.

LIST OF ILLUSTRATIONS.

VOL. II.

DOMBEY AND SON.

CHAPTER I.

NEW FACES.

THE major, more blue-faced and staring — more over-ripe, as it were, than ever — and giving vent, every now and then, to one of the horse's coughs, not so much of necessity as in a spontaneous explosion of importance, walked arm in arm with Mr. Dombey up the sunny side of the way, with his cheeks swelling over his tight stock, his legs majestically wide apart, and his great head wagging from side to side, as if he were remonstrating within himself for being such a captivating object. They had not walked many yards before the major encountered somebody he knew, nor many yards farther before the major encountered somebody else he knew, but he merely shook his fingers at them as he passed, and led Mr. Dombey on: pointing out the localities as they went, and enlivening the walk with any current scandal suggested by them.

In this manner the major and Mr. Dombey were walking arm in arm, much to their own satisfaction, when they beheld advancing towards them a wheeled chair, in which a lady was seated, indolently steering her carriage by a kind of rudder in front, while it was propelled by some unseen power in the rear. Although the lady was not young, she was very blooming in the face — quite rosy — and her dress and attitude were perfectly juvenile. Walking by the side of the chair, and carrying her gossamer parasol with a proud and weary air, as if so great an effort must be soon abandoned, and the parasol dropped, sauntered a much younger lady, very handsome, very haughty, very wilful, who tossed her head and drooped her eyelids, as though, if there were anything in all the world worth looking into, save a mirror, it certainly was not the earth or sky.

"Why, what the devil have we here, sir?" cried the major, stopping as this little cavalcade drew near.

"My dearest Edith!" drawled the lady in the chair, "Major Bagstock!"

The major no sooner heard the voice than he relinquished Mr. Dombey's arm, darted forward, took the hand of the lady in the chair, and pressed it to his lips. With no less gallantry the major folded both his gloves upon his heart, and bowed low to the other lady. And now, the chair having stopped, the motive power became visible in the shape of a flushed page pushing behind, who seemed to have in part outgrown and in part outpushed his strength, for when he stood upright he was tall, and wan, and thin, and his plight appeared the more forlorn from his having injured the shape of his hat, by butting at the carriage with his head to urge it forward, as is sometimes done by elephants in Oriental countries.

"Joe Bagstock," said the major to both ladies, "is a proud and happy man for the rest of his life."

"You false creature!" said the old lady in the chair insipidly. "Where do you come from? I can't bear you."

"Then suffer old Joe to present a friend, ma'am," said the major promptly, "as a reason for being tolerated. Mr. Dombey, Mrs. Skewton." The lady in the chair was gracious. "Mr. Dombey, Mrs. Granger." The lady with the parasol was faintly conscious of Mr. Dombey's taking off his hat, and bowing low. "I am delighted, sir," said the major, "to have this opportunity."

The major seemed in earnest, for he looked at all the three, and leered in his ugliest manner.

"Mrs. Skewton, Dombey," said the major, "makes havoc in the heart of old Josh."

Mr. Dombey signified that he didn't wonder at it.

"You perfidious goblin," said the lady in the chair, "I have done! How long have you been here, bad man?"

"One day," replied the major.

"And can you be a day, or even a minute," returned the lady, slightly settling her false curls and false eyebrows with her fan, and showing her false teeth, set off by her false complexion, "in the garden of what's-its-name —"

"Eden, I suppose, mamma," interrupted the younger lady scornfully.

"My dear Edith," said the other, "I cannot help it. I never can remember those frightful names — without having your whole soul and being inspired by the sight of Nature; by the perfume," said Mrs. Skewton, rustling a handkerchief that was faint and sickly with essences, "of her artless breath, you creature?"

The discrepancy between Mrs. Skewton's fresh enthusiasm of words and forlornly faded manner was hardly less observable than that between her age, which was about seventy, and her dress, which would have been youthful for twenty-seven. Her attitude in the wheeled chair (which she never varied) was one in which she had been taken in a barouche, some fifty years before, by a then fashionable artist, who had appended to his published sketch the name of Cleopatra: in consequence of a discovery made by the critics of the time, that it bore an exact resemblance to that princess as she reclined on board her galley. Mrs. Skewton was a beauty then, and bucks threw wine-glasses over their heads by dozens in her honor. The beauty and the barouche had both passed away, but she still preserved the attitude, and, for this reason expressly, maintained the wheeled chair and the butting page: there being nothing whatever, except the attitude, to prevent her from walking.

"Mr. Dombey is devoted to Nature, I trust?" said Mrs. Skewton, settling her diamond brooch. And by the way, she chiefly lived upon the reputation of some diamonds, and her family connections.

"My friend Dombey, ma'am," returned the major, "may be devoted to her in secret, but a man who is paramount in the greatest city in the universe —"

"No one can be a stranger," said Mrs. Skewton, "to Mr. Dombey's immense influence."

As Mr. Dombey acknowledged the compliment with a bend of his head, the younger lady, glancing at him, met his eyes.

"You reside here, madam?" said Mr. Dombey, addressing her.

"No, we have been to a great many places. To Harrogate, and Scarborough, and into Devonshire. We have been visiting and resting here and there. Mamma likes change."

"Edith, of course, does not," said Mrs. Skewton with a ghastly archness.

"I have not found that there is any change in such places," was the answer, delivered with supreme indifference.

"They libel me. There is only one change, Mr. Dombey," observed Mrs. Skewton with a mincing sigh, "for which I really care, and that I fear I shall never be permitted to enjoy. People cannot spare one. But seclusion and contemplation are my what's-his-name—"

"If you mean Paradise, mamma, you had better say so, to render yourself intelligible," said the younger lady.

"My dearest Edith," returned Mrs. Skewton, "you know that I am wholly dependent upon you for those odious names. I assure you, Mr. Dombey, Nature intended me for an Arcadian. I am thrown away in society. Cows are my passion. What I have ever sighed for has been to retreat to a Swiss farm, and live entirely surrounded by cows—and china."

This curious association of objects, suggesting a remembrance of the celebrated bull who got by mistake into a crockery shop, was received with perfect gravity by Mr. Dombey, who intimated his opinion that Nature was, no doubt, a very respectable institution.

"What I want," drawled Mrs. Skewton, pinching her shrivelled throat, "is heart." It was frightfully true in one sense, if not in that in which she used the phrase. "What I want is frankness, confidence, less conventionality, and freer play of soul. We are so dreadfully artificial."

We were, indeed.

"In short," said Mrs. Skewton, "I want Nature everywhere. It would be so extremely charming."

"Nature is inviting us away now, mamma, if you are ready," said the younger lady, curling her handsome lip. At this hint, the wan page, who had been surveying the party over the top of the chair, vanished behind it, as if the ground had swallowed him up.

"Stop a moment, Withers!" said Mrs. Skewton as the chair began to move; calling to the page with all the languid dignity with which she had called in days of yore to a coachman with a wig, cauliflower nosegay, and silk stockings. "Where are you staying, abomination?"

The major was staying at the Royal Hotel, with his friend Dombey.

"You may come and see us any evening when you are good," lisped Mrs. Skewton. "If Mr. Dombey will honor us, we shall be happy. Withers, go on!"

The major again pressed to his blue lips the tips of the fingers that were disposed on the ledge of the wheeled chair with careful carelessness; after the Cleopatra model: and Mr. Dombey bowed. The elder lady honored them both with a very gracious smile and a girlish wave of her hand; the younger lady with the very slightest inclination of her head that common courtesy allowed.

The last glimpse of the wrinkled face of the

mother, with that patched color on it which the sun made infinitely more haggard and dismal than any want of color could have been, and of the proud beauty of the daughter with her graceful figure and erect deportment, engendered such an involuntary disposition on the part of both the major and Mr. Dombey to look after them, that they both turned at the same moment. The page, nearly as much aslant as his own shadow, was toiling after the chair, uphill, like a slow battering-ram; the top of Cleopatra's bonnet was fluttering in exactly the same corner to the inch as before; and the Beauty, loitering by herself a little in advance, expressed in all her elegant form, from head to foot, the same supreme disregard of everything and everybody.

"I tell you what, sir," said the major as they resumed their walk again, "if Joe Bagstock were a younger man, there's not a woman in the world whom he'd prefer for Mrs. Bagstock to that woman. By George, sir!" said the major, "she's superb!"

"Do you mean the daughter?" inquired Mr. Dombey.

"Is Joey B. a turnip, Dombey," said the major, "that he should mean the mother?"

"You were complimentary to the mother," returned Mr. Dombey.

"An ancient flame, sir," chuckled Major Bagstock. "De-vilish ancient. I humor her."

"She impresses me as being perfectly genteel," said Mr. Dombey.

"Genteel, sir!" said the major, stopping short, and staring in his companion's face. "The Honorable Mrs. Skewton, sir, is sister to the late Lord Feenix, and aunt to the present lord. The family are not wealthy — they're poor, indeed — and she lives upon a small jointure; but if you come to blood, sir!" The major gave a flourish with his stick, and walked on again, in despair of being able to say what you came to, if you came to that.

"You addressed the daughter, I observed," said Mr. Dombey after a short pause, "as Mrs. Granger."

"Edith Skewton, sir," returned the major, stopping short again, and punching a mark in the ground with his cane to represent her, "married (at eighteen) Granger of Ours;" whom the major indicated by another punch. "Granger, sir," said the major, tapping the last ideal portrait, and rolling his head emphatically, "was Colonel of Ours; a de-vilish handsome fellow, sir, of forty-one. He died, sir, in the second year of his marriage." The major ran the representative of the deceased Granger through and through the body with his walking-stick, and went on again, carrying his stick over his shoulder.

"How long is this ago?" asked Mr. Dombey, making another halt.

"Edith Granger, sir," replied the major, shutting one eye, putting his head on one side, passing his cane into his left hand, and smoothing his shirt-frill with his right, "is at this present time not quite thirty. And damme, sir," said the major, shouldering his stick once more and walking on again, "she's a peerless woman!"

"Was there any family?" asked Mr. Dombey presently.

"Yes, sir," said the major. "There was a boy."

Mr. Dombey's eyes sought the ground, and a shade came over his face.

"Who was drowned, sir," pursued the major, "when a child of four or five years old."

"Indeed?" said Mr. Dombey, raising his head.

"By the upsetting of a boat in which his nurse had no business to have put him," said the major. "That's *his* history. Edith Granger is Edith Granger still; but if tough old Joey B., sir, were a little younger and a little richer, the name of that immortal paragon should be Bagstock."

The major heaved his shoulders and his cheeks, and laughed more like an over-fed Mephistophiles than ever, as he said the words.

"Provided the lady made no objection, I suppose?" said Mr. Dombey coldly.

"By Gad, sir," said the major, "the Bagstock breed are not accustomed to that sort of obstacle. Though it's true enough that Edith might have married twen-ty times, but for being proud, sir, proud."

Mr. Dombey seemed, by his face, to think no worse of her for that.

"It's a great quality after all," said the major. "By the Lord, it's a high quality! Dombey! You are proud yourself, and your friend, old Joe, respects you for it, sir."

With this tribute to the character of his ally, which seemed to be wrung from him by the force of circumstances and the irresistible tendency of their conversation, the major closed the subject, and glided into a general exposition of the extent to which he had been beloved and doted on by splendid women and brilliant creatures.

On the next day but one, Mr. Dombey and the
major encountered the Honorable Mrs. Skewton
and her daughter in the Pump-room; on the day
after, they met them again very near the place
where they had met them first.   After meeting
them thus three or four times in all, it became a
point of mere civility to old acquaintances that the
major should go there one evening.   Mr. Dombey
had not originally intended to pay visits, but, on
the major announcing this intention, he said he
would have the pleasure of accompanying him.   So
the major told the native to go round before dinner,
and say, with his and Mr. Dombey's compliments,
that they would have the honor of visiting the
ladies that same evening, if the ladies were alone.
In answer to which message, the native brought
back a very small note with a very large quantity
of scent about it, indited by the Honorable Mrs.
Skewton to Major Bagstock, and briefly saying,
" You are a shocking bear, and I have a great mind
not to forgive you, but if you are very good indeed,"
which was underlined, "you may come.   Compliments (in which Edith unites) to Mr. Dombey."

The Honorable Mrs. Skewton and her daughter,
Mrs. Granger, resided, while at Leamington, in lodgings that were fashionable enough and dear enough,
but rather limited in point of space and conven-
iences; so that the Honorable Mrs. Skewton, being
in bed, had her feet in the window and her head in
the fireplace, while the Honorable Mrs. Skewton's
maid was quartered in a closet within the drawing-
room, so extremely small, that, to avoid developing
the whole of its accommodations, she was obliged
to writhe in and out of the door like a beautiful

serpent. Withers, the wan page, slept out of the house immediately under the tiles at a neighboring milk-shop; and the wheeled chair, which was the stone of that young Sisyphus, passed the night in a shed belonging to the same dairy, where new-laid eggs were produced by the poultry connected with the establishment, who roosted on a broken donkey-cart — persuaded, to all appearance, that it grew there, and was a species of tree.

Mr. Dombey and the major found Mrs. Skewton arranged, as Cleopatra, among the cushions of a sofa; very airily dressed; and certainly not resembling Shakespeare's Cleopatra, whom age could not wither. On their way upstairs they had heard the sound of a harp, but it had ceased on their being announced, and Edith now stood beside it, handsomer and haughtier than ever. It was a remarkable characteristic of this lady's beauty that it appeared to vaunt and assert itself without her aid, and against her will. She knew that she was beautiful: it was impossible that it could be otherwise: but she seemed with her own pride to defy her very self.

Whether she held cheap, attractions that could only call forth admiration that was worthless to her, or whether she designed to render them more precious to admirers by this usage of them, those to whom they *were* precious seldom paused to consider.

"I hope, Mrs. Granger," said Mr. Dombey, advancing a step towards her, "we are not the cause of your ceasing to play?"

" *You?* Oh, no!"

"Why do you not go on, then, my dearest Edith?" said Cleopatra.

"I left off as I began — of my own fancy."

The exquisite indifference of her manner in say-ing this: an indifference quite removed from dul-ness or insensibility, for it was pointed with proud purpose: was well set off by the carelessness with which she drew her hand across the strings, and came from that part of the room.

"Do you know, Mr. Dombey," said her languish-ing mother, playing with a hand-screen, "that occa-sionally my dearest Edith and myself actually almost differ —"

"Not quite, sometimes, mamma?" said Edith.

"Oh, never quite, my darling! Fie, fie, it would break my heart," returned her mother, making a faint attempt to pat her with the screen, which Edith made no movement to meet. " — About these cold conventionalities of manner that are observed in little things? Why are we not more natural? Dear me! With all those yearnings, and gushings, and impulsive throbbings that we have implanted in our souls, and which are so very charm-ing, why are we not more natural?"

Mr. Dombey said it was very true, very true.

"We could be more natural, I suppose, if we tried?" said Mrs. Skewton.

Mr. Dombey thought it possible.

"Devil a bit, ma'am," said the major. "We couldn't afford it. Unless the world was peopled with J. B.'s — tough and blunt old Joes, ma'am, plain red herrings with hard roes, sir — we couldn't afford it. It wouldn't do."

"You naughty infidel," said Mrs. Skewton, "be mute."

"Cleopatra commands," returned the major, kiss-ing his hand, "and Antony Bagstock obeys."

"The man has no sensitiveness," said Mrs. Skewton, cruelly holding up the hand-screen so as to shut the major out. "No sympathy. And what do we live for *but* sympathy? What else is so extremely charming? Without that gleam of sunshine on our cold, cold earth," said Mrs. Skewton, arranging her lace tucker, and complacently observing the effect of her bare lean arm, looking upward from the wrist, "how could we possibly bear it? In short, obdurate man!" glancing at the major round the screen, "I would have my world all heart; and Faith is so excessively charming, that I won't allow you to disturb it, do you hear?"

The major replied that it was hard in Cleopatra to require the world to be all heart, and yet to appropriate to herself the hearts of all the world; which obliged Cleopatra to remind him that flattery was insupportable to her, and that, if he had the boldness to address her in that strain any more, she would positively send him home.

Withers the Wan, at this period, handing round the tea, Mr. Dombey again addressed himself to Edith.

"There is not much company here, it would seem?" said Mr. Dombey in his own portentous, gentlemanly way.

"I believe not. We see none."

"Why, really," observed Mrs. Skewton from her couch, "there are no people here just now with whom we care to associate."

"They have not enough heart," said Edith with a smile. The very twilight of a smile: so singularly were its light and darkness blended.

"My dearest Edith rallies me, you see!" said her

mother, shaking her head: which shook a little of
itself sometimes, as if the palsy twinkled now and
then in opposition to the diamonds. "Wicked one!"

"You have been here before, if I am not mistaken?" said Mr. Dombey. Still to Edith.

"Oh, several times. I think we have been everywhere."

"A beautiful country!"

"I suppose it is. Everybody says so."

"Your cousin Feenix raves about it, Edith," interposed her mother from her couch.

The daughter slightly turned her graceful head,
and raising her eyebrows by a hair's breadth, as if
her cousin Feenix were of all the mortal world the
least to be regarded, turned her eyes again towards
Mr. Dombey.

"I hope, for the credit of my good taste, that I
am tired of the neighborhood," she said.

"You have almost reason to be, madam," he replied, glancing at a variety of landscape drawings,
of which he had already recognized several as repre-
senting neighboring points of view, and which were
strewn abundantly about the room, "if these beautiful productions are from your hand."

She gave him no reply, but sat in a disdainful
beauty, quite amazing.

"Have they that interest?" said Mr. Dombey.
"Are they yours?"

"Yes."

"And you play, I already know."

"Yes."

"And sing?"

"Yes."

She answered all these questions with a strange

reluctance; and with that remarkable air of opposition to herself, already noticed as belonging to her beauty. Yet she was not embarrassed, but wholly self-possessed. Neither did she seem to wish to avoid the conversation, for she addressed her face, and — so far as she could — her manner also, to him; and continued to do so when he was silent.

"You have many resources against weariness at least," said Mr. Dombey.

"Whatever their efficiency may be," she returned, "you know them all now. I have no more."

"May I hope to prove them all?" said Mr. Dombey with solemn gallantry, laying down a drawing he had held, and motioning towards the harp.

"Oh, certainly! If you desire it!"

She rose as she spoke, and crossing by her mother's couch, and directing a stately look towards her, which was instantaneous in its duration, but inclusive (if any one had seen it) of a multitude of expressions, among which that of the twilight smile, without the smile itself, overshadowed all the rest, went out of the room.

The major, who was quite forgiven by this time, had wheeled a little table up to Cleopatra, and was sitting down to play piquet with her. Mr. Dombey, not knowing the game, sat down to watch them for his edification until Edith should return.

"We are going to have some music, Mr. Dombey, I hope?" said Cleopatra.

"Mrs. Granger has been kind enough to promise so," said Mr. Dombey.

"Ah! That's very nice. Do you propose, major?"

"No, ma'am," said the major. "Couldn't do it."

"You're a barbarous being," replied the lady,

"and my hand's destroyed. You are fond of music, Mr. Dombey?"

"Eminently so," was Mr. Dombey's answer.

"Yes. It's very nice," said Cleopatra, looking at her cards. "So much heart in it — undeveloped recollections of a previous state of existence — and all that — which is so truly charming. Do you know," simpered Cleopatra, reversing the knave of clubs, who had come into her game with his heels uppermost, "that if anything could tempt me to put a period to my life, it would be curiosity to find out what it's all about, and what it means; there are so many provoking mysteries, really, that are hidden from us. Major, you to play!"

The major played; and Mr. Dombey, looking on for his instruction, would soon have been in a state of dire confusion, but that he gave no attention to the game whatever, and sat wondering instead when Edith would come back.

She came at last, and sat down to her harp, and Mr. Dombey rose and stood beside her, listening. He had little taste for music, and no knowledge of the strain she played, but he saw her bending over it, and perhaps he heard among the sounding strings some distant music of his own, that tamed the monster of the iron road, and made it less inexorable.

Cleopatra had a sharp eye, verily, at piquet. It glistened like a bird's, and did not fix itself upon the game, but pierced the room from end to end, and gleamed on harp, performer, listener, everything.

When the haughty beauty had concluded, she arose, and receiving Mr. Dombey's thanks and compliments in exactly the same manner as before, went, with scarcely any pause, to the piano, and began there.

Edith Granger, any song but that! Edith Granger, you are very handsome, and your touch upon the keys is brilliant, and your voice is deep and rich; but not the air that his neglected daughter sang to his dead son!

Alas! he knows it not; and if he did, what airs of hers would stir him, rigid man? Sleep, lonely Florence, sleep! Peace in thy dreams, although the night has turned dark, and the clouds are gathering, and threaten to discharge themselves in hail!

CHAPTER II.

MR. CARKER the manager sat at his desk, smooth and soft as usual, reading those letters which were reserved for him to open, backing them occasionally with such memoranda and references as their business purport required, and parcelling them out into little heaps for distribution through the several departments of the house. The post had come in heavy that morning, and Mr. Carker the manager had a good deal to do.

The general action of a man so engaged — pausing to look over a bundle of papers in his hand, dealing them round in various portions, taking up another bundle and examining its contents with knitted brows and pursed-out lips — dealing, and sorting, and pondering by turns — would easily suggest some whimsical resemblance to a player at cards. The face of Mr. Carker the manager was in good keeping with such a fancy. It was the face of a man who studied his play warily; who made himself master of all the strong and weak points of the game; who registered the cards in his mind as they fell about him, knew exactly what was on them, what they missed, and what they made; who was crafty to find out what the other players held, and who never betrayed his own hand.

The letters were in various languages, but Mr. Carker the manager read them all. If there had been anything in the offices of Dombey and Son that he could *not* read, there would have been a card wanting in the pack. He read almost at a glance, and made combinations of one letter with another and one business with another as he went on, adding new matter to the heaps — much as a man would know the cards at sight, and work out their combinations in his mind after they were turned. Something too deep for a partner, and much too deep for an adversary, Mr. Carker the manager sat in the rays of the sun that came down slanting on him through the skylight, playing his game alone.

And although it is not among the instincts, wild or domestic, of the cat tribe to play at cards, feline from sole to crown was Mr. Carker the manager, as he basked in the strip of summer light and warmth that shone upon his table and the ground as if they were a crooked dial-plate, and himself the only figure on it. With hair and whiskers deficient in color at all times, but feebler than common in the rich sunshine, and more like the coat of a sandy tortoise-shell cat; with long nails, nicely pared and sharpened; with a natural antipathy to any speck of dirt, which made him pause sometimes and watch the falling motes of dust, and rub them off his smooth white hand or glossy linen: Mr. Carker the manager, sly of manner, sharp of tooth, soft of foot, watchful of eye, oily of tongue, cruel of heart, nice of habit, sat with a dainty steadfastness and patience at his work, as if he were waiting at a mouse's hole.

At length the letters were disposed of, excepting one which he reserved for a particular audience. Having locked the more confidential correspondence in a drawer, Mr. Carker the manager rang his bell.

" Why do *you* answer it ? " was his reception of his brother.

" The messenger is out, and I am the next," was the submissive reply.

"You are the next?" muttered the manager. "Yes! Creditable to me! There l"

Pointing to the heaps of opened letters, he turned disdainfully away in his elbow-chair, and broke the seal of that one which he held in his hand.

"I am sorry to trouble you, James," said the brother, gathering them up, " but — "

" Oh! You have something to say. I knew that. Well? "

Mr. Carker the manager did not raise his eyes or turn them on his brother, but kept them on his letter, though without opening it.

"Well ? " he repeated sharply.

"I am uneasy about Harriet."

"Harriet who? What Harriet? I know nobody of that name."

" She is not well, and has changed very much of late."

"She changed very much a great many years ago," replied the manager; " and that is all I have to say."

"I think if you would hear me — "

"Why should I hear you, Brother John?" returned the manager, laying a sarcastic emphasis on those two words, and throwing up his head, but not lifting his eyes. " I tell you, Harriet Carker made her choice many years ago between her two brothers. She may repent it, but she must abide by it."

"Don't mistake me. I do not say she *does* repent it. It would be black ingratitude in me to hint at such a thing," returned the other. "Though, believe me, James, I am as sorry for her sacrifice as you."

"As I?" exclaimed the manager. "As I?"

"As sorry for her choice — for what you call her choice — as you are angry at it," said the junior.

"Angry?" repeated the other, with a wide show of his teeth.

"Displeased. Whatever word you like best. You know my meaning. There is no offence in my intention."

"There is offence in everything you do," replied his brother, glancing at him with a sudden scowl, which in a moment gave place to a wider smile than the last. "Carry those papers away, if you please. I am busy."

His politeness was so much more cutting than his wrath, that the junior went to the door. But stopping at it, and looking round, he said, —

"When Harriet tried in vain to plead for me with you, on your first just indignation, and my first disgrace; and when she left you, James, to follow my broken fortunes, and devote herself, in her mistaken affection, to a ruined brother, because, without her, he had no one, and was lost; she was young and pretty. I think if you could see her now — if you would go and see her — she would move your admiration and compassion."

The manager inclined his head, and showed his teeth, as who should say, in answer to some careless small-talk, "Dear me! Is that the case?" but said never a word.

"We thought in those days: you and I both: that she would marry young, and lead a happy and light-hearted life," pursued the other. "Oh, if you knew how cheerfully she cast those hopes away; how cheerfully she has gone forward on the path she took, and never once looked back; you never could say again that her name was strange in your ears. Never!"

Again the manager inclined his head, and showed his teeth, and seemed to say, "Remarkable indeed! You quite surprise me!" And again he uttered never a word.

"May I go on?" said John Carker mildly.

"On your way?" replied his smiling brother. "If you will have the goodness."

John Carker, with a sigh, was passing slowly out at the door, when his brother's voice detained him for a moment on the threshold.

"If she has gone and goes her own way cheerfully," he said, throwing the still unfolded letter on his desk, and putting his hands firmly in his pockets, "you may tell her that I go as cheerfully on mine. If she has never once looked back, you may tell her that I have, sometimes, to recall her taking part with you, and that my resolution is no easier to wear away" — he smiled very sweetly here — "than marble."

"I tell her nothing of you. We never speak about you. Once a year, on your birthday, Harriet says always, 'Let us remember James by name, and wish him happy,' but we say no more."

"Tell it, then, if you please," returned the other, "to yourself. You can't repeat it too often, as a lesson to you to avoid the subject in speaking to me. I know no Harriet Carker. There is no such person. *You* may have a sister: make much of her. I have none."

Mr. Carker the manager took up the letter again, and waved it with a smile of mock courtesy towards the door. Unfolding it as his brother withdrew, and looking darkly after him as he left the room, he once more turned round in his elbow-chair, and applied himself to a diligent perusal of its contents.

It was in the writing of his great chief, Mr. Dombey, and dated from Leamington. Though he was a quick reader of all other letters, Mr. Carker read this slowly; weighing the words as he went, and bringing every tooth in his head to bear upon them. When he had read it through once, he turned it over again, and picked out these passages. "I find myself benefited by the change, and am not yet inclined to name any time for my return." "I wish, Carker, you would arrange to come down once and see me here, and let me know how things are going on, in person." "I omitted to speak to you about young Gay. If not gone per Son and Heir, or if Son and Heir still lying in the Docks, appoint some other young man, and keep him in the City for the present. I am not decided." "Now that's unfortunate," said Mr. Carker the manager, expanding his mouth, as if it were made of india-rubber: "for he's far away!"

Still that passage, which was in a postscript, attracted his attention and his teeth once more.

"I think," he said, "my good friend Captain Cut-

tle mentioned something about being towed along
in the wake of that day. What a pity he's so far
away!"

He refolded the letter, and was sitting trifling
with it, standing it long-wise and broad-wise on his
table, and turning it over and over on all sides —
doing pretty much the same thing, perhaps, by its
contents — when Mr. Perch the messenger knocked
softly at the door, and coming in on tiptoe, bending
his body at every step as if it were the delight of
his life to bow, laid some papers on the table.

"Would you please to be engaged, sir?" asked
Mr. Perch, rubbing his hands, and deferentially putting his head on one side, like a man who felt he
had no business to hold it up in such a presence,
and would keep it as much out of the way as
possible.

"Who wants me?"

"Why, sir," said Mr. Perch in a soft voice, "really
nobody, sir, to speak of at present. Mr. Gills, the
Ship's Instrument-maker, sir, has looked in about a
little matter of payment, he says; but I mentioned
to him, sir, that you was engaged several deep;
several deep."

Mr. Perch coughed once behind his hand, and
waited for further orders.

"Anybody else?"

"Well, sir," said Mr. Perch, "I wouldn't of my
own self take the liberty of mentioning, sir, that
there was anybody else; but that same young lad
that was here yesterday, sir, and last week, has been
hanging about the place; and it looks, sir," added
Mr. Perch, stopping to shut the door, "dreadful
unbusiness-like to see him whistling to the spar-

rows down the court, and making of 'em answer him."

"You said he wanted something to do, didn't you, Perch?" asked Mr. Carker, leaning back in his chair, and looking at that officer.

"Why, sir," said Mr. Perch, coughing behind his hand again, "his expression certainly were that he was in wants of a sitiwation, and that he considered something might be done for him about the Docks, being used to fishing with a rod and line; but —" Mr. Perch shook his head very dubiously indeed.

"What does he say when he comes?" asked Mr. Carker.

"Indeed, sir," said Mr. Perch, coughing another cough behind his hand, which was always his resource as an expression of humility when nothing else occurred to him, "his observation generally air that he would humbly wish to see one of the gentlemen, and that he wants to earn a living. But you see, sir," added Perch, dropping his voice to a whisper, and turning, in the inviolable nature of his confidence, to give the door a thrust with his hand and knee, as if that would shut it any more when it was shut already, "it's hardly to be bore, sir, that a common lad like that should come a-prowling here, and saying that his mother nursed our House's young gentleman, and that he hopes our House will give him a chance on that account. I am sure, sir,' observed Mr. Perch, "that although Mrs. Perch was at that time nursing as thriving a little girl, sir, as we've ever took the liberty of adding to our family, I wouldn't have made so free as drop a hint of her being capable of imparting nourishment, not if it was ever so!"

Mr. Carker grinned at him like a shark, but in an absent, thoughtful manner.

"Whether," submitted Mr. Perch after a short silence and another cough, "it mightn't be best for me to tell him, that if he was seen here any more he would be given into custody; and to keep to it! With respect to bodily fear," said Mr. Perch, "I'm so timid, myself, by nature, sir, and my nerves is so unstrung by Mrs. Perch's state, that I could take my affidavit easy."

"Let me see this fellow, Perch," said Mr. Carker. "Bring him in!"

"Yes, sir. Begging your pardon, sir," said Mr. Perch, hesitating at the door, "he's rough, sir, in appearance."

"Never mind. If he's there, bring him in. I'll see Mr. Gills directly. Ask him to wait!"

Mr. Perch bowed; and shutting the door as precisely and carefully as if he were not coming back for a week, went on his quest among the sparrows in the court. While he was gone Mr. Carker assumed his favorite attitude before the fireplace, and stood looking at the door; presenting, with his under lip tucked into the smile that showed his whole row of upper teeth, a singularly crouching appearance.

The messenger was not long in returning, followed by a pair of heavy boots that came bumping along the passage like boxes. With the unceremonious words, "Come along with you!"—a very unusual form of introduction from his lips—Mr. Perch then ushered into the presence a strong-built lad of fifteen, with a round red face, a round sleek head, round black eyes, round limbs, and round body, who, to carry out the general rotundity of his appearance, had a round hat in his hand, without a particle of brim to it.

Obedient to a nod from Mr. Carker, Perch had no sooner confronted the visitor with that gentleman than he withdrew. The moment they were face to face alone, Mr. Carker, without a word of preparation, took him by the throat, and shook him until his head seemed loose upon his shoulders.

The boy, who, in the midst of his astonishment, could not help staring wildly at the gentleman with so many white teeth, who was choking him, and at the office walls, as though determined, if he *were* choked, that his last look should be at the mysteries for his intrusion into which he was paying such a severe penalty, at last contrived to utter, —

"Come, sir! You let me alone, will you?"

"Let you alone!" said Mr. Carker. "What! I have got you, have I?" There was no doubt of that, and tightly too. "You dog," said Mr. Carker, through his set jaws, "I'll strangle you!"

Biler whimpered, Would he, though? Oh, no, he wouldn't — and what was he doing of — and why didn't he strangle somebody of his own size, and not *him?* But Biler was quelled by the extraordinary nature of his reception, and, as his head became stationary, and he looked the gentleman in the face, or rather in the teeth, and saw him snarling at him, he so far forgot his manhood as to cry.

"I haven't done nothing to you, sir," said Biler, otherwise Rob, otherwise Grinder, and always Toodle.

"You young scoundrel!" replied Mr. Carker, slowly releasing him, and moving back a step into his favorite position. "What do you mean by daring to come here?"

"I didn't mean no harm, sir," whimpered Rob, putting one hand to his throat, and the knuckles of the other to his eyes. "I'll never come again, sir. I only wanted work."

"Work, young Cain that you are!" repeated Mr. Carker, eying him narrowly. "Ain't you the idlest vagabond in London?"

The impeachment, while it much affected Mr. Toodle junior, attached to his character so justly, that he could not say a word in denial. He stood looking at the gentleman, therefore, with a frightened, self-convicted, and remorseful air. As to his looking at him, it may be observed that he was fascinated by Mr. Carker, and never took his round eyes off him for an instant.

"Ain't you a thief?" said Mr. Carker, with his hands behind him in his pockets.

"No, sir," pleaded Rob.

"You are!" said Mr. Carker.

"I ain't indeed, sir," whimpered Rob. "I never did such a thing as thieve, sir, if you'll believe me. I know I've been going wrong, sir, ever since I took to bird-catching and walking-matching. I'm sure a cove might think," said Mr. Toodle junior, with a burst of penitence, "that singing birds was innocent company, but nobody knows what harm is in them little creeturs, and what they brings you down to."

They seemed to have brought *him* down to a velveteen jacket and trousers very much the worse for wear, a particularly small red waistcoat like a gorget, an interval of blue check, and the hat before mentioned.

"I ain't been home twenty times since them birds got their will of me," said Rob, "and that's ten months. How can I go home when everybody's miserable to see me? I wonder," said Biler, blubbering outright, and smearing his eyes with his coatcuff, "that I haven't been and drownded myself over and over again."

All of which, including his expression of surprise at not having achieved this last scarce performance, the boy said just as if the teeth of Mr. Carker drew it out of him, and he had no power of concealing anything with that battery of attraction in full play.

"You're a nice young gentleman!" said Mr. Carker, shaking his head at him. "There's hemp seed sown for *you*, my fine fellow!"

"I'm sure, sir," returned the wretched Biler, blubbering again, and again having recourse to his coatcuff, "I shouldn't care, sometimes, if it was growed too. My misfortunes all began in wagging, sir; but what could I do, exceptin' wag?"

"Excepting what?" said Mr. Carker.

"Wag, sir. Wagging from school."

"Do you mean pretending to go there, and not going?" said Mr. Carker.

"Yes, sir, that's wagging, sir," returned the quondam Grinder, much affected. "I was chivied through the streets, sir, when I went there, and pounded when I got there. So I wagged, and hid myself, and that began it."

"And you mean to tell me," said Mr. Carker, taking him by the throat again, holding him out at arm's length, and surveying him in silence for some moments, "that you want a place, do you?"

"I should be thankful to be tried, sir," returned Toodle junior faintly.

Mr. Carker the manager pushed him backwards into a corner — the boy submitting quietly, hardly venturing to breathe, and never once removing his eyes from his face — and rang the bell.

"Tell Mr. Gills to come here."

Mr. Perch was too deferential to express surprise or recognition of the figure in the corner: and Uncle Sol appeared immediately.

"Mr. Gills!" said Carker with a smile, "sit down. How do you do? You continue to enjoy your health, I hope?"

"Thank you, sir," returned Uncle Sol, taking out his pocket-book, and handing over some notes as he spoke. "Nothing ails me in body but old age. Twenty-five, sir."

"You are as punctual and exact, Mr. Gills," replied the smiling manager, taking a paper from one of his many drawers, and making an indorsement on it, while Uncle Sol looked over him, "as one of your own chronometers. Quite right."

"The Son and Heir has not been spoken, I find by the list, sir," said Uncle Sol, with a slight addition to the usual tremor in his voice.

"The Son and Heir has not been spoken," returned Carker. "There seems to have been tempestuous weather, Mr. Gills, and she has probably been driven out of her course."

"She is safe, I trust in Heaven!" said old Sol.

"She is safe, I trust in Heaven!" assented Mr. Carker in that voiceless manner of his: which made the observant young Toodle tremble again. "Mr. Gills," he added aloud, throwing himself back in his chair, "you must miss your nephew very much?"

Uncle Sol, standing by him, shook his head and heaved a deep sigh.

"Mr. Gills," said Carker, with his soft hand playing round his mouth, and looking up into the instrument-maker's face, "it would be company to you to have a young fellow in your shop just now, and it would be obliging me if you would give one house room for the present. No, to be sure," he added quickly, in anticipation of what the old man was going to say, "there's not much business doing there, I know: but you can make him clean the place out, polish up the instruments; drudge, Mr. Gills. That's the lad!"

Sol Gills pulled down his spectacles from his forehead to his eyes, and looked at Toodle junior standing upright in the corner: his head presenting the appearance (which it always did) of having been newly drawn out of a bucket of cold water; his small waistcoat rising and falling quickly in the play of his emotions; and his eyes intently fixed on Mr. Carker, without the least reference to his proposed master.

"Will you give him house room, Mr. Gills?" said the manager.

Old Sol, without being quite enthusiastic on the subject, replied that he was glad of any opportunity, however slight, to oblige Mr. Carker, whose wish on such a point was a command: and that the Wooden Midshipman would consider himself happy to receive in his berth any visitor of Mr. Carker's selecting.

Mr. Carker bared himself to the tops and bottoms

of his gums: making the watchful Toodle junior tremble more and more: and acknowledged the instrument-maker's politeness in his most affable manner.

"I'll dispose of him so, then, Mr. Gills," he answered, rising, and shaking the old man by the hand, "until I make up my mind what to do with him, and what he deserves. As I consider myself responsible for him, Mr. Gills," — here he smiled a wide smile at Rob, who shook before it, — "I shall be glad if you'll look sharply after him, and report his behavior to me. I'll ask a question or two of his parents as I ride home this afternoon — respectable people — to confirm some particulars in his own account of himself; and that done, Mr. Gills, I'll send him round to you to-morrow morning. Good-by."

His smile at parting was so full of teeth, that it confused old Sol, and made him vaguely uncomfortable. He went home, thinking of raging seas, foundering ships, drowning men, an ancient bottle of madeira never brought to light, and other dismal matter.

"Now, boy!" said Mr. Carker, putting his hand on young Toodle's shoulder, and bringing him out into the middle of the room. "You have heard me?"

Rob said, "Yes, sir."

"Perhaps you understand," pursued his patron, "that if you ever deceive or play tricks with me, you had better have drowned yourself indeed, once for all, before you came here?"

There was nothing in any branch of mental acquisitiou that Rob seemed to understand better than that.

"If you have lied to me," said Mr. Carker, "in anything, never come in my way again. If not, you may let me find you waiting for me somewhere near your mother's house this afternoon. I shall leave this at five o'clock, and ride there on horseback. Now, give me the address."

Rob repeated it slowly, as Mr. Carker wrote it down. Rob even spelt it over a second time, letter by letter, as if he thought that the omission of a dot or scratch would lead to his destruction. Mr. Carker then handed him out of the room: and Rob, keeping his round eyes fixed upon his patron to the last, vanished for the time being.

Mr. Carker the manager did a great deal of business in the course of the day, and bestowed his teeth upon a great many people. In the office, in the court, in the street, and on 'Change, they glistened and bristled to a terrible extent. Five o'clock arriving, and with it Mr. Carker's bay horse, they got on horseback, and went gleaming up Cheapside.

As no one can easily ride fast, even if inclined to do so, through the press and throng of the City at that hour, and as Mr. Carker was not inclined, he went leisurely along, picking his way among the carts and carriages, avoiding, whenever he could, the wetter and more dirty places in the over-watered road, and taking infinite pains to keep himself and his steed clean. Glancing at the passers-by while he was thus ambling on his way, he suddenly encountered the round eyes of the sleek-headed Rob intently fixed upon his face as if they had never been taken off, while the boy himself, with a pocket-handkerchief twisted up like a speckled eel, and girded round his waist, made a very conspicuous demonstration of being prepared to attend upon him, at whatever pace he might think proper to go.

This attention, however flattering, being one of an unusual kind, and attracting some notice from the other passengers, Mr. Carker took advantage of a clearer thoroughfare and a cleaner road, and broke into a trot. Rob immediately did the same. Mr. Carker presently tried a canter; Rob was still in attendance. Then a short gallop; it was all one to the boy. Whenever Mr. Carker turned his eyes to that side of the road, he still saw Toodle junior holding his course, apparently without distress, and working himself along by the elbows after the most approved manner of professional gentlemen who get over the ground for wagers.

Ridiculous as this attendance was, it was a sign of an influence established over the boy, and therefore Mr. Carker, affecting not to notice it, rode away into the neighborhood of Mr. Toodle's house. On his slackening his pace here, Rob appeared before him to point out the turnings; and when he called to a man at a neighboring gateway to hold his horse, pending his visit to the Buildings that had succeeded Staggs's Gardens, Rob dutifully held the stirrup while the manager dismounted.

"Now, sir," said Mr. Carker, taking him by the shoulder, "come along!"

The prodigal son was evidently nervous of visiting the parental abode: but Mr. Carker pushing him on before, he had nothing for it but to open the right door, and suffer himself to be walked into the midst of his brothers and sisters, mustered in overwhelming force round the family tea-table. At sight of the prodigal in the grasp of a stranger, these tender re-

lations united in a general howl, which smote upon
the prodigal's breast so sharply when he saw his
mother stand up among them, pale and trembling,
with the baby in her arms, that he lent his own
voice to the chorus.

Nothing doubting now that the stranger, if not
Mr. Ketch in person, was one of that company, the
whole of the young family wailed the louder, while
its more infantine members, unable to control the
transports of emotion appertaining to their time of
life, threw themselves on their backs like young birds
when terrified by a hawk, and kicked violently. At
length, poor Polly, making herself audible, said, with
quivering lips, "Oh, Rob, my poor boy, what have
you done at last?"

"Nothing, mother," cried Rob in a piteous voice;
"ask the gentleman!"

"Don't be alarmed," said Mr. Carker; "I want to
do him good."

At this announcement, Polly, who had not cried
yet, began to do so. The elder Toodles, who appeared to have been meditating a rescue, unclenched
their fists. The younger Toodles clustered round
their mother's gown, and peeped from under their
own chubby arms at their desperado brother and
his unknown friend. Everybody blessed the gentleman with the beautiful teeth, who wanted to do
good.

"This fellow," said Mr. Carker to Polly, giving
him a gentle shake, "is your son, eh, ma'am?"

"Yes, sir," sobbed Polly, with a courtesy; "yes,
sir."

"A bad son, I am afraid?" said Mr. Carker.

"Never a bad son to me, sir," returned Polly.

"To whom, then?" demanded Mr. Carker.

"He has been a little wild, sir," replied Polly, checking the baby, who was making convulsive efforts with his arms and legs to launch himself on Biler, through the ambient air, "and has gone with wrong companions; but I hope he has seen the misery of that, sir, and will do well again."

Mr. Carker looked at Polly, and the clean room and the clean children, and the simple Toodle face, combined of father and mother, that was reflected and repeated everywhere about him: and seemed to have achieved the real purpose of his visit.

"Your husband, I take it, is not at home?" he said.

"No, sir," replied Polly. "He's down the line at present."

The prodigal Rob seemed very much relieved to hear it: though still, in the absorption of all his faculties in his patron, he hardly took his eyes from Mr. Carker's face, unless for a moment at a time to steal a sorrowful glance at his mother.

"Then," said Mr. Carker, "I'll tell you how I have stumbled on this boy of yours, and who I am, and what I am going to do for him."

This Mr. Carker did in his own way: saying that he at first intended to have accumulated nameless terrors on his presumptuous head, for coming to the whereabout of Dombey and Son. That he had relented, in consideration of his youth, his professed contrition, and his friends. That he was afraid he took a rash step in doing anything for the boy, and one that might expose him to the censure of the prudent; but that he did it of himself and for himself, and risked the consequences single-handed; and that his mother's past connection with Mr. Dombey's family had nothing to do with it, and that Mr. Dombey had nothing to do with it, but that he, Mr. Carker, was the be-all and the end-all of this business. Taking great credit to himself for his goodness, and receiving no less from all the family then present, Mr. Carker signified, indirectly, but still pretty plainly, that Rob's implicit fidelity, attachment, and devotion were for evermore his due, and the least homage he could receive. And with this great truth Rob himself was so impressed, that, standing gazing on his patron with tears rolling down his cheeks, he nodded his shiny head until it seemed almost as loose as it had done under the same patron's hands that morning.

Polly, who had passed Heaven knows how many sleepless nights on account of this her dissipated first-born, and had not seen him for weeks and weeks, could have almost kneeled to Mr. Carker the manager, as to a good spirit — in spite of his teeth. But Mr. Carker rising to depart, she only thanked him with her mother's prayers and blessings; thanks so rich, when paid out of the heart's mint, especially for any service Mr. Carker had rendered, that he might have given back a large amount of change, and yet been overpaid.

As that gentleman made his way among the crowding children to the door, Rob retreated on his mother, and took her and the baby in the same repentant hug.

"I'll try hard, dear mother, now. Upon my soul I will!" said Rob.

"Oh, do, my dear boy! I am sure you will, for our sakes and your own!" cried Polly, kissing him.

"But you're coming back to speak to me, when you have seen the gentleman away?"

"I don't know, mother." Rob hesitated, and looked down. "Father — when's he coming home?"

"Not till two o'clock to-morrow morning."

"I'll come back, mother dear!" cried Rob. And passing through the shrill cry of his brothers and sisters in reception of this promise, he followed Mr. Carker out.

"What!" said Mr. Carker, who had heard this. "You have a bad father, have you?"

"No, sir!" returned Rob, amazed. "There ain't a better nor a kinder father going than mine is."

"Why don't you want to see him, then?" inquired his patron.

"There's such a difference between a father and a mother, sir," said Rob after faltering for a moment. "He couldn't hardly believe yet that I was going to do better — though I know he'd try to — but a mother — *she* always believes what's good, sir; at least, I know my mother does, God bless her!"

Mr. Carker's mouth expanded, but he said no more until he was mounted on his horse, and had dismissed the man who held it, when, looking down from the saddle steadily into the attentive and watchful face of the boy, he said, —

"You'll come to me to-morrow morning, and you shall be shown where that old gentleman lives; that old gentleman who was with me this morning; where you are going, as you heard me say."

"Yes, sir," returned Rob.

"I have a great interest in that old gentleman, and, in serving him, you serve me, boy, do you understand? Well," he added, interrupting him, for he saw his round face brighten when he was told that; "I see you do. I want to know all about that old gentleman, and how he goes on from day to day — for I am anxious to be of service to him — and especially who comes there to see him. Do you understand?"

Rob nodded his steadfast face, and said, "Yes, sir," again.

"I should like to know that he has friends who are attentive to him, and that they don't desert him — for he lives very much alone now, poor fellow; but that they are fond of him, and of his nephew who has gone abroad. There is a very young lady who may perhaps come to see him. I want particularly to know all about *her.*"

"I'll take care, sir," said the boy.

"And take care," returned his patron, bending forward to advance his grinning face closer to the boy's, and pat him on the shoulder with the handle of his whip: "take care you talk about affairs of mine to nobody but me."

"To nobody in the world, sir," replied Rob, shaking his head.

"Neither there," said Mr. Carker, pointing to the place they had just left, "nor anywhere else. I'll try how true and grateful you can be. I'll prove you!" Making this, by his display of teeth and by the action of his head, as much a threat as a promise, he turned from Rob's eyes, which were nailed upon him as if he had won the boy by a charm, body and soul, and rode away. But again becoming conscious, after trotting a short distance, that his devoted henchman, girt as before, was yielding him the same attendance, to the great amuse-

ment of sundry spectators, he reined up, and
ordered him off. To insure his obedience, he turned
in the saddle and watched him as he retired. It
was curious to see that even then Rob could not
keep his eyes wholly averted from his patron's face,
but, constantly turning and turning again to look
after him, involved himself in a tempest of buffet-
ings and jostlings from the other passengers in the
street: of which, in the pursuit of the one paramount idea, he was perfectly heedless.

Mr. Carker the manager rode on at a foot-pace,
with the easy air of one who had performed all the
business of the day in a satisfactory manner, and
got it comfortably off his mind. Complacent and
affable as man could be, Mr. Carker picked his way
along the streets, and hummed a soft tune as he
went. He seemed to purr: he was so glad.

And, in some sort, Mr. Carker, in his fancy, basked
upon a hearth too. Coiled up snugly at certain feet,
he was ready for a spring, or for a tear, or for a
scratch, or for a velvet touch, as the humor took
him and occasion served. Was there any bird in a
cage that came in for a share of his regards?

"A very young lady!" thought Mr. Carker the
manager, through his song. "Ay! when I saw her
last, she was a little child. With dark eyes and
hair, I recollect, and a good face; a very good face!
I dare say she's pretty."

More affable and pleasant yet, and humming his
song until his many teeth vibrated to it, Mr. Carker
picked his way along, and turned at last into the
shady street where Mr. Dombey's house stood. He
had been so busy, winding webs round good faces,
and obscuring them with meshes, that he hardly

thought of being at this point of his ride, until, glancing down the cold perspective of tall houses, he reined in his horse quickly within a few yards of the door. But to explain why Mr. Carker reined in his horse quickly, and what he looked at in no small surprise, a few digressive words are necessary.

Mr. Toots, emancipated from the Blimber thraldom, and coming into the possession of a certain portion of his worldly wealth, "which," as he had been wont, during his last half-year's probation, to communicate to Mr. Feeder every evening as a new discovery, "the executors couldn't keep him out of," had applied himself, with great diligence, to the science of Life. Fired with a noble emulation to pursue a brilliant and distinguished career, Mr. Toots had furnished a choice set of apartments; had established among them a sporting bower, embellished with the portraits of winning horses, in which he took no particle of interest; and a divan, which made him poorly. In this delicious abode Mr. Toots devoted himself to the cultivation of those gentle arts which refine and humanize existence, his chief instructor in which was an interesting character called the Game Chicken, who was always to be heard of at the bar of the Black Badger, wore a shaggy white great-coat in the warmest weather, and knocked Mr. Toots about the head three times a week, for the small consideration of ten-and-six per visit.

The Game Chicken, who was quite the Apollo of Mr. Toots's Pantheon, had introduced to him a marker who taught billiards, a Life Guard who taught fencing, a job-master who taught riding, a Cornish gentleman who was up to anything in the

athletic line, and two or three other friends connected no less intimately with the fine arts. Under
whose auspices Mr. Toots could hardly fail to
improve apace, and under whose tuition he went to
work.

But, however it came about, it came to pass, even
while these gentlemen had the gloss of novelty
upon them, that Mr. Toots felt, he didn't know how,
unsettled and uneasy. There were husks in his
corn, that even Game Chickens couldn't peck up;
gloomy giants in his leisure, that even Game
Chickens couldn't knock down. Nothing seemed to
do Mr. Toots so much good as incessantly leaving
cards at Mr. Dombey's door. No tax-gatherers in
the British dominions — that widespread territory
on which the sun never sets, and where the tax-
gatherer never goes to bed — was more regular and
persevering in his calls than Mr. Toots.

Mr. Toots never went upstairs; and always performed the same ceremonies, richly dressed for the
purpose, at the hall-door.

"Oh! Good-morning!" would be Mr. Toots's first
remark to the servant. "For Mr. Dombey," would
be Mr. Toots's next remark, as he handed in a card.
"For Miss Dombey," would be his next as he handed
in another.

Mr. Toots would then turn round as if to go away;
but the man knew him by this time, and knew he
wouldn't.

"Oh, I beg your pardon," Mr. Toots would say,
as if a thought had suddenly descended on him.
"Is the young woman at home?"

The man would rather think she was, but wouldn't
quite know. Then he would ring a bell that rang

upstairs, and would look up the staircase, and would say, Yes, she *was* at home, and was coming down. Then Miss Nipper would appear, and the man would retire.

"Oh! How de do?" Mr. Toots would say, with a chuckle and a blush.

Susan would thank him, and say she was very well.

"How's Diogenes going on?" would be Mr. Toots's second interrogation.

Very well indeed. Miss Florence was fonder and fonder of him every day. Mr. Toots was sure to hail this with a burst of chuckles, like the opening of a bottle of some effervescent beverage.

"Miss Florence is quite well, sir," Susan would add.

"Oh, it's of no consequence, thankee," was the invariable reply of Mr. Toots; and, when he had said so, he always went away very fast.

Now, it is certain that Mr. Toots had a filmy something in his mind, which led him to conclude that if he could aspire successfully, in the fulness of time, to the hand of Florence, he would be fortunate and blessed. It is certain that Mr. Toots, by some remote and roundabout road, had got to that point, and that there he made a stand. His heart was wounded; he was touched; he was in love. He had made a desperate attempt one night, and had sat up all night for the purpose, to write an acrostic on Florence, which affected him to tears in the conception. But he never proceeded in the execution further than the words, "For when I gaze" — the flow of imagination in which he had previously written down the initial letters of the other seven lines deserting him at that point.

Beyond devising that very artful and politic measure of leaving a card for Mr. Dombey daily, the brain of Mr. Toots had not worked much in reference to the subject that held his feelings prisoner. But deep consideration at length assured Mr. Toots that an important step to gain was the conciliation of Miss Susan Nipper, preparatory to giving her some inkling of his state of mind.

A little light and playful gallantry towards this lady seemed the means to employ, in that early chapter of the history, for winning her to his interests. Not being able quite to make up his mind about it, he consulted the Chicken — without taking that gentleman into his confidence; merely informing him that a friend in Yorkshire had written to him (Mr. Toots) for his opinion on such a question. The Chicken replying that his opinion always was, "Go in and win," and further, "When your man's before you, and your work cut out, go in and do it," Mr. Toots considered this a figurative way of supporting his own view of the case, and heroically resolved to kiss Miss Nipper next day.

Upon the next day, therefore, Mr. Toots, putting into requisition some of the greatest marvels that Burgess and Co. had ever turned out, went off to Mr. Dombey's upon this design. But his heart failed him so much as he approached the scene of action, that, although he arrived on the ground at three o'clock in the afternoon, it was six o'clock before he knocked at the door.

Everything happened as usual, down to the point when Susan said her young mistress was well, and Mr. Toots said it was of no consequence. To her amazement, Mr. Toots, instead of going off like

a rocket, after that observation, lingered and chuckled.

"Perhaps you'd like to walk upstairs, sir?" said Susan.

"Well, I think I will come in!" said Mr. Toots.

But, instead of walking upstairs, the bold Toots made an awkward plunge at Susan when the door was shut, and, embracing that fair creature, kissed her on the cheek.

"Go along with you," cried Susan, "or I'll tear your eyes out."

"Just another!" said Mr. Toots.

"Go along with you!" exclaimed Susan, giving him a push. "Innocents like you, too! Who'll begin next? Go along, sir!"

Susan was not in any serious strait, for she could hardly speak for laughing; but Diogenes, on the staircase, hearing a rustling against the wall and a shuffling of feet, and seeing through the banisters that there was some contention going on, and foreign invasion in the house, formed a different opinion, dashed down to the rescue, and in the twinkling of an eye had Mr. Toots by the leg.

Susan screamed, laughed, opened the street-door, and ran downstairs; the bold Toots tumbled staggering out into the street, with Diogenes holding on to one leg of his pantaloons, as if Burgess and Co. were his cooks, and had provided that dainty morsel for his holiday entertainment; Diogenes, shaken off, rolled over and over in the dust, got up again, whirled round the giddy Toots, and snapped at him: and all this turmoil, Mr. Carker, reining up his horse and sitting a little at a distance, saw, to his amazement, issue from the stately house of Mr. Dombey.

Mr. Carker remained watching the · discomfited
Toots, when Diogenes was called in, and the door
shut : and while that gentleman, taking refuge in a
doorway near at hand, bound up the torn leg of his
pantaloons with a costly silk handkerchief that had
formed part of his expensive outfit for the adven-
ture.

" I beg your pardon, sir," said Mr. Carker, riding
up, with his most propitiatory smile. " I hope you
are not hurt ? "

" Oh no, thank you," replied Mr. Toots, raising
his flushed face ; " it's of no consequence." Mr.
Toots would have signified, if he could, that he
liked it very much.

" If the dog's teeth have entered the leg,
sir — " began Carker, with a display of his own.

" No, thank you," said Mr. Toots ; " it's all quite
right.   It's very comfortable, thank you."

" I have the pleasure of knowing Mr. Dombey,"
observed Carker.

" Have you, though ? " rejoined the blushing
Toots.

" And you will allow me, perhaps, to apologize, in
his absence," said Mr. Carker, taking off his hat,
" for such a misadventure, and to wonder how it
can possibly have happened."

Mr. Toots is so much gratified by this politeness,
and the lucky chance of making friends with a
friend of Mr. Dombey, that he pulls out his card-
case, which he never loses an opportunity of using,
and hands his name and address to Mr. Carker:
who responds to that courtesy by giving him his
own, and with that they part.

As Mr. Carker picks his way so softly past the

house, glancing up at the windows, and trying to make out the pensive face behind the curtain looking at the children opposite, the rough head of Diogenes came clambering up close by it, and the dog, regardless of all soothing, barks and growls, and makes at him from that height, as if he would spring down and tear him limb from limb.

Well spoken, Di, so near your mistress! Another, and another, with your head up, your eyes flashing, and your vexed mouth worrying itself for want of him! Another, as he picks his way along! You have a good scent, Di, — cats, boy, cats!

CHAPTER III.

FLORENCE lived alone in the great dreary house, and day succeeded day, and still she lived alone; and the blank walls looked down upon her with a vacant stare, as if they had a Gorgon-like mind to stare her youth and beauty into stone.

No magic dwelling-place in magic story, shut up in the heart of a thick wood, was ever more solitary and deserted to the fancy than was her father's mansion in its grim reality, as it stood lowering on the street: always by night, when lights were shining from neighboring windows, a blot upon its scanty brightness; always by day a frown upon its never-smiling face.

There were not two dragon sentries keeping ward before the gate of this abode, as in magic legend are usually found on duty over the wronged innocence imprisoned: but besides a glowering visage, with its thin lips parted wickedly, that surveyed all comers from above the archway of the door, there was a monstrous fantasy of rusty iron curling and twisting like a petrifaction of an arbor over the threshold, budding in spikes and corkscrew points, and bearing, one on either side, two ominous extinguishers, that seemed to say, "Who enter here, leave light behind!" There were no talismanic characters engraven on the portal, but the house was now so neglected in appearance, that boys chalked the railings and the pavement — partienlarly round the corner where the side-wall was — and drew ghosts on the stable door; and, being sometimes driven off by Mr. Towlinson, made portraits of him, in return, with his ears growing out horizontally from under his hat. Noise ceased to be, within the shadow of the roof. The brass band that came into the street once a week, in the morning, never brayed a note in at those windows; but all such company, down to a poor little piping organ of weak intellect, with an imbecile party of automaton dancers waltzing in and out at folding doors, fell off from it with one accord, and shunned it as a hopeless place.

The spell upon it was more wasting than the spell that used to set enchanted houses sleeping once upon a time, but left their waking freshness unimpaired.

The passive desolation of disuse was everywhere silently manifest about it. Within doors, curtains, drooping heavily, lost their old folds and shapes, and hung like cumbrous palls. Hecatombs of furniture, still piled and covered up, shrunk like imprisoned and forgotten men, and changed insensibly. Mirrors were dim as with the breath of years. Patterns of carpets faded, and became perplexed and faint, like the memory of those years' trifling incidents. Boards, starting at unwonted footsteps, creaked and shook. Keys rusted in the locks of doors. Damp started on the walls, and, as the stains came out, the pictures seemed to go in and secrete themselves. Mildew and mould began to lurk in closets. Fungus-trees grew in corners of the cellars. Dust accumulated, nobody knew whence nor how; spiders, moths, and grubs were heard of every day. An exploratory black-beetle now and then was found immovable upon the stairs, or in an upper room, as wondering how he got there. Rats began to squeak and scuffle in the night-time, through dark galleries they mined behind the panelling.

The dreary magnificence of the state rooms, seen imperfectly by the doubtful light admitted through closed shutters, would have answered well enough for an enchanted abode. Such as the tarnished paws of gilded lions, stealthily put out from beneath their wrappers; the marble lineaments of busts on pedestals, fearfully revealing themselves through veils; the clocks that never told the time, or, if wound up by any chance, told it wrong, and struck unearthly numbers, which are not upon the dial; the accidental tinklings among the pendent lustres, more startling than alarm bells; the softened sounds and laggard air that made their way among these objects, and a phantom crowd of others, shrouded and hooded, and made spectral of shape. But, besides, there was the great staircase, where the lord of the place so rarely set his foot, and by which his little child had gone up to Heaven. There were other staircases and passages where no one went for weeks together; there were two closed rooms associated with dead members of the family, and with whispered recollections of them; and, to all the house but Florence, there was a gentle figure moving through the solitude and gloom, that gave to every lifeless thing a touch of present human interest and wonder.

For Florence lived alone in the deserted house, and day succeeded day, and still she lived alone, and the cold walls looked down upon her with a vacant stare, as if they had a Gorgon-like mind to stare her youth and beauty into stone.

The grass began to grow upon the roof, and in the crevices of the basement paving. A scaly, crumbling vegetation sprouted round the window-sills. Fragments of mortar lost their hold upon the insides of the unused chimneys, and came dropping down. The two trees with the smoky trunks were blighted high up, and the withered branches domineered above the leaves. Through the whole building, white had turned yellow, yellow nearly black; and, since the time when the poor lady died, it had slowly become a dark gap in the long monotonous street.

But Florence bloomed there, like the king's fair daughter in the story. Her books, her music, and her daily teachers were her only real companions, Susan Nipper and Diogenes excepted : of whom the former, in her attendance on the studies of her young mistress, began to grow quite learned herself, while the latter, softened possibly by the same influences, would lay his head upon the window-ledge, and placidly open and shut his eyes upon the street, all through a summer morning; sometimes pricking up his head to look with great significance after some noisy dog in a cart, who was barking his way along, and sometimes, with an exasperated and unaccountable recollection of his supposed enemy in

the neighborhood, rushing to the door, whence, after
a deafening disturbance, he would come jogging
back with a ridiculous complacency that belonged
to him, and lay his jaw upon the window-ledge
again, with the air of a dog who had done a public
service.

So Florence lived in her wilderness of a home,
within the circle of her innocent pursuits and
thoughts, and nothing harmed her. She could go
down to her father's rooms now, and think of him,
and suffer her loving heart humbly to approach him,
without fear of repulse. She could look upon the
objects that had surrounded him in his sorrow, and
could nestle near his chair, and not dread the glance
that she so well remembered. She could render
him such little tokens of her duty and service as
putting everything in order for him with her own
hands, binding little nosegays for his table, changing them as one by one they withered and he did
not come back, preparing something for him every
day, and leaving some timid mark of her presence
near his usual seat. To-day it was a little painted
stand for his watch; to-morrow she would be afraid
to leave it, and would substitute some other trifle
of her making not so likely to attract his eye.
Waking in the night, perhaps, she would tremble at
the thought of his coming home and angrily reject-
ing it, and would hurry down with slippered feet
and quickly-beating heart, and bring it away. At
another time she would only lay her face upon his
desk, and leave a kiss there, and a tear.

Still no one knew of this. Unless the household found it out when she was not there — and
they all held Mr. Dombey's rooms in awe — it was

as deep a secret in her breast as what had gone before it. Florence stole into those rooms at twilight, early in the morning, and at times when meals were served downstairs. And, although they were in every nook the better and the brighter for her care, she entered and passed out as quietly as any sunbeam, excepting that she left her light behind.

Shadowy company attended Florence up and down the echoing house, and sat with her in the dismantled rooms. As if her life were an enchanted vision, there arose out of her solitude ministering thoughts, that made it fanciful and unreal. She imagined so often what her life would have been if her father could have loved her, and she had been a favorite child, that sometimes, for the moment, she almost believed it was so, and, borne on by the current of that pensive fiction, seemed to remember how they had watched her brother in his grave together; how they had freely shared his heart between them; how they were united in the dear remembrance of him; how they often spoke about him yet; and her kind father, looking at her gently, told her of their common hope and trust in God. At other times she pictured to herself her mother yet alive. And oh, the happiness of falling on her neck, and clinging to her with the love and confidence of all her soul! And oh, the desolation of the solitary house again, with evening coming on, and no one there!

But there was one thought, scarcely shaped out to herself, yet fervent and strong within her, that upheld Florence when she strove, and filled her true young heart, so sorely tried, with constancy of purpose. Into her mind, as into all others contending with the great affliction of our mortal nature, there had stolen solemn wonderings and hopes, arising in the dim world beyond the present life, and murmuring, like faint music, of recognition in the far-off land between her brother and her mother : of some present consciousness in both of her : some love and commiseration for her : and some knowledge of her as she went her way upon the earth. It was a soothing consolation to Florence to give shelter to these thoughts, until one day—it was soon after she had last seen her father in his own room, late at night — the fancy came upon her, that, in weeping for his alienated heart, she might stir the spirits of the dead against him. Wild, weak, childish as it may have been to think so, and to tremble at the half-formed thought, it was the impulse of her loving nature; and from that hour Florence strove against the cruel wound in her breast, and tried to think of him whose hand had made it only with hope.

Her father did not know — she held to it from that time — how much she loved him. She was very young, and had no mother, and had never learned, by some fault or misfortune, how.to express to him that she loved him. She would be patient, and would try to gain that art in time, and win him to a better knowledge of his only child.

This became the purpose of her life. The morning sun shone down upon the faded house, and found the resolution bright and fresh within the bosom of its solitary mistress. Through all the duties of the day it animated her; for Florence hoped that the more she knew, and the more accomplished she became, the more glad he would be when he came to know and like her. Sometimes she wondered, with a swelling heart and rising tear, whether she was proficient enough in anything to surprise him when they should become companions. Sometimes she tried to think if there were any kind of knowledge that would bespeak his interest more readily than another. Always: at her books, her music, and her work: in her morning walks, and in her nightly prayers: she had her engrossing aim in view. Strange study for a child, to learn the road to a hard parent's heart.

There were many careless loungers through the street, as the summer evening deepened into night, who glanced across the road at the sombre house, and saw the youthful figure at the window, such a contrast to it, looking upward at the stars as they began to shine, who would have slept the worse if they had known on what design she mused so steadfastly. The reputation of the mansion as a haunted house would not have been the gayer with some humble dwellers elsewhere, who were struck by its external gloom in passing and repassing on their daily avocations, and so named it, if they could have read its story in the darkening face. But Florence held her sacred purpose, unsuspected and unaided: and studied only how to bring her father to the understanding that she loved him, and made no appeal against him in any wandering thought.

Thus Florence lived alone in the deserted house, and day succeeded day, and still she lived alone, and the monotonous walls looked down upon her with a stare, as if they had a Gorgon-like intent to stare her youth and beauty into stone.

Susan Nipper stood opposite to her young mistress, one morning, as she folded and sealed a note she had been writing: and showed in her looks an approving knowledge of its contents.

"Better late than never, dear Miss Floy," said Susan, "and I do say, that even a visit to them old Skettleses will be a godsend."

"It is very good of Sir Barnet and Lady Skettles, Susan," returned Florence, with a mild correction of that young lady's familiar mention of the family in question, "to repeat their invitation so kindly."

Miss Nipper, who was perhaps the most thorough-going partisan on the face of the earth, and who carried her partisanship into all matters, great or small, and perpetually waged war with it against society, screwed up her lips and shook her head, as a protest against any recognition of disinterestedness in the Skettleses, and a plea in bar that they would have valuable consideration for their kindness in the company of Florence.

"They know what they're about, if ever people did," murmured Miss Nipper, drawing in her breath, "oh! trust them Skettleses for that!"

"I am not very anxious to go to Fulham, Susan, I confess," said Florence thoughtfully; "but it will be right to go. I think it will be better."

"Much better," interposed Susan, with another emphatic shake of her head.

"And so," said Florence, "though I would prefer to have gone when there was no one there, instead of in this vacation-time, when it seems there are some young people staying in the house, I have thankfully said yes."

"For which *I* say, Miss Floy, Oh be joyful!" returned Susan. "Ah! h—h!"

This last ejaculation, with which Miss Nipper frequently wound up a sentence at about that epoch of time, was supposed, below the level of the hall, to have a general reference to Mr. Dombey, and to be expressive of a yearning in Miss Nipper to favor that gentleman with a piece of her mind. But she never explained it; and it had, in consequence, the charm of mystery, in addition to the advantage of the sharpest expression.

"How long it is before we have any news of Walter, Susan!" observed Florence after a moment's silence.

"Long indeed, Miss Floy!" replied her maid. "And Perch said, when he came just now to see for letters — but what signifies what *he* says?" exclaimed Susan, reddening and breaking off. "Much *he* knows about it!"

Florence raised her eyes quickly, and a flush overspread her face.

"If I hadn't," said Susan Nipper, evidently struggling with some latent anxiety and alarm, and looking full at her young mistress, while endeavoring to work herself into a state of resentment with the unoffending Mr. Perch's image, "if I hadn't more manliness than that insipidest of his sex, I'd never take pride in my hair again, but turn it up behind my ears, and wear coarse caps, without a bit of border, until death released me from my insignificance, I may not be a Amazon, Miss Floy, and wouldn't so demean myself by such disfigurement, but anyways I'm not a giver up, I hope."

"Give up! What?" cried Florence, with a face of terror.

"Why, nothing, miss," said Susan. "Good gracious, nothing! It's only that wet curl-paper of a man Perch, that any one might almost make away with, with a touch, and really it would be a blessed event for all parties if some one *would* take pity on him, and would have the goodness!"

"Does he give up the ship, Susan?" inquired Florence, very pale.

"No, miss," returned Susan; "I should like to see him make so bold as to do it to my face! No, miss, but he goes on about some bothering ginger that Mr. Walter was to send to Mrs. Perch, and shakes his dismal head, and says he hopes it may be coming; anyhow, he says, it can't come now in time for the intended occasion, but may do for next, which really," said Miss Nipper, with aggravated scorn, "puts me out of patience with the man, for though I can bear a great deal, I am not a camel, neither am I," added Susan, after a moment's consideration, "if I know myself, a dromedary neither."

"What else does he say, Susan?" inquired Florence earnestly. "Won't you tell me?"

"As if I wouldn't tell you anything, Miss Floy, and everything!" said Susan. "Why, miss, he says that there begins to be a general talk about the ship, and that they have never had a ship on that voyage half so long unheard of, and that the captain's wife was at the office yesterday, and seemed a little put out about it, but any one could say that, we knew nearly that before."

"I must visit Walter's uncle," said Florence hurriedly, "before I leave home. I will go and see him this morning. Let us walk there directly, Susan."

Miss Nipper having nothing to urge against the proposal, but being perfectly acquiescent, they were soon equipped, and in the streets, and on their way towards the little Midshipman.

The state of mind in which poor Walter had gone to Captain Cuttle's, on the day when Brogley the broker came into possession, and when there seemed to him to be an execution in the very steeples, was pretty much the same as that in which Florence now took her way to Uncle Sol's; with this difference, that Florence suffered the added pain of thinking that she had been, perhaps, the innocent occasion of involving Walter in peril, and all to whom he was dear, herself included, in an agony of suspense. For the rest, uncertainty and danger seemed written upon everything. The weather-cocks on spires and housetops were mysterious with hints of stormy wind, and pointed, like so many ghostly fingers, out to dangerous seas, where fragments of great wrecks were drifting, perhaps, and helpless men were rocked upon them into a sleep as deep as the unfathomable waters. When Florence came into the City, and passed gentlemen who were talking together, she dreaded to hear them speaking of the ship, and saying it was lost. Pictures and prints of vessels fighting with the rolling waves filled her with alarm. The smoke and clouds, though moving gently, moved too fast for her apprehensions, and made her fear there was a tempest blowing at that moment on the ocean.

Susan Nipper may or may not have been affected similarly, but having her attention much engaged in struggles with boys, whenever there was any press of people — for, between that grade of humankind and herself there was some natural animosity, that invariably broke out whenever they came together — it would seem that she had not much leisure on the road for intellectual operations.

Arriving in good time abreast of the Wooden Midshipman on the opposite side of the way, and waiting for an opportunity to cross the street, they were a little surprised at first to see, at the instrument-maker's door, a round-headed lad, with his chubby face addressed towards the sky, who, as they looked at him, suddenly thrust into his capacious mouth two fingers of each hand, and, with the assistance of that machinery, whistled, with astonishing shrillness, to some pigeons at a considerable elevation in the air.

"Mrs. Richards's eldest, miss!" said Susan, "and the worrit of Mrs. Richards's life!"

As Polly had been to tell Florence of the resuscitated prospects of her son and heir, Florence was prepared for the meeting; so, a favorable moment presenting itself, they both hastened across, without any further contemplation of Mrs. Richards's bane. That sporting character, unconscious of their approach, again whistled with his utmost might, and then yelled, in a rapture of excitement, "Strays! Whoo-oop! Strays!" which identification had such an effect upon the conscience-stricken pigeons, that instead of going direct to some town in the north of England, as appeared to have been their original intention, they began to wheel and falter; whereupon Mrs. Richards's first-born pierced them with another whistle, and again yelled, in a voice that rose above the turmoil of the street, "Strays! Whoo-oop! Strays!"

From this transport he was abruptly recalled to terrestrial objects by a poke from Miss Nipper, which sent him into the shop.

"Is this the way you show your penitence, when Mrs. Richards has been fretting for you months and months?" said Susan, following the poke. "Where's Mr. Gills?"

Rob, who smoothed his first rebellious glance at Miss Nipper when he saw Florence following, put his knuckles to his hair, in honor of the latter, and said to the former, that Mr. Gills was out.

"Fetch him home," said Miss Nipper with authority, "and say that my young lady's here."

"I don't know where he's gone," said Rob.

"Is *that* your penitence?" cried Susan, with stinging sharpness.

"Why, how can I go and fetch him when I don't know where to go?" whimpered the baited Rob. "How can you be so unreasonable?"

"Did Mr. Gills say when he should be home?" asked Florence.

"Yes, miss," replied Rob, with another application of his knuckles to his hair. "He said he should be home early in the afternoon; in about a couple of hours from now, miss."

"Is he very anxious about his nephew?" inquired Susan.

"Yes, miss," returned Rob, preferring to address himself to Florence, and slighting Nipper; "I should say he was, very much so. He ain't indoors, miss, not a quarter of an hour together. He can't settle in one place five minutes. He goes about like a — just like a stray," said Rob, stooping to get a glimpse of the pigeons through the window,

and checking himself, with his fingers half-way to
his mouth, on the verge of another whistle.

"Do you know a friend of Mr. Gills called Captain Cuttle?" inquired Florence after a moment's
reflection.

"Him with a hook, miss?" rejoined Rob, with
an illustrative twist of his left hand. "Yes, miss.
He was here the day before yesterday."

"Has he not been here since?" asked Susan.

"No, miss," returned Rob, still addressing his
reply to Florence.

"Perhaps Walter's uncle has gone there, Susan,"
observed Florence, turning to her.

"To Captain Cuttle's, miss?" interposed Rob.
"No, he's not gone there, miss. Because he left
particular word that, if Captain Cuttle called, I
should tell him how surprised he was not to have
seen him yesterday, and should make him stop till
he came back."

"Do you know where Captain Cuttle lives?" asked
Florence.

Rob replied in the affirmative, and turning to a
greasy parchment book on the shop desk, read the
address aloud.

Florence again turned to her maid, and took counsel with her in a low voice, while Rob the round-
eyed, mindful of his patron's secret charge, looked
on and listened. Florence proposed that they should
go to Captain Cuttle's house; hear from his own
lips what he thought of the absence of any tidings
of the Son and Heir; and bring him, if they could,
to comfort Uncle Sol. Susan at first objected
slightly, on the score of distance; but a hackney
coach being mentioned by her mistress, withdrew

that opposition, and gave in her assent. There were some minutes of discussion between them before they came to this conclusion, during which the staring Rob paid close attention to both speakers, and inclined his ear to each by turns, as if he were appointed arbitrator of the arguments.

In fine, Rob was despatched for a coach, the visitors keeping shop meanwhile; and when he brought it, they got into it, leaving word for Uncle Sol that they would be sure to call again on their way back. Rob, having stared after the coach until it was as invisible as the pigeons had now become, sat down behind the desk with a most assiduous demeanor; and, in order that he might forget nothing of what had transpired, made notes of it on various small scraps of paper, with a vast expenditure of ink. There was no danger of these documents betraying anything, if accidentally lost; for, long before a word was dry, it became as profound a mystery to Rob as if he had had no part whatever in its production.

While he was yet busy with these labors, the hackney coach, after encountering unheard-of difficulties from swivel-bridges, soft roads, impassable canals, caravans of casks, settlements of scarlet beans and little wash-houses, and many such obstacles abounding in that country, stopped at the corner of Brig Place. Alighting here, Florence and Susan Nipper walked down the street, and sought out the abode of Captain Cuttle.

It happened by evil chance to be one of Mrs. Mac-Stinger's great cleaning days. On these occasions Mrs. MacStinger was knocked up by the policeman at a quarter before three in the morning, and rarely succumbed before twelve o'clock next night. The chief object of this institution appeared to be, that Mrs. MacStinger should move all the furniture into the back-garden at early dawn, walk about the house in pattens all day, and move the furniture back again after dark. These ceremonies greatly fluttered those doves the young MacStingers, who were not only unable at such times to find any resting-place for the soles of their feet, but generally came in for a good deal of pecking from the maternal bird during the progress of the solemnities.

At the moment when Florence and Susan Nipper presented themselves at Mrs. MacStinger's door, that worthy but redoubtable female was in the act of conveying Alexander MacStinger, aged two years and three months, along the passage for forcible deposition in a sitting posture on the street pavement; Alexander being black in the face with holding his breath after punishment, and a cool paving-stone being usually found to act as a powerful restorative in such cases.

The feelings of Mrs. MacStinger, as a woman and a mother, were outraged by the look of pity for Alexander which she observed in Florence's face. Therefore, Mrs. MacStinger asserting those finest emotions of our nature, in preference to weakly gratifying her curiosity, shook and buffeted Alexander, both before and during the application of the paving-stone, and took no further notice of the strangers.

"I beg your pardon, ma'am," said Florence when the child had found his breath again, and was using it. "Is this Captain Cuttle's house?"

"No," said Mrs. MacStinger.

"Not Number Nine?" asked Florence, hesitating.

"Who said it wasn't Number Nine?" said Mrs. MacStinger.

Susan Nipper instantly struck in, and begged to inquire what Mrs. MacStinger meant by that, and if she knew whom she was talking to.

Mrs. MacStinger, in retort, looked at her all over. "What do *you* want with Captain Cuttle, I should wish to know?" said Mrs. MacStinger.

"Should you? Then I'm sorry that you won't be satisfied," returned Miss Nipper.

"Hush, Susan! If you please!" said Florence. "Perhaps you can have the goodness to tell us where Captain Cuttle lives, ma'am, as he don't live here."

"Who says he don't live here?" retorted the implacable MacStinger. "I said it wasn't Cap'en Cuttle's house — and it ain't his house — and forbid it that it ever should be his house — for Cap'en Cuttle don't know how to keep a house — and don't deserve to have a house — it's *my* house — and when I let the upper floor to Cap'en Cuttle, oh, I do a thankless thing, and cast pearls before swine!"

Mrs. MacStinger pitched her voice for the upper windows in offering these remarks, and cracked off each clause sharply by itself, as if from a rifle possessing an infinity of barrels. After the last shot, the captain's voice was heard to say, in feeble remonstrance from his own room, "Steady below!"

"Since you want Cap'en Cuttle, there he is!" said Mrs. MacStinger, with an angry motion of her hand. On Florence making bold to enter without any more parley, and on Susan following, Mrs. MacStinger recommenced her pedestrian exercise in

VOL. II.–5.

pattens, and Alexander MacStinger (still on the
paving-stone), who had stopped in his crying to
attend to the conversation, began to wail again,
entertaining himself during that dismal performance, which was quite mechanical, with a general
survey of the prospect, terminating in the hackney
coach.

The captain in his own apartment was sitting
with his hands in his pockets, and his legs drawn
up under his chair, on a very small, desolate island,
lying about midway in an ocean of soap and water.
The captain's windows had been cleaned, the walls
had been cleaned, the stove had been cleaned, and
everything, the stove excepted, was wet, and shining
with soft soap and sand: the smell of which dry-
saltery impregnated the air. In the midst of the
dreary scene, the captain, cast away upon his island,
looked round on the waste of waters with a rueful
countenance, and seemed waiting for some friendly
bark to come that way, and take him off.

But when the captain, directing his forlorn visage
towards the door, saw Florence appear with her
maid, no words can describe his astonishment.
Mrs. MacStinger's eloquence having rendered all
other sounds but imperfectly distinguishable, he
had looked for no rarer visitor than the potboy or
the milkman; wherefore, when Florence appeared,
and, coming to the confines of the island, put her
hand in his, the captain stood up aghast, as if he
supposed her, for the moment, to be some young
member of the Flying Dutchman's family.

Instantly recovering his self-possession, however,
the captain's first care was to place her on dry land,
which he happily accomplished with one motion of

his arm. Issuing forth, then, upon the main, Captain Cuttle took Miss Nipper round the waist, and bore her to the island also. Captain Cuttle, then, with great respect and admiration, raised the hand of Florence to his lips, and standing off a little (for the island was not large enough for three), beamed on her from the soap and water like a new description of Triton.

"You are amazed to see us, I am sure," said Florence with a smile.

The inexpressibly gratified captain kissed his hook in reply, and growled, as if a choice and delicate compliment were included in the words, "Stand by! Stand by!"

"But I couldn't rest," said Florence, "without coming to ask you what you think about dear Walter —who is my brother now — and whether there is anything to fear, and whether you will not go and console his poor uncle every day, until we have some intelligence of him?"

At these words Captain Cuttle, as by an involuntary gesture, clapped his hand to his head, on which the hard glazed hat was not, and looked discomfited.

"Have you any fears for Walter's safety?" inquired Florence, from whose face the captain (so enraptured he was with it) could not take his eyes: while she, in her turn, looked earnestly at him, to be assured of the sincerity of his reply.

"No, Heart's Delight," said Captain Cuttle, "I am not afeard. Wal'r is a lad as'll go through a deal o' hard weather. Wal'r is a lad as'll bring as much success to that 'ere brig as a lad is capable on. Wal'r," said the captain, his eyes glistening with the praise of his young friend, and his hook raised

.to announce a beautiful quotation, "is what you may call a out'ard and visible sign of a in'ard and spirited grasp, and when found make a note of."

Florence, who did not quite understand this, though the captain evidently thought it full of meaning, and highly satisfactory, mildly looked to him for something more.

"I am not afeard, my Heart's Delight," resumed the captain. "There's been most uncommon bad weather in them latitudes, there's no denyin', and they have drove and drove, and been beat off, maybe t'other side the world. But the ship's a good ship, and the lad's a good lad; and it ain't easy, thank the Lord," the captain made a little bow, "to break up hearts of oak, whether they're in brigs or buzzums. Here we have 'em both ways, which is bringing it up with a round turn, and so I ain't a bit afeard as yet."

"As yet?" repeated Florence.

"Not a bit," returned the captain, kissing his iron hand; "and afore I begin to be, my Heart's Delight, Wal'r will have wrote home from the island, or from some port or another, and made all taut and ship-shape. And with regard to old Sol Gills," here the captain became solemn, "who I'll stand by, and not desert until death doe us part, and when the stormy winds do blow, do blow, do blow — overhaul the catechism," said the captain parenthetically, "and there you'll find them expressions — if it would console Sol Gills to have the opinion of a seafaring man as has got a mind equal to any undertaking that he puts it alongside of, and as was all but smashed in his 'prenticeship, and of which the name is Bunsby, that 'ere man shall give him such an opinion in his own parlor as'll stun him. Ah!" said Captain Cuttle, vauntingly, "as much as if he'd gone and knocked his head again a door!"

"Let us take this gentleman to see him, and let us hear what he says," cried Florence. "Will you go with us now? We have a coach here."

Again the captain clapped his hand to his head, on which the hard glazed hat was not, and looked discomfited. But at this instant a most remarkable phenomenon occurred. The door opening without any note of preparation, and apparently of itself, the hard glazed hat in question skimmed into the room like a bird, and alighted heavily at the captain's feet. The door then shut as violently as it had opened, and nothing ensued in explanation of the prodigy.

Captain Cuttle picked up his hat, and having turned it over with a look of interest and welcome, began to polish it on his sleeve. While doing so, the captain eyed his visitors intently, and said in a low voice, —

"You see I should have bore down on Sol Gills yesterday, and this morning, but she — she took it away and kept it. That's the long and short of the subject."

"Who did, for goodness' sake?" asked Susan Nipper.

"The lady of the house, my dear," returned the captain in a gruff whisper, and making signals of secrecy. "We had some words about the swabbing of these here planks, and she — in short," said the captain, eying the door, and relieving himself with a long breath, "she stopped my liberty."

"Oh! I wish she had me to deal with!" said

Susan, reddening with the energy of the wish.
" I'd stop her ! "

" Would you, do you think, my dear ? " rejoined
the captain, shaking his head doubtfully, but regarding the desperate courage of the fair aspirant
with obvious admiration. " I don't know. It's
difficult navigation. She's very hard to carry on
with, my dear. You never can tell how she'll head,
you see. She's full one minute, and round upon
you next. And when she *is* a Tartar," said the
captain, with the perspiration breaking out upon
his forehead — There was nothing but a whistle
emphatic enough for the conclusion of the sentence,
so the captain whistled tremulously. After which
he again shook his head, and recurring to his admiration of Miss Nipper's devoted bravery, timidly repeated, " Would you, do you think, my dear ? ".

Susan only replied with a bridling smile, but that
was so very full of defiance, that there is no knowing how long Captain Cuttle might have stood entranced in its contemplation, if Florence in her
anxiety had not again proposed their immediately
resorting to the oracular Bunsby. Thus reminded
of his duty, Captain Cuttle put on the glazed hat
firmly, took up another knobby stick, with which he
had supplied the place of that one given to Walter,
and offering his arm to Florence, prepared to cut
his way through the enemy.

It turned out, however, that Mrs. MacStinger had
already changed her course, and that she headed, as
the captain had remarked she often did, in quite a
new direction. For, when they got downstairs, they
found that exemplary woman beating the mats on
the door-steps, with Alexander, still upon the pav-

ing-stone, dimly looming through a fog of dust; and so absorbed was Mrs. MacStinger in her household occupation, that when Captain Cuttle and his visitors passed, she beat the harder, and neither by word nor gesture showed any consciousness of their vicinity. The captain was so well pleased with this easy escape — although the effect of the door-mats on him was like a copious administration of snuff, and made him sneeze until the tears ran down his face — that he could hardly believe his good fortune; but more than once, between the door and the hackney coach, looked over his shoulder, with an obvious apprehension of Mrs. MacStinger's giving chase yet.

However, they got to the corner of Brig Place without any molestation from that terrible fire-ship; and the captain mounting the coach-box — for his gallantry would not allow him to ride inside with the ladies, though besought to do so — piloted the driver on his course for Captain Bunsby's vessel, which was called the Cautious Clara, and was lying hard by Ratcliff.

Arrived at the wharf off which this great commander's ship was jammed in among some five hundred companions, whose tangled rigging looked like monstrous cobwebs half swept down, Captain Cuttle appeared at the coach window, and invited Florence and Miss Nipper to accompany him on board; observing that Bunsby was to the last degree soft-hearted in respect of ladies, and that nothing would so much tend to bring his expansive intellect into a state of harmony as their presentation to the Cautious Clara.

Florence readily consented; and the captain, taking her little hand in his prodigious palm, led her, with a mixed expression of patronage, paternity, pride, and ceremony, that was pleasant to see, over several very dirty decks, until, coming to the Clara, they found that cautious craft (which lay outside the tier) with her gangway removed, and half a dozen feet of river interposed between herself and her nearest neighbor. It appeared, from Captain Cuttle's explanation, that the great Bunsby, like himself, was cruelly treated by his landlady, and that when her usage of him for the time being was so hard that he could bear it no longer, he set this gulf between them as a last resource.

" Clara a-hoy ! " cried the captain, putting a hand to each side of his mouth.

" A-hoy ! " cried a boy, like the captain's echo, tumbling up from below.

" Bunsby aboard ? " cried the captain, hailing the boy in a stentorian voice, as if he were half a mile off instead of two yards.

" Ay, ay ! " cried the boy in the same tone.

The boy then shoved out a plank to Captain Cuttle, who adjusted it carefully, and led Florence across; returning presently for Miss Nipper. So they stood upon the deck of the Cautious Clara, in whose standing rigging divers fluttering articles of dress were curing, in company with a few tongues and some mackerel.

Immediately there appeared, coming slowly up above the bulkhead of the cabin, another bulkhead — human and very large — with one stationary eye in the mahogany face, and one revolving one, on the principle of some lighthouses. This head was decorated with shaggy hair, like oakum, which had no governing inclination towards the north, east, west, or south, but inclined to all four quarters of the compass, and to every point upon it. The head was followed by a perfect desert of chin, and by a shirt collar and neckerchief, and by a dreadnaught pilot coat, and by a pair of dreadnaught pilot trousers, whereof the waistband was so very broad and high, that it became a succedaneum for a waistcoat: being ornamented, near the wearer's breast-bone, with some massive wooden buttons, like backgammon men. As the lower portions of these pantaloons became revealed, Bunsby stood confessed; his hands in their pockets, which were of vast size; and his gaze directed, not to Captain Cuttle or the ladies, but the masthead.

The profound appearance of this philosopher, who was bulky and strong, and on whose extremely red face an expression of taciturnity sat enthroned, not inconsistent with his character, in which that quality was proudly conspicuous, almost daunted Captain Cuttle, though on familiar terms with him. Whispering to Florence that Bunsby had never in his life expressed surprise, and was considered not to know what it meant, the captain watched him as he eyed his masthead, and afterwards swept the horizon; and when the revolving eye seemed to be coming round in his direction said, —

"Bunsby, my lad, how fares it?"

A deep, gruff, husky utterance, which seemed to have no connection with Bunsby, and certainly had not the least effect upon his face, replied, "Ay, ay, shipmet, how goes it?" At the same time Bunsby's right hand and arm, emerging from a pocket, shook the captain's, and went back again.

"Bunsby," said the captain, striking home at once, "here you are; a man of mind, and a man as can give an opinion. Here's a young lady as wants to take that opinion, in regard of my friend Wal'r; likewise my t'other friend, Sol Gills, which is a character for you to come within hail of, being a man of science, which is the mother of inwention, and knows no law. Bunsby, will you wear, to oblige me, and come along with us?"

The great commander, who seemed, by the expression of his visage, to be always on the lookout for something in the extremest distance, and to have no ocular knowledge of anything within ten miles, made no reply whatever.

"Here is a man," said the captain, addressing himself to his fair auditors, and indicating the commander with his outstretched hook, "that has fell down more than any man alive; that has had more accidents happen to his own self than the Seaman's Hospital to all hands; that took as many spars and bars and bolts about the outside of his head, when he was young, as you'd want a order for on Chatham Yard to build a pleasure yacht with; and yet that got his opinions in that way, it's my belief, for there ain't nothing like 'em afloat or ashore."

The stolid commander appeared, by a very slight vibration in his elbows, to express some satisfaction in this encomium; but if his face had been as distant as his gaze was, it could hardly have enlightened the beholders less in reference to anything that was passing in his thoughts.

"Shipmet," said Bunsby all of a sudden, and stooping down to look out under some interposing spar, "what'll the ladies drink?"

Captain Cuttle, whose delicacy was shocked by such an inquiry in connection with Florence, drew the sage aside, and seeming to explain in his ear, accompanied him below; where, that he might not take offence, the captain drank a dram himself, which Florence and Susan, glancing down the open skylight, saw the sage, with difficulty finding room for himself between his berth and a very little brass fireplace, serve out for self and friend. They soon reappeared on deck, and Captain Cuttle, triumphing in the success of his enterprise, conducted Florence back to the coach, while Bunsby followed, escorting Miss Nipper, whom he hugged upon the way (much to that young lady's indignation) with his pilot-coated arm, like a blue bear.

The captain put his oracle inside, and gloried so much in having secured him, and having got that mind into a hackney coach, that he could not refrain from often peeping in at Florence through the little window behind the driver, and testifying his delight in smiles, and also in taps upon his forehead, to hint to her that the brain of Bunsby was hard at it. In the meantime, Bunsby, still hugging Miss Nipper (for his friend, the captain, had not exaggerated the softness of his heart), uniformly preserved his gravity of deportment, and showed no other consciousness of her or anything.

Uncle Sol, who had come home, received them at the door, and ushered them immediately into the little back-parlor, strangely altered by the absence of Walter. On the table, and about the room, were the charts and maps on which the heavy-hearted instrument-maker had again and again tracked the missing vessel across the sea, and on which, with a pair of compasses that he still had in his hand, he had been measuring, a minute before, how far she must have driven, to have driven here or there: and trying to demonstrate that a long time must elapse before hope was exhausted.

"Whether she can have run," said Uncle Sol, looking wistfully over the chart; "but no, that's almost impossible. Or whether she can have been forced by stress of weather — but that's not reasonably likely. Or whether there is any hope she so far changed her course as — but even I can hardly hope that!" With such broken suggestions, poor old Uncle Sol roamed over the great sheet before him, and could not find a speck of hopeful probability in it large enough to set one small point of the compasses upon.

Florence saw immediately — it would have been difficult to help seeing — that there was a singular indescribable change in the old man, and that, while his manner was far more restless and unsettled than usual, there was yet a curious contradictory decision in it that perplexed her very much. She fancied once that he spoke wildly, and at random; for, on her saying she regretted not to have seen him when she had been there before that morning, he at first replied that he had been to see her, and directly afterwards seemed to wish to recall that answer.

"You have been to see me?" said Florence. "To-day?"

"Yes, my dear young lady," returned Uncle Sol, looking at her and away from her in a confused manner. "I wished to see you with my own eyes, and to hear you with my own ears, once more before — " There he stopped.

"Before when? Before what?" said Florence, putting her hand upon his arm.

"Did I say 'before'?" replied old Sol. "If I did, I must have meant before we should have news of my dear boy."

"You are not well," said Florence tenderly. "You have been so very anxious. I am sure you are not well."

"I am as well," returned the old man, shutting up his right hand, and holding it out to show her: "as well and firm as any man at my time of life can hope to be. See! It's steady. Is its master not as capable of resolution and fortitude as many a younger man? I think so. We shall see."

There was that in his manner more than in his words, though they remained with her too, which impressed Florence so much, that she would have confided her uneasiness to Captain Cuttle at that moment, if the captain had not seized that moment for expounding the state of circumstances on which the opinion of the sagacious Bunsby was requested, and entreating that profound authority to deliver the same.

Bunsby, whose eye continued to be addressed to somewhere about the half-way house between London and Gravesend, two or three times put out his rough right arm, as seeking to wind it, for inspiration, round the fair form of Miss Nipper; but that young female having withdrawn herself in displeasure to the opposite side of the table, the soft heart of the commander of the Cautious Clara met with no response to its impulses. After sundry failures in this wise, the commander, addressing himself to nobody, thus spake; or rather, the voice within him said of its own accord, and quite independent of himself, as if he were possessed by a gruff spirit :

" My name's Jack Bunsby ! "

" He was christened John," cried the delighted Captain Cuttle. " Hear him ! "

" And what I says," pursued the voice after some deliberation, " I stands to."

The captain, with Florence on his arm, nodded at the auditory, and seemed to say, " Now he's coming out. This is what I meant when I brought him."

" Whereby," proceeded the voice, " why not ? If so, what odds ? Can any man say otherwise ? No. Awast then ! "

When it had pursued its train of argument to this point, the voice stopped and rested. It then proceeded very slowly, thus :

" Do I believe that this here Son and Heir's gone down, my lads ? Mayhap. Do I say so ? Which ? If a skipper stands out by Sen' George's Channel, making for the Downs, what's right ahead of him ? The Goodwins. He isn't forced to run upon the Goodwins, but he may. The bearings of this observation lays in the application on it. That ain't no part of my duty. Awast then, keep a bright lookout for'ard, and good luck to you ! "

The voice here went out of the back-parlor, and into the street, taking the commander of the Cautious Clara with it, and accompanying him on board again with all convenient expedition, where he immediately turned in, and refreshed his mind with a nap.

The students of the sage's precepts, left to their

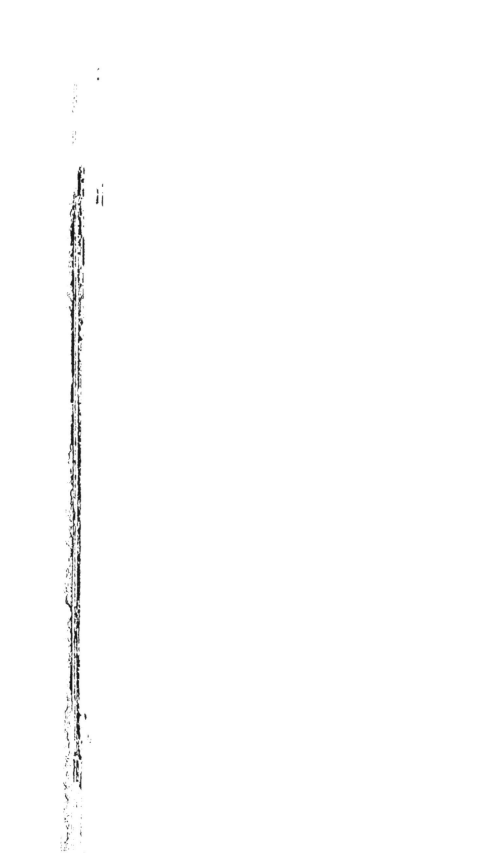

own application of his wisdom — upon a principle
which was the main leg of the Bunsby tripod, as
it is perchance of some other oracular stools —
looked at one another in a little uncertainty; while
Rob the Grinder, who had taken the innocent freedom of peering in, and listening, through the skylight in the roof, came softly down from the leads,
in a state of very dense confusion. Captain Cuttle,
however, whose admiration of Bunsby was, if possible, enhanced by the splendid manner in which he
had justified his reputation and come through this
solemn reference, proceeded to explain that Bunsby
meant nothing but confidence, that Bunsby had no
misgivings; and that such an opinion as that man
had given, coming from such a mind as his, was
Hope's own anchor, and with good roads to cast it
in. Florence endeavored to believe that the captain
was right; but the Nipper, with her arms tight
folded, shook her head in resolute denial, and had
no more trust in Bunsby than in Mr. Perch himself.

The philosopher seemed to have left Uncle Sol
pretty much where he had found him, for he still
went roaming about the watery world, compasses in
hand, and discovering no rest for them. It was in
pursuance of a whisper in his ear from Florence,
while the old man was absorbed in this pursuit,
that Captain Cuttle laid his heavy hand upon his
shoulder.

"What cheer, Sol Gills?" cried the captain
heartily.

"But so-so, Ned," returned the instrument-maker.
"I have been remembering, all this afternoon, that
on the very day when my boy entered Dombey's

House, and came home late to dinner, sitting just
there where you stand, we talked of storm and
shipwreck, and I could hardly turn him from the
subject."

But meeting the eyes of Florence, which were
fixed with earnest scrutiny upon his face, the old
man stopped and smiled.

"Stand by, old friend!" cried the captain. "Look
alive! I tell you what, Sol Gills; arter I've convoyed
Heart's Delight safe home"—here the captain kissed
his hook to Florence,—"I'll come back and take you
in tow for the rest of this blessed day. You'll come
and eat your dinner along with me, Sol, somewheres
or other."

"Not to-day, Ned!" said the old man quickly, and
appearing to be unaccountably startled by the propo-
sitiou. "Not to-day. I couldn't do it!"

"Why not?" returned the captain, gazing at him
in astonishment.

"I—I have so much to do. I—I mean to think
of, and arrange. I couldn't do it, Ned, indeed. I
must go out again, and be alone, and turn my mind
to many things to-day."

The captain looked at the instrument-maker, and
looked at Florence, and again at the instrument-
maker. "To-morrow, then," he suggested at last.

"Yes, yes. To-morrow," said the old man.
"Think of me to-morrow. Say to-morrow."

"I shall come here early, mind, Sol Gills," stipu-
lated the captain.

"Yes, yes. The first thing to-morrow morning,"
said old Sol; "and now good-by, Ned Cuttle, and
God bless you!"

Squeezing both the captain's hands with uncommon fervor as he said it, the old man turned to Florence, folded hers in his own, and put them to his lips; then hurried her out to the coach with very singular precipitation. Altogether, he made such an effect on Captain Cuttle that the captain lingered behind, and instructed Rob to be particularly gentle and attentive to his master until the morning; which injunction he strengthened with the payment of one shilling down, and the promise of another sixpence before noon next day. This kind office performed, Captain Cuttle, who considered himself the natural and lawful body-guard of Florence, mounted the box with a mighty sense of his trust, and escorted her home. At parting, he assured her that he would stand by Sol Gills, close and true; and once again inquired of Susan Nipper, unable to forget her gallant words in reference to Mrs. MacStinger, "Would you, do you think, my dear, though?"

When the desolate house had closed upon the two, the captain's thoughts reverted to the old instrument-maker, and he felt uncomfortable. Therefore, instead of going home, he walked up and down the street several times, and, eking out his leisure until evening, dined late at a certain angular little tavern in the City, with a public parlor like a wedge, to which glazed hats much resorted. The captain's principal intention was to pass Sol Gills's after dark, and look in through the window: which he did. The parlor door stood open, and he could see his old friend writing busily and steadily at the table within, while the little Midshipman, already sheltered from the night dews, watched him from the counter; under which Rob the Grinder made his own bed, prepara-

tory to shutting the shop. Re-assured by the tran-
quillity that reigned within the precincts of the
wooden mariner, the captain headed for Brig Place,
resolving to weigh anchor betimes in the morning.

CHAPTER IV.

SIR BARNET and Lady Skettles, very good people, resided in a pretty villa at Fulham, on the banks of the Thames; which was one of the most desirable residences in the world when a rowing-match happened to be going past, but had its little inconveniences at other times, among which may be enumerated the occasional appearance of the river in the drawing-room, and the contemporaneous disappearance of the lawn and shrubbery.

Sir Barnet Skettles expressed his personal consequence chiefly through an antique gold snuff-box, and a ponderous silk pocket-handkerchief, which he had an imposing manner of drawing out of his pocket like a banner, and using with both hands at once. Sir Barnet's object in life was constantly to extend the range of his acquaintance. Like a heavy body dropped into water — not to disparage so worthy a gentleman by the comparison — it was in the nature of things that Sir Barnet must spread an ever-widening circle about him, until there was no room left. Or, like a sound in air, the vibration of which, according to the speculation of an ingenious modern philosopher, may go on travelling for-

ever through the interminable fields of space, nothing but coming to the end of his moral tether could
stop Sir Barnet Skettles in his voyage of discovery
through the social system.

Sir Barnet was proud of making people acquainted
with people. He liked the thing for its own sake,
and it advanced his favorite object too. For example, if Sir Barnet had the good fortune to get
hold of a raw recruit, or a country gentleman, and
ensnared him to his hospitable villa, Sir Barnet
would say to him, on the morning after his arrival,
"Now, my dear sir, is there anybody you would
like to know? Who is there you would wish to
meet? Do you take any interest in writing people, or in painting or sculpturing people, or in acting
people, or in anything of that sort?" Possibly the
patient answered yes, and mentioned somebody of
whom Sir Barnet had no more personal knowledge
than of Ptolemy the Great. Sir Barnet replied that
nothing on earth was easier, as he knew him very
well: immediately called on the aforesaid somebody,
left his card, wrote a short note, — "My dear sir —
penalty of your eminent position — friend at my
house naturally desirous — Lady Skettles and myself participate — trust that, genius being superior
to ceremonies, you will do us the distinguished favor
of giving us the pleasure," &c. &c. — and so killed
a brace of birds with one stone, dead as door-nails.

With the snuff-box and banner in full force, Sir
Barnet Skettles propounded his usual inquiry to
Florence on the first morning of her visit. When
Florence thanked him, and said there was no one in
particular whom she desired to see, it was natural
she should think with a pang of poor lost Walter.

When Sir Barnet Skettles, urging his kind offer, said, "My dear Miss Dombey, are you sure you can remember no one whom your good papa—to whom I beg you to present the best compliments of myself and Lady Skettles when you write—might wish you to know?" it was natural, perhaps, that her poor head should droop a little, and that her voice should tremble as it softly answered in the negative.

Skettles junior, much stiffened as to his cravat, and sobered down as to his spirits, was at home for the holidays, and appeared to feel himself aggrieved by the solicitude of his excellent mother that he should be attentive to Florence. Another and a deeper injury under which the soul of young Barnet chafed was the company of Doctor and Mrs. Blimber, who had been invited on a visit to the parental roof-tree, and of whom the young gentleman often said he would have preferred their passing the vacation at Jericho.

"Is there anybody *you* can suggest, now, Doctor Blimber?" said Sir Barnet Skettles, turning to that gentleman.

"You are very kind, Sir Barnet," returned Doctor Blimber. "Really I am not aware that there is, in particular. I like to know my fellow-men in general, Sir Barnet. What does Terence say? Any one who is the parent of a son is interesting to *me*."

"Has Mrs. Blimber any wish to see any remarkable person?" asked Sir Barnet courteously.

Mrs. Blimber replied, with a sweet smile and a shake of her sky-blue cap, that if Sir Barnet could have made her known to Cicero, she would have troubled him: but such an introduction not being feasible, and she already enjoying the friendship of himself and his amiable lady, and possessing, with the Doctor her husband, their joint confidence in regard to their dear son — here young Barnet was observed to curl his nose — she asked no more.

Sir Barnet was fain, under these circumstances, to content himself for the time with the company assembled. Florence was glad of that; for she had a study to pursue among them, and it lay too near her heart, and was too precious and momentous, to yield to any other interest.

There were some children staying in the house. Children who were as frank and happy with fathers and with mothers as those rosy faces opposite home. Children who had no restraint upon their love, and freely showed it. Florence sought to learn their secret; sought to find out what it was she had missed; what simple art they knew, and she knew not; how she could be taught by them to show her father that she loved him, and to win his love again.

Many a day did Florence thoughtfully observe these children. On many a bright morning did she leave her bed when the glorious sun rose, and walking up and down upon the river's bank, before any one in the house was stirring, look up at the windows of their rooms, and think of them, asleep, so gently tended and affectionately thought of. Florence would feel more lonely then than in the great house all alone; and would think sometimes that she was better there than here, and that there was greater peace in hiding herself than in mingling with others of her age, and finding how unlike them all she was. But attentive to her study, though it touched her to the quick at every little leaf she turned in the hard book, Florence remained among them, and tried, with patient hope, to gain the knowledge that she wearied for.

Ah! how to gain it? how to know the charm in its beginning? There were daughters here who rose up in the morning, and lay down to rest at night, possessed of fathers' hearts already. They had no repulse to overcome, no coldness to dread, no frown to smooth away. As the morning advanced, and the windows opened one by one, and the dew began to dry upon the flowers and grass, and youthful feet began to move upon the lawn, Florence, glancing round at the bright faces, thought, What was there she could learn from these children? It was too late to learn from them; each could approach her father fearlessly, and put up her lips to meet the ready kiss, and wind her arm about the neck that bent down to caress her. *She* could not begin by being so bold. Oh! could it be that there was less and less hope as she studied more and more?

She remembered well that even the old woman who had robbed her when a little child — whose image and whose house, and all she had said and done, were stamped upon her recollection, with the enduring sharpness of a fearful impression made at that early period of life — had spoken fondly of her daughter, and how terribly even she had cried out in the pain of hopeless separation from her child. But her own mother, she would think again, when she recalled this, had loved her well. Then, sometimes, when her thoughts reverted swiftly to the void between herself and her father, Florence would tremble, and the tears would start upon her face, as she pictured to herself her mother living on, and coming also to dislike her, because of her wanting the unknown grace that should conciliate that father naturally, and had never done so from her cradle. She knew that this imagination did wrong to her mother's memory, and had no truth in it, or base to rest upon; and yet she tried so hard to justify him, and to find the whole blame in herself, that she could not resist its passing, like a wild cloud, through the distance of her mind.

There came among the other visitors, soon after Florence, one beautiful girl, three or four years younger than she, who was an orphan child, and who was accompanied by her aunt, a gray-haired lady, who spoke much to Florence, and who greatly liked (but that they all did) to hear her sing of an evening, and would always sit near her at that time, with motherly interest. They had only been two days in the house when Florence, being in an arbor in the garden one warm morning, musingly observant of a youthful group upon the turf, through some intervening boughs, and wreathing flowers for the head of one little creature among them who was the pet and plaything of the rest, heard this same lady and her niece, in pacing up and down a sheltered nook close by, speak of herself.

" Is Florence an orphan like me, aunt ? " said the child.

" No, my love. She has no mother, but her father is living."

" Is she in mourning for her poor mamma now ? " inquired the child quickly.

" No ; for her only brother."

" Has she no other brother ? "

" None."

" No sister ? "

" None."

" I am very, very sorry ! " said the little girl.

As they stopped soon afterwards to watch some boats, and had been silent in the meantime, Florence, who had risen when she heard her name, and had gathered up her flowers to go and meet them, that they might know of her being within hearing, resumed her seat and work, expecting to hear no more; but the conversation recommenced next moment.

" Florence is a favorite with every one here, and deserves to be, I am sure," said the child earnestly. " Where is her papa ? "

The aunt replied, after a moment's pause, that she did not know. Her tone of voice arrested Florence, who had started from her seat again; and held her fastened to the spot, with her work hastily caught up to her bosom, and her two hands saving it from being scattered on the ground.

" He is in England, I hope, aunt ? " said the child.

" I believe so. Yes; I know he is, indeed."

" Has he ever been here ? "

" I believe not. No."

" Is he coming here to see her ? "

" I believe not."

" Is he lame, or blind, or ill, aunt ? " asked the child.

The flowers that Florence held to her breast began to fall when she heard those words, so wonderingly spoken. She held them closer; and her face hung down upon them.

" Kate," said the lady after another moment of silence, " I will tell you the whole truth about

Florence as I have heard it, and believe it to be. Tell no one else, my dear, because it may be little known here, and your doing so would give her pain."

"I never will!" exclaimed the child.

"I know you never will," returned the lady. "I can trust you as myself. I fear then, Kate, that Florence's father cares little for her, very seldom sees her, never was kind to her in her life, and now quite shuns her and avoids her. She would love him dearly if he would suffer her, but he will not — though for no fault of hers; and she is greatly to be loved and pitied by all gentle hearts."

More of the flowers that Florence held fell scattering on the ground; those that remained were wet, but not with dew; and her face dropped upon her laden hands.

"Poor Florence! Dear, good Florence!" cried the child.

"Do you know why I have told you this, Kate?" said the lady.

"That I may be very kind to her, and take great care to try to please her. Is that the reason, aunt?"

"Partly," said the lady, "but not all. Though we see her so cheerful: with a pleasant smile for every one; ready to oblige us all, and bearing her part in every amusement here: she can hardly be quite happy. Do you think she can, Kate?"

"I am afraid not," said the little girl.

"And you can understand," pursued the lady, "why her observation of children who have parents who are fond of them and proud of them — like many here just now — should make her sorrowful in secret?"

"Yes, dear aunt," said the child, "I understand that very well. Poor Florence!"

More flowers strayed upon the ground, and those she yet held to her breast trembled as if a wintry wind were rustling them.

"My Kate," said the lady, whose voice was serious, but very calm and sweet, and had so impressed Florence from the first moment of her hearing it, "of all the youthful people here, you are her natural and harmless friend; you have not the innocent means that happier children have —"

"There are none happier, aunt!" exclaimed the child, who seemed to cling about her.

"— As other children have, dear Kate, of reminding her of her misfortune. Therefore I would have you, when you try to be her little friend, try all the more for that, and feel that the bereavement you sustained — thank Heaven! before you knew its weight — gives you claim and hold upon poor Florence."

"But I am not without a parent's love, aunt, and I never have been," said the child, "with you."

"However that may be, my dear," returned the lady, "your misfortune is a lighter one than Florence's; for not an orphan in the wide world can be so deserted as the child who is an outcast from a living parent's love."

The flowers were scattered on the ground like dust; the empty hands were spread upon the face; and orphaned Florence, shrinking down upon the ground, wept long and bitterly.

But true of heart, and resolute in her good purpose, Florence held to it as her dying mother held by her upon the day that gave Paul life. He did

not know how much she loved him.   However long
the time in coming, and however slow the interval,
she must try to bring that knowledge to her father's
heart one day or other.   Meantime, she must be
careful in no thoughtless word, or look, or burst of
feeling awakened by any chance circumstance, to
complain against him, or to give occasion for these
whispers to his prejudice.

Even in the response she made the orphan child,
to whom she was attracted strongly, and whom she
had such occasion to remember, Florence was mindful of him.   If she singled her out too plainly
(Florence thought) from among the rest, she would
confirm — in one mind certainly : perhaps in more
— the belief that he was cruel and unnatural.   Her
own delight was no set-off to this.   What she had
overheard was a reason, not for soothing herself,
but for saving him; and Florence did it, in pursuance of the study of her heart.

She did so always.   If a book were read aloud,
and there were anything in the story that pointed
at an unkind father, she was in pain for their application of it to him ; not for herself.   So with any
trifle of an interlude that was acted, or picture that
was shown, or game that was played, among them.
The occasions for such tenderness towards him were
so many, that her mind misgave her often, it would
indeed be better to go back to the old house, and
live again within the shadow of its dull walls, undisturbed.   How few who saw sweet Florence, in her
spring of womanhood, the modest little queen of
those small revels, imagined what a load of sacred
care lay heavy in her breast !   How few of those
who stiffened in her father's freezing atmosphere

suspected what a heap of fiery coals was piled upon his head!

Florence pursued her study patiently, and failing to acquire the secret of the nameless grace she sought among the youthful company who were assembled in the house, often walked out alone, in the early morning, among the children of the poor. But still she found them all too far advanced to learn from. They had won their household places long ago, and did not stand without, as she did, with a bar across the door.

There was one man whom she several times observed at work very early, and often with a girl of about her own age seated near him. He was a very poor man, who seemed to have no regular employment, but now went roaming about the banks of the river when the tide was low, looking out for bits and scraps in the mud; and now worked at the unpromising little patch of garden ground before his cottage; and now tinkered up a miserable old boat that belonged to him; or did some job of that kind for a neighbor, as chance occurred. Whatever the man's labor, the girl was never employed; but sat, when she was with him, in a listless, moping state, and idle.

Florence had often wished to speak to this man; yet she had never taken courage to do so, as he made no movement towards her. But one morning when she happened to come upon him suddenly, from a by-path among some pollard willows which terminated in the little shelving piece of stony ground that lay between his dwelling and the water, where he was bending over a fire he had made to calk the old boat which was lying bottom upwards close by, he raised his head at the sound of her footstep, and gave her Good-morning.

"Good-morning," said Florence, approaching nearer; "you are at work early."

"I'd be glad to be often at work earlier, miss, if I had work to do."

"Is it so hard to get?" asked Florence.

"*I* find it so," replied the man.

Florence glanced to where the girl was sitting, drawn together, with her elbows on her knees, and her chin on her hands, and said, —

"Is that your daughter?"

He raised his head quickly, and looking towards the girl with a brightened face, nodded to her, and said "Yes." Florence looked towards her too, and gave her a kind salutation; the girl muttered something in return, ungraciously and sullenly.

"Is she in want of employment also?" said Florence.

The man shook his head. "No, miss," he said. "I work for both."

"Are there only you two, then?" inquired Florence.

"Only us two," said the man. "Her mother has been dead these ten year. Martha!" (he lifted up his head again, and whistled to her) "won't you say a word to the pretty young lady?"

The girl made an impatient gesture with her cowering shoulders, and turned her head another way. Ugly, misshapen, peevish, ill-conditioned, ragged, dirty — but beloved! Oh, yes! Florence had seen her father's look towards her, and she knew whose look it had no likeness to.

"I'm afraid she's worse this morning, my poor

girl!" said the man, suspending his work, and contemplating his ill-favored child with a compassion
that was the more tender for being rough.

"She is ill, then?" said Florence.

The man drew a deep sigh. "I don't believe my
Martha's had five short days' good health," he
answered, looking at her still, "in as many long
years."

"Ay! and more than that, John," said a neighbor,
who had come down to help him with the boat.

"More than that you say, do you?" cried the
other, pushing back his battered hat, and drawing
his hand across his forehead. "Very like. It seems
a long, long time."

"And the more the time," pursued the neighbor,
"the more you've favored and humored her, John,
till she's got to be a burden to herself and every
body else."

"Not to me," said her father, falling to his work
again. "Not to me."

Florence could feel — who better? — how truly
he spoke. She drew a little closer to him, and
would have been glad to touch his rugged hand, and
thank him for his goodness to the miserable object
that he looked upon with eyes so different from any
other man's.

"Who would favor my poor girl — to call it favor-
ing — if I didn't?" said the father.

"Ay, ay," cried the neighbor. "In reason, John.
But you! You rob yourself to give to her. You
bind yourself hand and foot on her account. You
make your life miserable along of her. And what
does *she* care? You don't believe she knows it?"

The father lifted up his head again, and whistled

to her. Martha made the same impatient gesture with her crouching shoulders in reply; and he was glad and happy.

"Only for that, miss," said the neighbor with a smile, in which there was more of secret sympathy than he expressed; "only to get that, he never lets her out of his sight!"

"Because the day'll come, and has been coming a long while," observed the other, bending low over his work, "when to get half as much from that unfort'nate child of mine — to get the trembling of a finger, or the waving of a hair — would be to raise the dead."

Florence softly put some money near his hand on the old boat, and left him.

And now Florence began to think, if she were to fall ill, if she were to fade like her dear brother, would he then know that she had loved him; would she then grow dear to him; would he come to her bedside, when she was weak and dim of sight, and take her into his embrace, and cancel all the past? Would he so forgive her in that changed condition, for not having been able to lay open her childish heart to him, as to make it easy to relate with what emotions she had gone out of his room that night; what she had meant to say if she had had the courage; and how she had endeavored, afterwards, to learn the way she never knew in infancy?

Yes, she thought, if she were dying, he would relent. She thought, that if she lay, serene and not unwilling to depart, upon the bed that was curtained round with recollections of their darling boy, he would be touched home, and would say, "Dear

Florence, live for me, and we will love each other as we might have done, and be as happy as we might have been these many years!" She thought that if she heard such words from him, and had her arms clasped round him, she could answer with a smile, "It is too late for anything but this; I never could be happier, dear father!" and so leave him, with a blessing on her lips.

The golden water she remembered on the wall appeared to Florence, in the light of such reflections, only as a current flowing on to rest, and to a region where the dear ones, gone before, were waiting, hand-in-hand: and often, when she looked upon the darker river rippling at her feet, she thought with awful wonder, but not terror, of that river which her brother had so often said was bearing him away.

The father and his sick daughter were yet fresh in Florence's mind, and, indeed, that incident was not a week old, when Sir Barnet and his lady, going out walking in the lanes one afternoon, proposed to her to bear them company. Florence readily consenting, Lady Skettles ordered out young Barnet as a matter of course. For nothing delighted Lady Skettles so much as beholding her eldest son with Florence on his arm.

Barnet, to say the truth, appeared to entertain an opposite sentiment on the subject, and on such occasions frequently expressed himself audibly, though indefinitely, in reference to "a parcel of girls." As it was not easy to ruffle her sweet temper, however, Florence generally reconciled the young gentleman to his fate after a few minutes, and they strolled on amicably; Lady Skettles and Sir Barnet following, in a state of perfect complacency and high gratification.

This was the order of procedure on the afternoon in question : and Florence had almost succeeded in overruling the present objections of Skettles junior to his destiny, when a gentleman on horseback came riding by, looked at them earnestly as he passed, drew in his rein, wheeled round, and came riding back again, hat in hand.

The gentleman had looked particularly at Florence ; and when the little party stopped, on his riding back, he bowed to her before saluting Sir Barnet and his lady.   Florence had no remembrance of having ever seen him, but she started involuntarily when he came near her, and drew back.

" My horse is perfectly quiet, I assure you," said the gentleman.

It was not that, but something in the gentleman himself — Florence could not have said what — that made her recoil as if she had been stung.

" I have the honor to address Miss Dombey, I believe ? " said the gentleman with a most persuasive smile.   On Florence inclining her head, he added, " My name is Carker.   I can hardly hope to be remembered by Miss Dombey except by name. Carker."

Florence, sensible of a strange inclination to shiver, though the day was hot, presented him to her host and hostess; by whom he was very graciously received.

" I beg pardon," said Mr. Carker, "a thousand times !   But I am going down to-morrow morning to Mr. Dombey, at Leamington, and if Miss Dombey

can intrust me with any commission, need I say how *very* happy I shall be?"

Sir Barnet, immediately divining that Florence would desire to write a letter to her father, proposed to return, and besought Mr. Carker to come home and dine in his riding gear. Mr. Carker had the misfortune to be engaged for dinner, but if Miss Dombey wished to write, nothing would delight him more than to accompany them back, and to be her faithful slave in waiting as long as she pleased. As he said this with his widest smile, and bent down close to her to pat his horse's neck, Florence, meeting his eyes, saw, rather than heard him say, "There is no news of the ship!"

Confused, frightened, shrinking from him, and not even sure that he had said those words, for he seemed to have shown them to her in some extraordinary manner through his smile instead of uttering them, Florence faintly said that she was obliged to him, but she would not write; she had nothing to say.

"Nothing to send, Miss Dombey?" said the man of teeth.

"Nothing," said Florence, "but my — but my dear love — if you please."

Disturbed as Florence was, she raised her eyes to his face with an imploring and expressive look, that plainly besought him, if he knew — which he as plainly did — that any message between her and her father was an uncommon charge, but that one most of all, to spare her. Mr. Carker smiled and bowed low, and being charged by Sir Barnet with the best compliments of himself and Lady Skettles, took his leave, and rode away; leaving a favorable impression on that worthy couple. Florence was seized with such a shudder as he went, that Sir Barnet, adopting the popular superstition, supposed somebody was passing over her grave. Mr. Carker, turning a corner on the instant, looked back, and bowed, and disappeared, as if he rode off to the churchyard straight to do it.

CHAPTER V.

CAPTAIN CUTTLE, though no sluggard, did not turn so early on the morning after he had seen Sol Gills, through the shop-window, writing in the parlor, with the Midshipman upon the counter, and Rob the Grinder making up his bed below it, but that the clock struck six as he raised himself on his elbow, and took a survey of his little chamber. The captain's eyes must have done severe duty, if he usually opened them as wide on awaking as he did that morning; and were but roughly rewarded for their vigilance, if he generally rubbed them half as hard. But the occasion was no common one, for Rob the Grinder had certainly never stood in the doorway of Captain Cuttle's bedroom before, and in it he stood then, panting at the captain, with a flushed and tousled air of bed about him, that greatly heightened both his color and expression.

"Holloa!" roared the captain. "What's the matter?"

Before Rob could stammer a word in answer, Captain Cuttle turned out, all in a heap, and covered the boy's mouth with his hand.

"Steady, my lad," said the captain; "don't ye speak a word to me as yet!"

The captain, looking at his visitor in great consternation, gently shouldered him into the next
room, after laying this injunction upon him; and
disappearing for a few moments, forthwith returned
in the blue suit. Holding up his hand in token of
the injunction not yet being taken off, Captain
Cuttle walked up to the cupboard, and poured himself out a dram ; a counterpart of which he handed
to the messenger. The captain then stood himself
up in a corner, against the wall, as if to forestall
the possibility of being knocked backward by the
communication that was to be made to him; and
having swallowed his liquor, with his eyes fixed on
the messenger, and his face as pale as his face could
be, requested him to "heave ahead."

"Do you mean tell you, captain ?" asked Rob,
who had been greatly impressed by these precautions.

"Ay !" said the captain.

"Well, sir," said Rob, "I ain't got much to tell.
But look here !"

Rob produced a bundle of keys. The captain
surveyed them, remained in his corner, and surveyed the messenger.

"And look here !" pursued Rob.

The boy produced a sealed packet, which Captain
Cuttle stared at as he had stared at the keys.

"When I woke this morning, captain," said Rob,
"which was about a quarter after five, I found these
on my pillow. The shop-door was unbolted and unlocked, and Mr. Gills gone."

"Gone !" roared the captain.

"Flowed, sir," returned Rob.

The captain's voice was so tremendous, and he

came out of his corner with such way on him, that
Rob retreated before him into another corner:
holding out the keys and packet, to prevent himself
from being run down.

"'For Captain Cuttle,' sir," cried Rob, "is on the
keys, and on the packet too. Upon my word and
honor, Captain Cuttle, I don't know anything more
about it. I wish I may die if I do! Here's a sitiwation for a lad that's just got a sitiwation," cried
the unfortunate Grinder, screwing his cuff into his
face: "his master bolted with his place, and him
blamed for it!"

These lamentations had reference to Captain
Cuttle's gaze, or rather glare, which was full of
vague suspicions, threatenings, and denunciations.
Taking the proffered packet from his hand, the
captain opened it and read as follows:—

"My dear Ned Cuttle. Enclosed is my will"—
the captain turned it over with a doubtful look
—"and testament.— Where's the testament?"
said the captain, instantly impeaching the ill-fated
Grinder. "What have you done with that, my
lad?"

"*I* never see it," whimpered Rob. "Don't keep
on suspecting an innocent lad, captain. *I* never
touched the testament."

Captain Cuttle shook his head, implying that
somebody must be made answerable for it; and
gravely proceeded:—

"Which don't break open for a year, or until you
have decisive intelligence of my dear Walter, who
is dear to you, Ned, too, I am sure." The captain
paused and shook his head in some emotion; then,
as a re-establishment of his dignity in this trying

position, looked with exceeding sternness at the Grinder. "If you should never hear of me, or see me more, Ned, remember an old friend as he will remember you to the last—kindly; and at least until the period I have mentioned has expired, keep a home in the old place for Walter. There are no debts, the loan from Dombey's House is paid off, and all my keys I send with this. Keep this quiet, and make no inquiry for me; it is useless. So no more, dear Ned, from your true friend, Solomon Gills." The captain took a long breath, and then read these words, written below: "The boy Rob, well recommended, as I told you, from Dombey's House. If all else should come to the hammer, take care, Ned, of the little Midshipman."

To convey to posterity any idea of the manner in which the captain, after turning this letter over and over, and reading it a score of times, sat down in his chair, and held a court-martial on the subject in his own mind, would require the united genius of all the great men who, discarding their own untoward days, have determined to go down to posterity, and have never got there. At first the captain was too much confounded and distressed to think of anything but the letter itself; and even when his thoughts began to glance upon the various attendant facts, they might, perhaps, as well have occupied themselves with their former theme, for any light they reflected on them. In this state of mind, Captain Cuttle having the Grinder before the court, and no one else, found it a great relief to decide, generally, that he was an object of suspicion: which the captain so clearly expressed in his visage, that Rob remonstrated.

"Oh, don't, captain!" cried the Grinder. "I wonder how you can! What have I done to be looked at like that?"

"My lad," said Captain Cuttle, "don't you sing out afore you're hurt. And don't you commit yourself, whatever you do."

"I haven't been and committed nothing, captain," answered Rob.

"Keep her free, then," said the captain impressively, "and ride easy."

With a deep sense of the responsibility imposed upon him, and the necessity of thoroughly fathoming this mysterious affair, as became a man in his relations with the parties, Captain Cuttle resolved to go down and examine the premises, and to keep the Grinder with him. Considering that youth as under arrest at present, the captain was in some doubt whether it might not be expedient to handcuff him, or tie his ankles together, or attach a weight to his legs, but not being clear as to the legality of such formalities, the captain decided merely to hold him by the shoulder all the way, and knock him down if he made any objection.

However, he made none, and consequently got to the instrument-maker's house without being placed under any more stringent restraint. As the shutters were not yet taken down, the captain's first care was to have the shop opened; and, when the daylight was freely admitted, he proceeded, with its aid, to further investigation.

The captain's first care was to establish himself in a chair in the shop, as president of the solemn tribunal that was sitting within him; and to require Rob to lie down in his bed under the counter, show exactly where he discovered the keys and packet when he awoke, how he found the door when he went to try it, how he started off to Brig Place — cautiously preventing the latter imitation from being carried farther than the threshold — and so on to the end of the chapter. When all this had been done several times, the captain shook his head, and seemed to think the matter had a bad look.

Next, the captain, with some indistinct idea of finding a body, instituted a strict search over the whole house ; groping in the cellars with a lighted candle, thrusting his hook behind doors, bringing his head into violent contact with beams, and covering himself with cobwebs. Mounting up to the old man's bedroom, they found that he had not been in bed on the previous night, but had merely lain down on the coverlet, as was evident from the impression yet remaining there.

" And *I* think, captain," said Rob, looking round the room, " that when Mr. Gills was going in and out so often, these last few days, he was taking little things away piecemeal, not to attract attention."

" Ay l " said the captain mysteriously. " Why so, my lad ? "

" Why," returned Rob, looking about, " I don't see his shaving tackle. Nor his brushes, captain. Nor no shirts. Nor yet his shoes."

As each of these articles was mentioned, Captain Cuttle took particular notice of the corresponding department of the Grinder, lest he should appear to have been in recent use, or should prove to be in present possession thereof. But Rob had no occasion to shave, certainly was not brushed, and wore the clothes he had worn for a long time past, beyond all possibility of mistake.

" And what should you say," said the captain — "not committing yourself — about his time of sheering off ? Hey ? "

" Why, I think, captain," returned Rob, "that he must have gone pretty soon after I began to snore."

" What o'clock was that ? " said the captain, prepared to be very particular about the exact time.

" How can I tell, captain ? " answered Rob. " I only know that I'm a heavy sleeper at first, and a light one towards morning; and if Mr. Gills had come through the shop near daybreak, though ever so much on tiptoe, I'm pretty sure I should have heard him shut the door at all events."

On mature consideration of this evidence, Captain Cuttle began to think, that the instrument-maker must have vanished of his own accord; to which logical conclusion he was assisted by the letter addressed to himself, which, as being unquestionably in the old man's handwriting, would seem, with no great forcing, to bear the construction, that he arranged of his own will to go, and so went. The captain had next to consider where and why ? and, as there was no way whatsoever that he saw to the solution of the first difficulty, he confined his meditations to the second.

Remembering the old man's curious manner, and the farewell he had taken of him: unaccountably fervent at the time, but quite intelligible now: a terrible apprehension strengthened on the captain, that, overpowered by his anxieties and regrets for Walter, he had been driven to commit suicide. Unequal to the wear and tear of daily life, as he had often professed himself to be, and shaken as he no doubt was by the uncertainty and deferred hope he had undergone, it seemed no violently strained misgiving, but only too probable.

Free from debt, and with no fear for his personal liberty, or the seizure of his goods, what else but such a state of madness could have hurried him away alone and secretly? As to his carrying some apparel with him, if he had really done so — and they were not even sure of that — he might have done so, the captain argued, to prevent inquiry, to distract attention from his probable fate, or to ease the very mind that was now revolving all these possibilities. Such, reduced into plain language, and condensed within a small compass, was the final result and substance of Captain Cuttle's deliberations; which took a long time to arrive at this pass, and were, like some more public deliberations, very discursive and disorderly.

Dejected and despondent in the extreme, Captain Cuttle felt it just to release Rob from the arrest in which he had placed him, and to enlarge him, subject to a kind of honorable inspection which he still resolved to exercise; and having hired a man, from Brogley the broker, to sit in the shop during their absence, the captain, taking Rob with him, issued forth upon a dismal quest after the mortal remains of Solomon Gills.

Not a station-house, or bone-house, or workhouse in the metropolis escaped a visitation from the hard glazed hat. Along the wharves, among the shipping, on the bank-side, up the river, down the river, here, there, everywhere, it went gleaming where men were thickest, like the hero's helmet in an epic battle. For a whole week the captain read of all the found and missing people in all the newspapers and handbills, and went forth on expeditions at all hours of the day to identify Solomon Gills, in poor little ship-boys who had fallen overboard, and in tall foreigners with dark beards who had taken poison — "to make sure," Captain Cuttle said, "that it warn't him." It is a sure thing that it never was, and that the good captain had no other satisfaction.

Captain Cuttle at last abandoned these attempts as hopeless, and set himself to consider what was to be done next. After several new perusals of his poor friend's letter, he considered that the maintenance of "a home in the old place for Walter" was the primary duty imposed upon him. Therefore, the captain's decision was, that he would keep house on the premises of Solomon Gills himself, and would go into the instrument business, and see what came of it.

But, as this step involved the relinquishment of his apartments at Mrs. MacStinger's, and he knew that resolute woman would never hear of his deserting them, the captain took the desperate determination of running away.

"Now, look ye here, my lad," said the captain to Rob when he had matured this notable scheme; "to-morrow, I sha'n't be found in this here road-stead till night — not till arter midnight p'rhaps. But you keep watch till you hear me knock, and the moment you do, turn to and open the door."

"Very good, captain," said Rob.

"You'll continue to be rated on these here books," pursued the captain condescendingly, "and I don't say but what you may get promotion, if you and me should pull together with a will. But the moment you hear me knock to-morrow night, whatever time it is, turn to and show yourself smart with the door."

"I'll be sure to do it, captain," replied Rob.

"Because, you understand," resumed the captain, coming back again to enforce this charge upon his mind, "there may be, for anything I can say, a chase; and I might be took while I was waiting, if you didn't show yourself smart at the door."

Rob again assured the captain that he would be prompt and wakeful; and the captain, having made this prudent arrangement, went home to Mrs. MacStinger's for the last time.

The sense the captain had of its being the last time, and of the awful purpose hidden beneath his blue waistcoat, inspired him with such a mortal dread of Mrs. MacStinger, that the sound of that lady's foot downstairs, at any time of the day, was sufficient to throw him into a fit of trembling. It fell out, too, that Mrs. MacStinger was in a charming temper — mild and placid as a house-lamb; and Captain Cuttle's conscience suffered terrible twinges when she came up to inquire if she could cook him nothing for his dinner.

"A nice small kidney-pudding, now, Cap'en Cuttle," said his landlady; "or a sheep's heart. Don't mind my trouble."

"No, thankee, ma'am," returned the captain.

"Have a roast fowl," said Mrs. MacStinger, "with a bit of weal stuffing and some egg sauce. Come, Cap'en Cuttle! Give yourself a little treat!"

"No, thankee, ma'am," returned the captain very humbly.

"I'm sure you're out of sorts, and want to be stimulated," said Mrs. MacStinger. "Why not have, for once in a way, a bottle of sherry wine?"

"Well, ma'am," rejoined the captain, "if you'd be so good as take a glass or two, I think I would try that. Would you do me the favor, ma'am," said the captain, torn to pieces by his conscience, "to accept a quarter's rent ahead?"

"And why so, Cap'en Cuttle?" retorted Mrs. MacStinger — sharply as the captain thought.

The captain was frightened to death. "If you would, ma'am," he said with submission, "it would oblige me. I can't keep my money very well. It pays itself out. I should take it kind if you'd comply."

"Well, Cap'en Cuttle," said the unconscious Mac-Stinger, rubbing her hands, "you can do as you please. It's not for me, with my family, to refuse, no more than it is to ask."

"And would you, ma'am," said the captain, taking down the tin canister, in which he kept his cash, from the top shelf of the cupboard, "be so good as offer eighteen-pence apiece to the little family all round? If you could make it convenient, ma'am, to pass the word presently for them children to come for'ard in a body, I should be glad to see 'em."

These innocent MacStingers were so many daggers to the captain's breast, when they appeared in a swarm, and tore at him with the confiding trustfulness he so little deserved. The eye of Alexander MacStinger, who had been his favorite, was insup-

portable to the captain; the voice of Juliana Mac-
Stinger, who was the picture of her mother, made a
coward of him.

Captain Cuttle kept up appearances, nevertheless,
tolerably well, and for an hour or two was very
hardly used and roughly handled by the young Mac-
Stingers : who, in their childish frolics, did a little
damage also to the glazed hat, by sitting in it, two
at a time, as in a nest, and drumming on the inside
of the crown with their shoes. At length the captain sorrowfully dismissed them : taking leave of
these cherubs with the poignant remorse and grief
of a man who was going to execution.

In the silence of night the captain packed up his
heavier property in a chest, which he locked, intend-
ing to leave it there, in all probability forever, but
on the forlorn chance of one day finding a man sufficiently bold and desperate to come and ask for it.
Of his lighter necessaries the captain made a bundle;
and disposed his plate about his person, ready for
flight. At the hour of midnight, when Brig Place
was buried in slumber, and Mrs. MacStinger was
lulled in sweet oblivion, with her infants around
her, the guilty captain, stealing down on tiptoe in
the dark, opened the door, closed it softly after him,
and took to his heels.

Pursued by the image of Mrs. MacStinger springing out of bed, and, regardless of costume, following
and bringing him back; pursued also by a consciousness of his enormous crime; Captain Cuttle held
on at a great pace, and allowed no grass to grow
under his feet between Brig Place and the instrument-maker's door. It opened when he knocked —
for Rob was on the watch — and, when it was bolted

and locked behind him, Captain Cuttle felt comparatively safe.

"Whew!" cried the captain, looking round him.
"It's a breather!"

"Nothing the matter, is there, captain?" cried
the gaping Rob.

"No, no!" said Captain Cuttle after changing
color, and listening to a passing footstep in the
street. "But mind ye, my lad; if any lady, except
either of them two as you see t'other day, ever
comes and asks for Cap'en Cuttle, be sure to report
no person of that name known, nor never heard of
here; observe them orders, will you?"

"I'll take care, captain," returned Rob.

"You might say — if you liked," hesitated the
captain, "that you read in the paper that a cap'en
of that name was gone to Australia, emigrating
along with a whole ship's complement of people as
had all swore never to come back no more."

Rob nodded his understanding of these instructions; and Captain Cuttle, promising to make a
man of him if he obeyed orders, dismissed him,
yawning, to his bed under the counter, and went
aloft to the chamber of Solomon Gills.

What the captain suffered next day, whenever a
bonnet passed, or how often he darted out of the
shop to elude imaginary MacStingers, and sought
safety in the attic, cannot be told. But, to avoid
the fatigues attendant on this means of self-preservation, the captain curtained the glass door of communication between the shop and parlor on the inside,
fitted a key to it from the bunch that had been sent
to him; and cut a small hole of espial in the wall.
The advantage of this fortification is obvious. On

a bonnet appearing, the captain instantly slipped into his garrison, locked himself up, and took a secret observation of the enemy. Finding it a false alarm, the captain instantly slipped out again. And the bonnets in the streets were so very numerous, and alarms were so inseparable from their appearance, that the captain was almost incessantly slipping in and out all day long.

Captain Cuttle found time, however, in the midst of this fatiguing service, to inspect the stock; in connection with which he had the general idea (very laborious to Rob) that too much friction could not be bestowed upon it, and that it could not be made too bright. He also ticketed a few attractive-looking articles at a venture, at prices ranging from ten shillings to fifty pounds, and exposed them in the window, to the great astonishment of the public.

After effecting these improvements, Captain Cuttle, surrounded by the instruments, began to feel scientific : and looked up at the stars at night through the skylight, when he was smoking his pipe in the little back-parlor before going to bed, as if he had established a kind of property in them. As a tradesman in the City, too, he began to have an interest in the Lord Mayor and the Sheriffs, and in public companies; and felt bound to read the quotations of the Funds every day, though he was unable to make out, on any principle of navigation, what the figures meant, and could have very well dispensed with the fractions. Florence the captain waited on, with his strange news of Uncle Sol, immediately after taking possession of the Midshipman; but she was away from home. So the captain sat himself down in his altered station of life, with no company but Rob the Grinder; and losing count of time, as men do when great changes come upon them, thought musingly of Walter, and of Solomon Gills, and even of Mrs. MacStinger herself, as among the things that had been.

CHAPTER VI.

"Your most obedient, sir," said the major. "Damme, sir, a friend of my friend Dombey's is a friend of mine, and I'm glad to see you!"

"I am infinitely obliged, Carker," explained Mr. Dombey, "to Major Bagstock for his company and conversation. Major Bagstock has rendered me great service, Carker."

Mr. Carker the manager, hat in hand, just arrived at Leamington, and just introduced to the major, showed the major his whole double range of teeth, and trusted he might take the liberty of thanking him with all his heart for having effected so great an improvement in Mr. Dombey's looks and spirits.

"By Gad, sir," said the major in reply, "there are no thanks due to me, for it's a give-and-take affair. A great creature like our friend Dombey, sir," said the major, lowering his voice, but not lowering it so much as to render it inaudible to that gentleman, "cannot help improving and exalting his friends. He strengthens and invigorates a man, sir, does Dombey, in his moral nature."

Mr. Carker snapped at the expression. In his

moral nature. Exactly. The very words he had been on the point of suggesting.

"But when my friend Dombey, sir," added the major, "talks to you of Major Bagstock, I must crave leave to set him and you right. He means plain Joe, sir — Joey B. — Josh Bagstock — Joseph — rough and tough old J., sir. At your service."

Mr. Carker's excessively friendly inclinations towards the major, and Mr. Carker's admiration of his roughness, toughness, and plainness, gleamed out of every tooth in Mr. Carker's head.

"And now, sir," said the major, "you and Dombey have the devil's own amount of business to talk over."

"By no means, major," observed Mr. Dombey.

"Dombey," said the major defiantly, "I know better; a man of your mark — the Colossus of commerce — is not to be interrupted. Your moments are precious. We shall meet at dinner-time. In the interval old Joseph will be scarce. The dinner hour is a sharp seven, Mr. Carker."

With that, the major, greatly swollen as to his face, withdrew; but immediately putting in his head at the door again, said, —

"I beg your pardon. Dombey, have you any message to 'em ?"

Mr. Dombey, in some embarrassment, and not without a glance at the courteous keeper of his business confidence, intrusted the major with his compliments.

"By the Lord, sir," said the major, "you must make it something warmer than that, or old Joe will be far from welcome."

"Regards then, if you will, major," returned Mr. Dombey.

"Damme, sir," said the major, shaking his shoulders and his great cheeks jocularly : "make it something warmer than that."

"What you please, then, major," observed Mr. Dombey.

"Our friend is sly, sir, sly, sir, de-vilish sly," said the major, staring round the door at Carker. "So is Bagstock." But stopping in the midst of a chuckle, and drawing himself up to his full height, the major solemnly exclaimed, as he struck himself on the chest, "Dombey! I envy your feelings. God bless you!" and withdrew.

"You must have found the gentleman a great resource," said Carker, following him with his teeth.

"Very great indeed," said Mr. Dombey.

"He has friends here, no doubt," pursued Carker. "I perceive, from what he has said, that you go into society here. Do you know," smiling horribly, "I am so very glad that you go into society!"

Mr. Dombey acknowledged this display of interest on the part of his second in command by twirling his watch-chain, and slightly moving his head.

"You were formed for society," said Carker. "Of all the men I know, you are the best adapted by nature and by position for society. Do you know, I have been frequently amazed that you should have held it at arm's length so long!"

"I have had my reasons, Carker. I have been alone, and indifferent to it. But you have great social qualifications yourself, and are the more likely to have been surprised."

"Oh! *I!*" returned the other with ready self-disparagement. "It's quite another matter in the case of a man like me. I don't come into comparison with *you*."

Mr. Dombey put his hand to his neckcloth, settled his chin in it, coughed, and stood looking at his faithful friend and servant for a few moments in silence.

"I shall have the pleasure, Carker," said Mr. Dombey at length: making as if he swallowed something a little too large for his throat: "to present you to my — to the major's friends. Highly agreeable people."

"Ladies among them, I presume?" insinuated the smooth manager.

"They are all — that is to say, they are both — ladies," replied Mr. Dombey.

"Only two?" smiled Carker.

"There are only two. I have confined my visits to their residence, and have made no other acquaintance here."

"Sisters, perhaps?" quoth Carker.

"Mother and daughter," replied Mr. Dombey.

As Mr. Dombey dropped his eyes, and adjusted his neckcloth again, the smiling face of Mr. Carker the manager became in a moment, and without any stage of transition, transformed into a most intent and frowning face, scanning his closely and with an ugly sneer. As Mr. Dombey raised his eyes, it changed back, no less quickly, to its old expression, and showed him every gum of which it stood possessed.

"You are very kind," said Carker. "I shall be delighted to know them. Speaking of daughters, I have seen Miss Dombey."

There was a sudden rush of blood to Mr. Dombey's face.

"I took the liberty of waiting on her," said Carker, "to inquire if she could charge me with any little commission. I am not so fortunate as to be the bearer of any but her — but her dear love."

Wolf's face that it was then, with even the hot tongue revealing itself through the stretched mouth, as the eyes encountered Mr. Dombey's!

"What business intelligence is there ? " inquired the latter gentleman after a silence, during which Mr. Carker had produced some memoranda and other papers.

"There is very little," returned Carker. "Upon the whole, we have not had our usual good fortune of late, but that is of little moment to you. At Lloyd's they give up the Son and Heir for lost. Well, she was insured from her keel to her mast-head."

"Carker," said Mr. Dombey, taking a chair near him, "I cannot say that young man, Gay, ever impressed me favorably — "

"Nor me," interposed the manager.

" — But I wish," said Mr. Dombey, without heeding the interruption, "he had never gone on board that ship. I wish he had never been sent out."

"It is a pity you didn't say so in good time, is it not ? " retorted Carker coolly. "However, I think it's all for the best. I really think it's all for the best. Did I mention that there was something like a little confidence between Miss Dombey and myself ? "

"No," said Mr. Dombey sternly.

"I have no doubt," returned Mr. Carker after an

impressive pause, "that, wherever Gay is, he is much better where he is than at home here. If I were, or could be, in your place, I should be satisfied of that. I am quite satisfied of it myself. Miss Dombey is confiding and young — perhaps hardly proud enough for your daughter — if she have a fault. Not that that is much, though, I am sure. Will you check these balances with me?"

Mr. Dombey leaned back in his chair, instead of bending over the papers that were laid before him, and looked the manager steadily in the face. The manager, with his eyelids slightly raised, affected to be glancing at his figures, and to await the leisure of his principal. He showed that he affected this, as if from great delicacy, and with a design to spare Mr. Dombey's feelings; and the latter, as he looked at him, was cognizant of his intended consideration, and felt that, but for it, this confidential Carker would have said a great deal more, which he, Mr. Dombey, was too proud to ask for. It was his way in business, often. Little by little, Mr. Dombey's gaze relaxed, and his attention became diverted to the papers before him; but, while busy with the occupation they afforded him, he frequently stopped, and looked at Mr. Carker again. Whenever he did so, Mr. Carker was demonstrative, as before, in his delicacy, and impressed it on his great chief more and more.

While they were thus engaged; and, under the skilful culture of the manager, angry thoughts in reference to poor Florence brooded and bred in Mr. Dombey's breast, usurping the place of the cold dislike that generally reigned there; Major Bagstock, much admired by the old ladies of Leamington, and followed by the native, carrying the usual amount of light baggage, straddled along the shady side of the way, to make a morning call on Mrs. Skewton. It being mid-day when the major reached the bower of Cleopatra, he had the good fortune to find his princess on her usual sofa, languishing over a cup of coffee, with the room so darkened and shaded for her more luxurious repose, that Withers, who was in attendance on her, loomed like a phantom page.

"What insupportable creature is this coming in?" said Mrs. Skewton. "I cannot bear it. Go away, whoever you are!"

"You have not the heart to banish J. B., ma'am!" said the major, halting midway to remonstrate, with his cane over his shoulder.

"Oh, it's you, is it? On second thoughts, you may enter," observed Cleopatra.

The major entered accordingly, and, advancing to the sofa, pressed her charming hand to his lips.

"Sit down," said Cleopatra, listlessly waving her fan, "a long way off. Don't come too near me, for I am frightfully faint and sensitive this morning, and you smell of the sun. You are absolutely tropical."

"By George, ma'am," said the major, "the time has been when Joseph Bagstock has been grilled and blistered by the sun; the time was when he was forced, ma'am, into such full blow, by high hot-house heat in the West Indies, that he was known as the Flower. A man never heard of Bagstock, ma'am, in those days; he heard of the Flower — the Flower of Ours. The Flower may have faded, more or less, ma'am," observed the major, dropping into a much nearer chair than had been indicated by his cruel divinity, " but it is a tough plant yet, and constant as the evergreen."

Here the major, under cover of the dark room, shut up one eye, rolled his head like a harlequin, and, in his great self-satisfaction, perhaps, went nearer to the confines of apoplexy than he had ever gone before.

" Where is Mrs. Granger ? " inquired Cleopatra of her page.

Withers believed she was in her own room.

" Very well," said Mrs. Skewton. " Go away, and shut the door. I am engaged."

As Withers disappeared, Mrs. Skewton turned her head languidly towards the major, without otherwise moving, and asked him how his friend was.

" Dombey, ma' am," returned the major, with a facetious gurgling in his throat, " is as well as a man in his condition *can* be. His condition is a desperate one, ma'am. He is touched, is Dombey. Touched!" cried the major. " He is bayoneted through the body."

Cleopatra cast a sharp look at the major, that contrasted forcibly with the affected drawl in which she presently said : —

" Major Bagstock, although I know but little of the world, — nor can I really regret my inexperience, for I fear it is a false place :. full of withering conventionalities : where nature is but little regarded, and where the music of the heart, and the gushing of the soul, and all that sort of thing, which is so truly poetical, is seldom heard, — I cannot misunderstand your meaning. There is an

allusion to Edith — to my extremely dear child,"
said Mrs. Skewton, tracing the outline of her eyebrows with her forefinger, "in your words, to which
the tenderest of chords vibrates excessively!"

"Bluntness, ma'am," returned the major, "has
ever been the characteristic of the Bagstock breed.
You are right. Joe admits it."

"And that allusion," pursued Cleopatra, "would
involve one of the most — if not positively *the*
most touching, and thrilling, and sacred emotions
of which our sadly fallen nature is susceptible, I
conceive."

The major laid his hand upon his lips, and wafted
a kiss to Cleopatra, as if to identify the emotion in
question.

"I feel that I am weak. I feel that I am wanting in that energy which should sustain a mamma:
not to say a parent: on such a subject," said Mrs.
Skewton, trimming her lips with the laced edge of
her pocket-handkerchief; "but I can hardly approach
a topic so excessively momentous to my dearest
Edith without a feeling of faintness. Nevertheless,
bad man, as you have boldly remarked upon it, and
as it has occasioned me great anguish:" Mrs.
Skewton touched her left side with her fan: "I will
not shrink from my duty."

The major, under cover of the dimness, swelled,
and swelled, and rolled his purple face about, and
winked his lobster eye, until he fell into a fit of
wheezing, which obliged him to rise and take a turn
or two about the room, before his fair friend could
proceed.

"Mr. Dombey," said Mrs. Skewton, when she at
length resumed, "was obliging enough, now many

weeks ago, to do us the honor of visiting here; in company, my dear major, with yourself. I acknowledge — let me be open — that it is my failing to be the creature of impulse, and to wear my heart, as it were, outside. I know my failing full well. My enemy cannot know it better. But I am not penitent; I would rather not be frozen by the heartless world, and am content to bear this imputation justly."

Mrs. Skewton arranged her tucker, pinched her wiry throat to give it a soft surface, and went on with great complacency.

"It gave me (my dearest Edith too, I am sure) infinite pleasure to receive Mr. Dombey. As a friend of yours, my dear major, we were naturally disposed to be prepossessed in his favor; and I fancied that I observed an amount of heart in Mr. Dombey, that was excessively refreshing."

"There is devilish little heart in Dombey now, ma'am," said the major.

"Wretched man!" cried Mrs. Skewton, looking at him languidly, "pray be silent."

"J. B. is dumb, ma'am," said the major.

"Mr. Dombey," pursued Cleopatra, smoothing the rosy hue upon her cheeks, "accordingly repeated his visit; and possibly finding some attraction in the simplicity and primitiveness of our tastes — for there is always a charm in Nature — it is so very sweet — became one of our little circle every evening. Little did I think of the awful responsibility into which I plunged when I encouraged Mr. Dombey — to — "

"To beat up these quarters, ma'am," suggested Major Bagstock.

"Coarse person!" said Mrs. Skewton, "you anticipate my meaning, though in odious language."

Here Mrs. Skewton rested her elbow on the little
table at her side, and suffering her wrist to droop in
what she considered a graceful and becoming manner, dangled her fan to and fro, and lazily admired
her hand while speaking.

"The agony I have endured," she said mincingly,
"as the truth has by degrees dawned upon me, has
been too exceedingly terrific to dilate upon. My
whole existence is bound up in my sweetest Edith;
and to see her change from day to day — my beautiful pet, who has positively garnered up her heart
since the death of that most delightful creature,
Granger — is the most affecting thing in the world."

Mrs. Skewton's world was not a very trying one,
if one might judge of it by the influence of its
most affecting circumstance upon her; but this by
the way.

"Edith," simpered Mrs. Skewton, "who is the
perfect pearl of my life, is said to resemble me. I
believe we *are* alike."

"There is one man in the world who never will
admit that any one resembles you, ma'am," said the
major; "and that man's name is old Joe Bagstock."

Cleopatra made as if she would brain the flatterer
with her fan, but relenting, smiled upon him and
proceeded, —

"If my charming girl inherits any advantages
from me, wicked one!" — the major was the wicked
one — "she inherits also my foolish nature. She
has great force of character — mine has been said
to be immense, though I don't believe it — but once
moved, she is susceptible and sensitive to the last

extent. What are my feelings when I see her pining! They destroy me."

The major, advancing his double chin, and pursing up his blue lips into 'a soothing expression, affected the profoundest sympathy.

"The confidence," said Mrs. Skewton, "that has subsisted between us — the free development of soul, and openness of sentiment — is touching to think of. We have been more like sisters than mamma and child."

"J. B.'s own sentiment," observed the major, "expressed by J. B. fifty thousand times!"

"Do not interrupt, rude man!" said Cleopatra. "What are my feelings, then, when I find that there is one subject avoided by us! That there is a what's-his-name — a gulf — opened between us! That my own artless Edith is changed to me! They are of the most poignant description, of course."

The major left his chair, and took one nearer to the little table.

"From day to day I see this, my dear major," proceeded Mrs. Skewton. "From day to day I feel this. From hour to hour I reproach myself for that excess of faith and trustfulness which has led to such distressing consequences; and almost from minute to minute, I hope that Mr. Dombey may explain himself, and relieve the torture I undergo, which is extremely wearing. But nothing happens, my dear major; I am the slave of remorse — take care of the coffee-cup: you are so very awkward — my darling Edith is an altered being; and I really don't see what is to be done, or what good creature I can advise with."

Major Bagstock, encouraged, perhaps, by the softened and confidential tone into which Mrs. Skewton, after several times lapsing into it for a moment, seemed now to have subsided for good, stretched out his hand across the little table, and said with a leer, —

"Advise with Joe, ma'am."

"Then, you aggravating monster," said Cleopatra, giving one hand to the major, and tapping his knuckles with her fan, which she held in the other, "why don't you talk to me? You know what I mean. Why don't You tell me something to the purpose?"

The major laughed, and kissed the hand she had bestowed upon him, and laughed again immensely.

"Is there as much Heart in Mr. Dombey as I gave him credit for?" languished Cleopatra tenderly. "Do you think he is in earnest, my dear major? Would you recommend his being spoken to, or his being left alone? Now tell me, like a dear man, what you would advise."

"Shall we marry him to Edith Granger, ma'am?" chuckled the major hoarsely.

"Mysterious creature!" returned Cleopatra, bringing her fan to bear upon the major's nose. "How can *we* marry him?"

"Shall we marry him to Edith Granger, ma'am, I say?" chuckled the major again.

Mrs. Skewton returned no answer in words, but smiled upon the major with so much archness and vivacity, that that gallant officer, considering himself challenged, would have imprinted a kiss on her exceedingly red lips, but for her interposing the fan with a very winning and juvenile dexterity. It might have been in modesty; it might have been in apprehension of some danger to their bloom.

"Dombey, ma'am," said the major, "is a great catch."

"Oh, mercenary wretch!" cried Cleopatra with a little shriek, "I am shocked."

"And Dombey, ma'am," pursued the major, thrusting forward his head, and extending his eyes, "is in earnest. Joseph says it; Bagstock knows it; J. B. keeps him to the mark. Leave Dombey to himself, ma'am. Dombey is safe, ma'am. Do as you have done; do no more; and trust to J. B. for the end."

"You really think so, my dear major?" returned Cleopatra, who had eyed him very cautiously and very searchingly, in spite of her listless bearing.

"Sure of it, ma'am," rejoined the major. "Cleopatra the peerless, and her Antony Bagstock, will often speak of this triumphantly, when sharing the elegance and wealth of Edith Dombey's establishment. Dombey's right-hand man, ma'am," said the major, stopping abruptly in a chuckle, and becoming serious, "has arrived."

"This morning?" said Cleopatra.

"This morning, ma'am," returned the major. "And Dombey's anxiety for his arrival, ma'am, is to be referred — take J. B.'s word for this, for Joe is de-vilish sly" — the major tapped his nose, and screwed up one of his eyes tight; which did not enhance his native beauty — "to his desire that what is in the wind should become known to him, without Dombey's telling and consulting him. For Dombey is as proud, ma'am," said the major, "as Lucifer."

VOL. II.-9.

"A charming quality," lisped Mrs. Skewton; "reminding one of dearest Edith."

"Well, ma'am," said the major, "I have thrown out hints already, and the right-hand man understands 'em; and I'll throw out more before the day is done. Dombey projected this morning a ride to Warwick Castle, and to Kenilworth, to-morrow, to be preceded by a breakfast with us. I undertook the delivery of this invitation. Will you honor us so far, ma'am?" said the major, swelling with shortness of breath and slyness, as he produced a note, addressed to the Honorable Mrs. Skewton, by favor of Major Bagstock, wherein hers ever faithfully, Paul Dombey, besought her and her amiable and accomplished daughter to consent to the proposed excursion; and in a postscript unto which, the same ever faithfully Paul Dombey entreated to be recalled to the remembrance of Mrs. Granger.

"Hush!" said Cleopatra suddenly, "Edith!"

The loving mother can scarcely be described as resuming her insipid and affected air when she made this exclamation; for she had never cast it off; nor was it likely that she ever would or could, in any other place than in the grave. But hurriedly dismissing whatever shadow of earnestness, or faint confession of a purpose, laudable or wicked, that her face, or voice, or manner, had, for the moment, betrayed, she lounged upon the couch, her most insipid and most languid self again, as Edith entered the room.

Edith, so beautiful and stately, but so cold and so repelling. Who, slightly acknowledging the presence of Major Bagstock, and directing a keen glance at her mother, drew back the curtain from a window, and sat down there, looking out.

"My dearest Edith," said Mrs. Skewton, "where on earth have you been? I have wanted you, my love, most sadly."

"You said you were engaged, and I stayed away," she answered, without turning her head.

"It was cruel to old Joe, ma'am," said the major in his gallantry.

"It was very cruel, I know," she said, still looking out — and said with such calm disdain that the major was discomfited, and could think of nothing in reply.

"Major Bagstock, my darling Edith," drawled her mother, "who is generally the most useless and disagreeable creature in the world : as you know — "

"It is surely not worth while, mamma," said Edith, looking round, "to observe these forms of speech. We are quite alone. We know each other."

The quiet scorn that sat upon her handsome face — a scorn that evidently lighted on herself, no less than them — was so intense and deep, that her mother's simper, for the instant, though of a hardy constitution, drooped before it.

"My darling girl — " she began again.

"Not woman yet?" said Edith with a smile.

"How very odd you are to-day, my dear! Pray let me say, my love, that Major Bagstock has brought the kindest of notes from Mr. Dombey, proposing that we should breakfast with him to-morrow, and ride to Warwick and Kenilworth. Will you go, Edith?"

"Will I go?" she repeated, turning very red, and breathing quickly as she looked round at her mother.

"I knew you would, my own," observed the latter carelessly. "It is, as you say, quite a form to ask. Here is Mr. Dombey's letter, Edith."

"Thank you. I have no desire to read it," was her answer.

"Then perhaps I had better answer it myself," said Mrs. Skewton, "though I had thought of asking *you* to be my secretary, darling." As Edith made no movement and no answer, Mrs. Skewton begged the major to wheel her little table nearer, and to set open the desk it contained, and to take out pen and paper for her; all which congenial offices of gallantry the major discharged with much submission and devotion.

"Your regards, Edith, my dear?" said Mrs. Skewton, pausing, pen in hand, at the postscript.

"What you will, mamma," she answered, without turning her head, and with supreme indifference.

Mrs. Skewton wrote what she would, without seeking for any more explicit directions, and handed her letter to the major, who, receiving it as a precious charge, made a show of laying it near his heart, but was fain to put it in the pocket of his pantaloons on account of the insecurity of his waistcoat. The major then took a very polished and chivalrous farewell of both ladies, which the elder one acknowledged in her usual manner, while the younger, sitting with her face addressed to the window, bent her head so slightly that it would have been a greater compliment to the major to have made no sign at all, and to have left him to infer that he had not been heard or thought of.

"As to alteration in her, sir," mused the major on his way back: on which expedition — the afternoon being sunny and hot — he ordered the native and the light baggage to the front, and walked in the shadow of that expatriated prince: "as to alteration, sir, and pining, and so forth, that won't go down with Joseph Bagstock. None of that, sir. It won't do here. But as to there being something of a division between 'em — or a gulf as the mother calls it — damme, sir, that seems true enough. And it's odd enough! Well, sir!" panted the major, "Edith Granger and Dombey are well matched; let 'em fight it out! Bagstock backs the winner."

The major, by saying these latter words aloud, in the vigor of his thoughts, caused the unhappy native to stop, and turn round, in the belief that he was personally addressed. Exasperated to the last degree by this act of insubordination, the major (though he was swelling with enjoyment of his own humor, at the moment of its occurrence) instantly thrust his cane among the native's ribs, and continued to stir him up at short intervals, all the way to the hotel.

Nor was the·major less exasperated as he dressed for dinner, during which operation the dark servant underwent the pelting of a shower of miscellaneous objects, varying in size from a boot to a hair-brush, and including everything that came within his master's reach. For the major plumed himself on having the native in a perfect state of drill, and visited the least departure from strict discipline with this kind of fatigue duty. Add to this, that he maintained the native about his person as a counter-irritant against the gout, and all other vexatious, mental as well as bodily; and the native would appear to have earned his pay — which was not large.

At length the major, having disposed of all the missiles that were convenient to his hand, and having called the native so many new names as must have given him great occasion to marvel at the resources of the English language, submitted to have his cravat put on; and being dressed, and finding himself in a brisk flow of spirits after this exercise, went downstairs to enliven "Dombey" and his right-hand man.

Dombey was not yet in the room, but the right-hand man was there, and his dental treasures were, as usual, ready for the major.

"Well, sir!" said the major. "How have you passed the time since I had the happiness of meeting you? Have you walked at all?"

"A saunter of barely half an hour's duration," returned Carker. "We have been so much occupied."

"Business, eh?" said the major.

"A variety of little matters necessary to be gone through," replied Carker. "But do you know — this is quite unusual with me, educated in a distrustful school, and who am not generally disposed to be communicative," he said, breaking off, and speaking in a charming tone of frankness — "but I feel quite confidential with you, Major Bagstock."

"You do me honor, sir," returned the major. "You may be."

"Do you know, then," pursued Carker, "that I have not found my friend — our friend, I ought rather to call him — "

"Meaning Dombey, sir?" cried the major. "You see me, Mr. Carker, standing here! J. B.?"

He was puffy enough to see, and blue enough; and Mr. Carker intimated that he had that pleasure.

"Then you see a man, sir, who would go through fire and water to serve Dombey," returned Major Bagstock.

Mr. Carker smiled, and said he was sure of it. "Do you know, major," he proceeded: "to resume where I left off: that I have not found our friend so attentive to business to-day as usual?"

"No?" observed the delighted major.

"I have found him a little abstracted, and with his attention disposed to wander," said Carker.

"By Jove, sir," cried the major, "there's a lady in the case."

"Indeed, I begin to believe there really is," returned Carker. "I thought you might be jesting when you seemed to hint at it; for I know you military men —"

The major gave the horse's cough, and shook his head and shoulders, as much as to say, "Well! we *are* gay dogs, there's no denying." He then seized Mr. Carker by the button-hole, and with starting eyes whispered in his ear that she was a woman of extraordinary charms, sir. That she was a young widow, sir. That she was of a fine family, sir. That Dombey was over head and ears in love with her, sir, and that it would be a good match on both sides; for she had beauty, blood, and talent, and Dombey had fortune; and what more could any couple have? Hearing Mr. Dombey's footsteps without, the major cut himself short by saying that Mr. Carker would see her to-morrow morning, and would judge for himself; and between his mental excitement, and the exertion of saying all this in wheezy whispers, the major sat gurgling in the throat and watering at the eyes until dinner was ready.

The major, like some other noble animals, exhibited himself to great advantage at feeding-time. On this occasion he shone resplendent at one end of the table, supported by the milder lustre of Mr. Dombey at the other; while Carker on one side lent his ray to either light, or suffered it to merge into both, as occasion arose.

During the first course or two the major was usually grave; for the native, in obedience to general orders, secretly issued, collected every sauce and cruet round him, and gave him a great deal to do, in taking out the stoppers, and mixing up the contents in his plate. Besides which, the native had private zests and flavors on a side-table, with which the major daily scorched himself; to say nothing of strange machines out of which he spurted unknown liquids into the major's drink. But on this occasion, Major Bagstock, even amidst these many occupations, found time to be social; and his sociality consisted in excessive slyness for the behoof of Mr. Carker, and the betrayal of Mr. Dombey's state of mind.

"Dombey," said the major, "you don't eat. What's the matter?"

"Thank you," returned that gentleman, "I am doing very well; I have no great appetite to-day."

"Why, Dombey, what's become of it?" asked the major. "Where's it gone? You haven't left it with our friends, I'll swear, for I can answer for their having none to-day at luncheon. I can answer for one of 'em, at least; I won't say which."

Then the major winked at Carker, and became so frightfully sly, that his dark attendant was obliged to pat him on the back, without orders, or he would probably have disappeared under the table.

In a later stage of the dinner: that is to say, when the native stood at the major's elbow, ready to serve the first bottle of champagne: the major became still slyer.

"Fill this to the brim, you scoundrel," said the major, holding up his glass. "Fill Mr. Carker's to the brim too. And Mr. Dombey's too. By Gad, gentlemen," said the major, winking at his new friend, while Mr. Dombey looked into his plate with a conscious air, "we'll consecrate this glass of wine to a divinity whom Joe is proud to know, and at a distance humbly and reverently to admire. Edith," said the major, "is her name; angelic Edith!"

"To angelic Edith!" cried the smiling Carker.

"Edith, by all means," said Mr. Dombey.

The entrance of the waiters with new dishes caused the major to be slyer yet, but in a more serious vein. "For though, among ourselves, Joe Bagstock mingles jest and earnest on this subject, sir," said the major, laying his finger on his lips, and speaking half apart to Carker, "he holds that name too sacred to be made the property of these fellows, or of any fellows. Not a word, sir, while they are here!"

This was respectful and becoming on the major's part, and Mr. Dombey plainly felt it so. Although embarrassed, in his own frigid way, by the major's allusions, Mr. Dombey had no objection to such rallying, it was clear, but rather courted it. Perhaps the major had been pretty near the truth when he had divined, that morning, that the great man who was too haughty formally to consult with or confide

in his prime minister on such a matter yet wished
him to be fully possessed of it. Let this be how it
may, he often glanced at Mr. Carker while the major
plied his light artillery, and seemed watchful of its
effect upon him.

But the major, having secured an attentive listener,
and a smiler who had not his match in all the world
— "in short, a de-vilish intelligent and agreeable
fellow," as he often afterwards declared — was not
going to let him off with a little slyness personal to
Mr. Dombey. Therefore, on the removal of the
cloth, the major developed himself as a choice spirit
in the broader and more comprehensive range of
narrating regimental stories, and cracking regimental
jokes, which he did with such prodigal exuberance,
that Carker was (or feigned to be) quite exhausted
with laughter and admiration: while Mr. Dombey
looked on over his starched cravat, like the major's
proprietor, or like a stately showman who was glad
to see his bear dancing well.

When the major was too hoarse with meat and
drink, and the display of his social powers, to
render himself intelligible any longer, they ad-
journed to coffee. After which, the major inquired
of Mr. Carker the manager, with little apparent
hope of an answer in the affirmative, if he played
piquet.

"Yes, I play piquet a little," said Mr. Carker.

"Backgammon, perhaps?" observed the major,
hesitating.

"Yes, I play backgammon a little too," replied
the man of teeth.

"Carker plays at all games, I believe," said Mr.
Dombey, laying himself on a sofa like a man of

wood without a hinge or a joint in him; "and plays them well."

In sooth, he played the two in question to such perfection, that the major was astonished, and asked him, at random, if he played chess.

"Yes, I play chess a little," answered Carker. "I have sometimes played, and won a game — it's a mere trick — without seeing the board."

"By Gad, sir!" said the major, staring, "you're a contrast to Dombey, who plays nothing."

"Oh! *He!*" returned the manager. "*He* has never had occasion to acquire such little arts. To men like me they are sometimes useful. As at present, Major Bagstock, when they enable me to take a hand with you."

It might be only the false mouth, so smooth and wide; and yet there seemed to lurk, beneath the humility and subserviency of this short speech, a something like a snarl; and, for a moment, one might have thought that the white teeth were prone to bite the hand they fawned upon. But the major thought nothing about it; and Mr. Dombey lay meditating, with his eyes half shut, during the whole of the play, which lasted until bedtime.

By that time, Mr. Carker, though the winner, had mounted high into the major's good opinion, insomuch that when he left the major at his own room before going to bed, the major, as a special attention, sent the native — who always rested on a mattress spread upon the ground at his master's door — along the gallery, to light him to bis room in state.

There was a faint blur on the surface of the mirror in Mr. Carker's chamber, and its reflection was, perhaps, a false one. But it showed, that night,

the image of a man who saw, in his fancy, a crowd
of people slumbering on the ground at his feet, like
the poor native at his master's door : who picked his
way among them : looking down maliciously enough :
but trod upon no upturned face — as yet.

CHAPTER VII.

MR. CARKER the manager rose with the lark, and went out walking in the summer day. His meditations — and he meditated with contracted brows while he strolled along — hardly seemed to soar as high as the lark, or to mount in that direction; rather they kept close to their nest upon the earth, and looked about among the dust and worms. But there was not a bird in the air, singing unseen, farther beyond the reach of human eye than Mr. Carker's thoughts. He had his face so perfectly under control, that few could say more, in distinct terms, of its expression, than that it smiled or that it pondered. It pondered now, intently. As the lark rose higher, he sank deeper in thought. As the lark poured out her melody clearer and stronger, he fell into a graver and profounder silence. At length, when the lark came headlong down, with an accumulating stream of song, and dropped among the green wheat near him, rippling in the breath of the morning like a river, he sprang up from his reverie, and looked round with a sudden smile, as courteous and as soft as if he had had numerous observers to propitiate; nor did he relapse after being thus awakened; but clearing his face, like one who bethought himself that it might otherwise wrinkle and tell tales, went smiling on, as if for practice.

Perhaps with an eye to first impressions, Mr. Carker was very carefully and trimly dressed that morning. Though always somewhat formal in his dress, in imitation of the great man whom he served, he stopped short of the extent of Mr. Dombey's stiffness: at once, perhaps, because he knew it to be ludicrous, and because, in doing so, he found another means of expressing his sense of the difference and distance between them. Some people quoted him, indeed, in this respect, as a pointed commentary, and not a flattering one, on his icy patron — but the world is prone to misconstruction, and Mr. Carker was not accountable for its bad propensity.

Clean and florid: with his light complexion fading, as it were, in the sun, and his dainty step enhancing the softness of the turf: Mr. Carker the manager strolled about meadows and green lanes, and glided among avenues of trees, until it was time to return to breakfast. Taking a nearer way back, Mr. Carker pursued it, airing his teeth, and said aloud as he did so, "Now to see the second Mrs. Dombey!"

He had strolled beyond the town, and re-entered it by a pleasant walk, where there was a deep shade of leafy trees, and where there were a few benches here and there for those who chose to rest. It not being a place of general resort at any hour, and wearing, at that time of the still morning, the air of being quite deserted and retired, Mr. Carker had it, or thought he had it, all to himself. So, with the whim of an idle man, to whom there yet remained twenty minutes for reaching a destination easily accessible in ten, Mr. Carker threaded the great boles of the trees, and went passing in and out, before this one and behind that, weaving a chain of footsteps on the dewy ground.

But he found he was mistaken in supposing there was no one in the grove; for, as he softly rounded the trunk of one large tree, on which the obdurate bark was knotted and overlapped like the hide of a rhinoceros or some kindred monster of the ancient days before the flood, he saw an unexpected figure sitting on a bench near at hand, about which, in another moment, he would have wound the chain he was making.

It was that of a lady elegantly dressed and very handsome, whose dark proud eyes were fixed upon the ground, and in whom some passion or struggle was raging. For, as she sat looking down, she held a corner of her under lip within her mouth, her bosom heaved, her nostril quivered, her head trembled, indignant tears were on her cheek, and her foot was set upon the moss as though she would have crushed it into nothing. And yet almost the selfsame glance that showed him this, showed him the selfsame lady rising with a scornful air of weariness and lassitude, and turning away with nothing expressed in face or figure but careless beauty and imperious disdain.

A withered and very ugly old woman, dressed not so much like a gypsy as like any of that medley race of vagabonds who tramp about the country, begging, and stealing, and tinkering, and weaving rushes, by turns, or all together, had been observing the lady too; for, as she rose, this second figure, strangely confronting the first, scrambled up from the ground — out of it, it almost appeared — and stood in the way.

"Let me tell your fortune, my pretty lady," said the old woman, munching with her jaws, as if the Death's head beneath her yellow skin were impatient to get out.

"I can tell it for myself," was the reply.

"Ay, ay, pretty lady; but not right. You didn't tell it right when you were sitting there. I see you! Give me a piece of silver, pretty lady, and I'll tell your fortune true. There's riches, pretty lady, in your face."

"I know," returned the lady, passing her with a dark smile and a proud step. "I knew it before."

"What! You won't give me nothing?" cried the old woman. "You won't give me nothing to tell your fortune, pretty lady? How much will you give me *not* to tell it, then? Give me something, or I'll call it after you!" croaked the old woman passionately.

Mr. Carker, whom the lady was about to pass close, slinking against his tree as she crossed to gain the path, advanced so as to meet her, and pulling off his hat as she went by, bade the old woman hold her peace. The lady acknowledged his interference with an inclination of the head, and went her way.

"You give me something, then, or I'll call it after her!" screamed the old woman, throwing up her arms, and pressing forward against his outstretched hand. "Or come," she added, dropping her voice suddenly, looking at him earnestly, and seeming in a moment to forget the object of her wrath, "give me something, or I'll call it after *you!*"

"After *me*, old lady?" returned the manager, putting his hand in his pocket.

"Yes," said the woman, steadfast in her scrutiny, and holding out her shrivelled hand. "*I* know!"

"What do you know?" demanded Carker, throwing her a shilling. "Do you know who the handsome lady is?"

Munching like that sailor's wife of yore, who had chestnuts in her lap, and scowling like the witch who asked for some in vain, the old woman picked the shilling up, and going backwards, like a crab, or like a heap of crabs: for her alternately expanding and contracting hands might have represented two of that species, and her creeping face some half a dozen more: crouched on the veinous root of an old tree, pulled out a short black pipe from within the crown of her bonnet, lighted it with a match, and smoked in silence, looking fixedly at her questioner.

Mr. Carker laughed and turned upon his heel.

"Good!" said the old woman. "One child dead, and one child living: one wife dead, and one wife coming. Go and meet her!"

In spite of himself, the manager looked round again, and stopped. The old woman, who had not removed her pipe, and was munching and mumbling while she smoked, as if in conversation with an invisible familiar, pointed with her finger in the direction he was going, and laughed.

"What was that you said, Bedlamite?" he demanded.

The woman mumbled, and chattered, and smoked, and still pointed before him; but remained silent.

Muttering a farewell that was not complimentary, Mr. Carker pursued his way; but as he turned out of that place, and looked over his shoulder at the root of the old tree, he could yet see the finger pointing before him, and thought he heard the woman screaming, " Go and meet her ! "

Preparations for a choice repast were completed, he found, at the hotel; and Mr. Dombey, and the major, and the breakfast were awaiting the ladies. Individual constitution has much to do with the development of such facts, no doubt; but, in this case, appetite carried it hollow over the tender passion; Mr. Dombey being very cool and collected, and the major fretting and fuming in a state of violent heat and irritation. At length the door was thrown open by the native, and, after a pause, occupied by her languishing along the gallery, a very blooming, but not very youthful, lady appeared.

" My dear Mr. Dombey," said the lady, " I am afraid we are late, but Edith has been out already, looking for a favorable point of view for a sketch, and kept me waiting for her. Falsest of majors," giving him her little finger, " how do you do ? "

" Mrs. Skewton," said Mr. Dombey, " let me gratify my friend Carker " — Mr. Dombey unconsciously emphasized the word friend, as saying, " No, really; I do allow him to take credit for that distinction " — " by presenting him to you. You have heard me mention Mr. Carker."

" I am charmed, I am sure," said Mrs. Skewton graciously.

Mr. Carker was charmed, of course. Would he have been more charmed on Mr. Dombey's behalf, if Mrs. Skewton had been (as he at first supposed

her) the Edith whom they had toasted over-
night?

"Why, where, for Heaven's sake, is Edith?" exclaimed Mrs. Skewton, looking round. "Still at the
door, giving Withers orders about the mounting of
those drawings! My dear Mr. Dombey, will you
have the kindness — "

Mr. Dombey was already gone to seek her. Next
moment he returned, bearing on his arm the same
elegantly dressed and very handsome lady whom
Mr. Carker had encountered underneath the trees.

"Carker — " began Mr. Dombey. But their recognition of each other was so manifest, that Mr.
Dombey stopped, surprised.

"I am obliged to the gentleman," said Edith with
a stately bend, "for sparing me some annoyance
from an importunate beggar just now."

"I am obliged to my good fortune," said Mr.
Carker, bowing low, "for the opportunity of rendering so slight a service to one whose servant I am
proud to be."

As her eye rested on him for an instant, and then
lighted on the ground, he saw in its bright and
searching glance a suspicion that he had not come
up at the moment of his interference, but had
secretly observed her sooner. As he saw that, she
saw in *his* eye that her distrust was not without
foundation.

"Really," cried Mrs. Skewton, who had taken this
opportunity of inspecting Mr. Carker through her
glass, and satisfying herself (as she lisped audibly
to the major) that he was all heart; "really, now,
this is one of the most enchanting coincidences that
I ever heard of. The idea! My dearest Edith,

there is such an obvious destiny in it, that really one might almost be induced to cross one's arms upon one's frock, and say, like those wicked Turks, there is no What's-his-name but Thingummy, and What-you-may-call-it is his prophet!"

Edith deigned no revision of this extraordinary quotation from the Koran, but Mr. Dombey felt it necessary to offer a few polite remarks.

"It gives me great pleasure," said Mr. Dombey with cumbrous gallantry, "that a gentleman so nearly connected with myself as Carker is, should have had the honor and happiness of rendering the least assistance to Mrs. Granger." Mr. Dombey bowed to her. "But it gives me some pain, and it occasions me to be really envious of Carker;" he unconsciously laid stress on these words, as sensible that they must appear to involve a very surprising proposition; "envious of Carker, that I had not that honor and that happiness myself." Mr. Dombey bowed again. Edith, saving for a curl of her lip, was motionless.

"By the Lord, sir," cried the major, bursting into speech at sight of the waiter, who was come to announce breakfast, "it's an extraordinary thing to me that no one can have the honor and happiness of shooting all such beggars through the head without being brought to book for it. But here's an arm for Mrs. Granger, if she'll do J. B. the honor to accept it; and the greatest service Joe can render you, ma'am, just now, is, to lead you in to table!"

With this, the major gave his arm to Edith; Mr. Dombey led the way with Mrs. Skewton; Mr. Carker went last, smiling on the party.

"I am quite rejoiced, Mr. Carker," said the lady mother at breakfast, after another approving survey of him through her glass, "that you have timed your visit so happily as to go with us to-day. It is the most enchanting expedition!"

"Any expedition would be enchanting in such society," returned Carker; "but I believe it is, in itself, full of interest."

"Oh!" cried Mrs. Skewton with a faded little scream of rapture, "the Castle is charming!—associations of the middle ages—and all that—which is so truly exquisite. Don't you dote upon the middle ages, Mr. Carker?"

"Very much indeed," said Mr. Carker.

"Such charming times!" cried Cleopatra. "So full of faith! So vigorous and forcible! So picturesque! So perfectly removed from commonplace! Oh, dear! If they would only leave us a little more of the poetry of existence in these terrible days!"

Mrs. Skewton was looking sharp after Mr. Dombey all the time she said this, who was looking at Edith: who was listening, but who never lifted up her eyes.

"We are dreadfully real, Mr. Carker," said Mrs. Skewton; "are we not?"

Few people had less reason to complain of their reality than Cleopatra, who had as much that was false about her as could well go to the composition of anybody with a real individual existence. But Mr. Carker commiserated our reality nevertheless, and agreed that we were very hardly used in that regard.

"Pictures at the Castle quite divine!" said Cleopatra. "I hope you dote upon pictures?"

"I assure you, Mrs. Skewton," said Mr. Dombey, with solemn encouragement of his manager, "that Carker has a very good taste for pictures; quite a natural power of appreciating them. He is a very creditable artist himself. He will be delighted, I am sure, with Mrs. Granger's taste and skill."

"Damme, sir!" cried Major Bagstock, "my opinion is, that you're the Admirable Carker, and can do anything."

"Oh!" smiled Carker with humility, "you are much too sanguine, Major Bagstock. I can do very little. But Mr. Dombey is so generous in his estimation of any trivial accomplishment a man like myself may find it almost necessary to acquire, and to which, in his very different sphere, he is far superior, that —" Mr. Carker shrugged his shoulders, deprecating further praise, and said no more.

All this time Edith never raised her eyes, unless to glance towards her mother when that lady's fervent spirit shone forth in words. But, as Carker ceased, she looked at Mr. Dombey for a moment. For a moment only; but with a transient gleam of scornful wonder on her face, not lost on one observer, who was smiling round the board.

Mr. Dombey caught the dark eyelash in its descent, and took the opportunity of arresting it.

"You have been to Warwick often, unfortunately?" said Mr. Dombey.

"Several times."

"The visit will be tedious to you, I am afraid."

"Oh, no; not at all."

"Ah! You are like your cousin Feenix, my dearest Edith," said Mrs. Skewton. "He has been to Warwick Castle fifty times, if he has been there once; yet if he came to Leamington to-morrow — I wish he would, dear angel! — he would make his fifty-second visit next day."

"We are all enthusiastic, are we not, mamma?" said Edith, with a cold smile.

"Too much so for our peace, perhaps, my dear," returned her mother; "but we won't complain. Our own emotions are our recompense. If, as your cousin says, the sword wears out the what's-its-name — "

"The scabbard, perhaps," said Edith.

"Exactly — a little too fast, it is because it is bright and glowing, you know, my dearest love."

Mrs. Skewton heaved a gentle sigh, supposed to cast a shadow on the surface of that dagger of lath, whereof her susceptible bosom was the sheath: and leaning her head on one side, in the Cleopatra manner, looked with pensive affection on her darling child.

Edith had turned her face towards Mr. Dombey when he first addressed her, and had remained in that attitude while speaking to her mother, and while her mother spoke to her, as though offering him her attention, if he had anything more to say. There was something in the manner of this simple courtesy: almost defiant, and giving it the character of being rendered on compulsion, or as a matter of traffic to which she was a reluctant party: again not lost upon that same observer who was smiling round the board. It set him thinking of her as he had first seen her, when she had believed herself to be alone among the trees.

Mr. Dombey, having nothing else to say, proposed — the breakfast being now finished, and the major gorged, like any boa constrictor — that they should start. A barouche being in waiting, according to the orders of that gentleman, the two ladies, the major, and himself took their seats in it; the native and the wan page mounted the box, Mr. Towlinson being left behind; and Mr. Carker, on horseback, brought up the rear.

Mr. Carker cantered behind the carriage, at the distance of a hundred yards or so, and watched it, during all the ride, as if he were a cat indeed, and its four occupants mice. Whether he looked to one side of the road or to the other — over distant landscape, with its smooth undulations, windmills, corn, grass, bean fields, wild flowers, farmyards, hayricks, and the spire among the wood — or upward in the sunny air, where butterflies were sporting round his head, and birds were pouring out their songs — or downward, where the shadows of the branches interlaced, and made a trembling carpet on the road — or onward, where the overhanging trees formed aisles and arches, dim with the softened light that steeped through leaves — one corner of his eye was ever on the formal head of Mr. Dombey, ad-dressed towards him, and the feather in the bonnet, drooping so neglectfully and scornfully between them: much as he had seen the haughty eyelids droop; not least so when the face met that now fronting it. Once, and once only, did his wary glance release these objects; and that was when a leap over a low hedge, and a gallop across a field, enabled him to anticipate the carriage coming by the road, and to be standing ready, at the journey's end, to hand the ladies out. Then, and but then, he met her glance for an instant in her first surprise; but when he touched her, in alighting, with his soft white hand, it overlooked him altogether as before.

Mrs. Skewton was bent on taking charge of Mr. Carker herself, and showing him the beauties of the Castle. She was determined to have his arm, and the major's too. It would do that incorrigible creature: who was the most barbarous infidel in point of poetry: good to be in such company. This chance arrangement left Mr. Dombey at liberty to escort Edith: which he did: stalking before them through the apartments with a gentlemanly solemnity.

"Those darling bygone times, Mr. Carker," said Cleopatra, "with their delicious fortresses, and their dear old dungeons, and their delightful places of torture, and their romantic vengeances, and their picturesque assaults and sieges, and everything that makes life truly charming! How dreadfully we have degenerated!"

"Yes, we have fallen off deplorably," said Mr. Carker.

The peculiarity of their conversation was, that Mrs. Skewton, in spite of her ecstasies, and Mr. Carker, in spite of his urbanity, were both intent on watching Mr. Dombey and Edith. With all their conversational endowments, they spoke somewhat distractedly, and at random in consequence.

"We have no faith left, positively," said Mrs. Skewton, advancing her shrivelled ear; for Mr. Dombey was saying something to Edith. "We have no faith in the dear old barons, who were the most delightful creatures — or in the dear old priests, who were the most warlike of men — or even in the days of that inestimable Queen Bess, upon the wall there,

which were so extremely golden! Dear creature!
She was all heart! And that charming father of
hers! I hope you dote on Harry the Eighth!"

"I admire him very much," said Carker.

"So bluff!" cried Mrs. Skewton, "wasn't he?
So burly. So truly English. Such a picture, too,
he makes, with his dear little peepy eyes, and his
benevolent chin!"

"Ah, ma'am!" said Carker, stopping short; "but
if you speak of pictures, there's a composition!
What gallery in the world can produce the counterpart of that?"

As the smiling gentleman thus spake, he pointed
through a doorway to where Mr. Dombey and Edith
were standing alone in the centre of another room.

They were not interchanging a word or a look.
Standing together, arm in arm, they had the appearance of being more divided than if seas had rolled
between them. There was a difference even in the
pride of the two, that removed them farther from
each other than if one had been the proudest and
the other the humblest specimen of humanity in all
creation. He, self-important, unbending, formal,
austere. She, lovely and graceful in an uncommon
degree, but totally regardless of herself and him
and everything around, and spurning her own attractions with her haughty brow and lip, as if they
were a badge or livery she hated. So unmatched
were they, and opposed: so forced and linked
together by a chain which adverse hazard and mis-
chance had forged: that fancy might have imagined
the pictures on the walls around them startled by
the unnatural conjunction, and observant of it in
their several expressions. Grim knights and war-

riors looked scowling on them. A churchman, with his hand upraised, denounced the mockery of such a couple coming to God's altar. Quiet waters in landscapes, with the sun reflected in their depths, asked, if better means of escape were not at hand, was there no drowning left? Ruins cried, "Look here, and see what We are, wedded to uncongenial Time!" Animals, opposed by nature, worried one another, as a moral to them. Loves and Cupids took to flight afraid, and Martyrdom had no such torment in its painted history of suffering.

Nevertheless, Mrs. Skewton was so charmed by the sight to which Mr. Carker invoked her attention, that she could not refrain from saying, half aloud, how sweet, how very full of soul it was! Edith, overhearing, looked round, and flushed indignant scarlet to her hair.

"My dearest Edith knows I was admiring her!" said Cleopatra, tapping her, almost timidly, on the back with her parasol. "Sweet pet!"

Again Mr. Carker saw the strife he had witnessed so unexpectedly among the trees. Again he saw the haughty languor and indifference come over it, and hide it like a cloud.

She did not raise her eyes to him; but, with a slight peremptory motion of them, seemed to bid her mother come near. Mrs. Skewton thought it expedient to understand the hint, and, advancing quickly with her two cavaliers, kept near her daughter from that time.

Mr. Carker now, having nothing to distract his attention, began to discourse upon the pictures, and to select the best, and point them out to Mr. Dombey: speaking with his usual familiar recognition of Mr. Dombey's greatness, and rendering homage by adjusting his eyeglass for him, or finding out the right place in his catalogue, or holding his stick, or the like. These services did not so much originate with Mr. Carker, in truth, as with Mr. Dombey himself, who was apt to assert his chieftainship by saying, with subdued authority, and in an easy way — for him — "Here, Carker, ˙have the goodness to assist me, will you?" which the smiling gentleman always did with pleasure.

They made the tour of the pictures, the walls, crow's nest, and so forth; and as they were still one little party, and the major was rather in the shade, being sleepy during the process of digestion, Mr. Carker became communicative and agreeable. At first he addressed himself for the most part to Mrs. Skewton; but as that sensitive lady was in such ecstasies with the works of art, after the first quarter of an hour, that she could do nothing but yawn (they were such perfect inspirations, she observed as a reason for that mark of rapture), he transferred his attentions to Mr. Dombey. Mr. Dombey said little beyond an occasional "Very true, Carker," or "Indeed, Carker?" but he tacitly encouraged Carker to proceed, and inwardly approved of his behavior very much: deeming it as well that somebody should talk, and thinking that his remarks, which were, as one might say, a branch of the parent establishment, might amuse Mrs. Granger. Mr. Carker, who possessed an excellent discretion, never took the liberty of addressing that lady direct; but she seemed to listen, though she never looked at him; and once or twice, when he was emphatic in his peculiar humility, the twilight smile stole over her face, not as a light, but as a deep black shadow.

Warwick Castle being at length pretty well exhansted, and the major very much so: to say nothing of Mrs. Skewton, whose peculiar demonstrations of delight had become very frequent indeed: the carriage was again put in requisition, and they rode to several admired points of view in the neighborhood. Mr. Dombey ceremoniously observed, of one of these, that a sketch, however slight, from the fair hand of Mrs. Granger would be a remembrance to him of that agreeable day: though he wanted no artificial remembrance, he was sure (here Mr. Dombey made another of his bows), which he must always highly value. Withers the lean, having Edith's sketch-book under his arm, was immediately called upon by Mrs. Skewton to produce the same: and the carriage stopped, that Edith might make the drawing, which Mr. Dombey was to put away among his treasures.

"But I am afraid I trouble you too much," said Mr. Dombey.

"By no means. Where would you wish it taken from?" she answered, turning to him with the same enforced attention as before.

Mr. Dombey, with another bow, which cracked the starch in his cravat, would beg to leave that to the artist.

"I would rather you chose for yourself," said Edith.

"Suppose, then," said Mr. Dombey, "we say from here. It appears a good spot for the purpose, or — Carker, what do *you* think?"

There happened to be in the foreground, at some

little distance, a grove of trees, not unlike that in which Mr. Carker had made his chain of footsteps in the morning, and with a seat under one tree, greatly resembling, in the general character of its situation, the point where his chain had broken.

"Might I venture to suggest to Mrs. Granger," said Carker, "that that is an interesting — almost a curious — point of view ? "

She followed the direction of his riding whip with her eyes, and raised them quickly to his face. It was the second glance they had exchanged since their introduction; and would have been exactly like the first, but that its expression was plainer.

"Would you like that ? " said Edith to Mr. Dombey.

"I shall be charmed," said Mr. Dombey to Edith.

Therefore the carriage was driven to the spot where Mr. Dombey was to be charmed; and Edith, without moving from her seat, and opening her sketch-book with her usual proud indifference, began to sketch.

" My pencils are all pointless," she said, stopping and turning them over.

"Pray allow me," said Mr. Dombey. "Or Carker will do it better, as he understands these things. Carker, have the goodness to see to these pencils for Mrs. Granger."

Mr. Carker rode up close to the carriage door on Mrs. Granger's side, and letting the rein fall on his horse's neck, took the pencils from her hand with a smile and a bow, and sat in the saddle leisurely mending them. Having done so, he begged to be allowed to hold them, and to hand them to her as they were required; and thus Mr. Carker, with many

commendations of Mrs. Granger's extraordinary skill
— especially in trees — remained close at her side,
looking over the drawing as she made it. Mr.
Dombey, in the meantime, stood bolt-upright in
the carriage like a highly respectable ghost, looking on too; while Cleopatra and the major dallied
as two ancient doves might do.

" Are you satisfied with that, or shall I finish it a
little more ? " said Edith, showing the sketch to
Mr. Dombey.

Mr. Dombey begged that it might not be touched;
it was perfection.

" It is most extraordinary," said Carker, bringing
every one of his red gums to bear upon his praise.
" I was not prepared for anything so beautiful, and
so unusual altogether."

This might have applied to the sketcher no less
than to the sketch: but Mr. Carker's manner was
openness itself — not as to his mouth alone, but as
to his whole spirit. So it continued to be while the
drawing was laid aside for Mr. Dombey, and while
the sketching materials were put up; then he
handed in the pencils (which were received with
a distant acknowledgment of his help, but without
a look), and tightening his rein, fell back, and followed the carriage again.

Thinking, perhaps, as he rode, that even this
trivial sketch had been made and delivered to its
owner as if it had been bargained for and bought.
Thinking, perhaps, that although she had assented
with such perfect readiness to his request, her
haughty face, bent over the drawing, or glancing
at the distant objects represented in it, had been
the face of a proud woman, engaged in a sordid and

miserable transaction. Thinking, perhaps, of such
things : but smiling certainly, and while he seemed
to look about him freely, in enjoyment of the air and
exercise, keeping always that sharp corner of his
eye upon the carriage.

A stroll among the haunted ruins of Kenilworth,
and more rides to more points of view : most of
which, Mrs. Skewton reminded Mr. Dombey, Edith
had already sketched, as he had seen in looking
over her drawings : brought the day's expedition
to a close. Mrs. Skewton and Edith were driven
to their own lodgings; Mr. Carker was graciously
invited by Cleopatra to return thither with Mr.
Dombey and the major, in the evening, to hear
some of Edith's music; and the three gentlemen
repaired to their hotel to dinner.

The dinner was the counterpart of yesterday's, except that the major was twenty-four hours more triumphant and less mysterious. Edith was toasted
again. Mr. Dombey was again agreeably embarrassed.
And Mr. Carker was full of interest and praise.

There were no other visitors at Mrs. Skewton's.
Edith's drawings were strewn about the room a little
more abundantly than usual, perhaps; and Withers,
the wan page, handed round a little stronger tea.
The harp was there; the piano was there; and Edith
sang and played. But even the music was paid by
Edith to Mr. Dombey's order, as it were, in the same
uncompromising way. As thus.

"Edith, my dearest love," said Mrs. Skewton, half
an hour after tea, "Mr. Dombey is dying to hear you,
I know."

"Mr. Dombey has life enough left to say so for
himself, mamma, I have no doubt."

"I shall be immensely obliged," said Mr. Dombey.
"What do you wish?"

"Piano?" hesitated Mr. Dombey.

"Whatever you please. You have only to choose."

Accordingly, she began with the piano. It was the same with the harp; the same with her singing; the same with the selection of the pieces that she sang and played. Such frigid and constrained, yet prompt and pointed, acquiescence with the wishes he imposed upon her, and on no one else, was sufficiently remarkable to penetrate through all the mysteries of piquet, and impress itself on Mr. Carker's keen attention. Nor did he lose sight of the fact that Mr. Dombey was evidently proud of his power, and liked to show it.

Nevertheless, Mr. Carker played so well — some games with the major, and some with Cleopatra, whose vigilance of eye in respect of Mr. Dombey and Edith no lynx could have surpassed — that he even heightened his position in the lady mother's good graces; and when, on taking leave, he regretted that he would be obliged to return to London next morning, Cleopatra trusted: community of feeling not being met with every day: that it was far from being the last time they would meet.

"I hope so," said Mr. Carker, with an expressive look at the couple in the distance, as he drew towards the door, following the major. "I think so."

Mr. Dombey, who had taken a stately leave of Edith, bent, or made some approach to a bend, over Cleopatra's couch, and said, in a low voice, —

"I have requested Mrs. Granger's permission to call on her to-morrow morning — for a purpose — and she has appointed twelve o'clock. May I hope to have the pleasure of finding you at home, madam, afterwards?"

Cleopatra was so much fluttered and moved by hearing this, of course, incomprehensible speech, that she could only shut her eyes, and shake her head, and give Mr. Dombey her hand; which Mr. Dombey, not exactly knowing what to do with, dropped.

"Dombey, come along!" cried the major, looking in at the door. "Damme, sir, old Joe has a great mind to propose an alteration in the name of the Royal Hotel, and that it should be called the Three Jolly Bachelors, in honor of ourselves and Carker." With this the major slapped Mr. Dombey on the back, and winking over his shoulder at the ladies, with a frightful tendency of blood to the head, carried him off.

Mrs. Skewton reposed on her sofa, and Edith sat apart, by her harp, in silence. The mother, trifling with her fan, looked stealthily at the daughter more than once, but the daughter, brooding gloomily with downcast eyes, was not to be disturbed.

Thus they remained for a long hour, without a word, until Mrs. Skewton's maid appeared, according to custom, to prepare her gradually for night. At night she should have been a skeleton, with dart and hour-glass, rather than a woman, this attendant; for her touch was as the touch of Death. The painted object shrivelled underneath her hand; the form collapsed, the hair dropped off, the arched dark eyebrows changed to scanty tufts of gray; the pale lips shrunk, the skin became cadaverous and loose; an old, worn, yellow, nodding woman, with red eyes, alone remained in Cleopatra's place, huddled up, like a slovenly bundle, in a greasy flannel gown.

The very voice was changed, as it addressed Edith, when they were alone again.

" Why don't you tell me," it said sharply, " that he is coming here to-morrow by appointment ? "

" Because you know it," returned Edith, " mother."

The mocking emphasis she laid on that one word!

" You know he has bought me," she resumed. " Or that he will to-morrow. He has considered of his bargain; he has shown it to his friend; he is even rather proud of it; he thinks that it will suit him, and may be had sufficiently cheap; and he will buy to-morrow. God, that I have lived for this, and that I feel it! "

Compress into one handsome face the conscious self-abasement and the burning indignation of a hundred women, strong in passion and in pride; and there it hid itself with two white shuddering arms.

" What do you mean ? " returned the angry mother. " Haven't you from a child — "

" A child ! " said Edith, looking at her. " When was I a child ? What childhood did you ever leave to me ? I was a woman — artful, designing, mercenary, laying snares for men — before I knew myself or you, or even understood the base and wretched aim of every new display I learnt. You gave birth to a woman. Look upon her. She is in her pride to-night."

And, as she spoke, she struck her hand upon her beautiful bosom, as though she would have beaten down herself.

" Look at me," she said, " who have never known

what it is to have an honest heart, and love. Look at me, taught to scheme and plot when children play, and married in my youth — an old age of design — to one for whom I had no feeling but indifference. Look at me, whom he left a widow, dying before his inheritance descended to him — a judgment on you, well deserved! — and tell me what has been my life for ten years since."

"We have been making every effort to endeavor to secure to you a good establishment," rejoined her mother. "That has been your life. And now you have got it."

"There is no slave in a market, there is no horse in a fair, so shown and offered and examined and paraded, mother, as I have been, for ten shameful years," cried Edith, with a burning brow, and the same bitter emphasis on the one word. "Is it not so? Have I been made the by-word of all kinds of men? Have fools, have profligates, have boys, have dotards, dangled after me, and one by one rejected me, and fallen off, because you were too plain, with all your cunning — yes, and too true, with all those false pretences — until we have almost come to be notorious? The license of look and touch," she said with flashing eyes, "have I submitted to it, in half the places of resort upon the map of England? Have I been hawked and vended here and there, until the last grain of self-respect is dead within me, and I loathe myself? Has *this* been my late childhood? I had none before. Do not tell me that I had, to-night, of all nights in my life!"

"You might have been well married," said her mother, "twenty times at least, Edith, if you had given encouragement enough."

"No! Who takes me, refuse that I am, and as I well deserve to be," she answered, raising her head, and trembling in her energy of shame and stormy pride, "shall take me, as this man does, with no art of mine put forth to lure him. He sees me at the auction, and he thinks it well to buy me. Let him! When he came to view me — perhaps to bid — he required to see the roll of my accomplishments. I gave it to him. When he would have me show one of them, to justify his purchase to his men, I require of him to say which he demands, and I exhibit it. I will do no more. He makes the purchase of his own will, and with his own sense of its worth, and the power of his money; and I hope it may never disappoint him. *I* have not vaunted and pressed the bargain; neither have you, so far as I have been able to prevent you."

"You talk strangely to-night, Edith, to your own mother."

"It seems so to me; stranger to me than to you," said Edith. "But my education was completed long ago. I am too old now, and have fallen too low, by degrees, to take a new course, and to stop yours, and to help myself. The germ of all that purifies a woman's breast, and makes it true and good, has never stirred in mine, and I have nothing else to sustain me when I despise myself." There had been a touching sadness in her voice, but it was gone when she went on to say, "So, as we are genteel and poor, I am content that we should be made rich by these means; all I say is, I have kept the only purpose I have had the strength to form — I had almost said the power, with you at my side, mother — and have not tempted this man on."

"This man! You speak," said her mother, "as if you hated him."

"And you thought I loved him, did you not?" she answered, stopping on her way across the room, and looking round. "Shall I tell you," she continued, with her eyes fixed on her mother, "who already knows us thoroughly, and reads us right, and before whom I have even less of self-respect or confidence than before my own inward self: being so much degraded by his knowledge of me?"

"This is an attack, I suppose," returned her mother coldly, "on poor, unfortunate what's-his-name — Mr. Carker. Your want of self-respect and confidence, my dear, in reference to that person (who is very agreeable, it strikes me), is not likely to have much effect on your establishment. Why do you look at me so hard? Are you ill?"

Edith suddenly let fall her face as if it had been stung, and, while she pressed her hands upon it, a terrible tremble crept over her whole frame. It was quickly gone; and with her usual step she passed out of the room.

The maid, who should have been a skeleton, then re-appeared, and giving one arm to her mistress, who appeared to have taken off her manner with her charms, and to have put on paralysis with her flannel gown, collected the ashes of Cleopatra, and carried them away, ready for to-morrow's revivification.

CHAPTER VIII.

ALTERATIONS.

"So the day has come at length, Susan," said Florence to the excellent Nipper, "when we are going back to our quiet home!"

Susan drew in her breath with an amount of expression not easily described, and further relieving her feelings with a smart cough, answered, "Very quiet indeed, Miss Floy, no doubt. Excessive so."

"When I was a child," said Florence thoughtfully, and after musing for some moments, "did you ever see that gentleman who has taken the trouble to ride down here to speak to me, now, three times, — three times I think, Susan?"

"Three times, miss," returned the Nipper. "Once when you was out a-walking with them Sket—"

Florence gently looked at her, and Miss Nipper checked herself.

"With Sir Barnet and his lady, I mean to say, miss, and the young gentleman. And two evenings since then."

"When I was a child, and when company used to come to visit papa, did you ever see that gentleman at home, Susan?" asked Florence.

"Well, miss," returned her maid after considering, "I really couldn't say I ever did. When your poor dear ma died, Miss Floy, I was very new in the family, you see, and *my* element"—the Nipper bridled, as opining that her merits had been always designedly extinguished by Mr. Dombey—"was the floor below the attics."

"To be sure," said Florence, still thoughtfully; "you are not likely to have known who came to the house. I quite forgot."

"Not, miss, but what we talked about the family and visitors," said Susan, "and but what I heard much said, although the nurse before Mrs. Richards *did* make unpleasant remarks when I was in company, and hint at little Pitchers, but that could only be attributed, poor thing," observed Susan with composed forbearance, "to habits of intoxication, for which she was required to leave, and did."

Florence, who was seated at her chamber window, with her face resting on her hand, sat looking out, and hardly seemed to hear what Susan said, she was so lost in thought.

"At all events, miss," said Susan, "I remember very well that this same gentleman, Mr. Carker, was almost, if not quite, as great a gentleman with your papa then as he is now. It used to be said in the house, then, miss, that he was at the head of all your pa's affairs in the City, and managed the whole, and that your pa minded him more than anybody, which, begging your pardon, Miss Floy, he might easy do, for he never minded anybody else. I knew that, Pitcher as I might have been."

Susan Nipper, with an injured remembrance of the

nurse before Mrs. Richards, emphasized "Pitcher" strongly.

"And that Mr. Carker has not fallen off, miss," she pursued, "but has stood his ground, and kept his credit with your pa, I know from what is said among our people by that Perch, whenever he comes to the house, and though he's the weakest reed in the world, Miss Floy, and no one can have a moment's patience with the man, he knows what goes on in the City tolerably well, and says that your pa does nothing without Mr. Carker, and leaves all to Mr. Carker, and acts according to Mr. Carker, and has Mr. Carker always at his elbow, and I do believe that he believes (that washiest of Perches) that after your pa, the Emperor of India is the child unborn to Mr. Carker."

Not a word of this was lost on Florence, who, with an awakened interest in Susan's speech, no longer gazed abstractedly on the prospect without, but looked at her, and listened with attention.

"Yes, Susan," she said when that young lady had concluded. "He is in papa's confidence, and is his friend, I am sure."

Florence's mind ran high on this theme, and had done for some days. Mr. Carker, in the two visits with which he had followed up his first one, had assumed a confidence between himself and her — a right on his part to be mysterious and stealthy, in telling her that the ship was still unheard of — a kind of mildly restrained power and authority over her — that made her wonder, and caused her great uneasiness. She had no means of repelling it, or of freeing herself from the web he was gradually winding about her : for that would have required some art and knowledge of the world, opposed to such address as his; and Florence had none. True, he said no more to her than that there was no news of the ship, and that he feared the worst; but how he came to know that she was interested in the ship, and why he had the right to signify his knowledge to her so insidiously and darkly, troubled Florence very much.

This conduct on the part of Mr. Carker, and her habit of often considering it with wonder and uneasiness, began to invest him with an uncomfortable fascination in Florence's thoughts. A more distinct remembrance of his features, voice, and manner: which she sometimes courted, as a means of reducing him to the level of a real personage, capable of exerting no greater charm over her than another: did not remove the vague impression. And yet he never frowned, or looked upon her with an air of dislike or animosity, but was always smiling and serene.

Again, Florence, in pursuit of her strong purpose with reference to her father, and her steady resolution to believe that she was herself unwittingly to blame for their so cold and distant relations, would recall to mind that this gentleman was his confidential friend, and would think, with an anxious heart, could her struggling tendency to dislike and fear him be a part of that misfortune in her which had turned her father's love adrift, and left her so alone ? She dreaded that it might be; sometimes believed it was: then she resolved that she would try to conquer this wrong feeling; persuaded herself that she was honored and encouraged by the notice of her father's friend; and hoped that patient observation of him and trust in him would lead her bleeding feet along that stony road which ended in her father's heart.

Thus, with no one to advise her — for she could advise with no one without seeming to complain against him — gentle Florence tossed on an uneasy sea of doubt and hope; and Mr. Carker, like a scaly monster of the deep, swam down below, and kept his shining eye upon her.

Florence had a new reason in all this for wishing to be at home again. Her lonely life was better suited to her course of timid hope and doubt: and she feared, sometimes, that in her absence she might miss some hopeful chance of testifying her affection for her father. Heaven knows, she might have set her mind at rest, poor child! on this point; but her slighted love was fluttering within her, and, even in her sleep, it flew away in dreams, and nestled, like a wandering bird come home, upon her father's neck.

Of Walter she thought often. Ah! how often, when the night was gloomy, and the wind was blowing round the house! But hope was strong in her breast. It is so difficult for the young and ardent, even with such experience as hers, to imagine youth and ardor quenched like a weak flame, and the bright day of life merging into night at noon, that hope was strong yet. Her tears fell frequently for Walter's sufferings, but rarely for his supposed death, and never long.

She had written to the old instrument-maker, but had received no answer to her note: which, indeed, required none. Thus matters stood with Florence on the morning when she was going home, gladly, to her old secluded life.

Doctor and Mrs. Blimber, accompanied (much against his will), by their valued charge, Master Barnet, were already gone back to Brighton, where that young gentleman and his fellow-pilgrims to Parnassus were then, no doubt, in the continual resumption of their studies. The holiday time was past and over; most of the juvenile guests at the villa had taken their departure; and Florence's long visit was come to an end.

There was one guest, however, albeit not resident within the house, who had been very constant in his attention to the family, and who still remained devoted to them. This was Mr. Toots, who, after renewing, some weeks ago, the acquaintance he had had the happiness of forming with Skettles junior, on the night when he burst the Blimberian bonds and soared into freedom with his ring on, called regularly every other day, and left a perfect pack of cards at the hall-door; so many, indeed, that the ceremony was quite a deal on the part of Mr. Toots, and a hand at whist on the part of the servant.

Mr. Toots likewise, with the bold and happy idea of preventing the family from forgetting him (but there is reason to suppose that this expedient originated in the teeming brain of the Chicken), had established a six-oared cutter, manned by aquatic friends of the Chicken's, and steered by that illustrious character in person, who wore a bright red fireman's coat for the purpose, and concealed the perpetual black eye with which he was afflicted beneath a green shade. Previous to the institution of this equipage, Mr. Toots sounded the Chicken on a hypothetical case, as, supposing the Chicken to be enamoured of a young lady named Mary, and to have conceived the intention of starting a boat of his own, what would he call that boat? The Chicken replied, with divers strong asseverations, that he would either christen it Poll or The Chicken's Delight. Improving on this idea, Mr. Toots, after deep study and the exercise of much invention, resolved to call his boat The Toots's Joy, as a delicate compliment to Florence, of which no man knowing the parties could possibly miss the appreciation.

Stretched on a crimson cushion in his gallant bark, with his shoes in the air, Mr. Toots, in the exercise of his project, had come up the river day after day, and week after week, and had flitted to and fro, near Sir Barnet's garden, and had caused his crew to cut across and across the river at sharp angles, for his better exhibition to any lookers-out from Sir Barnet's windows, and had had such evolutions performed by the Toots's Joy as had filled all the neighboring part of the water-side with astonishment. But, whenever he saw any one in Sir Barnet's garden on the brink of the river, Mr. Toots always feigned to be passing there by a combination of coincidences of the most singular and unlikely description.

"How are you, Toots?" Sir Barnet would say, waving his hand from the lawn, while the artful Chicken steered close in shore.

"How de do, Sir Barnet?" Mr. Toots would answer. "What a surprising thing that I should see *you* here!"

Mr. Toots, in his sagacity, always said this, as if, instead of that being Sir Barnet's house, it were some deserted edifice on the banks of the Nile or Ganges.

"I never was so surprised!" Mr. Toots would exclaim. — "Is Miss Dombey there?"

Whereupon Florence would appear, perhaps.

"Oh, Diogenes is quite well, Miss Dombey," Mr. Toots would cry. "I called to ask this morning."

"Thank you very much!" the pleasant voice of Florence would reply.

"Won't you come ashore, Toots?" Sir Barnet would say then. "Come! you're in no hurry. Come and see us."

"Oh, it's of no consequence, thank you!" Mr. Toots would blushingly rejoin. "I thought Miss Dombey might like to know, that's all. Good-by!" And poor Mr. Toots, who was dying to accept the invitation, but hadn't the courage to do it, signed to the Chicken with an aching heart, and away went the Joy, cleaving the water like an arrow.

The Joy was lying in a state of extraordinary splendor, at the garden steps, on the morning of Florence's departure. When she went downstairs to take leave, after her talk with Susan, she found Mr. Toots awaiting her in the drawing-room.

"Oh, how de do, Miss Dombey?" said the stricken Toots, always dreadfully disconcerted when the desire of his heart was gained, and he was speaking to her. "Thank you, I'm very well indeed, I hope you're the same; so was Diogenes yesterday."

"You are very kind," said Florence.

"Thank you, it's of no consequence," retorted Mr. Toots. "I thought perhaps you wouldn't mind, in this fine weather, coming home by water, Miss Dombey. There's plenty of room in the boat for your maid."

"I am very much obliged to you," said Florence, hesitating. "I really am — but I would rather not."

"Oh, it's of no consequence," retorted Mr. Toots. "Good-morning!"

"Won't you wait and see Lady Skettles?" asked Florence kindly.

"Oh, no, thank you," returned Mr. Toots, "it's of no consequence at all."

So shy was Mr. Toots on such occasions, and so flurried! But Lady Skettles entering at the moment, Mr. Toots was suddenly seized with a passion for asking her how she did, and hoping she was very well; nor could Mr. Toots by any possibility leave off shaking hands with her until Sir Barnet appeared: to whom he immediately clung with the tenacity of desperation.

"We are losing to-day, Toots," said Sir Barnet, turning towards Florence, "the light of our house, I assure you."

"Oh, it's of no conseq— I mean yes, to be sure," faltered the embarrassed Toots. "Good-morning!"

Notwithstanding the emphatic nature of this farewell, Mr. Toots, instead of going away, stood leering about him vacantly. Florence, to relieve him, bade adieu, with many thanks, to Lady Skettles, and gave her arm to Sir Barnet.

"May I beg of you, my dear Miss Dombey," said her host as he conducted her to the carriage, "to present my best compliments to your dear papa?"

It was distressing to Florence to receive the commission, for she felt as if she were imposing on Sir Barnet, by allowing him to believe that a kindness rendered to her was rendered to her father. As she could not explain, however, she bowed her head and thanked him; and again she thought that the dull home, free from such embarrassments, and such reminders of her sorrow, was her natural and best retreat.

Such of her late friends and companions as were yet remaining at the villa came running from within, and from the garden, to say good-by. They were all attached to her, and very earnest in taking leave of her. Even the household were sorry for her going, and the servants came nodding and courtesying round the carriage door. As Florence looked round on the kind faces, and saw among them those of Sir Barnet and his lady, and of Mr. Toots, who was chuckling and staring at her from a distance, she was reminded of the night when Paul and she had come from Doctor Blimber's: and, when the carriage drove away, her face was wet with tears.

Sorrowful tears, but tears of consolation too; for all the softer memories connected with the dull old house to which she was returning made it dear to her as they rose up. How long it seemed since she had wandered through the silent rooms: since she had last crept, softly and afraid, into those her father occupied: since she had felt the solemn but yet soothing influence of the beloved dead in every action of her daily life! This new farewell reminded her, besides, of her parting with poor Walter: of his looks and words that night: and of the gracious blending she had noticed in him of tenderness for those he left behind, with courage and high spirit. His little history was associated with the old house, too, and gave it a new claim and hold upon her heart.

Even Susan Nipper softened towards the home of so many years as they were on their way towards it. Gloomy as it was, and rigid justice as she rendered to its gloom, she forgave it a great deal. "I shall be glad to see it again, I don't deny, miss," said the Nipper. "There ain't much in it to boast of, but I wouldn't have it burnt or pulled down, neither!"

"You'll be glad to go through the old rooms, won't you, Susan?" said Florence, smiling.

"Well, miss," returned the Nipper, softening more and more towards the house as they approached it nearer, "I won't deny but what I shall, though I shall hate 'em again to-morrow, very likely."

Florence felt that, for her, there was greater peace within it than elsewhere. It was better and easier to keep her secret shut up there, among the tall dark walls, than to carry it abroad into the light, and try to hide it from a crowd of happy eyes. It was better to pursue the study of her loving heart alone, and find no new discouragements in loving hearts about her. It was easier to hope, and pray, and love on, all uncared for, yet with constancy and patience, in the tranquil sanctuary of such remembrances: although it mouldered, rusted, and decayed about her: than in a new scene, let its gayety be what it would. She welcomed back her old enchanted dream of life, and longed for the old dark door to close upon her once again.

Full of such thoughts, they turned into the long and sombre street. Florence was not on that side of the carriage which was nearest to her home, and, as the distance lessened between them and it, she looked out of her window for the children over the way.

She was thus engaged, when an exclamation from Susan caused her to turn quickly round.

"Why, gracious me!" cried Susan, breathless, "where's our house?"

"Our house!" said Florence.

Susan, drawing in her head from the window, thrust it out again, drew it in again as the carriage stopped, and stared at her mistress in amazement.

There was a labyrinth of scaffolding raised all round the house, from the basement to the roof. Loads of bricks and stones, and heaps of mortar, and piles of wood, blocked up half the width and length of the broad street at the side. Ladders were raised against the walls; laborers were climbing up and down; men were at work upon the steps of the scaffolding; painters and decorators were busy inside; great rolls of ornamental paper were being delivered from a cart at the door; an upholsterer's wagon also stopped the way; no furniture was to be seen through the gaping and broken windows in any of the rooms; nothing but workmen, and the implements of their several trades, swarming from the kitchens to the garrets. Inside and outside alike: bricklayers, painters, carpenters, masons: hammer, hod, brush, pickaxe, saw, and trowel: all at work together, in full chorus.

Florence descended from the coach, half doubting if it were, or could be, the right house, until she recognized Towlinson, with a sunburnt face, standing at the door to receive her.

"There is nothing the matter?" inquired Florence.

"Oh, no, miss!"

"There are great alterations going on."

"Yes, miss, great alterations," said Towlinson.

Florence passed him as if she were in a dream, and hurried upstairs. The garish light was in the long-darkened drawing-room, and there were steps and platforms, and men in paper caps, in the high places. Her mother's picture was gone with the rest of the movables, and on the mark where it had been was scrawled in chalk, "This room in panel. Green and gold." The staircase was a labyrinth of posts and planks like the outside of the house, and a whole Olympus of plumbers and glaziers was reclining in various attitudes on the skylight. Her own room was not yet touched within, but there were beams and boards raised against it without, balking the daylight. She went up swiftly to that other bedroom, where the little bed was; and a dark giant of a man, with a pipe in his mouth, and his head tied up in a pocket-handkerchief, was staring in at the window.

It was here that Susan Nipper, who had been in quest of Florence, found her, and said, would she go downstairs to her papa, who wished to speak to her?

"At home! and wishing to speak to me!" cried Florence, trembling.

Susan, who was infinitely more distraught than Florence herself, repeated her errand; and Florence, pale and agitated, hurried down again without a moment's hesitation. She thought upon the way down, would she dare to kiss him? The longing of her heart resolved her, and she thought she would.

Her father might have heard that heart beat when

it came into his presence. One instant, and it would have beat against his breast —

But he was not alone. There were two ladies there; and Florence stopped. Striving so hard with her emotion, that if her brute friend Di had not burst in and overwhelmed her with his caresses as a welcome home — at which one of the ladies gave a little scream, and that diverted her attention from herself — she would have swooned upon the floor.

"Florence," said her father, putting out his hand: so stiffly that it held her off: "how do you do?"

Florence took the hand between her own, and putting it timidly to her lips, yielded to its withdrawal. It touched the door, in shutting it, with quite as much endearment as it had touched her.

"What dog is that?" said Mr. Dombey, displeased.

"It is a dog, papa — from Brighton."

"Well!" said Mr. Dombey; and a cloud passed over his face, for he understood her.

"He is very good-tempered," said Florence, addressing herself with her natural grace and sweetness to the two lady strangers. "He is only glad to see me. Pray forgive him."

She saw in the glance they interchanged that the lady who had screamed, and who was seated, was old; and that the other lady, who stood near her papa, was very beautiful, and of an elegant figure.

"Mrs. Skewton," said her father, turning to the first, and holding out his hand, "this is my daughter Florence."

"Charming, I am sure," observed the lady, putting

up her glass. "So natural! My darling Florence, you must kiss me. if you please."

Florence. having done so. turned towards the other lady. by whom her father stood waiting.

"Edith." said Mr. Dombey, "this is my daughter Florence. Florence, this lady will soon be your mamma."

Florence started, and looked up at the beautiful face in a conflict of emotions, among which the tears that name awakened struggled for a moment with surprise. interest. admiration. and an indefinable sort of fear. Then she cried out. "Oh. papa, may you be happy! may you be very, very happy all your life!" and then fell weeping on the lady's bosom.

There was a short silence. The beautiful lady, who at first had seemed to hesitate whether or no she should advance to Florence, held her to her breast. and pressed the hand with which she clasped her. close about her waist. as if to re-assure her and comfort her. Not one word passed the lady's lips. She bent her head down over Florence, and she kissed her on the cheek, but she said no word.

"Shall we go on through the rooms." said Mr. Dombey. "and see how our workmen are doing? Pray allow me. my dear madam."

He said this in offering his arm to Mrs. Skewton, who had been looking at Florence through her glass, as though picturing to herself what she might be made. by the infusion — from her own copious storehouse. no doubt — of a little more Heart and Nature. Florence was still sobbing on the lady's breast. and holding to her. when Mr. Dombey was heard to say from the conservatory, —

"Let us ask Edith. Dear me, where is she?"

"Edith, my dear!" cried Mrs. Skewton, "where are you? Looking for Mr. Dombey, somewhere, I know. We are here, my love."

The beautiful lady released her hold of Florence, and pressing her lips once more upon her face, withdrew hurriedly, and joined them. Florence remained standing in the same place : happy, sorry, joyful, and in tears, she knew not how or how long, but all at once : when her new mamma came back, and took her in her arms again.

"Florence," said the lady hurriedly, and looking into her face with great earnestness, "you will not begin by hating me?"

"By hating you, mamma?" cried Florence, winding her arm round her neck, and returning the look.

"Hush! Begin by thinking well of me," said the beautiful lady. "Begin by believing that I will try to make you happy, and that I am prepared to love you, Florence. Good-by. We shall meet again soon. Good-by! Don't stay here now!"

Again she pressed her to her breast — she had spoken in a rapid manner, but firmly — and Florence saw her rejoin them in the other room.

And now Florence began to hope that she would learn from her new and beautiful mamma how to gain her father's love; and in her sleep that night, in her lost old home, her own mamma smiled radiantly upon the hope, and blessed it. Dreaming Florence!

CHAPTER IX.

Miss Tox, all unconscious of any such rare appearances, in connection with Mr. Dombey's house, as scaffoldings and ladders, and men with their heads tied up in pocket-handkerchiefs, glaring in at the windows like flying genii or strange birds, having breakfasted one morning, at about this eventful period of time, on her customary viands; to wit, one French roll rasped, one egg new laid (or warranted to be), and one little pot of tea, wherein was infused one little silver scoopful of that herb on behalf of Miss Tox, and one little silver scoopful on behalf of the teapot — a flight of fancy in which good housekeepers delight; went upstairs to set forth the Bird Waltz on the harpsichord, to water and arrange the plants, to dust the knick-knacks, and, according to her daily custom, to make her little drawing-room the garland of Princess's Place.

Miss Tox endued herself with the pair of ancient gloves, like dead leaves, in which she was accustomed to perform these avocations — hidden from human sight at other times in a table drawer — and went methodically to work; beginning with the Bird Waltz; passing, by a natural association of ideas, to her bird — a very high-shouldered canary, stricken in years, and much rumpled, but a piercing singer, as Princess's Place well knew; taking, next in order, the little china ornaments, paper fly-cages, and so forth; and coming round, in good time, to the plants, which generally required to be snipped here and there with a pair of scissors, for some botanical reason that was very powerful with Miss Tox.

Miss Tox was slow in coming to the place this morning. The weather was warm, the wind southerly; and there was a sigh of the summer-time in Princess's Place, that turned Miss Tox's thoughts upon the country. The potboy attached to the Princess's Arms had come out with a can, and trickled water, in a flowing pattern, all over Princess's Place, and it gave the weedy ground a fresh scent — quite a growing scent, Miss Tox said. There was a tiny blink of sun peeping in from the great street round the corner, and the smoky sparrows hopped over it and back again, brightening as they passed: or bathed in it like a stream, and became glorified sparrows, unconnected with chimneys. Legends in praise of Ginger Beer, with pictorial representations of thirsty customers submerged in the effervescence, or stunned by the flying corks, were conspicuous in the window of the Princess's Arms. They were making late hay somewhere out of town; and though the fragrance had a long way to come, and many counter-fragranees to contend with among the dwellings of the poor (may God reward the worthy gentlemen who stickle for the plague as part and parcel of the wisdom of our ancestors, and who do their little best to keep those dwellings miserable!), yet it was wafted faintly into Princess's Place, whispering of Nature and her wholesome air, as such things will, even unto prisoners and captives, and those who are desolate and oppressed.

Miss Tox sat down upon the window-seat, and thought of her good papa deceased — Mr. Tox, of the Customs Department of the public service; and of her childhood, passed at a seaport, among a considerable quantity of cold tar, and some rusticity. She fell into a softened remembrance of meadows in old time, gleaming with buttercups, like so many inverted firmaments of golden stars; and how she had made chains of dandelion stalks for youthful vowers of eternal constancy, dressed chiefly in nankeen; and how soon those fetters had withered and broken.

Sitting on the window-seat, and looking out upon the sparrows and the blink of sun, Miss Tox thought likewise of her good mamma deceased — sister to the owner of the powdered head and pigtail — of her virtues, and her rheumatism. And when a man with bulgy legs, and a rough voice, and a heavy basket on his head that crushed his hat into a mere black muffin, came crying flowers down Princess's Place, making his timid little roots of daisies shudder in the vibration of every yell he gave, as though he had been an ogre hawking little children, summer recollections were so strong upon Miss Tox that she shook her head, and murmured, she would be comparatively old before she knew it — which seemed likely.

In her pensive mood, Miss Tox's thoughts went wandering on Mr. Dombey's track; probably because

the major had returned home to his lodgings oppo-
site, and had just bowed to her from his window.
What other reason could Miss Tox have for connect-
ing Mr. Dombey with her summer days and dandelion
fetters? Was he more cheerful? thought Miss
Tox. Was he reconciled to the decrees of fate?
Would he ever marry again; and if yes, whom?
What sort of person now?

A flush — it was warm weather — overspread Miss
Tox's face as, while entertaining these meditations,
she turned her head, and was surprised by the
reflection of her thoughtful image in the chimney-
glass. Another flush succeeded when she saw a
little carriage drive into Princess's Place, and make
straight for her own door. Miss Tox arose, took up
her scissors hastily, and so coming, at last, to the
plants, was very busy with them when Mrs. Chick
entered the room.

"How is my sweetest friend?" exclaimed Miss
Tox with open arms.

A little stateliness was mingled with Miss Tox's
sweetest friend's demeanor, but she kissed Miss Tox,
and said, "Lucretia, thank you, I am pretty well. I
hope you are the same. Hem!"

Mrs. Chick was laboring under a peculiar little
monosyllabic cough; a sort of primer, or easy introduction to the art of coughing.

"You call very early, and how kind that is, my
dear!" pursued Miss Tox. "Now, have you breakfasted?"

"Thank you, Lucretia," said Mrs. Chick, "I have.
I took an early breakfast" — the good lady seemed
curious on the subject of Princess's Place, and looked
all round it as she spoke — "with my brother, who
has come home."

"He is better, I trust, my love?" faltered Miss Tox.

"He is greatly better, thank you. Hem!"

"My dear Louisa must be careful of that cough," remarked Miss Tox.

"It's nothing," returned Mrs. Chick. "It's merely change of weather. We must expect change."

"Of weather?" asked Miss Tox in her simplicity.

"Of everything," returned Mrs. Chick. "Of course we must. It's a world of change. Any one would surprise me very much, Lucretia, and would greatly alter my opinion of their understanding, if they attempted to contradict or evade what is so perfectly evident. Change!" exclaimed Mrs. Chick with severe philosophy. "Why, my gracious me, what is there that does *not* change? Even the silk-worm, who I am sure might be supposed not to trouble itself about such subjects, changes into all sorts of unexpected things continually."

"My Louisa," said the mild Miss Tox, "is ever happy in her illustrations."

"You are so kind, Lucretia," returned Mrs. Chick, a little softened, "as to say so, and to think so, I believe. I hope neither of us may ever have any cause to lessen our opinion of the other, Lucretia."

"I am sure of it," returned Miss Tox.

Mrs. Chick coughed as before, and drew lines on the carpet with the ivory end of her parasol. Miss Tox, who had experience of her fair friend, and knew that under the pressure of any slight fatigue or vexation she was prone to a discursive kind of irritability, availed herself of the pause to change the subject.

"Pardon me, my dear Louisa," said Miss Tox,

"but have I caught sight of the manly form of Mr. Chick in the carriage?"

"He is there," said Mrs. Chick, "but pray leave him there. He has his newspaper, and would be quite contented for the next two hours. Go on with your flowers, Lucretia, and allow me to sit here and rest."

"My Louisa knows," observed Miss Tox, "that, between friends like ourselves, any approach to ceremony would be out of the question. Therefore —" Therefore Miss Tox finished the sentence, not in words, but action; and putting on her gloves again, which she had taken off, and arming herself once more with her scissors, began to snip and clip among the leaves with microscopic industry.

"Florence has returned home also," said Mrs. Chick, after sitting silent for some time, with her head on one side, and her parasol sketching on the floor; "and really Florence is a great deal too old now to continue to lead that solitary life to which she has been accustomed. Of course she is. There can be no doubt about it. I should have very little respect, indeed, for anybody who could advocate a different opinion. Whatever my wishes might be, I *could not* respect them. We cannot command our feelings to such an extent as that."

Miss Tox assented, without being particular as to the intelligibility of the proposition.

"If she's a strange girl," said Mrs. Chick, "and if my brother Paul cannot feel perfectly comfortable in her society, after all the sad things that have happened, and all the terrible disappointments that have been undergone, then, what is the reply? That he must make an effort. That he is bound to make

an effort. We have always been a family remarkable
for effort. Paul is at the head of the family; almost
the only representative of it left—for what am I?
—I am of no consequence—"

" My dearest love!" remonstrated Miss Tox.

Mrs. Chick dried her eyes, which were, for the
moment, overflowing; and proceeded,—

"—And consequently he is more than ever bound
to make an effort. And though his having done so
comes upon me with a sort of shock—for mine is a
very weak and foolish nature; which is anything
but a blessing, I am sure; I often wish my heart
was a marble slab, or a paving-stone—"

" My sweet Louisa!" remonstrated Miss Tox again.

"—Still, it is a triumph to me to know that he is
so true to himself, and to his name of Dombey;
although, of course, I always knew he would be. I
only hope," said Mrs. Chick after a pause, "that she
may be worthy of the name too."

Miss Tox filled a little green watering-pot from a
jug, and happening to look up when she had done
so, was so surprised by the amount of expression
Mrs. Chick had conveyed into her face, and was
bestowing upon her, that she put the little watering-pot on the table for the present, and sat down
near it.

" My dear Louisa," said Miss Tox, "will it be the
least satisfaction to you if I venture to observe, in
reference to that remark, that I, as a humble individual, think your sweet niece in every way most
promising?"

" What do you mean, Lucretia?" returned Mrs.
Chick with increased stateliness of manner. "To
what remark of mine, my dear, do you refer?"

"Her being worthy of her name, my love," replied Miss Tox.

"If," said Mrs. Chick with solemn patience, "I have not expressed myself with clearness, Lucretia, the fault, of course, is mine. There is, perhaps, no reason why I should express myself at all, except the intimacy that has subsisted between us, and which I very much hope, Lucretia — confidently hope — nothing will occur to disturb. Because, why should I do anything else? There is no reason; it would be absurd. But I wish to express myself clearly, Lucretia; and therefore, to go back to that remark, I must beg to say that it was not intended to relate to Florence in any way."

"Indeed!" returned Miss Tox.

"No," said Mrs. Chick shortly and decisively.

"Pardon me, my dear," rejoined her meek friend; "but I cannot have understood it. I fear I am dull."

Mrs. Chick looked round the room and over the way; at the plants, at the birds, at the watering-pot, at almost everything within view, except Miss Tox; and finally, dropping her glance upon Miss Tox, for a moment, on its way to the ground, said, looking meanwhile with elevated eyebrows at the carpet, —

"When I speak, Lucretia, of her being worthy of the name, I speak of my brother Paul's second wife. I believe I have already said, in effect, if not in the very words I now use, that it is his intention to marry a second wife."

Miss Tox left her seat in a hurry, and returned to her plants; clipping among the stems and leaves with as little favor as a barber working at so many pauper heads of hair.

"Whether she will be fully sensible of the distinction conferred upon her," said Mrs. Chick in a lofty tone, "is quite another question. I hope she may be. We are bound to think well of one another in this world, and I hope she may be. I have not been advised with, myself. If I had been advised with, I have no doubt my advice would have been cavalierly received, and therefore it is infinitely better as it is. I much prefer it as it is."

Miss Tox, with head bent down, still clipped among the plants. Mrs. Chick, with energetic shakings of her own head from time to time, continued to hold forth, as if in defiance of somebody.

"If my brother Paul had consulted with me, which he sometimes does — or rather, sometimes used to do; for he will naturally do that no more now, and this is a circumstance which I regard as a relief from responsibility," said Mrs. Chick hysterically, " for I thank Heaven I am not jealous: " here Mrs. Chick again shed tears: "if my brother Paul had come to me, and had said, 'Louisa, what kind of qualities would you advise me to look out for in a wife?' I should certainly have answered, 'Paul, you must have family, you must have beauty, you must have dignity, you must have connection.' Those are the words I should have used. You might have led me to the block immediately afterwards," said Mrs. Chick, as if that consequence were highly probable, "but I should have used them. I should have said, 'Paul! You to marry a second time without family! You to marry without beauty! You to marry without dignity! You to marry without connection! There is nobody in the world, not mad, who could dream of daring to entertain such a preposterous idea!'"

Miss Tox stopped clipping; and, with her head among the plants, listened attentively. Perhaps Miss Tox thought there was hope in this exordium, and in the warmth of Mrs. Chick.

"I should have adopted this course of argument," pursued the discreet lady, "because I trust I am not a fool. I make no claim to be considered a person of superior intellect — though I believe some people have been extraordinary enough to consider me so; one so little humored as I am would very soon be disabused of any such notion; but I trust I am not a downright fool. And to tell ME," said Mrs. Chick with ineffable disdain, "that my brother, Paul Dombey, could ever contemplate the possibility of uniting himself to anybody — I don't care who" — she was more sharp and emphatic in that short clause than in any other part of her discourse — "not possessing these requisites, would be to insult what understanding I *have* got, as much as if I was to be told that I was born and bred an elephant. Which I *may* be told next," said Mrs. Chick with resignation. "It wouldn't surprise me at all. I expect it."

In the moment's silence that ensued, Miss Tox's scissors gave a feeble clip or two; but Miss Tox's face was still invisible, and Miss Tox's morning gown was agitated. Mrs. Chick looked sideways at her, through the intervening plants, and went on to say, in a tone of bland conviction, and as one dwelling on a point of fact that hardly required to be stated, —

"Therefore, of course my brother Paul has done what was to be expected of him, and what anybody might have foreseen he would do, if he entered the marriage state again. I confess it takes me rather by surprise, however gratifying; because, when Paul went out of town, I had no idea at all that he would form any attachment out of town, and he certainly had no attachment when he left here. However, it seems to be extremely desirable in every point of view. I have no doubt the mother is a most genteel and elegant creature, and I have no right whatever to dispute the policy of her living with them: which is Paul's affair, not mine; and as to Paul's choice, herself, I have only seen her picture yet, but that is beautiful indeed. Her name is beautiful too," said Mrs. Chick, shaking her head with energy, and arranging herself in her chair; "Edith is at once uncommon, as it strikes me, and distinguished. Consequently, Lucretia, I have no doubt you will be happy to hear that the marriage is to take place immediately — of course you will:" great emphasis again: "and that you are delighted with this change in the condition of my brother, who has shown you a great deal of pleasant attention at various times."

Miss Tox made no verbal answer, but took up the little watering-pot with a trembling hand, and looked vacantly round, as if considering what article of furniture would be improved by the contents. The room-door opening at this crisis of Miss Tox's feelings, she started, laughed aloud, and fell into the arms of the person entering; happily insensible alike of Mrs. Chick's indignant countenance, and of the major at his window over the way, who had his double-barrelled eyeglass in full action, and whose face and figure were dilated with Mephistophilean joy.

Not so the expatriated native, amazed supporter of Miss Tox's swooning form, who, coming straight upstairs with a polite inquiry touching Miss Tox's health (in exact pursuance of the major's malicious instructions), had accidentally arrived in the very nick of time to catch the delicate burden in his arms, and to receive the contents of the little watering-pot in his shoe; both of which circumstances, coupled with his consciousness of being closely watched by the wrathful major, who had threatened the usual penalty in regard of every bone of his skin in case of any failure, combined to render him a moving spectacle of mental and bodily distress.

For some moments this afflicted foreigner remained clasping Miss Tox to his heart, with an energy of action in remarkable opposition to his disconcerted face, while that poor lady trickled slowly down upon him the very last sprinklings of the little watering-pot, as if he were a delicate exotic (which, indeed, he was), and might be almost expected to blow while the gentle rain descended. Mrs. Chick, at length recovering sufficient presence of mind to interpose, commanded him to drop Miss Tox upon the sofa and withdraw; and the exile promptly obeying, she applied herself to promote Miss Tox's recovery.

But none of that gentle concern which usually characterizes the daughters of Eve in their tending of each other; none of that freemasonry in fainting, by which they are generally bound together in a mysterious bond of sisterhood; was visible in Mrs. Chick's demeanor. Rather, like the executioner who restores the victim to sensation previous to proceeding with the torture (or was wont to do so in the good old times for which all true men wear perpetual mourning) did Mrs. Chick administer the

smelling-bottle, the slapping on the hands, the dashing of cold water on the face, and the other proved remedies. And when, at length, Miss Tox opened her eyes, and gradually became restored to animation and consciousness, Mrs. Chick drew off as from a criminal, and reversing the precedent of the murdered King of Denmark, regarded her more in anger than in sorrow.

"Lucretia!" said Mrs. Chick. "I will not attempt to disguise what I feel. My eyes are opened all at once. I wouldn't have believed this, if a saint had told it to me."

"I am foolish to give way to faintness," Miss Tox faltered. "I shall be better presently."

"You will be better presently, Lucretia!" repeated Mrs. Chick with exceeding scorn. "Do you suppose I am blind? Do you imagine I am in my second childhood? No, Lucretia! I am obliged to you!"

Miss Tox directed an imploring, helpless kind of look towards her friend, and put her handkerchief before her face.

"If any one had told me this yesterday," said Mrs. Chick with majesty, "or even half an hour ago, I should have been tempted, I almost believe, to strike them to the earth. Lucretia Tox, my eyes are opened to you all at once. The scales" — here Mrs. Chick cast down an imaginary pair, such as are commonly used in grocers' shops — "have fallen from my sight. The blindness of my confidence is past, Lucretia. It has been abused and played upon, and evasion is quite out of the question now, I assure you."

"Oh! to what do you allude so cruelly, my love?" asked Miss Tox through her tears.

"Lucretia," said Mrs. Chick, "ask your own heart. I must entreat you not to address me by any such familiar term as you have just used, if you please. I have some self-respect left, though you may think otherwise."

"Oh, Louisa!" cried Miss Tox. "How can you speak to me like that?"

"How can I speak to you like that?" retorted Mrs. Chick, who, in default of having any particular argument to sustain herself upon, relied principally on such repetitions for her most withering effects. "Like that! You may well say like that, indeed!"

Miss Tox sobbed pitifully.

"The idea!" said Mrs. Chick, "of your having basked at my brother's fireside like a serpent, and wound yourself, through me, almost into his confidence, Lucretia, that you might, in secret, entertain designs upon him, and dare to aspire to contemplate the possibility of his uniting himself to *you!* Why, it is an idea," said Mrs. Chick with sarcastic dignity, "the absurdity of which almost relieves its treachery."

"Pray, Louisa," urged Miss Tox, "do not say such dreadful things."

"Dreadful things!" repeated Mrs. Chick. "Dreadful things! Is it not a fact, Lucretia, that you have just now been unable to command your feelings even before me, whose eyes you had so completely closed?"

"I have made no complaint," sobbed Miss Tox. "I have said nothing. If I have been a little overpowered by your news, Louisa, and have ever had any lingering thought that Mr. Dombey was inclined to be particular towards me, surely *you* will not condemn me."

"She is going to say," said Mrs. Chick, addressing herself to the whole of the furniture, in a comprehensive glance of resignation and appeal, "she is going to say — I know it — that I have encouraged her!"

"I don't wish to exchange reproaches, dear Louisa," sobbed Miss Tox. "Nor do I wish to complain. But, in my own defence —"

"Yes," cried Mrs. Chick, looking round the room with a prophetic smile, "that's what she's going to say. I knew it. You had better say it. Say it openly! Be open, Lucretia Tox," said Mrs. Chick with desperate sternness, "whatever you are."

"— In my own defence," faltered Miss Tox, "and only in my own defence against your unkind words, my dear Louisa, I would merely ask you if you haven't often favored such a fancy, and even said it might happen, for anything we could tell?"

"There is a point," said Mrs. Chick, rising, not as if she were going to stop at the floor, but as if she were about to soar up high into her native skies, "beyond which endurance becomes ridiculous, if not culpable. I can bear much; but not too much. What spell was on me when I came into this house this day, I don't know; but I had a presentiment — a dark presentiment," said Mrs. Chick with a shiver, "that something was going to happen. Well may I have had that foreboding, Lucretia, when my confidence of many years is destroyed in an instant, when my eyes are opened all at once, and when I find you revealed in your true colors. Lucretia, I have been mistaken in you. It is better for us both that this subject should end here. I wish you well, and I shall ever wish you well. But, as an individual

who desires to be true to herself in her own poor
position, whatever that position may be, or may not
be — and as the sister of my brother — and as the
sister-in-law of my brother's wife — and as a connection by marriage of my brother's wife's mother
— may I be permitted to add, as a Dombey?.— I
can wish you nothing else but good-morning."

These words delivered with cutting suavity, tem-
pered and chastened by a lofty air of moral recti-
tude, carried the speaker to the door.   There she
inclined her head in a ghostly and statue-like manner, and so withdrew to her carriage, to seek comfort and consolation in the arms of Mr. Chick, her
lord.

Figuratively speaking, that is to say ; for the arms
of Mr. Chick were full of his newspaper.   Neither
did that gentleman address his eyes towards his wife
otherwise than by stealth.   Neither did he offer any
consolation whatever.   In short, he sat reading, and
humming fag-ends of tunes, and sometimes glancing
furtively at her without delivering himself of a
word, good, bad, or indifferent.

In the meantime Mrs. Chick sat swelling and bridling, and tossing her head, as if she were still repeating that solemn formula of farewell to Lucretia Tox.
At length she said aloud, " Oh, the extent to which
her eyes had been opened that day ! "

" To which your eyes have been opened, my dear ! "
repeated Mr. Chick.

" Oh, don't talk to me ! " said Mrs. Chick.   " If
you can bear to see me in this state, and not ask
me what the matter is, you had better hold your
tongue for ever."

" What *is* the matter, my dear ? " asked Mr. Chick.

"To think," said Mrs. Chick in a state of soliloquy, "that she should ever have conceived the base idea of connecting herself with our family by a marriage with Paul! To think that when she was playing at horses with that dear child who is now in his grave — I never liked it at the time — she should have been hiding such a double-faced design! I wonder she was never afraid that something would happen to her. She is fortunate if nothing does."

"I really thought, my dear," said Mr. Chick slowly, after rubbing the bridge of his nose for some time with his newspaper, "that you had gone on the same tack yourself, all along, until this morning; and had thought it would be a convenient thing enough, if it could have been brought about."

Mrs. Chick instantly burst into tears, and told Mr. Chick that, if he wished to trample upon her with his boots, he had better do it.

"But with Lucretia Tox I have done," said Mrs. Chick, after abandoning herself to her feelings for some minutes, to Mr. Chick's great terror. "I can bear to resign Paul's confidence in favor of one who, I hope and trust, may be deserving of it, and with whom he has a perfect right to replace poor Fanny if he chooses; I can bear to be informed, in Paul's cool manner, of such a change in his plans, and never to be consulted until all is settled and determined; but deceit I can *not* bear, and with Lucretia Tox I have done. It is better as it is," said Mrs. Chick piously; "much better. It would have been a long time before I could have accommodated myself comfortably with her, after this; and I really don't know, as Paul is going to be very grand, and these are people of condition, that she would have been quite presentable, and might not have compromised myself. There's a providence in everything; everything works for the best; I have been tried to-day, but, upon the whole, I don't regret it."

In which Christian spirit Mrs. Chick dried her eyes, and smoothed her lap, and sat as became a person calm under a great wrong. Mr. Chick, feeling his unworthiness, no doubt, took an early opportunity of being set down at a street corner and walking away whistling, with his shoulders very much raised, and his hands in his pockets.

While poor excommunicated Miss Tox, who, if she were a fawner and toad-eater, was at least an honest and a constant one, and had ever borne a faithful friendship towards her impeacher, and had been truly absorbed and swallowed up in devotion to the magnificence of Mr. Dombey — while poor excommunicated Miss Tox watered her plants with her tears, and felt that it was winter in Princess's Place.

CHAPTER X.

ALTHOUGH the enchanted house was no more, and the working world had broken into it, and was hammering and crashing and tramping up and down stairs all day long, keeping Diogenes in an incessant paroxysm of barking from sunrise to sunset — evidently convinced that his enemy had got the better of him at last, and was then sacking the premises in triumphant defiance — there was, at first, no other great change in the method of Florence's life. At night, when the workpeople went away, the house was dreary and deserted again; and Florence, listening to their voices echoing through the hall and staircase as they departed, pictured to herself the cheerful homes to which they were returning, and the children who were waiting for them, and was glad to think that they were merry and well pleased to go.

She welcomed back the evening silence as an old friend, but it came now with an altered face, and looked more kindly on her. Fresh hope was in it. The beautiful lady who had soothed and caressed her, in the very room in which her heart had been so wrung, was a spirit of promise to her. Soft

shadows of the bright life dawning, when her
father's affection should be gradually won, and all,
or much, should be restored of what she had lost on
the dark day when a mother's love had faded with
a mother's last breath on her cheek, moved about
her in the twilight, and were welcome company.
Peeping at the rosy children her neighbors, it was
a new and precious sensation to think that they
might soon speak together and know each other:
when she would not fear, as of old, to show herself
before them lest they should be grieved to see her
in her black dress sitting there alone!

In her thoughts of her new mother, and in the
love and trust overflowing her pure heart towards
her, Florence loved her own dead mother more and
more.   She had no fear of setting up a rival in her
breast.   The new flower sprang from the deep-
planted and long-cherished root, she knew.   Every
gentle word that had fallen from the lips of the
beautiful lady sounded to Florence like an echo of
the voice long hushed and silent.   How could she
love that memory less for living tenderness, when it
was her memory of all parental tenderness and
love ?

Florence was, one day, sitting reading in her
room, and thinking of the lady and her promised
visit soon — for her book turned on a kindred sub-
jcet — when, raising her eyes, she saw her standing
in the doorway.

"Mamma!" cried Florence, joyfully meeting her.
"Come again!"

"Not mamma yet," returned the lady with a serious smile, as she encircled Florence's neck with her
arm.

"But very soon to be," cried Florence.

"Very soon now, Florence : very soon."

Edith bent her head a little so as to press the blooming cheek of Florence against her own, and for some few moments remained thus silent. There was something so very tender in her manner, that Florence was even more sensible of it than on the first occasion of their meeting.

She led Florence to a chair beside her, and sat down ; Florence looking in her face, quite wondering at its beauty, and willingly leaving her hand in hers.

"Have you been alone, Florence, since I was here last ? "

"Oh, yes !" smiled Florence hastily.

She hesitated and cast down her eyes ; for her new mamma was very earnest in her look, and the look was intently and thoughtfully fixed upon her face.

"I — I — am used to be alone," said Florence. "I don't mind it at all. Di and I pass whole days together sometimes." Florence might have said whole weeks and months.

"Is Di your maid, love ? "

"My dog, mamma," said Florence, laughing. "Susan is my maid."

"And these are your rooms," said Edith, looking round. "I was not shown these rooms the other day. We must have them improved, Florence. They shall be made the prettiest in the house."

"If I might change them, mamma," returned Florence, "there is one upstairs, I should like much better."

"Is this not high enough, dear girl ? " asked Edith, smiling.

"The other was my brother's room," said Florence, "and I am very fond of it. I would have spoken to papa about it when I came home, and found the workmen here, and everything changing; but —"

Florence dropped her eyes, lest the same look should make her falter again.

" — But I was afraid it might distress him; and as you said you would be here again soon, mamma, and are the mistress of everything, I determined to take courage and ask you."

Edith sat looking at her, with her brilliant eyes intent upon her face, until, Florence raising her own, she, in her turn, withdrew her gaze, and turned it on the ground. It was then that Florence thought how different this lady's beauty was from what she had supposed. She had thought it of a proud and lofty kind; yet her manner was so subdued and gentle, that if she had been of Florence's own age and character it scarcely could have invited confidence more.

Except when a constrained and singular reserve crept over her; and then she seemed (but Florence hardly understood this, though she could not choose but notice it and think about it) as if she were humbled before Florence, and ill at ease. When she had said that she was not her mamma yet, and when Florence had called her the mistress of everything there, this change in her was quick and startling; and now, while the eyes of Florence rested on her face, she sat as though she would have shrunk and hidden from her, rather than as one about to love and cherish her, in right of such a near connection.

She gave Florence her ready promise about her new room, and said she would give directions about it herself. She then asked some questions concerning poor Paul; and, when they had sat in conversation for some time, told Florence she had come to take her to her own home.

"We have come to London now, my mother and I," said Edith, "and you shall stay with us until I am married. I wish that we should know and trust each other, Florence."

"You are very kind to me," said Florence, "dear mamma. How much I thank you!"

"Let me say now, for it may be the best opportunity," continued Edith, looking round to see that they were quite alone, and speaking in a lower voice, "that when I am married, and have gone away for some weeks, I shall be easier at heart if you will come home here. No matter who invites you to stay elsewhere, come home here. It is better to be alone than — What I would say is," she added, checking herself, "that I know well you are best at home, dear Florence."

"I will come home on the very day, mamma."

"Do so. I rely on that promise. Now prepare to come with me, dear girl. You will find me downstairs when you are ready."

Slowly and thoughtfully did Edith wander alone through the mansion of which she was so soon to be the lady: and little heed took she of all the elegance and splendor it began to display. The same indomitable haughtiness of soul, the same proud scorn expressed in eye and lip, the same fierce beauty, only tamed by a sense of its own little worth, and of the little worth of everything around

it, went through the grand saloons and halls, that
had got loose among the shady trees, and raged and
rent themselves. The mimic roses on the walls and
floors were set round with sharp thorns, that tore
her breast; in every scrap of gold, so dazzling to
the eye, she saw some hateful atom of her purchase-
money; the broad, high mirrors showed her at full
length, a woman with a noble quality yet dwelling
in her nature, who was too false to her better self,
and too debased and lost, to save herself. She believed that all this was so plain, more or less, to all
eyes, that she had no resource or power of self-as-
sertion but in pride: and with this pride, which tor-
tured her own heart night and day, she fought her
fate out, braved it, and defied it.

Was this the woman whom Florence — an innocent girl, strong only in her earnestness and simple
truth — could so impress and quell, that by her side
she was another creature, with her tempest of passion hushed, and her very pride itself subdued?
Was this the woman who now sat beside her in a
carriage, with her arms entwined, and who, while
she courted and entreated her to love and trust her,
drew her fair head to nestle on her breast, and would
have laid down life to shield it from wrong or harm?

Oh, Edith! it were well to die, indeed, at such a
time! Better and happier far, perhaps, to die so,
Edith, than to live on to the end!

The Honorable Mrs. Skewton, who was thinking
of anything rather than of such sentiments — for,
like many genteel persons who have existed at various times, she set her face against death altogether,
and objected to the mention of any such low and
levelling upstart — had borrowed a house in Brook

Street, Grosvenor Square, from a stately relative (one of the Feenix brood), who was out of town, and who did not object to lending it, in the handsomest manner, for nuptial purposes, as the loan implied his final release and acquittance from all further loans and gifts to Mrs. Skewton and her daughter. It being necessary, for the credit of the family, to make a handsome appearance at such a time, Mrs. Skewton, with the assistance of an accommodating tradesman resident in the parish of Mary-le-bone, who lent out all sorts of articles to the nobility and gentry, from a service of plate to an army of footmen, clapped into this house a silver-headed butler (who was charged extra on that account, as having the appearance of an ancient family retainer), two very tall young men in livery, and a select staff of kitchen servants; so that a legend arose, downstairs, that Withers the page, released at once from his numerous household duties, and from the propulsion of the wheeled chair (inconsistent with the metropolis), had been several times observed to rub his eyes and pinch his limbs, as if he misdoubted his having overslept himself at the Leamington milkman's, and being still in a celestial dream. A variety of requisites in plate and china being also conveyed to the same establishment from the same convenient source, with several miscellaneous articles, including a neat chariot and a pair of bays, Mrs. Skewton cushioned herself on the principal sofa, in the Cleopatra attitude, and held her court in fair state.

"And how," said Mrs. Skewton, on the entrance of her daughter and her charge, "is my charming Florence? You must come and kiss me, Florence, if you please, my love."

Florence was timidly stooping to pick out a place in the white part of Mrs. Skewton's face, when that lady presented her ear, and relieved her of her difficulty.

"Edith, my dear," said Mrs. Skewton, "positively, I— Stand a little more in the light, my sweetest Florence, for a moment."

Florence blushingly complied.

"You don't remember, dearest Edith," said her mother, "what you were when you were about the same age as our exceedingly precious Florence, or a few years younger ? "

"I have long forgotten, mother."

"For, positively, my dear," said Mrs. Skewton, "I do think that I see a decided resemblance to what you were then, in our extremely fascinating young friend. And it shows," said Mrs. Skewton in a lower voice, which conveyed her opinion that Florence was in a very unfinished state, "what cultivation will do."

"It does, indeed," was Edith's stern reply.

Her mother eyed her sharply for a moment, and feeling herself on unsafe ground, said, as a diversion, —

"My charming Florence, you must come and kiss me once more, if you please, my love."

Florence complied, of course, and again imprinted her lips on Mrs. Skewton's ear.

"And you have heard, no doubt, my darling pet," said Mrs. Skewton, detaining her hand, "that your papa, whom we all perfectly adore and dote upon, is to be married to my dearest Edith this day week ? "

"I knew it would be very soon," returned Florence, "but not exactly when."

"My darling Edith," urged her mother gayly, "is it possible you have not told Florence?"

"Why should I tell Florence?" she returned, so suddenly and harshly, that Florence could scarcely believe it was the same voice.

Mrs. Skewton then told Florence, as another and safer diversion, that her father was coming to dinner, and that he would no doubt be charmingly surprised to see her; as he had spoken last night of dressing in the City, and had known nothing of Edith's design, the execution of which, according to Mrs. Skewton's expectation, would throw him into a perfect ecstasy. Florence was troubled to hear this; and her distress became so keen, as the dinner hour approached, that if she had known how to frame an entreaty to be suffered to return home, without involving her father in her explanation, she would have hurried back on foot, bareheaded, breathless, and alone, rather than incur the risk of meeting his displeasure.

As the time drew nearer, she could hardly breathe. She dared not approach a window, lest he should see her from the street. She dared not go upstairs to hide her emotion, lest, in passing out at the door, she should meet him unexpectedly; besides which dread, she felt as though she never could come back again if she were summoned to his presence. In this conflict of her fears, she was sitting by Cleopatra's couch, endeavoring to understand and to reply to the bald discourse of that lady, when she heard his foot upon the stair.

"I hear him now!" cried Florence, starting. "He is coming!"

Cleopatra, who in her juvenility was always playfully disposed, and who in her self-engrossment did not trouble herself about the nature of this agitation, pushed Florence behind her couch, and dropped a shawl over her, preparatory to giving Mr. Dombey a rapture of surprise. It was so quickly done that in a moment Florence heard his awful step in the room.

He saluted his intended mother-in-law and his intended bride. The strange sound of his voice thrilled through the whole frame of his child.

"My dear Dombey," said Cleopatra, "come here and tell me how your pretty Florence is."

"Florence is very well," said Mr. Dombey, advancing towards the couch.

"At home?"

"At home," said Mr. Dombey.

"My dear Dombey," returned Cleopatra with bewitching vivacity; "now are you sure you are not deceiving me? I don't know what my dearest Edith will say to me when I make such a declaration, but, upon my honor, I am afraid you are the falsest of men, my dear Dombey."

Though he had been; and had been detected on the spot in the most enormous falsehood that was ever said or done; he could hardly have been more disconcerted than he was when Mrs. Skewton plucked the shawl away, and Florence, pale and trembling, rose before him like a ghost. He had not yet recovered his presence of mind when Florence had run up to him, clasped her hands round his neck, kissed his face, and hurried out of the room. He looked round as if to refer the matter to somebody else, but Edith had gone after Florence instantly.

"Now, confess, my dear Dombey," said Mrs. Skewton, giving him her hand, "that you never were more surprised and pleased in your life."

"I never was more surprised," said Mr. Dombey.

"Nor pleased, my dearest Dombey?" returned Mrs. Skewton, holding up her fan.

"I — yes, I am exceedingly glad to meet Florence here," said Mr. Dombey. He appeared to consider gravely about it for a moment, and then said, more decidedly, "Yes, I really am very glad indeed to meet Florence here."

"You wonder how she comes here," said Mrs. Skewton, "don't you?"

"Edith, perhaps —" suggested Mr. Dombey.

"Ah! wicked guesser!" replied Cleopatra, shaking her head. "Ah! cunning, cunning man! One shouldn't tell these things; your sex, my dear Dombey, are so vain, and so apt to abuse our weaknesses; but, you know my open soul — Very well: immediately."

This was addressed to one of the very tall young men who announced dinner.

"But Edith, my dear Dombey," she continued in a whisper, "when she cannot have you near her — and, as I tell her, she cannot expect that always — will at least have near her something or somebody belonging to you. Well, how extremely natural that is! And, in this spirit, nothing would keep her from riding off to-day to fetch our darling Florence. Well, how excessively charming that is!"

As she waited for an answer, Mr. Dombey answered, "Eminently so."

"Bless you, my dear Dombey, for that proof of heart!" cried Cleopatra, squeezing his hand. "But I am growing too serious! Take me downstairs, like an angel, and let us see what these people intend to give us for dinner. Bless you, dear Dombey!"

Cleopatra skipping off her couch with tolerable briskness after the last benediction, Mr. Dombey took her arm in his, and led her ceremoniously downstairs; one of the very tall young men on hire, whose organ of veneration was imperfectly developed, thrusting his tongue into his cheek, for the entertainment of the other very tall young man on hire, as the couple turned into the dining-room.

Florence and Edith were already there, and sitting side by side. Florence would have risen when her father entered, to resign her chair to him; but Edith openly put her hand upon her arm, and Mr. Dombey took an opposite place at the round table.

The conversation was almost entirely sustained by Mrs. Skewton. Florence hardly dared to raise her eyes, lest they should reveal the traces of tears; far less dared to speak; and Edith never uttered one word, unless in answer to a question. Verily, Cleopatra worked hard for the establishment that was so nearly clutched; and verily it should have been a rich one to reward her!

"And so your preparations are nearly finished at last, my dear Dombey?" said Cleopatra, when the dessert was put upon the table, and the silver-headed butler had withdrawn. "Even the lawyer's preparations!"

"Yes, madam," replied Mr. Dombey; "the deed of settlement, the professional gentlemen inform me, is now ready, and, as I was mentioning to you, Edith has only to do us the favor to suggest her own time for its execution."

Edith sat like a handsome statue; as cold, as silent, and as still.

"My dearest love," said Cleopatra, "do you hear what Mr. Dombey says? Ah, my dear Dombey!" aside to that gentleman, "how her absence, as the time approaches, reminds me of the days when that most agreeable of creatures, her papa, was in your situation!"

"I have nothing to suggest. It shall be when you please," said Edith, scarcely looking over the table at Mr. Dombey.

"To-morrow?" suggested Mr. Dombey.

"If you please."

"Or would next day," said Mr. Dombey, "suit your engagements better?"

"I have no engagements. I am always at your disposal. Let it be when you like."

"No engagements, my dear Edith!" remonstrated her mother, "when you are in a most terrible state of flurry all day long, and have a thousand and one appointments with all sorts of tradespeople!"

"They are of your making," returned Edith, turning on her, with a slight contraction of her brow. "You and Mr. Dombey can arrange between you."

"Very true indeed, my love, and most considerate of you!" said Cleopatra. "My darling Florence, you must really come and kiss me once more, if you please, my dear!"

Singular coincidence that these gushes of interest in Florence hurried Cleopatra away from almost every dialogue in which Edith had a share, however trifling! Florence had certainly never undergone so much embracing, and perhaps had never been, unconsciously, so useful in her life.

Mr. Dombey was far from quarrelling, in his own breast, with the manner of his beautiful betrothed. He had that good reason for sympathy with haughtiness and coldness which is found in a fellow-feeling. It flattered him to think how these deferred to him in Edith's case, and seemed to have no will apart from his. It flattered him to picture to himself this proud and stately woman doing the honors of his house, and chilling his guests after his own manner. The dignity of Dombey and Son would be heightened and maintained, indeed, in such hands.

So thought Mr. Dombey when he was left alone at the dining-table, and mused upon his past and future fortunes : finding no uncongeniality in an air of scant and gloomy state that pervaded the room, in color a dark brown, with black hatchments of pictures blotching the walls, and twenty-four black chairs, with almost as many nails in them as so many coffins, waiting like mutes upon the threshold of the Turkey carpet; and two exhausted negroes holding up two withered branches of candelabra on the sideboard, and a musty smell prevailing, as if the ashes of ten thousand dinners were entombed in the sarcophagus below it. The owner of the house lived much abroad ; the air of England seldom agreed long with a member of the Feenix family ; and the room had gradually put itself into deeper and still deeper mourning for him, until it was become so funereal as to want nothing but a body in it to be quite complete.

No bad representation of the body, for the nonce, in his unbending form, if not in his attitude, Mr. Dombey looked down into the cold depths of the Dead Sea of mahogany on which the fruit dishes and decanters lay at anchor; as if the subjects of his thoughts were rising towards the surface one by one, and plunging down again. Edith was there in all her majesty of brow and figure; and close to her came Florence, with her timid head turned to him, as it had been, for an instant, when she left the room; and Edith's eyes upon her, and Edith's hand put out protectingly. A little figure in a low armchair came springing next into the light, and looked upon him wonderingly, with its bright eyes and its old-young face, gleaming as in the flickering of an evening fire. Again came Florence close upon it, and absorbed his whole attention. Whether as a foredoomed difficulty and disappointment to him; whether as a rival who had crossed him in his way, and might again; whether as his child, of whom, in his successful wooing, he could stoop to think, as claiming, at such a time, to be no more estranged; or whether as a hint to him that the mere appearance of caring for his own blood should be maintained in his new relations; he best knew. Indifferently well, perhaps, at best; for marriage company and marriage altars, and ambitious scenes — still blotted here and there with Florence — always Florence — turned up so fast, and so confusedly, that he rose, and went upstairs, to escape them.

It was quite late at night before candles were brought; for at present they made Mrs. Skewton's head ache, she complained; and in the meantime Florence and Mrs. Skewton talked together (Cleopatra being very anxious to keep her close to herself), or Florence touched the piano softly for Mrs. Skewton's delight; to make no mention of a few occasions, in the course of the evening, when that affectionate lady was impelled to solicit another kiss, and which always happened after Edith had said anything. They were not many, however, for Edith sat apart by an open window during the whole time (in spite of her mother's fears that she would take cold), and remained there until Mr. Dombey took leave. He was serenely gracious to Florence when he did so; and Florence went to bed in a room within Edith's, so happy and hopeful, that she thought of her late self as if it were some other poor deserted girl who was to be pitied for her sorrow; and, in her pity, sobbed herself to sleep.

The week fled fast. There were drives to milliners, dressmakers, jewellers, lawyers, florists, pastry-cooks; and Florence was always of the party. Florence was to go to the wedding. Florence was to cast off her mourning, and to wear a brilliant dress on the occasion. The milliner's intentions on the subject of this dress — the milliner was a Frenchwoman, and greatly resembled Mrs. Skewton — were so chaste and elegant, that Mrs. Skewton bespoke one like it for herself. The milliner said it would become her to admiration, and that all the world would take her for the young lady's sister.

The week fled faster. Edith looked at nothing and cared for nothing. Her rich dresses came home, and were tried on, and were loudly commended by Mrs. Skewton and the milliners, and were put away without a word from her. Mrs. Skewton made their plans for every day, and executed them. Sometimes Edith sat in the carriage when they went to make purchases: sometimes, when it was absolutely necessary, she went into the shops. But

Mrs. Skewton conducted the whole business, whatever it happened to be; and Edith looked on as uninterested and with as much apparent indifference as if she had no concern in it. Florence might perhaps have thought she was haughty and listless, but that she was never so to her. So Florence quenched her wonder in her gratitude whenever it broke out, and soon subdued it.

The week fled faster. It had nearly winged its flight away. The last night of the week, the night before the marriage, was come. In the dark room — for Mrs. Skewton's head was no better yet, though she expected to recover permanently to-morrow — were that lady, Edith, and Mr. Dombey. Edith was at her open window, looking out into the street; Mr. Dombey and Cleopatra were talking softly on the sofa. It was growing late; and Florence, being fatigued, had gone to bed.

"My dear Dombey," said Cleopatra, "you will leave me Florence to-morrow, when you deprive me of my sweetest Edith?"

Mr. Dombey said he would with pleasure.

"To have her about me here while you are both at Paris, and to think that, at her age, I am assisting in the formation of her mind, my dear Dombey," said Cleopatra, "will be a perfect balm to me in the extremely shattered state to which I shall be reduced."

Edith turned her head suddenly. Her listless manner was exchanged, in a moment, to one of burning interest, and, unseen in the darkness, she attended closely to their conversation.

Mr. Dombey would be delighted to leave Florence in such admirable guardianship.

"My dear Dombey," returned Cleopatra, "a thousand thanks for your good opinion. I feared you were going, with malice aforethought, as the dreadful lawyers say — those horrid prosers! — to condemn me to utter solitude."

"Why do me so great an injustice, my dear madam?" said Mr. Dombey.

"Because my charming Florence tells me so positively she must go home to-morrow," returned Cleopatra, "that I began to be afraid, my dearest Dombey, you were quite a Bashaw."

"I assure you, madam!" said Mr. Dombey, "I have laid no commands on Florence; and if I had, there are no commands like your wish."

"My dear Dombey," replied Cleopatra, "what a courtier you are! Though I'll not say so, either; for courtiers have no heart, and yours pervades your charming life and character. And are you really going so early, my dear Dombey?"

Oh, indeed! it was late, and Mr. Dombey feared he must.

"Is this a fact, or is it all a dream?" lisped Cleopatra. "Can I believe, my dearest Dombey, that you are coming back to-morrow morning to deprive me of my sweet companion; my own Edith?"

Mr. Dombey, who was accustomed to take things literally, reminded Mrs. Skewton that they were to meet first at the church.

"The pang," said Mrs. Skewton, "of consigning a child, even to you, my dear Dombey, is one of the most excruciating imaginable: and combined with a naturally delicate constitution, and the extreme stupidity of the pastrycook who has undertaken the breakfast, is almost too much for my poor strength. But I shall rally, my dear Dombey, in the morning; do not fear for me, or be uneasy on my account. Heaven bless you! My dearest Edith!" she cried archly. "Somebody is going, pet."

Edith, who had turned her head again towards the window, and whose interest in their conversation had ceased, rose up in her place, but made no advance towards him, and said nothing. Mr. Dombey, with a lofty gallantry adapted to his dignity and the occasion, betook his creaking boots towards her, put her hand to his lips, and said, "To-morrow morning I shall have the happiness of claiming this hand as Mrs. Dombey's," and bowed himself solemnly out.

Mrs. Skewton rang for candles as soon as the house-door had closed upon him. With the candles appeared her maid, with the juvenile dress that was to delude the world to-morrow. The dress had savage retribution in it, as such dresses ever have, and made her infinitely older and more hideous than her greasy flannel gown. But Mrs. Skewton tried it on with mincing satisfaction; smirked at her cadaverous self in the glass, as she thought of its killing effect upon the major; and suffering her maid to take it off again, and to prepare her for repose, tumbled into ruins like a house of painted cards.

All this time Edith remained at the dark window, looking out into the street. When she and her mother were at last left alone, she moved from it for the first time that evening, and came opposite to her. The yawning, shaking, peevish figure of the mother, with her eyes raised to confront the proud, erect form of the daughter, whose glance of fire was bent downward upon her, had a conscious air upon it, that no levity or temper could conceal.

"I am tired to death," said she. "You can't be trusted for a moment. You are worse than a child. Child! No child would be half so obstinate and undutiful."

"Listen to me, mother," returned Edith, passing these words by with a scorn that would not descend to trifle with them. "You must remain alone here until I return."

"Must remain alone here, Edith, until you return?" repeated her mother.

"Or in that name upon which I shall call to-morrow to witness what I do, so falsely and so shamefully, I swear I will refuse the hand of this man in the church. If I do not, may I fall dead upon the pavement!"

The mother answered with a look of quick alarm, in no degree diminished by the look she met.

"It is enough," said Edith steadily, "that we are what we are. I will have no youth and truth dragged down to my level. I will have no guileless nature undermined, corrupted, and perverted, to amuse the leisure of a world of mothers. You know my meaning. Florence must go home."

"You are an idiot, Edith," cried her angry mother. "Do you expect there can ever be peace for you in that house till she is married, and away?"

"Ask me, or ask yourself, if I ever expect peace in that house," said her daughter, "and you know the answer."

"And am I to be told to-night, after all my pains and labor, and when you are going, through me, to be rendered independent," her mother almost shrieked in her passion, while her palsied head shook like a leaf, "that there is corruption and contagion in me, and that I am not fit company for a girl? What are you, pray? What are you?"

"I have put the question to myself," said Edith, ashy pale, and pointing to the window, "more than once when I have been sitting there, and something in the faded likeness of my sex has wandered past outside; and God knows I have met with my reply. Oh, mother, mother, if you had but left me to my natural heart when I too was a girl — a younger girl than Florence — how different I might have been!"

Sensible that any show of anger was useless here, her mother restrained herself, and fell a-whimpering, and bewailed that she had lived too long, and that her only child had cast her off, and that duty towards parents was forgotten in these evil days, and that she had heard unnatural taunts, and cared for life no longer.

"If one is to go on living through continual scenes like this," she whined, "I am sure it would be much better for me to think of some means of putting an end to my existence. Oh! The idea of your being my daughter, Edith, and addressing me in such a strain!"

"Between us, mother," returned Edith mournfully, "the time for mutual reproaches is past."

"Then why do you revive it?" whimpered her mother. "You know that you are lacerating me in

the cruelest manner. You know how sensitive I
am to unkindness. At such a moment, too, when
I have so much to think of, and am naturally anxious to appear to the best advantage! I wonder at
you, Edith. To make your mother a fright upon
your wedding day!"

Edith bent the same fixed look upon her as she
sobbed and rubbed her eyes; and said in the same
low, steady voice, which had neither risen nor fallen
since she first addressed her, "I have said that
Florence must go home."

"Let her go!" cried the afflicted and affrighted
parent hastily. "I am sure I am willing she should
go. What is the girl to me?"

"She is so much to me, that rather than communicate, or suffer to be communicated, to her one
grain of the evil that is in my breast, mother, I
would renounce you, as I would (if you gave me
cause) renounce him in the church to-morrow,"
replied Edith. "Leave her alone. She shall not,
while I can interpose, be tampered with and tainted
by the lessons I have learned. This is no hard
condition on this bitter night."

"If you had proposed it in a filial manner, Edith," whined her mother, "perhaps not;
very likely not. But such extremely cutting
words —"

"They are past and at an end between us now,"
said Edith. "Take your own way, mother; share
as you please in what you have gained; spend,
enjoy, make much of it; and be as happy as you
will. The object of our lives is won. Henceforth
let us wear it silently. My lips are closed upon the
past from this hour. I forgive you your part in

to-morrow's wickedness. May God forgive my own!"

Without a tremor in her voice or frame, and passing onward with a foot that set itself upon the neck of every soft emotion, she bade her mother goodnight, and repaired to her own room.

But not to rest: for there was no rest in the tumult of her agitation when alone. To and fro, and to and fro, and to and fro again, five hundred times, among the splendid preparations for her adornment on the morrow; with her dark hair shaken down, her dark eyes flashing with a raging light, her broad white bosom red with the cruel grasp of the relentless hand with which she spurned it from her, pacing up and down with an averted head, as if she would avoid the sight of her own fair person, and divorce herself from its companionship. Thus, in the dead time of the night before her bridal, Edith Granger wrestled with her unquiet spirit, tearless, friendless, silent, proud, and uncomplaining.

At length it happened that she touched the open door which led into the room where Florence lay.

She started, stopped, and looked in.

A light was burning there, and showed her Florence in her bloom of innocence and beauty, fast asleep. Edith held her breath, and felt herself drawn on towards her.

Drawn nearer, nearer, nearer yet; at last, drawn so near, that stooping down, she pressed her lips to the gentle hand that lay outside the bed, and put it softly to her neck. Its touch was like the prophet's rod of old upon the rock. Her tears sprung forth beneath it, as she sunk upon her knees, and laid her aching head and streaming hair upon the pillow by its side.

Thus Edith Granger passed the night before her bridal. Thus the sun found her on her bridal morning.

CHAPTER XI.

THE WEDDING.

DAWN, with its passionless blank face, steals shivering to the church beneath which lies the dust of little Paul and his mother, and looks in at the windows. It is cold and dark. Night crouches yet upon the pavement, and broods, sombre and heavy, in nooks and corners of the building. The steeple clock, perched up above the houses, emerging from beneath another of the countless ripples in the tide of time that regularly roll and break on the eternal shore, is grayly visible like a stone beacon, recording how the sea flows on; but within doors, dawn, at first, can only peep at night, and see that it is there.

Hovering feebly round the church, and looking in, dawn moans and weeps for its short reign, and its tears trickle on the window glass, and the trees against the church wall bow their heads, and wring their many hands in sympathy. Night, growing pale before it, gradually fades out of the church, but lingers in the vaults below, and sits upon the coffins. And now comes bright day, burnishing the steeple-clock, and reddening the spire, and drying up the tears of dawn, and stifling its complaining; and the scared dawn, following the night, and chasing it from its last refuge, shrinks into the vaults itself, and hides, with a frightened face, among the dead, until night returns, refreshed, to drive it out.

And now, the mice, who have been busier with the Prayer-books than their proper owners, and with the hassocks, more worn by their little teeth than by human knees, hide their bright eyes in their holes, and gather close together in affright at the resounding clashing of the church door. For the beadle, that man of power, comes early this morning with the sexton; and Mrs. Miff the wheezy little pew-opener — a mighty dry old lady, sparely dressed, with not an inch of fulness anywhere about her — is also here, and has been waiting at the church gate half an hour, as her place is, for the beadle.

A vinegary face has Mrs. Miff, and a mortified bonnet, and eke a thirsty soul for sixpences and shillings. Beckoning to stray people to come into pews has given Mrs. Miff an air of mystery; and there is reservation in the eye of Mrs. Miff, as always knowing of a softer seat, but having her suspicions of the fee. There is no such fact as Mr. Miff, nor has there been these twenty years, and Mrs. Miff would rather not allude to him. He held some bad opinions, it would seem, about free seats; and though Mrs. Miff hopes he may be gone upward, she couldn't positively undertake to say so.

Busy is Mrs. Miff this morning at the church door, beating and dusting the altar cloth, the carpet, and the cushions; and much has Mrs. Miff to say about the wedding they are going to have. Mrs. Miff is told that the new furniture and alterations in the house cost full five thousand pound, if they cost a penny; and Mrs. Miff has heard, upon the best authority, that the lady hasn't got a sixpence wherewithal to bless herself. Mrs. Miff remembers, likewise, as if it had happened yesterday, the first wife's funeral, and then the christening, and then the other funeral; and Mrs. Miff says, By the by, she'll soap-and-water that 'ere tablet presently, against the company arrive. Mr. Sownds, the beadle, who is sitting in the sun upon the church steps all this time (and seldom does anything else, except in cold weather, sitting by the fire), approves of Mrs. Miff's discourse, and asks if Mrs. Miff has heard it said that the lady is uncommon handsome? The information Mrs. Miff has received being of this nature, Mr. Sownds the beadle, who, though orthodox and corpulent, is still an admirer of female beauty, observes, with unction, Yes, he hears she is a spanker — an expression that seems somewhat forcible to Mrs. Miff, or would from any lips but those of Mr. Sownds the beadle.

In Mr. Dombey's house, at this same time, there is great stir and bustle, more especially among the women: not one of whom has had a wink of sleep since four o'clock, and all of whom were full dressed before six. Mr. Towlinson is an object of greater consideration than usual to the housemaid, and the cook says at breakfast-time that one wedding makes many, which the housemaid can't believe, and don't think true at all. Mr. Towlinson reserves his sentiments on this question; being rendered something gloomy by the engagement of a foreigner with whiskers (Mr. Towlinson is whiskerless himself), who has been hired to accompany the happy pair to Paris, and who is busy packing the

new chariot. In respect of this personage, Mr. Towlinson admits, presently, that he never knew of any
good that ever come of foreigners; and being
charged by the ladies with prejudice, says, Look at
Bonaparte, who was at the head of 'em, and see
what *he* was always up to! Which the housemaid
says is very true.

The pastrycook is hard at work in the funereal
room in Brook Street, and the very tall young men
are busy looking on. One of the very tall young
men already smells of sherry, and his eyes have a
tendency to become fixed in his head, and to stare
at objects without seeing them. The very tall
young man is conscious of this failing in himself;
and informs his comrade that it's his "exciseman."
The very tall young man would say excitement, but
his speech is hazy.

The men who play the bells have got scent of
the marriage; and the marrow-bones and cleavers
too; and a brass band too. The first are practising
in a back-settlement near Battle Bridge; the second
put themselves in communication, through their
chief, with Mr. Towlinson, to whom they offer
terms to be bought off; and the third, in the person of an artful trombone, lurks and dodges round
the corner, waiting for some traitor tradesman to
reveal the place and hour of breakfast for a bribe.
Expectation and excitement extend further yet, and
take a wider range. From Balls Pond Mr. Perch
brings Mrs. Perch to spend the day with Mr. Dombey's servants, and accompany them, surreptitiously,
to see the wedding. In Mr. Toots's lodgings, Mr.
Toots attires himself as if he were at least the
bridegroom: determined to behold the spectacle in

splendor from a secret corner of the gallery, and thither to convey the Chicken. For it is Mr. Toots's desperate intent to point out Florence to the Chicken, then and there, and openly to say, "Now, Chicken, I will not deceive you any longer; the friend I have sometimes mentioned to you is myself; Miss Dombey is the object of my passion; what are your opinions, Chicken, in this state of things, and what, on the spot, do you advise?" The so-much-to-be-astonished Chicken, in the meanwhile, dips his beak into a tankard of strong beer in Mr. Toots's kitchen, and pecks up two pounds of beefsteaks. In Princess's Place, Miss Tox is up and doing; for she too, though in sore distress, is resolved to put a shilling in the hands of Mrs. Miff, and see the ceremony, which has a cruel fascination for her, from some lonely corner. The quarters of the Wooden Midshipman are all alive; for Captain Cuttle, in his ankle-jacks and with a huge shirt collar, is seated at his breakfast, listening to Rob the Grinder as he reads the marriage service to him beforehand, under orders, to the end that the captain may perfectly understand the solemnity he is about to witness: for which purpose the captain gravely lays injunctions on his chaplain, from time to time, to "put about," or to "overhaul that 'ere article again," or to stick to his own duty, and leave the Amens to him, the captain; one of which he repeats, whenever a pause is made by Rob the Grinder, with sonorous satisfaction. Besides all this, and much more, twenty nursery-maids in Mr. Dombey's street alone have promised twenty families of little women, whose instinctive interest in nuptials dates from their cradles, that they shall go

and see the marriage. Truly Mr. Sownds the
beadle has good reason to feel himself in office, as
he suns his portly figure on the church steps, waiting for the marriage hour. Truly Mrs. Miff has
cause to pounce on an unlucky dwarf child, with a
giant baby, who peeps in at the porch, and drive her
forth with indignation.

Cousin Feenix has come over from abroad expressly
to attend the marriage. Cousin Feenix was a man
about town forty years ago; but he is still so juvenile
in figure and in manner, and so well got up, that
strangers are amazed when they discover latent
wrinkles in his lordship's face, and crows' feet in his
eyes; and when they first observe him, not exactly
certain, as he walks across a room, of going quite
straight to where he wants to go. But Cousin
Feenix, getting up at half-past seven o'clock or so,
is quite another thing from Cousin Feenix got up:
and very dim indeed he looks while being shaved at
Long's Hotel, in Bond Street.

Mr. Dombey leaves his dressing-room, amidst a
general whisking away of the women on the staircase, who disperse in all directions, with a great
rustling of skirts, except Mrs. Perch, who being
(but that she always is) in an interesting situation,
is not nimble, and is obliged to face him, and is ready
to sink with confusion as she courtesies — may
Heaven avert all evil consequences from the house
of Perch! Mr. Dombey walks up to the drawing-
room to bide his time. Gorgeous are Mr. Dombey's
new blue coat, fawn-colored pantaloons, and lilac
waistcoat; and a whisper goes about the house that
Mr. Dombey's hair is curled.

A double knock announces the arrival of the

major, who is gorgeous too, and wears a whole geranium in his buttonhole, and has his hair curled
tight and crisp, as well the native knows.

"Dombey!" says the major, putting out both
hands, "how are you?"

"Major," says Mr. Dombey, "how are You?"

"By Jove, sir," says the major, "Joey B. is in
such case this morning, sir," — and here he hits
himself hard upon the breast, — "in such case this
morning, sir, that, damme, Dombey, he has half a
mind to make a double marriage of it, sir, and take
the mother."

Mr. Dombey smiles; but faintly, even for him;
for Mr. Dombey feels that he is going to be related
to the mother, and that, under those circumstances,
she is not to be joked about.

"Dombey," says the major, seeing this, "I give
you joy. I congratulate you, Dombey. By the
Lord, sir," says the major, "you are more to be
envied, this day, than any man in England!"

Here, again, Mr. Dombey's assent is qualified;
because he is going to confer a great distinction on
a lady; and, no doubt, she is to be envied most.

"As to Edith Granger, sir," pursues the major,
"there is not a woman in all Europe but might —
and would, sir, you will allow Bagstock to add —
and would — give her ears, and her earrings too, to
be in Edith Granger's place."

"You are good enough to say so, major," says
Mr. Dombey.

"Dombey," returns the major, "you know it.
Let us have no false delicacy. You know it. Do
you know it, or do you not, Dombey?" says the
major, almost in a passion.

"Oh, really, major —"

"Damme, sir," retorts the major, "do you know that fact, or do you not? Dombey! Is old Joe your friend? Are we on that footing of unreserved intimacy, Dombey, that may justify a man — a blunt old Joseph B., sir — in speaking out; or am I to take open order, Dombey, and to keep my distance, and to stand on forms?"

"My dear Major Bagstock," says Mr. Dombey with a gratified air, "you are quite warm."

"By Gad, sir," says the major, "I am warm. Joseph B. does not deny it, Dombey. He is warm. This is an occasion, sir, that calls forth all the honest sympathies remaining in an old, infernal, battered, used-up, invalided J. B. carcass. And I tell you what, Dombey — at such a time a man must blurt out what he feels, or put a muzzle on; and Joseph Bagstock tells you to your face, Dombey, as he tells his club behind your back, that he never will be muzzled when Paul Dombey is in question. Now, damme, sir," concludes the major with great firmness, "what do you make of that?"

"Major," says Mr. Dombey, "I assure you that I am really obliged to you. I had no idea of checking your too partial friendship."

"Not too partial, sir!" exclaims the choleric major. "Dombey, I deny it!"

"Your friendship I will say, then," pursues Mr. Dombey, "on any account. Nor can I forget, major, on such an occasion as the present, how much I am indebted to it."

"Dombey," says the major, with appropriate action, "that is the hand of Joseph Bagstock; of plain old Joey B., sir, if you like that better! That is the hand of which his Royal Highness the late Duke of York did me the honor to observe, sir, to his Royal Highness the late Duke of Kent, that it was the hand of Josh; a rough and tough, and possibly an up-to-snuff, old vagabond. Dombey, may the present moment be the least unhappy of our lives! God bless you!"

Now enters Mr. Carker, gorgeous likewise, and smiling like a wedding-guest indeed. He can scarcely let Mr. Dombey's hand go, he is so congratulatory; and he shakes the major's hand so heartily at the same time, that his voice shakes too, in accord with his arms, as it comes sliding from between his teeth.

"The very day is auspicious," says Mr. Carker. "The brightest and most genial weather! I hope I am not a moment late?"

"Punctual to your time, sir," says the major.

"I am rejoiced, I am sure," says Mr. Carker. "I was afraid I might be a few seconds after the appointed time, for I was delayed by a procession of wagons; and I took the liberty of riding round to Brook Street"—this to Mr. Dombey—"to leave a few poor rarities of flowers for Mrs. Dombey. A man in my position, and so distinguished as to be invited here, is proud to offer some homage in acknowledgment of his vassalage: and, as I have no doubt Mrs. Dombey is overwhelmed with what is costly and magnificent,"—with a strange glance at his patron,—"I hope the very poverty of my offering may find favor for it."

"Mrs. Dombey that is to be," returns Mr. Dombey condescendingly, "will be very sensible of your attention, Carker, I am sure."

"And if she is to be Mrs. Dombey this morning,

sir," says the major, putting down his coffee-cup, and looking at his watch, "it's high time we were off!"

Forth, in a barouche, ride Mr. Dombey, Major Bagstock, and Mr. Carker to the church. Mr. Sownds the beadle has long risen from the steps, and is in waiting with his cocked hat in his hand. Mrs. Miff courtesies and proposes chairs in the vestry. Mr. Dombey prefers remaining in the church. As he looks up at the organ, Miss Tox in the gallery shrinks behind the fat leg of a cherubim on a monument, with cheeks like a young Wind. Captain Cuttle, on the contrary, stands up, and waves his hook, in token of welcome and encouragement. Mr. Toots informs the Chicken, behind his hand, that the middle gentleman, he in the fawn-colored pantaloons, is the father of his love. The Chicken hoarsely whispers Mr. Toots that he's as stiff a cove as ever he see, but that it is within the resources of Science to double him up with one blow in the waistcoat.

Mr. Sownds and Mrs. Miff are eying Mr. Dombey from a little distance, when the noise of approaching wheels is heard, and Mr. Sownds goes out; Mrs. Miff meeting Mr. Dombey's eye as it is withdrawn from the presumptuous maniac upstairs, who salutes him with so much urbanity, drops a courtesy, and informs him that she believes his " good lady " is come. Then there is a crowding and a whispering at the door, and the good lady enters with a haughty step.

There is no sign upon her face of last night's suffering; there is no trace in her manner of the woman on the bended knees, reposing her wild head upon the pillow of the sleeping girl. That girl, all gentle and lovely, is at her side — a striking contrast to her own disdainful and defiant figure, standing there, composed, erect, inscrutable of will, resplendent and majestic in the zenith of its charms, yet beating down, and treading on, the admiration that it challenges.

There is a pause while Mr. Sownds the beadle glides into the vestry for the clergyman and clerk. At this juncture, Mrs. Skewton speaks to Mr. Dombey; more distinctly and emphatically than her custom is, and moving, at the same time, close to Edith.

"My dear Dombey," says the good mamma, "I fear I must relinquish darling Florence after all, and suffer her to go home, as she herself proposed. After my loss of to-day, my dear Dombey, I feel I shall not have spirits, even for her society."

"Had she not better stay with you?" returns the bridegroom.

"I think not, my dear Dombey. No, I think not. I shall be better alone. Besides, my dearest Edith will be her natural and constant guardian when you return, and I had better not encroach upon her trust, perhaps. She might be jealous. Eh, dear Edith?"

The affectionate mamma presses her daughter's arm as she says this: perhaps entreating her attention earnestly.

"To be serious, my dear Dombey," she resumes, "I will relinquish our dear child, and not inflict my gloom upon her. We have settled that just now. She fully understands, dear Dombey. Edith, my dear, she fully understands."

Again the good mother presses her daughter's

arm.   Mr. Dombey offers no additional remonstrance; for the clergyman and clerk appear; and
Mrs. Miff, and Mr. Sownds the beadle, group the
party in their proper places at the altar rails.

"Who giveth this woman to be married to this
man ?"

Cousin Feenix does that. He has come from
Baden-Baden on purpose. "Confound it," Cousin
Feenix says — good-natured creature, Cousin Feenix
— "when we *do* get a rich City fellow into the
family, let us show him some attention; let us do
something for him."

"*I* give this woman to be married to this man,"
saith Cousin Feenix, therefore. Cousin Feenix,
meaning to go in a straight line, but turning off
sideways by reason of his wilful legs, gives the
wrong woman to be married to this man at first —
to wit, a bridesmaid of some condition, distantly
connected with the family, and ten years Mrs. Skewton's junior — but Mrs. Miff, interposing her mortified bonnet, dexterously turns him back, and runs
him, as on casters, full at the "good lady;" whom
Cousin Feenix giveth to be married to this man
accordingly.

And will they in the sight of Heaven — ?

Ay, that they will: Mr. Dombey says he will.
And what says Edith ?   *She* will.

So, from that day forward, for better for worse,
for richer for poorer, in sickness and in health, to
love and to cherish, till death do them part, they
plight their troth to one another, and are married.

In a firm, free hand the bride subscribes her name
in the register when they adjourn to the vestry.
"There ain't a many ladies comes here," Mrs. Miff

says with a courtesy — to look at Mrs. Miff, at such a season, is to make her mortified bonnet go down with a dip — "writes their names like this good lady!" Mr. Sownds the beadle thinks it is a truly spanking signature, and worthy of the writer — this, however, between himself and conscience.

Florence signs too, but unapplauded, for her hand shakes. All the party sign; Cousin Feenix last; who puts his noble name into a wrong place, and enrols himself as having been born that morning.

The major now salutes the bride right gallantly, and carries out that branch of military tactics in reference to all the ladies: notwithstanding Mrs. Skewton's being extremely hard to kiss, and squeaking shrilly in the sacred edifice. The example is followed by Cousin Feenix, and even by Mr. Dombey. Lastly, Mr. Carker, with his white teeth glistening, approaches Edith, more as if he meant to bite her than to taste the sweets that linger on her lips.

There is a glow upon her proud cheek, and a flashing in her eyes, that may be meant to stay him; but it does not, for he salutes her as the rest have done, and wishes her all happiness.

"If wishes," says he in a low voice, "are not superfluous, applied to such a union."

"I thank you, sir," she answers, with a curled lip and a heaving bosom.

But, does Edith feel still, as on the night when she knew that Mr. Dombey would return to offer his alliance, that Carker knows her thoroughly, and reads her right, and that she is more degraded by his knowledge of her than by aught else? Is it for this reason that her haughtiness shrinks beneath his smile, like snow within the hand that grasps it firmly, and that her imperious glance droops in meeting his, and seeks the ground ?

"I am proud to see," says Mr. Carker, with a servile stooping of his neck, which the revelations making by his eyes and teeth proclaim to be a lie, " I am proud to see that my humble offering is graced by Mrs. Dombey's hand, and permitted to hold so favored a place in so joyful an occasion."

Though she bends her head in answer, there is something in the momentary action of her hand, as if she would crush the flowers it holds, and fling them, with contempt, upon the ground. But, she puts the hand through the arm of her new husband, who has been standing near, conversing with the major, and is proud again, and motionless, and silent.

The carriages are once more at the church-door. Mr. Dombey, with his bride upon his arm, conducts her through the twenty families of little women who are on the steps, and every one of whom remembers the fashion and the color of her every article of dress from that moment, and reproduces it on her doll, who is for ever being married. Cleopatra and Cousin Feenix enter the same carriage. The major hands into a second carriage Florence, and the bridesmaid who so narrowly escaped being given away by mistake, and then enters it himself, and is followed by Mr. Carker. Horses prance and caper; coachmen and footmen shine in fluttering favors, flowers, and new-made liveries. Away they dash and rattle through the streets; and, as they pass along, a thousand heads are turned to look at them, and a thousand sober moralists revenge themselves for not being married too, that morning, by reflecting that these people little think such happiness can't last.

Miss Tox emerges from behind the cherubim's leg when all is quiet, and comes slowly down from the gallery. Miss Tox's eyes are red, and her pocket-handkerchief is damp. She is wounded, but not exasperated, and she hopes they may be happy. She quite admits to herself the beauty of the bride, and her own comparatively feeble and faded attractions; but the stately image of Mr. Dombey, in his lilac waistcoat and his fawn-colored pantaloons, is present to her mind, and Miss Tox weeps afresh, behind her veil, on her way home to Princess's Place. Captain Cuttle, having joined in all the amens and responses with a devout growl, feels much improved by his religious exercises; and, in a peaceful frame of mind, pervades the body of the church, glazed hat in hand, and reads the tablet to the memory of little Paul. The gallant Mr. Toots, attended by the faithful Chicken, leaves the building in torments of love. The Chicken is as yet unable to elaborate a scheme for winning Florence, but his first idea has gained possession of him, and he thinks the doubling up of Mr. Dombey would be a move in the right direction. Mr. Dombey's servants come out of their hiding-places, and prepare to rush to Brook Street, when they are delayed by symptoms of indisposition on the part of Mrs. Perch, who entreats a glass of water and becomes alarming; Mrs. Perch gets better soon, however, and is borne away; and Mrs. Miff, and Mr. Sownds the beadle, sit upon the steps to count what they have gained by the affair, and talk it over, while the sexton tolls a funeral.

Now, the carriages arrive at the bride's residence, and the players on the bells begin to jingle, and the band strikes up, and Mr. Punch, that model of connubial bliss, salutes his wife. Now, the people run and push, and press round in a gaping throng, while Mr. Dombey, leading Mrs. Dombey by the hand, advances solemnly into the Feenix halls. Now, the rest of the wedding-party alight, and enter after them. And why does Mr. Carker, passing through the people to the hall-door, think of the old woman who called to him in the grove that morning? Or why does Florence, as she passes, think, with a tremble, of her childhood; when she was lost, and of the visage of Good Mrs. Brown?

Now, there are more congratulations on this happiest of days, and more company, though not much; and now they leave the drawing-room, and range themselves at table in the dark brown dining-room, which no confectioner can brighten up, let him garnish the exhausted negroes with as many flowers and love-knots as he will.

The pastrycook has done his duty like a man, though, and a rich breakfast is set forth. Mr. and Mrs. Chick have joined the party, among others. Mrs. Chick admires that Edith should be, by nature, such a perfect Dombey; and is affable and confidential to Mrs. Skewton, whose mind is relieved of a great load, and who takes her share of the champagne. The very tall young man, who suffered from excitement early, is better; but a vague sentiment of repentance has seized upon him, and he hates the other very tall young man, and wrests dishes from him by violence, and takes a grim delight in disobliging the company. The company

are cool and calm, and do not outrage the black hatchments of pictures looking down upon them by any excess of mirth. Cousin Feenix and the major are the gayest there; but Mr. Carker has a smile for the whole table. He has an especial smile for the bride, who very, very seldom meets it.

Cousin Feenix rises when the company have breakfasted, and the servants have left the room; and wonderfully young he looks with his white wristbands almost covering his hands (otherwise rather bony), and the bloom of the champagne in his cheeks.

"Upon my honor," says Cousin Feenix, "although it's an unusual sort of thing in a private gentleman's house, I must beg leave to call upon you to drink what is usually called a — in fact, a toast."

The major very hoarsely indicates his approval. Mr. Carker, bending his head forward over the table in the direction of Cousin Feenix, smiles and nods a great many times.

"A — in fact, it's not a —" Cousin Feenix beginning again, thus, comes to a dead stop.

"Hear, hear!" says the major in a tone of conviction.

Mr. Carker softly claps his hands, and bending forward over the table again, smiles and nods a great many more times than before, as if he were particularly struck by this last observation, and desired personally to express his sense of the good it has done him.

"It is," says Cousin Feenix, "an occasion, in fact, when the general usages of life may be a little departed from without impropriety; and although I never was an orator in my life, and when I was in

the House of Commons, and had the honor of sec-
onding the address, was — in fact, was laid up for a
fortnight with the consciousness of failure — "

The major and Mr. Carker are so much delighted
by this fragment of personal history, that Cousin
Feenix laughs, and, addressing them individually,
goes on to say, —

"And, in point of fact, when I was devilish ill —
still, you know, I feel that a duty devolves upon
me.   And when a duty devolves upon an English-
man, he is bound to get out of it, in my opinion, in
the best way he can.   Well! our family has had the
gratification, to-day, of connecting itself, in the
person of my lovely and accomplished relative,
whom I now see — in point of fact, present — "

Here there is general applause.

"Present," repeats Cousin Feenix, feeling that it
is a neat point which will bear repetition, — "with
one who — that is to say, with a man at whom the
finger of scorn can never — in fact, with my honorable friend Dombey, if he will allow me to call him
so."

Cousin Feenix bows to Mr. Dombey; Mr. Dombey
solemnly returns the bow; everybody is more or
less gratified and affected by this extraordinary, and
perhaps unprecedented, appeal to the feelings.

"I have not," says Cousin Feenix, "enjoyed those
opportunities which I could have desired, of cultivating the acquaintance of my friend Dombey, and
studying those qualities which do equal honor to his
head, and, in point of fact, to his heart; for it has
been my misfortune to be, as we used to say in my
time at the House of Commons, when it was not the
custom to allude to the Lords, and when the order

of parliamentary proceedings was perhaps better observed than it is now — to be in — in point of fact," says Cousin Feenix, cherishing his joke with great slyness, and finally bringing it out with a jerk, "'in another place!'"

The major falls into convulsions, and is recovered with difficulty.

"But I know sufficient of my friend Dombey," resumes Cousin Feenix in a graver tone, as if he had suddenly become a sadder and a wiser man, "to know that he is, in point of fact, what may be emphatically called a — a merchant — a British merchant — and a — and a man. And although I have been resident abroad for some years (it would give me great pleasure to receive my friend Dombey, and everybody here, at Baden-Baden, and to have an opportunity of making 'em known to the Grand Duke), still I know enough, I flatter myself, of my lovely and accomplished relative, to know that she possesses every requisite to make a man happy, and that her marriage with my friend Dombey is one of inclination and affection on both sides."

Many smiles and nods from Mr. Carker.

"Therefore," says Cousin Feenix, "I congratulate the family of which I am a member on the acquisition of my friend Dombey. I congratulate my friend Dombey on his union with my lovely and accomplished relative, who possesses every requisite to make a man happy; and I take the liberty of calling on you all, in point of fact, to congratulate both my friend Dombey, and my lovely and accomplished relative on the present occasion."

The speech of Cousin Feenix is received with great applause, and Mr. Dombey returns thanks on

behalf of himself and Mrs. Dombey. J. B. shortly
afterwards proposes Mrs. Skewton. The breakfast
languishes when that is done, the violated hatchments are avenged, and Edith rises to assume her
travelling dress.

All the servants, in the meantime, have been
breakfasting below. Champagne has grown too
common among them to be mentioned, and roast
fowls, raised pies, and lobster salad have become
mere drugs. The very tall young man has recovered
his spirits, and again alludes to the exciseman.
His comrade's eye begins to emulate his own, and
he too stares at objects without taking cognizance
thereof. There is a general redness in the faces of
the ladies; in the face of Mrs. Perch particularly,
who is joyous and beaming, and lifted so far above
the cares of life, that if she were asked just now to
direct a wayfarer to Balls Pond, where her own
cares lodge, she would have some difficulty in recall-
ing the way. Mr. Towlinson has proposed the
happy pair; to which the silver-headed butler has
responded neatly, and with emotion; for he half
begins to think he *is* an old retainer of the family,
and that he is bound to be affected by these changes.
The whole party, and especially the ladies, are very
frolicsome. Mr. Dombey's cook, who generally
takes the lead in society, has said, it is impossible
to settle down after this, and why not go, in a party,
to the play ? Everybody (Mrs. Perch included) has
agreed to this; even the native, who is tigerish in
his drink, and who alarms the ladies (Mrs. Perch
particularly) by the rolling of his eyes. One of the
very tall young men has even proposed a ball after
the play, and it presents itself to no one (Mrs.

Perch included) in the light of an impossibility. Words have arisen between the housemaid and Mr. Towlinson; she, on the authority of an old saw, asserting marriages to be made in heaven: he affecting to trace the manufacture elsewhere; he supposing that she says so, because she thinks of being married her own self; she saying, Lord forbid, at any rate, that she should ever marry *him*. To calm these flying taunts, the silver-headed butler rises to propose the health of Mr. Towlinson, whom to know is to esteem, and to esteem is to wish well settled in life with the object of his choice, wherever (here the silver-headed butler eyes the housemaid) she may be. Mr. Towlinson returns thanks in a speech replete with feeling, of which the peroration turns on foreigners, regarding whom he says they may find favor, sometimes, with weak and inconstant intellects that can be led away by hair, but all he hopes is, he may never hear of no foreigner never boning nothing out of no travelling chariot. The eye of Mr. Towlinson is so severe and so expressive here, that the housemaid is turning hysterical, when she and all the rest, roused by the intelligence that the Bride is going away, hurry upstairs to witness her departure.

The chariot is at the door; the Bride is descending to the hall, where Mr. Dombey waits for her. Florence is ready on the staircase to depart too; and Miss Nipper, who has held a middle state between the parlor and the kitchen, is prepared to accompany her. As Edith appears, Florence hastens towards her, to bid her farewell.

Is Edith cold, that she should tremble? Is there anything unnatural or unwholesome in the touch of

Florence, that the beautiful form recedes and con-
tracts, as if it could not bear it ?   Is there so much
hurry in this going away, that Edith, with a wave
of her hand, sweeps on, and is gone ?

Mrs. Skewton, overpowered by her feelings as a
mother, sinks on her sofa in the Cleopatra attitude,
when the clatter of the chariot wheels is lost, and
sheds several tears.   The major, coming with the rest
of the company from table, endeavors to comfort her;
but she will not be comforted on any terms, and so
the major takes his leave.   Cousin Feenix takes his
leave, and Mr. Carker takes his leave.   The guests
all go away.   Cleopatra, left alone, feels a little
giddy from her strong emotion, and falls asleep.

Giddiness prevails below-stairs too.   The very
tall young man, whose excitement came on so
soon, appears to have his head glued to the table
in the pantry, and cannot be detached from it.   A
violent revulsion has taken place in the spirits of
Mrs. Perch, who is low on account of Mr. Perch;
and tells cook that she fears he is not so much
attached to his home as he used to be, when they
were only nine in family.   Mr. Towlinson has a
singing in his ears, and a large wheel going round
and round inside his head.   The housemaid wishes
it wasn't wicked to wish that one was dead.

There is a general delusion likewise, in these
lower regions, on the subject of time; everybody
conceiving that it ought to be, at the earliest, ten
o'clock at night, whereas it is not yet three in the
afternoon.   A shadowy idea of wickedness committed haunts every individual in the party; and each
one secretly thinks the other a companion in guilt,
whom it would be agreeable to avoid.   No man or

woman has the hardihood to hint at the projected visit to the play. Any one reviving the notion of the ball would be scouted as a malignant idiot.

Mrs. Skewton sleeps upstairs two hours afterwards, and naps are not yet over in the kitchen. The hatchments in the dining-room look down on crumbs, dirty plates, spillings of wine, half-thawed ice, stale discolored heel-taps, scraps of lobster, drumsticks of fowls, and pensive jellies, gradually resolving themselves into a lukewarm, gummy soup. The marriage is, by this time, almost as denuded of its show and garnish as the breakfast. Mr. Dombey's servants moralize so much about it, and are so repentant over their early tea at home, that, by eight o'clock or so, they settle down into confirmed seriousness; and Mr. Perch, arriving at that time from the City, fresh and jocular, with a white waistcoat and a comic song, ready to spend the evening, and prepared for any amount of dissipation, is amazed to find himself coldly received, and Mrs. Perch but poorly, and to have the pleasing duty of escorting that lady home by the next omnibus.

Night closes in. Florence, having rambled through the handsome house, from room to room, seeks her own chamber, where the care of Edith has surrounded her with luxuries and comforts; and, divesting herself of her handsome dress, puts on her old simple mourning for dear Paul, and sits down to read, with Diogenes winking and blinking on the ground beside her. But Florence cannot read to-night. The house seems strange and new, and there are loud echoes in it. There is a shadow on her heart: she knows not why or what: but it is heavy. Florence shuts her book, and gruff Diogenes, who takes that for a signal, puts his paws upon her lap, and rubs his ears against her caressing hands. But Florence cannot see him plainly in a little time, for there is a mist between her eyes and him, and her dead brother and dead mother shine in it like angels. Walter, too, poor, wandering, ship-wrecked boy, oh, where is he?

The major don't know; that's for certain; and don't care. The major, having choked and slumbered all the afternoon, has taken a late dinner at his club, and now sits over his pint of wine, driving a modest young man, with a fresh-colored face, at the next table (who would give a handsome sum to be able to rise and go away, but cannot do it), to the verge of madness, by anecdotes of Bagstock, sir, at Dombey's wedding, and old Joe's devilish gentle-manly friend, Lord Feenix. While Cousin Feenix, who ought to be at Long's, and in bed, finds him-self, instead, at a gaming-table, where his wilful legs have taken him, perhaps, in his own despite.

Night, like a giant, fills the church, from pave-ment to roof, and holds dominion through the silent hours. Pale dawn again comes peeping through the windows; and, giving place to day, sees night with-draw into the vaults, and follows it, and drives it out, and hides among the dead. The timid mice again cower close together when the great door clashes, and Mr. Sownds and Mrs. Miff, treading the circle of their daily lives, unbroken as a mar-riage ring, come in. Again the cocked hat and the mortified bonnet stand in the background at the marriage hour; and again this man taketh this woman, and this woman taketh this man, on the solemn terms:

"To have and to hold, from this day forward, for better for worse, for richer for poorer, in sickness and in health, to love and to cherish, until death do them part."

The very words that Mr. Carker rides into town repeating, with his mouth stretched to the utmost, as he picks his dainty way.

CHAPTER XII.

Honest Captain Cuttle, as the weeks flew over him in his fortified retreat, by no means abated any of his prudent provisions against surprise, because of the non-appearance of the enemy. The captain argued that his present security was too profound and wonderful to endure much longer; he knew that, when the wind stood in a fair quarter, the weather-cock was seldom nailed there; and he was too well acquainted with the determined and dauntless character of Mrs. MacStinger to doubt that that heroic woman had devoted herself to the task of his discovery and capture. Trembling beneath the weight of these reasons, Captain Cuttle lived a very close and retired life; seldom stirring abroad until after dark; venturing even then only into the obscurest streets; never going forth at all on Sundays; and, both within and without the walls of his retreat, avoiding bonnets, as if they were worn by raging lions.

The captain never dreamed that, in the event of his being pounced upon by Mrs. MacStinger in his walks, it would be possible to offer resistance. He felt that it could not be done. He saw himself, in his mind's eye, put meekly in a hackney coach, and carried off to his old lodgings. He foresaw that, once immured there, he was a lost man: his hat gone; Mrs. MacStinger watchful of him day and night; reproaches heaped upon his head before the infant family; himself the guilty object of suspicion and distrust: an ogre in the children's eyes, and in their mother's a detected traitor.

A violent perspiration and a lowness of spirits always came over the captain as this gloomy picture presented itself to his imagination. It generally did so previous to his stealing out of doors at night for air and exercise. Sensible of the risk he ran, the captain took leave of Rob, at those times, with the solemnity which became a man who might never return: exhorting him, in the event of his (the captain's) being lost sight of for a time, to tread in the paths of virtue, and keep the brazen instruments well polished.

But not to throw away a chance, and to secure to himself a means, in case of the worst, of holding communication with the external world, Captain Cuttle soon conceived the happy idea of teaching Rob the Grinder some secret signal, by which that adherent might make his presence and fidelity known to his commander in the hour of adversity. After much cogitation, the captain decided in favor of instructing him to whistle the marine melody, "Oh, cheerily, cheerily!" and Rob the Grinder attaining a point as near perfection in that accomplishment as a landsman could hope to reach, the captain impressed these mysterious instructions on his mind:

"Now, my lad, stand by! If ever I'm took—"

"Took, captain!" interposed Rob, with his round eyes wide open.

"Ah!" said Captain Cuttle darkly, "if ever I goes away, meaning to come back to supper, and don't come within hail again twenty-four hours arter my loss, go you to Brig Place, and whistle that 'ere tune near my old moorings — not as if you was a-meaning of it, you understand, but as if you'd drifted there promiscuous. If I answer in that tune, you sheer off, my lad, and come back four and twenty hours arterwards; if I answer in another tune, do you stand off and on, and wait till I throw out further signals. Do you understand them orders, now?"

"What am I to stand off and on of, captain?" inquired Rob. "The horse road?"

"Here's a smart lad for you!" cried the captain, eying him sternly, "as don't know his own native alphabet! Go away a bit and come back again alternate — d'ye understand that?"

"Yes, captain," said Rob.

"Very good, my lad, then," said the captain, relenting. "Do it!"

That he might do it the better, Captain Cuttle sometimes condescended, of an evening, after the shop was shut, to rehearse the scene: retiring into the parlor for the purpose, as into the lodgings of a supposititious MacStinger, and carefully observing the behavior of his ally, from the hole of espial he had cut in the wall. Rob the Grinder discharged himself of his duty with so much exactness and judgment, when thus put to the proof, that the captain presented him, at divers times, with seven sixpences, in token of satisfaction; and gradually felt stealing over his spirit the resignation of a man who had made provision for the worst, and taken every reasonable precaution against an unrelenting fate.

Nevertheless, the captain did not tempt ill-fortune by being a whit more venturesome than before. Though he considered it a point of good-breeding in himself, as a general friend of the family, to attend Mr. Dombey's wedding (of which he had heard from Mr. Perch), and to show that gentleman a pleasant and approving countenance from the gallery, he had repaired to the church in a hackney cabriolet with both windows up; and might have scrupled even to make that venture, in his dread of Mrs. MacStinger, but that the lady's attendance on the ministry of the Reverend Melchisedech rendered it peculiarly unlikely that she would be found in communion with the Establishment.

The captain got safe home again, and fell into the ordinary routine of his new life, without encountering any more direct alarm from the enemy than was suggested to him by the daily bonnets in the street. But, other subjects began to lie heavier on the captain's mind. Walter's ship was still unheard of. No news came of old Sol Gills. Florence did not even know of the old man's disappearance, and Captain Cuttle had not the heart to tell her. Indeed, the captain, as his own hopes of the generous, handsome, gallant-hearted youth whom he had loved, according to his rough manner, from a child, began to fade, and faded more and more from day to day, shrunk with instinctive pain from the thought of exchanging a word with Florence. If he had had good news to carry to her, the honest

captain would have braved the newly decorated
house and splendid furniture — though these, connected with the lady he had seen at church, were
awful to him — and made his way into her presence.
With a dark horizon gathering around their common
hopes, however, which darkened every hour, the
captain almost felt as if he were a new misfortune
and affliction to her; and was scarcely less afraid
of a visit from Florence than from Mrs. MacStinger
herself.

It was a chill, dark, autumn evening, and Captain
Cuttle had ordered a fire to be kindled in the little
back-parlor, now more than ever like the cabin of a
ship. The rain fell fast, and the wind blew hard;
and straying out on the housetop by that stormy
bedroom of his old friend, to take an observation of
the weather, the captain's heart died within him
when he saw how wild and desolate it was. Not
that he associated the weather of that time with
poor Walter's destiny, or doubted that, if Providence
had doomed him to be lost and shipwrecked, it was
over long ago; but that beneath an outward influence quite distinct from the subject-matter of his
thoughts, the captain's spirits sank, and his hopes
turned pale, as those of wiser men had often done
before him, and will often do again.

Captain Cuttle, addressing his face to the sharp
wind and slanting rain, looked up at the heavy scud
that was flying fast over the wilderness of housetops, and looked for something cheery there in vain.
The prospect near at hand was no better. In sundry tea-chests, and other rough boxes at his feet,
the pigeons of Rob the Grinder were cooing like so
many dismal breezes getting up. A crazy weather-

cock of a midshipman with a telescope at his eye, once visible from the street, but long bricked out, creaked and complained upon his rusty pivot as the shrill blast spun him round and round, and sported with him cruelly. Upon the captain's coarse blue vest the cold rain-drops started like steel beads; and he could hardly maintain himself aslant against the stiff nor'wester that came pressing against him, importunate to topple him over the parapet, and throw him on the pavement below. If there were any Hope alive that evening, the captain thought, as he held his hat on, it certainly kept house, and wasn't out of doors; so the captain, shaking his head in a despondent manner, went in to look for it.

Captain Cuttle descended slowly to the little back-parlor, and, seated in his accustomed chair, looked for it in the fire; but it was not there, though the fire was bright. He took out his tobacco-box and pipe, and, composing himself to smoke, looked for it in the red glow from the bowl, and in the wreaths of vapor that curled upward from his lips; but there was not so much as an atom of the rust of Hope's anchor in either. He tried a glass of grog; but melancholy truth was at the bottom of that well, and he couldn't finish it. He made a turn or two in the shop, and looked for Hope among the instruments; but they obstinately worked out reckonings for the missing ship, in spite of any opposition he could offer, that ended at the bottom of the lone sea.

The wind still rushing, and the rain still pattering, against the closed shutters, the captain brought to before the Wooden Midshipman upon the counter, and thought, as he dried the little officer's uniform

with his sleeve, how many years the Midshipman
had seen, during which few changes — hardly any
— had transpired among his ship's company ; how
the changes had come all together one day, as it
might be; and of what a sweeping kind they were.
Here was the little society of the back-parlor
broken up, and scattered far and wide. Here was
no audience for Lovely Peg, even if there had been
anybody to sing it, which there was not; for the
captain was as morally certain that nobody but he
could execute that ballad as he was that he had not
the spirit, under existing circumstances, to attempt
it. There was no bright face of "Wal'r" in the
house ; — here the captain transferred his sleeve for
a moment from the Midshipman's uniform to his
own cheek; — the familiar wig and buttons of Sol
Gills were a vision of the past; Richard Whitting-
ton was knocked on the head; and every plan and
project, in connection with the Midshipman, lay
drifting, without mast or rudder, on the waste of
waters.

As the captain, with a dejected face, stood revolving these thoughts, and polishing the Midshipman, partly in the tenderness of old acquaintance,
and partly in the absence of his mind, a knocking
at the shop-door communicated a frightful start to
the frame of Rob the Grinder seated on the counter,
whose large eyes had been intently fixed on the
captain's face, and who had been debating within
himself, for the five-hundredth time, whether the
captain could have done a murder, that he had such
an evil conscience, and was always running away.

"What's that ? " said Captain Cuttle softly.

" Somebody's knuckles, captain," answered Rob
the Grinder.

The captain, with an abashed and guilty air, immediately sneaked on tiptoe to the little parlor, and locked himself in. Rob, opening the door, would have parleyed with the visitor on the threshold, if the visitor had come in female guise; but the figure being of the male sex, and Rob's orders only applying to women, Rob held the door open, and allowed it to enter: which it did very quickly, glad to get out of the driving rain.

"A job for Burgess and Co. at any rate," said the visitor, looking over his shoulder compassionately at his own legs, which were very wet and covered with splashes. "Oh, how de do, Mr. Gills?"

The salutation was addressed to the captain, now emerging from the back-parlor with a most transparent and utterly futile affectation of coming out by accident.

"Thankee," the gentleman went on to say in the same breath; "I'm very well indeed myself, I'm much obliged to you. My name is Toots, — *Mister* Toots."

The captain remembered to have seen this young gentleman at the wedding, and made him a bow. Mr. Toots replied with a chuckle; and being embarrassed, as he generally was, breathed hard, shook hands with the captain for a long time, and then falling on Rob the Grinder, in the absence of any other resource, shook hands with him in a most affectionate and cordial manner.

"I say! I should like to speak a word to you, Mr. Gills, if you please," said Toots at length, with surprising presence of mind. "I say! Miss D. O. M., you know!"

. The captain, with responsive gravity and mystery,

immediately waved his hook towards the little parlor, whither Mr. Toots followed him.

"Oh! I beg your pardon, though," said Mr. Toots, looking up in the captain's face, as he sat down in a chair by the fire, which the captain placed for him; "you don't happen to know the Chicken at all; do you, Mr. Gills?"

"The Chicken?" said the captain.

"The Game Chicken," said Mr. Toots.

. The captain shaking his head, Mr. Toots explained that the man alluded to was the celebrated public character who had covered himself and his country with glory in his contest with the Nobby Shropshire One; but this piece of information did not appear to enlighten the captain very much.

"Because he's outside: that's all," said Mr. Toots. "But it's of no consequence; he won't get very wet, perhaps."

"I can pass the word for him in a moment," said the captain.

"Well, if you *would* have the goodness to let him sit in the shop with your young man," chuckled Mr. Toots, "I should be glad; because, you know, he's easily offended, and the damp's rather bad for his stamina. *I*'ll call him in, Mr. Gills."

With that, Mr. Toots, repairing to the shop-door, sent a peculiar whistle into the night, which produced a stoical gentleman in a shaggy white greatcoat and a flat-brimmed hat, with very short hair, a broken nose, and a considerable tract of bare and sterile country behind each ear.

"Sit down, Chicken," said Mr. Toots.

The compliant Chicken spat out some small pieces of straw on which he was regaling himself,

and took in a fresh supply from a reserve he carried in his hand.

"There ain't no drain of nothing short handy, is there?" said the Chicken generally. "This here sluicing night is hard lines to a man as lives on his condition."

Captain Cuttle proffered a glass of rum, which the Chicken, throwing back his head, emptied into himself, as into a cask, after proposing the brief sentiment, "Towards us!" Mr. Toots and the captain returning then to the parlor, and taking their seats before the fire, Mr. Toots began, —

"Mr. Gills — "

"Awast!" said the captain. "My name's Cuttle."

Mr. Toots looked greatly disconcerted, while the captain proceeded gravely, —

"Cap'en Cuttle is my name, and England is my nation, this here is my dwelling-place, and blessed be creation — Job," said the captain, as an index to his authority.

"Oh! I couldn't see Mr. Gills, could I?" said Mr. Toots; "because — "

"If you could see Sol Gills, young gen'l'm'n," said the captain impressively, and laying his heavy hand on Mr. Toots's knee, "old Sol, mind you — with your own eyes — as you sit there — you'd be welcomer to me than a wind astaru to a ship becalmed. But you can't see Sol Gills. And why can't you see Sol Gills?" said the captain, apprised by the face of Mr. Toots that he was making a profound impression on that gentleman's mind. "Because he's inwisible."

Mr. Toots, in his agitation, was going to reply

that it was of no consequence at all. But he corrected himself, and said, "Lor bless me!"

"That there man," said the captain, "has left me in charge here by a piece of writing, but though he was a'most as good as my sworn brother, I know no more where he's gone, or why he's gone — if so be to seek his nevy, or if so be along of being not quite settled in his mind — than you do. One morning, at daybreak, he went over the side," said the captain, "without a splash, without a ripple. I have looked for that man high and low, and never set eyes, nor ears, nor nothing else upon him, from that hour."

"But, good gracious, Miss Dombey don't know —" Mr. Toots began.

"Why, I ask you, as a feeling heart," said the captain, dropping his voice, "why should she know? Why should she be made to know until such time as there warn't any help for it? She took to old Sol Gills, did that sweet creetur, with a kindness, with a affability, with a — What's the good of saying so? You know her."

"I should hope so," chuckled Mr. Toots, with a conscious blush that suffused his whole countenance.

"And you come here from her?" said the captain.

"I should think so," chuckled Mr. Toots.

"Then all I need observe is," said the captain, "that you know a angel, and are chartered *by* a angel."

Mr. Toots instantly seized the captain's hand, and requested the favor of his friendship.

"Upon my word and honor," said Mr. Toots earnestly, "I should be very much obliged to you if you'd improve my acquaintance. I should like to know you, captain, very much. I really am in want of a friend, I am. Little Dombey was my friend at old Blimber's, and would have been now, if he'd have lived. The Chicken," said Mr. Toots in a forlorn whisper, "is very well — admirable in his way — the sharpest man, perhaps, in the world; there's not a move he isn't up to; everybody says so — but I don't know — he's not everything. So she *is* an angel, captain. If there is an angel anywhere, it's Miss Dombey. That's what I've always said. Really, though, you know," said Mr. Toots, "I should be very much obliged to you if you'd cultivate my acquaintance."

Captain Cuttle received this proposal in a polite manner, but still without committing himself to its acceptance; merely observing, "Ay, ay, my lad. We shall see, we shall see;" and reminding Mr. Toots of his immediate mission, by inquiring to what he was indebted for the honor of that visit.

"Why, the fact is," replied Mr. Toots, "that it's the young woman I come from. Not Miss Dombey — Susan, you know."

The captain nodded his head once, with a grave expression of face, indicative of his regarding that young woman with serious respect.

"And I'll tell you how it happens," said Mr. Toots. "You know, I go and call sometimes on Miss Dombey. I don't go there on purpose, you know, but I happen to be in the neighborhood very often; and when I find myself there, why — why, I call."

"Nat'rally," observed the captain.

"Yes," said Mr. Toots. "I called this afternoon. Upon my word and honor, I don't think it's possible to form an idea of the angel Miss Dombey was this afternoon."

The captain answered with a jerk of his head, implying that it might not be easy to some people, but was quite so to him.

"As I was coming out," said Mr. Toots, "the young woman, in the most unexpected manner, took me into the pantry."

The captain seemed, for the moment, to object to this proceeding; and leaning back in his chair, looked at Mr. Toots with a distrustful, if not threatening visage.

"Where she brought out," said Mr. Toots, "this newspaper. She told me that she had kept it from Miss Dombey all day, on account of something that was in it, about somebody that she and Dombey used to know; and then she read the passage to me. Very well. Then she said — Wait a minute; what was it she said, though?"

Mr. Toots, endeavoring to concentrate his mental powers on this question, unintentionally fixed the captain's eye, and was so much discomposed by its stern expression, that his difficulty in resuming the thread of his subject was enhanced to a painful extent.

"Oh!" said Mr. Toots after long consideration. "Oh, ah! Yes! She said that she hoped there was a bare possibility that it mightn't be true; and that as she couldn't very well come out herself, without surprising Miss Dombey, would I go down to Mr. Solomon Gills the Instrument-maker's in this street, who was the party's uncle, and ask whether he believed it was true, or had heard anything else in the City. She said, if he couldn't speak to me, no doubt Captain Cuttle could. By the by!" said Mr. Toots, as the discovery flashed upon him, "you, you know!"

The captain glanced at the newspaper in Mr. Toots's hand, and breathed short and hurriedly.

"Well," pursued Mr. Toots, "the reason why I'm rather late is, because I went up as far as Finchley first, to get some uncommonly fine chickweed that grows there, for Miss Dombey's bird. But I came on here directly afterwards. You've seen the paper, I suppose?"

The captain, who had become cautious of reading the news, lest he should find himself advertised at full length by Mrs. MacStinger, shook his head.

"Shall I read the passage to you?" inquired Mr. Toots.

The captain making a sign in the affirmative, Mr. Toots reads as follows, from the Shipping Intelligence:

"'Southampton. The bark Defiance, Henry James, Commander, arrived in this port to-day, with a cargo of sugar, coffee, and rum, reports that, being becalmed on the sixth day of her passage home from Jamaica, in'—in such and such a latitude, you know—" said Mr. Toots, after making a feeble dash at the figures, and tumbling over them.

"Ay!" cried the captain, striking his clenched hand on the table. "Heave ahead, my lad!"

"—Latitude," repeated Mr. Toots, with a startled glance at the captain, "and longitude so-and-so,—'the lookout observed, half an hour before sunset, some fragments of a wreck, drifting at about the distance of a mile. The weather being clear, and the bark making no way, a boat was hoisted out, with orders to inspect the same, when they were found to consist of sundry large spars, and a part of the main rigging of an English brig, of about five hundred tons burden, together with a portion of the stern, on which the words and letters "Son and H—— " were yet plainly legible. No vestige of any dead body was to be seen upon the floating fragments. Log of the Defiance states, that a breeze springing up in the night, the wreck was seen no more. There can be no doubt that all surmises as to the fate of the missing vessel, the Son and Heir, port of London, bound for Barbadoes, are now set at rest for ever; that she broke up in the last hurricane; and that every soul on board perished.' "

Captain Cuttle, like all mankind, little knew how much hope had survived within him under discouragement until he felt its death-shock. During the reading of the paragraph, and for a minute or two afterwards, he sat with his gaze fixed on the modest Mr. Toots like a man entranced; then, suddenly rising, and putting on his glazed hat, which, in his visitor's honor, he had laid upon the table, the captain turned his back, and bent his head down on the little chimney-piece.

"Oh, upon my word and honor," cried Mr. Toots, whose tender heart was moved by the captain's unexpected distress, "this is a most wretched sort of affair, this world is! Somebody's always dying, or going and doing something uncomfortable in it. I'm sure I never should have looked forward so much to coming into my property, if I had known this. I never saw such a world. It's a great deal worse than Blimber's."

Captain Cuttle, without altering his position, signed to Mr. Toots not to mind him; and presently turned round, with his glazed hat thrust back upon his ears, and his hand composing and smoothing his brown face.

"Wal'r, my dear lad," said the captain, "farewell! Wal'r, my child, my boy, and man, I loved you! He warn't my flesh and blood," said the captain, looking at the fire — "I ain't got none — but something of what a father feels when he loses a son, I feel in losing Wal'r. For why?" said the captain. "Because it ain't one loss, but a round dozen. Where's that there young schoolboy with the rosy face and curly hair, that used to be as merry in this here parlor, come round every week, as a piece of music? Gone down with Wal'r. Where's that there fresh lad, that nothing couldn't tire nor put out, and that sparkled up and blushed so, when we joked him about Heart's Delight, that he was beautiful to look at? Gone down with Wal'r. Where's that there man's spirit, all afire, that wouldn't see the old man hove down for a minute, and cared nothing for itself? Gone down with Wal'r. It ain't one Wal'r. There was a dozen Wal'rs that I knowed, and loved, all holding round his neck when he went down, and they're a-holding round mine now!"

Mr. Toots sat silent: folding and refolding the newspaper as small as possible upon his knee.

"And Sol Gills," said the captain, gazing at the fire, "poor nevyless old Sol, where are *you* got to? You was left in charge of me; his last words was,

'Take care of my uncle!' What came over *you*,
Sol, when you went and gave the go-by to Ned
Cuttle; and what am I to put in my accounts, that
he's a-looking down upon, respecting you? Sol
Gills, Sol Gills!" said the captain, shaking his head
slowly, "catch sight of that there newspaper, away
from home, with no one as knowed Wal'r by to say
a word; and broadside-to you broach, and down you
pitch, head foremost!"

Drawing a heavy sigh, the captain turned to Mr.
Toots, and roused himself to a sustained consciousness of that gentleman's presence.

"My lad," said the captain, "you must tell the
young woman honestly that this here fatal news is
too correct. They don't romance, you see, on such
p'ints. It's entered on the ship's log, and that's the
truest book as a man can write. To-morrow morning," said the captain, "I'll step out and make
inquiries; but they'll lead to no good. They can't
do it. If you'll give me a look-in in the forenoon,
you shall know what I have heerd; but tell the
young woman, from Cap'en Cuttle, that it's over.
Over!" And the captain, hooking off his glazed
hat, pulled his handkerchief out of the crown, wiped
his grizzled head despairingly, and tossed the handkerchief in again, with the indifference of deep
dejection.

"Oh! I assure you," said Mr. Toots, "really I am
dreadfully sorry. Upon my word I am, though I
wasn't acquainted with the party. Do you think
Miss Dombey will be very much affected, Captain
Gills — I mean Mr. Cuttle?"

"Why, Lord love you," returned the captain, with
something of compassion for Mr. Toots's innocence,

"when she warn't no higher than that, they were as fond of one another as two young doves."

"Were they, though!" said Mr. Toots, with a considerably lengthened face.

"They were made for one another," said the captain mournfully; "but what signifies that now?"

"Upon my word and honor," cried Mr. Toots, blurting out his words through a singular combination of awkward chuckles and emotion, "I'm even more sorry than I was before. You know, Captain Gills, I — I positively adore Miss Dombey; — I — I am perfectly sore with loving her;" the burst with which this confession forced itself out of the unhappy Mr. Toots bespoke the vehemence of his feelings; "but what would be the good of my regarding her in this manner, if I wasn't truly sorry for her feeling pain, whatever was the cause of it? Mine ain't a selfish affection, you know," said Mr. Toots, in the confidence engendered by his having been a witness of the captain's tenderness. "It's the sort of thing with me, Captain Gills, that if I could be run over or — or trampled upon — or — or thrown off a very high place — or anything of that sort — for Miss Dombey's sake, it would be the most delightful thing that could happen to me."

All this Mr. Toots said in a suppressed voice, to prevent its reaching the jealous ears of the Chicken, who objected to the softer emotions; which effort of restraint, coupled with the intensity of his feelings, made him red to the tips of his ears, and caused him to present such an affecting spectacle of disinterested love to the eyes of Captain Cuttle, that the good captain patted him consolingly on the back, and bade him cheer up.

"Thankee, Captain Gills," said Mr. Toots, "it's kind of you, in the midst of your own troubles, to say so. I'm very much obliged to you. As I said before, I really want a friend, and should be glad to have your acquaintance. Although I am very well off," said Mr. Toots with energy, "you can't think what a miserable beast I am. The hollow crowd, you know, when they see me with the Chicken, and characters of distinction like that, suppose me to be happy; but I'm wretched. I suffer for Miss Dombey, Captain Gills. I can't get through my meals; I have no pleasure in my tailor; I often cry when I'm alone. I assure you it'll be a satisfaction to me to come back to-morrow, or to come back fifty times."

Mr. Toots, with these words, shook the captain's hand; and disguising such traces of his agitation as could be disguised on so short a notice before the Chicken's penetrating glance, rejoined that eminent gentleman in the shop. The Chicken, who was apt to be jealous of his ascendancy, eyed Captain Cuttle with anything but favor as he took leave of Mr. Toots; but followed his patron without being otherwise demonstrative of his ill-will: leaving the captain oppressed with sorrow; and Rob the Grinder elevated with joy, on account of having had the honor of staring for nearly half an hour at the conqueror of the Nobby Shropshire One.

Long after Rob was fast asleep in his bed under the counter, the captain sat looking at the fire; and long after there was no fire to look at, the captain sat gazing on the rusty bars, with unavailing thoughts of Walter and old Sol crowding through his mind. Retirement to the stormy chamber at the top of the house brought no rest with it; and the captain rose up in the morning sorrowful and unrefreshed.

As soon as the City offices were open, the captain issued forth to the counting-house of Dombey and Son. But there was no opening of the Midshipman's windows that morning. Rob the Grinder, by the captain's orders, left the shutters closed, and the house was as a house of death.

It chanced that Mr. Carker was entering the office as Captain Cuttle arrived at the door. Receiving the manager's benison gravely and silently, Captain Cuttle made bold to accompany him into his own room.

"Well, Captain Cuttle," said Mr. Carker, taking up his usual position before the fireplace, and keeping on his hat, "this is a bad business."

"You have received the news as was in print yesterday, sir?" said the captain.

"Yes," said Mr. Carker, "we have received it. It was accurately stated. The underwriters suffer a considerable loss. We are very sorry. No help! Such is life!"

Mr. Carker pared his nails delicately with a penknife, and smiled at the captain, who was standing by the door looking at him.

"I excessively regret poor Gay," said Carker, "and the crew. I understand there were some of our very best men among 'em. It always happens so. Many men with families too. A comfort to reflect that poor Gay had no family, Captain Cuttle!"

The captain stood rubbing his chin, and looking at the manager. The manager glanced at the unopened letters lying on his desk, and took up the newspaper.

"Is there anything I can do for you, Captain Cuttle?" he asked, looking off it, with a smiling and expressive glance at the door.

"I wish you could set my mind at rest, sir, on something it's uneasy about," returned the captain.

"Ay!" exclaimed the manager, "what's that? Come, Captain Cuttle, I must trouble you to be quick, if you please. I am much engaged."

"Lookee here, sir," said the captain, advancing a step. "Afore my friend Wal'r went on this here disastrous voyage —"

"Come, come, Captain Cuttle," interposed the smiling manager, "don't talk about disastrous voyages in that way. We have nothing to do with disastrous voyages here, my good fellow. You must have begun very early on your day's allowance, captain, if you don't remember that there are hazards in all voyages, whether by sea or land. You are not made uneasy by the supposition that young what's-his-name was lost in bad weather that was got up against him in these offices — are you? Fie, captain! Sleep, and soda water, are the best cures for such uneasiness as that."

"My lad," returned the captain slowly, — "you are a'most a lad to me, and so I don't ask your pardon for that slip of a word, — if you find any pleasure in this here sport, you ain't the gentleman I took you for, and if you ain't the gentleman I took you for, maybe my mind has call to be uneasy. Now this is what it is, Mr. Carker. — Afore that poor lad went away, according to orders, he told me that he warn't a-going away for his own good or for promotion, he knowed. It was my belief that he was wrong, and I told him so, and I come here, your head governor being absent, to ask a question or two of you in a civil way, for my own satisfaction. Them questions you answered — free. Now, it'll ease my mind to know, when all is over, as it is, and when what can't be cured must be endoored — for which, as a scholar, you'll overhaul the book it's in, and thereof make a note — to know once more, in a word, that I warn't mistaken; that I warn't back'ard in my duty when I didn't tell the old man what Wal'r told me; and that the wind was truly in his sail when he h'isted of it for Barbadoes Harbor. Mr. Carker," said the captain in the goodness of his nature, "when I was here last, we was very pleasant together. If I ain't been altogether so pleasant myself this morning, on account of this poor lad, and if I have chafed again any observation of yours that I might have fended off, my name is Ed'ard Cuttle, and I ask your pardon."

"Captain Cuttle," returned the manager with all possible politeness, "I must ask you to do me a favor."

"And what is it, sir?" inquired the captain.

"To have the goodness to walk off, if you please," rejoined the manager, stretching forth his arm, "and to carry your jargon somewhere else."

Every knob in the captain's face turned white with astonishment and indignation; even the red rim on his forehead faded, like a rainbow among the gathering clouds.

"I tell you what, Captain Cuttle," said the manager, shaking his forefinger at him, and showing him all his teeth, but still amiably smiling, "I was much too lenient with you when you came here before. You belong to an artful and audacious set of people.

In my desire to save young what's-his-name from
being kicked out of this place, neck and crop, my
good captain, I tolerated you; but for once, and only
once. Now, go, my friend!"

The captain was absolutely rooted to the ground,
and speechless.

"Go," said the good-humored manager, gathering
up his skirts, and standing astride upon the hearth-
rug, "like a sensible fellow, and let us have no turning out, or any such violent measures. If Mr.
Dombey were here, captain, you might be obliged
to leave in a more ignominious manner, possibly. I
merely say, go!"

The captain, laying his ponderous hand upon his
chest, to assist himself in fetching a deep breath,
looked at Mr. Carker from head to foot, and looked
round the little room, as if he did not clearly understand where he was, or in what company.

"You are deep, Captain Cuttle," pursued Carker,
with the easy and vivacious frankness of a man of
the world who knew the world too well to be ruffled
by any discovery of misdoing, when it did not immediately concern himself; "but you are not quite out
of soundings, either — neither you nor your absent
friend, captain. What have you done with your
absent friend, hey?"

Again the captain laid his hand upon his chest.
After drawing another deep breath, he conjured himself to "stand by!" But in a whisper.

"You hatch nice little plots, and hold nice little
councils, and make nice little appointments, and
receive nice little visitors, too, captain, hey?" said
Carker, bending his brows upon him, without showing his teeth any the less: "but it's a bold measure

to come here afterwards. Not like your discretion! You conspirators, and hiders, and runners-away should know better than that. Will you oblige me by going?"

"My lad," gasped the captain in a choked and trembling voice, and with a curious action going on in the ponderous fist; "there's a many words I could wish to say to you, but I don't rightly know where they're stowed just at present. My young friend Wal'r was drownded only last night, according to my reckoning, and it puts me out, you see. But you and me will come alongside o' one another again, my lad," said the captain, holding up his hook, "if we live."

"It will be anything but shrewd in you, my good fellow, if we do," returned the manager with the same frankness; "for you may rely, I give you fair warning, upon my detecting and exposing you. I don't pretend to be a more moral man than my neighbors, my good captain; but the confidence of this House, or of any member of this House, is not to be abused and undermined while I have eyes and ears. Good-day!" said Mr. Carker, nodding his head.

Captain Cuttle, looking at him steadily (Mr. Carker looked full as steadily at the captain), went out of the office, and left him standing astride before the fire, as calm and pleasant as if there were no more spots upon his soul than on his pure white linen and his smooth sleek skin.

The captain glanced, in passing through the outer counting-house, at the desk where he knew poor Walter had been used to sit, now occupied by another young boy, with a face almost as fresh and hopeful

as his on the day when they tapped the famous last
bottle but one of the old madeira, in the little back-
parlor.   The association of ideas thus awakened did
the captain a great deal of good; it softened him in
the very height of his anger, and brought the tears
into his eyes.

Arrived at the Wooden Midshipman's again, and
sitting down in a corner of the dark shop, the captain's indignation, strong as it was, could make no
head against his grief.   Passion seemed not only to
do wrong and violence to the memory of the dead,
but to be infected by death, and to droop and decline
beside it.   All the living knaves and liars in the
world were nothing to the honesty and truth of one
dead friend.

The only thing the honest captain made out
clearly, in this state of mind, besides the loss of
Walter, was, that with him almost the whole world
of Captain Cuttle had been drowned.   If he reproached himself sometimes, and keenly too, for
having ever connived at Walter's innocent deceit, he
thought at least as often of the Mr. Carker whom
no sea could ever render up; and the Mr. Dombey,
whom he now began to perceive was as far beyond
human recall; and the "Heart's Delight," with whom
he must never foregather again; and the Lovely Peg,
that teak-built and trim ballad, that had gone ashore
upon a rock, and split into mere planks and beams
of rhyme.   The captain sat in the dark shop, thinking of these things, to the entire exclusion of his
own injury; and looking with as sad an eye upon
the ground, as if in contemplation of their actual
fragments as they floated past him.

But the captain was not unmindful, for all that,

of such decent and respectful observances in memory of poor Walter as he felt within his power. Rousing himself and rousing Rob the Grinder (who in the unnatural twilight was fast asleep), the captain sallied forth with his attendant at his heels, and the door-key in his pocket, and repairing to one of those convenient slop-selling establishments of which there is abundant choice at the eastern end of London, purchased on the spot two suits of mourning — one for Rob the Grinder, which was immensely too small, and one for himself, which was immensely too large. He also provided Rob with a species of hat, greatly to be admired for its symmetry and usefulness, as well as for a happy blending of the mariner with the coal-heaver; which is usually termed a sou'-wester; and which was something of a novelty in connection with the instrument business. In their several garments, which the vender declared to be such a miracle in point of fit as nothing but a rare combination of fortuitous circumstances ever brought about, and the fashion of which was unparalleled within the memory of the oldest inhabitant, the captain and Grinder immediately arrayed themselves: presenting a spectacle fraught with wonder to all who beheld it.

In this altered form the captain received Mr. Toots. "I'm took aback, my lad, at present," said the captain, "and will only confirm that there ill news. Tell the young woman to break it gently to the young lady, and for neither of 'em never to think of me no more — 'special, mind you, that is — though I will think of them, when night comes on a hurricane and seas is mountains rowling, for which overhaul your Doctor Watts, brother, and when found make a note on."

The captain reserved, until some fitter time, the consideration of Mr. Toots's offer of friendship, and thus dismissed him. Captain Cuttle's spirits were so low, in truth, that he half determined, that day, to take no further precautions against surprise from Mrs. MacStinger, but to abandon himself recklessly to chance, and be indifferent to what might happen. As evening came on, he fell into a better frame of mind, however; and spoke much of Walter to Rob the Grinder, whose attention and fidelity he likewise incidentally commended. Rob did not blush to hear the captain earnest in his praises, but sat staring at him, and affecting to snivel with sympathy, and making a feint of being virtuous, and treasuring up every word he said (like a young spy as he was) with very promising deceit.

When Rob had turned in, and was fast asleep, the captain trimmed the candle, put on his spectacles — he had felt it appropriate to take to spectacles on entering into the Instrument Trade, though his eyes were like a hawk's — and opened the Prayer-book at the Burial Service. And reading softly to himself, in the little back-parlor, and stopping now and then to wipe his eyes, the captain, in a true and simple spirit, committed Walter's body to the deep.

CHAPTER XIII.

TURN we our eyes upon two homes; not lying side by side, but wide apart, though both within easy range and reach of the great city of London.

The first is situated in the green and wooded country near Norwood. It is not a mansion; it is of no pretensions as to size; but it is beautifully arranged, and tastefully kept. The lawn, the soft, smooth slope, the flower garden, the clumps of trees where graceful forms of ash and willow are not wanting, the conservatory, the rustic veranda with sweet-smelling creeping plants entwined about the pillars, the simple exterior of the house, the well-ordered offices, though all upon the diminutive scale proper to a mere cottage, bespeak an amount of elegant comfort within, that might serve for a palace. This indication is not without warrant; for, within it is a house of refinement and luxury. Rich colors, excellently blended, meet the eye at every turn; in the furniture — its proportions admirably devised to suit the shapes and sizes of the small rooms; on the walls; upon the floors; tinging and subduing the light that comes in through the odd glass doors and windows here and there. There are a few choice prints and pictures, too; in quaint nooks and recesses there is no want of books; and there are games of skill and chance set forth on tables — fantastic chessmen, dice, backgammon, cards, and billiards.

And yet, amidst this opulence of comfort, there is something in the general air that is not well. Is it that the carpets and the cushions are too soft and noiseless, so that those who move or repose among them seem to act by stealth? Is it that the prints and pictures do not commemorate great thoughts or deeds, or render nature in the poetry of landscape, hall, or hut, but are of one voluptuous cast — mere shows of form and color — and no more? Is it that the books have all their gold outside, and that the titles of the greater part qualify them to be companions of the prints and pictures? Is it that the completeness and the beauty of the place are here and there belied by an affectation of humility, in some unimportant and inexpensive regard, which is as false as the face of the too-truly-painted portrait hanging yonder, or its original at breakfast in his easy-chair below it? Or is it that, with the daily breath of that original and master of all here, there issues forth some subtle portion of himself, which gives a vague expression of himself to everything about him?

It is Mr. Carker the manager who sits in the easy-chair. A gaudy parrot in a burnished cage upon the table tears at the wires with her beak, and goes walking, upside down, in its dome-top, shaking her house and screeching; but Mr. Carker is indifferent to the bird, and looks with a musing smile at a picture on the opposite wall.

"A most extraordinary accidental likeness, certainly," says he.

Perhaps it is a Juno; perhaps a Potiphar's wife; perhaps some scornful nymph — according as the picture-dealers found the market when they christened it. It is the figure of a woman, supremely handsome, who, turning away, but with her face addressed to the spectator, flashes her proud glance upon him.

It is like Edith.

With a passing gesture of his hand at the picture — what! a menace? No; yet something like it. A wave as of triumph? No; yet more like that. An insolent salute wafted from his lips? No; yet like that too — he resumes his breakfast, and calls to the chafing and imprisoned bird, who, coming down into a pendent gilded hoop within the cage, like a great wedding-ring, swings in it, for his delight.

The second home is on the other side of London, near to where the busy great north road of bygone days is silent and almost deserted, except by wayfarers who toil along on foot.. It is a poor, small house, barely and sparely furnished, but very clean; and there is even an attempt to decorate it, shown in the homely flowers trained about the porch and in the narrow garden. The neighborhood in which it stands has as little of the country to recommend it as it has of the town. It is neither of the town nor country. The former, like the giant in his travelling boots, has made a stride and passed it, and has set his brick-and-mortar heel a long way in advance; but the intermediate space between the giant's feet, as yet, is only blighted country, and not town; and here, among a few tall chimneys belching smoke all day and night, and among the brick-fields and the lanes where turf is cut, and where the fences tumble down, and where the dusty nettles grow, and where a scrap or two of hedge may yet be seen, and where the bird-catcher still comes occasionally, though he swears every time to come no more, this second home is to be found.

She who inhabits it is she who left the first in her devotion to an outcast brother. She withdrew from that home its redeeming spirit, and from its master's breast his solitary angel: but though his liking for her is gone, after this ungrateful slight as he considers it; and though he abandons her altogether in return, an old idea of her is not quite forgotten even by him. Let her flower garden, in which he never sets his foot, but which is yet maintained, among all his costly alterations, as if she had quitted it but yesterday, bear witness.

Harriet Carker has changed since then, and on her beauty there has fallen a heavier shade than Time of his unassisted self can cast, all-potent as he is — the shadow of anxiety and sorrow, and the daily struggle of a poor existence. But it is beauty still; and still a gentle, quiet, and retiring beauty that must be sought out, for it cannot vaunt itself; if it could, it would be what it is no more.

Yes. This slight, small, patient figure, neatly dressed in homely stuffs, and indicating nothing but the dull, household virtues, that had so little in common with the received idea of heroism and greatness, unless, indeed, any ray of them should shine through the lives of the great ones of the earth, when it becomes a constellation, and is tracked in heaven straightway — this slight, small, patient figure, leaning on the man still young, but worn and gray, is she his sister, who, of all the world, went over to him in his shame, and put her hand in his, and with a sweet composure and determination, led him hopefully upon his barren way.

"It is early, John," she said. "Why do you go so early?"

"Not many minutes earlier than usual, Harriet. If I have the time to spare, I should like, I think — it's a fancy — to walk once by the house where I took leave of him."

"I wish I had ever seen or known him, John."

"It is better as it is, my dear, remembering his fate."

"But I could not regret it more, though I had known him. Is not your sorrow mine? And if I had, perhaps you would feel that I was a better companion to you in speaking about him than I may seem now."

"My dearest sister! Is there anything within the range of rejoicing or regret, in which I am not sure of your companionship?"

"I hope you think not, John, for surely there is nothing!"

"How could you be better to me, or nearer to me then, than you are in this, or anything?" said her brother. "I feel that you did know him, Harriet, and that you shared my feelings towards him."

She drew the hand which had been resting on his shoulder round his neck, and answered, with some hesitation, —

"No, not quite."

"True, true," he said; "you think I might have done him no harm if I had allowed myself to know him better?"

"Think! I know it."

"Designedly, Heaven knows I would not," he replied, shaking his head mournfully : "but his reputation was too precious to be perilled by such association. Whether you share that knowledge, or do not, my dear —"

"I do not," she said quietly.

"It is still the truth, Harriet, and my mind is lighter when I think of him for that which made it so much heavier then." He checked himself in his tone of melancholy, and smiled upon her as he said "Good-by."

"Good-by, dear John! In the evening, at the old time and place, I shall meet you as usual on your way home. Good-by."

The cordial face she lifted up to his to kiss him was his home, his life, his universe, and yet it was a portion of his punishment and grief; for in the cloud he saw upon it — though serene and calm as any radiant cloud at sunset — and in the constancy and devotion of her life, and in the sacrifice she had made of ease, enjoyment, and hope, he saw the bitter fruits of his old crime, for ever ripe and fresh.

She stood at the door looking after him, with her hands loosely clasped in each other, as he made his way over the frowzy and uneven patch of ground which lay before their house, which had once (and not long ago) been a pleasant meadow, and was now a very waste, with a disorderly crop of beginnings of mean houses rising out of the rubbish, as if they had been unskilfully sown there. Whenever he looked back — as once or twice he did — her cordial face shone like a light upon his heart; but when he plodded on his way, and saw her not, the tears were in her eyes as she stood watching him.

Her pensive form was not long idle at the door. There was daily duty to discharge, and daily work to do — for such commonplace spirits, that are not heroic, often work hard with their hands — and Harriet was soon busy with her household tasks. These discharged, and the poor house made quite neat and orderly, she counted her little stock of money with an anxious face, and went out thoughtfully to buy some necessaries for their table, planning and contriving, as she went, how to save. So sordid are the lives of such low natures, who are not only not heroic to their valets and waiting-women, but have neither valets nor waiting-women to be heroic to withal!

While she was absent, and there was no one in the house, there approached it, by a different way from that the brother had taken, a gentleman, a very little past his prime of life, perhaps, but of a healthy, florid hue, an upright presence, and a bright, clear aspect, that was gracious and good-humored. His eyebrows were still black, and so was much of his hair; the sprinkling of gray observable among the latter graced the former very much, and showed his broad frank brow and honest eyes to great advantage.

After knocking once at the door, and obtaining no response, this gentleman sat down on a bench in the little porch to wait. A certain skilful action of his fingers as he hummed some bars, and beat time on the seat beside him, seemed to denote the musician; and the extraordinary satisfaction be derived from humming something very slow and long, which had no recognizable tune, seemed to denote that he was a scientific one.

The gentleman was still twirling a theme, which seemed to go round and round and round, and in and in and in, and to involve itself like a corkscrew twirled upon a table, without getting any nearer to anything, when Harriet appeared returning. He rose up as she advanced, and stood with his head uncovered.

"You are come again, sir!" she said, faltering.

"I take that liberty," he answered. "May I ask for five minutes of your leisure?"

After a moment's hesitation, she opened the door, and gave him admission to the little parlor. The gentleman sat down there, drew his chair to the table over against her, and said, in a voice that perfectly corresponded to his appearance, and with a simplicity that was very engaging, —

"Miss Harriet, you cannot be proud. You siguified to me, when I called t'other morning, that you were. Pardon me, if I say that I looked into your face while you spoke, and that it contradicted you. I look into it again," he added, laying his hand gently on her arm for an instant, "and it contradicts you more and more."

She was somewhat confused and agitated, and could make no ready answer.

"It is the mirror of truth," said her visitor, "and gentleness. Excuse my trusting to it, and returning."

His manner of saying these words divested them entirely of the character of compliments. It was so plain, grave, unaffected, and sincere, that she bent her head, as if at once to thank him and acknowledge his sincerity.

"The disparity between **our** ages," said the gentleman, "and the plainness of my purpose, empower me, I am glad to think, to speak my mind. That is my mind; and so you see me for the second time."

"There is a kind of pride, sir," she returned after a moment's silence, "or what may be supposed to be pride, which is mere duty. I hope I cherish no other."

"For yourself," he said.

"For myself."

"But — pardon me —" suggested the gentleman. "For your brother John?"

"Proud of his love I am," said Harriet, looking full upon her visitor, and changing her manner on the instant — not that it was less composed and quiet, but that there was a deep impassioned earnestness in it that made the very tremble in her voice a part of her firmness, "and proud of him. Sir, you who strangely know the story of his life, and repeated it to me when you were here last —"

"Merely to make my way into your confidence," interposed the gentleman. "For Heaven's sake, don't suppose —"

"I am sure," she said, "you revived it, in my hearing, with a kind and good purpose. I am quite sure of it."

"I thank you," returned her visitor, pressing her hand hastily. "I am much obliged to you. You do me justice, I assure you. You were going to say that I, who know the story of John Carker's life —"

"May think it pride in me," she continued, "when I say that I am proud of him! I *am*. You know the time was when I was not — when I could

not be — but that is past. The humility of many
years, the uncomplaining expiation, the true repentance, the terrible regret, the pain I know he has
even in my affection, which he thinks has cost me
dear, though Heaven knows I am happy, but for
his sorrow ! — oh, sir, after what I have seen, let me
conjure you, if you are in any place of power, and
are ever wronged, never, for any wrong, inflict a
punishment that cannot be recalled; while there
is a GOD above us to work changes in the hearts
he made."

"Your brother is an altered man," returned the
gentleman compassionately. "I assure you, I don't
doubt it."

"He was an altered man when he did wrong,"
said Harriet. "He is an altered man again, and is
his true self now, believe me, sir."

"But we go on," said her visitor, rubbing his
forehead, in an absent manner, with his hand, and
then drumming thoughtfully on the table, "we go
on in our clockwork routine, from day to day, and
can't make out, or follow, these changes. They —
they're a metaphysical sort of thing. We — we
haven't leisure for it. We — we haven't courage.
They're not taught at schools or colleges, and we
don't know how to set about it. In short, we are
so d——d business-like," said the gentleman, walking to the window and back, and sitting down again,
in a state of extreme dissatisfaction and vexation.

"I am sure," said the gentleman, rubbing his
forehead again, and drumming on the table as
before; "I have good reason to believe that a jog-
trot life, the same from day to day, would reconcile
one to anything. One don't see anything, one don't

hear anything, one don't know anything; that's the fact. We go on taking everything for granted, and so we go on, until whatever we do, good, bad, or indifferent, we do from habit. Habit is all I shall have to report, when I am called upon to plead to my conscience on my death-bed. 'Habit,' says I; 'I was deaf, dumb, blind, and paralytic to a million things, from habit.' 'Very business-like indeed, Mr. What's-your-name,' says Conscience, 'but it won't do here!'"

The gentleman got up and walked to the window again and back: seriously uneasy, though giving his uneasiness this peculiar expression.

"Miss Harriet," he said, resuming his chair, "I wish you would let me serve you. Look at me; I ought to look honest, for I know I am so at present. Do I?"

"Yes," she answered with a smile.

"I believe every word you have said," he returned. "I am full of self-reproach that I might have known this and seen this, and known you and seen you, any time these dozen years, and that I never have. I hardly know how I ever got here — creature that I am, not only of my own habit, but of other people's! But, having done so, let me do something. I ask it in all honor and respect. You inspire me with both, in the highest degree. Let me do something."

"We are contented, sir."

"No, no, not quite," returned the gentleman. "I think not quite. There are some little comforts that might smooth your life, and his. And his!" he repeated, fancying that had made some impression on her. "I have been in the habit of thinking that there was nothing wanting to be done for him; that it was all settled and over; in short, of not thinking at all about it. I am different now. Let me do something for him. You too," said the visitor with careful delicacy, "have need to watch your health closely, for his sake, and I fear it fails."

"Whoever you may be, sir," answered Harriet, raising her eyes to his face, "I am deeply grateful to you. I feel certain that, in all you say, you have no object in the world but kindness to us. But years have passed since we began this life; and to take from my brother any part of what has so endeared him to me, and so proved his better resolution — any fragment of the merit of his unassisted, obscure, and forgotten reparation — would be to diminish the comfort it will be to him and me, when that time comes to each of us, of which you spoke just now. I thank you better with these tears than any words. Believe it, pray."

The gentleman was moved, and put the hand she held out to his lips, much as a tender father might kiss the hand of a dutiful child. But more reverently.

"If the day should ever come," said Harriet, "when he is restored, in part, to the position he lost —"

"Restored!" cried the gentleman quickly. "How can that be hoped for? In whose hands does the power of any restoration lie? It is no mistake of mine, surely, to suppose that his having gained the priceless blessing of his life is one cause of the animosity shown to him by his brother."

"You touch upon a subject that is never breathed between us; not even between us," said Harriet.

"I beg your forgiveness," said the visitor. "I should have known it. I entreat you to forget that I have done so inadvertently. And now, as I dare urge no more — as I am not sure that I have a right to do so — though Heaven knows even that doubt may be habit," said the gentleman, rubbing his head, as despondently as before, "let me: though a stranger, yet no stranger: ask two favors."

"What are they?" she inquired.

"The first, that if you should see cause to change your resolution, you will suffer me to be as your right hand. My name shall then be at your service; it is useless now, and always insignificant."

"Our choice of friends," she answered, smiling faintly, "is not so great that I need any time for consideration. I can promise that."

"The second, that you will allow me sometimes, say every Monday morning, at nine o'clock — habit again — I must be business-like," said the gentleman, with a whimsical inclination to quarrel with himself on that head, "in walking past, to see you at the door or window. I don't ask to come in, as your brother will be gone out at that hour. I don't ask to speak to you. I merely ask to see, for the satisfaction of my own mind, that you are well, and without intrusion to remind you, by the sight of me, that you have a friend — an elderly friend, gray-haired already, and fast growing grayer — whom you may ever command."

The cordial face looked up in his; confided in it; and promised.

"I understand, as before," said the gentleman, rising, "that you purpose not to mention my visit to John Carker, lest he should be at all distressed

by my acquaintance with his history. I am glad of
it, for it is out of the ordinary course of things, and
—habit again!" said the gentleman, checking himself impatiently, "as if there were no better course
than the ordinary course!"

With that he turned to go, and walking, bareheaded, to the outside of the little porch, took leave
of her with such a happy mixture of unconstrained
respect and unaffected interest as no breeding could
have taught, no truth mistrusted, and nothing but a
pure and single heart expressed.

Many half-forgotten emotions were awakened in
the sister's mind by this visit. It was so very long
since any other visitor had crossed their threshold;
it was so very long since any voice of sympathy had
made sad music in her ears; that the stranger's figure remained present to her hours afterwards, when
she sat at the window, plying her needle; and his
words seemed newly spoken, again and again. He
had touched the spring that opened her whole life;
and if she lost him for a short space, it was only
among the many shapes of the one great recollection
of which that life was made.

Musing and working by turns; now constraining
herself to be steady at her needle for a long time
together, and now letting her work fall, unregarded,
on her lap, and straying wheresoever her busier
thoughts led, Harriet Carker found the hours glide
by her, and the day steal on. The morning, which
had been bright and clear, gradually became over-
cast; a sharp wind set in; the rain fell heavily;
and a dark mist, drooping over the distant town,
hid it from the view.

She often looked with compassion, at such a time,

upon the stragglers who came wandering into London by the great highway hard by, and who, footsore and weary, and gazing fearfully at the huge town before them, as if foreboding that their misery there would be but as a drop of water in the sea, or as a grain of sea-sand on the shore, went shrinking on, cowering before the angry weather, and looking as if the very elements rejected them. Day after day, such travellers crept past, but always, as she thought, in one direction — always towards the town. Swallowed up in one phase or other of its immensity, towards which they seemed impelled by a desperate fascination, they never returned. Food for the hospitals, the churchyards, the prison's, the river, fever, madness, vice, and death, — they passed on to the monster, roaring in the distance, and were lost.

The chill wind was howling, and the rain was falling, and the day was darkening moodily, when Harriet, raising her eyes from the work on which she had long since been engaged with unremitting constancy, saw one of these travellers approaching.

A woman. A solitary woman of some thirty years of age; tall; well formed; handsome; miserably dressed; the soil of many country roads in varied weather — dust, chalk, clay, gravel — clotted on her gray cloak by the streaming wet; no bonnet on her head, nothing to defend her rich black hair from the rain but a torn handkerchief; with the fluttering ends of which, and with her hair, the wind blinded her so that she often stopped to push them back, and look upon the way she was going.

She was in the act of doing so when Harriet observed her. As her hands, parting on her sunburnt forehead, swept across her face, and threw aside the

hindrances that encroached upon it, there was a reckless and regardless beauty in it: a dauntless and
depraved indifference to more than weather : a carelessness of what was cast upon her bare head from
heaven or earth : that, coupled with her misery and
loneliness, touched the heart of her fellow-woman.
She thought of all that was perverted and debased
within her, no less than without : of modest graces
of the mind, hardened and steeled, like these attractions of the person; of the many gifts of the Crea-
tor flung to the winds like the wild hair; of all the
beautiful ruin upon which the storm was beating and
the night was coming.

Thinking of this, she did not turn away with a
delicate indignation — too many of her own compas-
sionate and tender sex too often do — but pitied her.

Her fallen sister came on, looking far before her,
trying with her eager eyes to pierce the mist in
which the city was enshrouded, and glancing, now
and then, from side to side, with the bewildered and
uncertain aspect of a stranger. Though her tread
was bold and courageous, she was fatigued, and
after a moment of irresolution, sat down upon a
heap of stones; seeking no shelter from the rain,
but letting it rain on her as it would.

She was now opposite the house. Raising her
head after resting it for a moment on both hands,
her eyes met those of Harriet.

In a moment Harriet was at the door; and the
other, rising from her seat at her beck, came slowly,
and with no conciliatory look, towards her.

"Why do you rest in the rain?" said Harriet
gently.

"Because I have no other resting-place," was the
reply.

"But there are many places of shelter near here. This," referring to the little porch, "is better than where you were. You are very welcome to rest here."

The wanderer looked at her, in doubt and surprise, but without any expression of thankfulness; and sitting down, and taking off one of her worn shoes to beat out the fragments of stone and dust that were inside, showed that her foot was cut and bleeding.

Harriet uttering an expression of pity, the traveller looked up with a contemptuous and incredulous smile.

"Why, what's a torn foot to such as me ?" she said. "And what's a torn foot, in such as me, to such as you ?"

"Come in and wash it," answered Harriet mildly, "and let me give you something to bind it up."

The woman caught her arm, and, drawing it before her own eyes, hid them against it, and wept. Not like a woman, but like a stern man surprised into that weakness; with a violent heaving of her breast, and struggle for recovery, that showed how unusual the emotion was with her.

She submitted to be led into the house, and, evidently more in gratitude than in any care for herself, washed and bound the injured place. Harriet then put before her fragments of her own frugal dinner, and when she had eaten of them, though sparingly, besought her, before resuming her road (which she showed her anxiety to do), to dry her clothes before the fire. Again, more in gratitude than with any evidence of concern in her own behalf, she sat down in front of it, and unbinding the

handkerchief about her head, and letting her thick
wet hair fall down below her waist, sat drying it
with the palms of her hands, and looking at the
blaze.

"I dare say you are thinking," she said, lifting
her head suddenly, "that I used to be handsome
once. I believe I was—I know I was. Look
here!"

She held up her hair roughly with both hands;
seizing it as if she would have torn it out; then,
threw it down again, and flung it back as though it
were a heap of serpents.

"Are you a stranger in this place?" asked Harriet.

"A stranger!" she returned, stopping between
each short reply, and looking at the fire. "Yes.
Ten or a dozen years a stranger. I have had no
almanac where I have been. Ten or a dozen years.
I don't know this part. It's much altered since I
went away."

"Have you been far?"

"Very far. Months upon months over the sea,
and far away even then. I have been where con-
victs go," she added, looking full upon her enter-
tainer. "I have been one myself."

"Heaven help you and forgive you!" was the
gentle answer.

"Ah! Heaven help me and forgive me!" she
returned, nodding her head at the fire. "If man
would help some of us a little more, God would
forgive us all the sooner, perhaps."

But she was softened by the earnest manner, and
the cordial face so full of mildness and so free from
judgment of her, and said, less hardily,—

"We may be about the same age, you and I. If

I am older, it is not above a year or two. Oh, think of that!"

She opened her arms, as though the exhibition of her outward form would show the moral wretch she was; and letting them drop at her sides, hung down her head.

"There is nothing we may not hope to repair; it is never too late to amend," said Harriet. "You are penitent—"

"No," she answered. "I am not! I can't be. I am no such thing. Why should *I* be penitent, and all the world go free? They talk to me of my penitence. Who's penitent for the wrongs that have been done to me?"

She rose up, bound her handkerchief about her head, and turned to move away.

"Where are you going?" said Harriet.

"Yonder," she answered, pointing with her hand. "To London."

"Have you any home to go to?"

"I think I have a mother. She's as much a mother as her dwelling is a home," she answered with a bitter laugh.

"Take this," cried Harriet, putting money in her hand. "Try to do well. It is very little, but for one day it may keep you from harm."

"Are you married?" said the other faintly, as she took it.

"No. I live here with my brother. We have not much to spare, or I would give you more."

"Will you let me kiss you?"

Seeing no scorn or repugnance in her face, the object of her charity bent over her as she asked the question, and pressed her lips against her cheek.

Once more she caught her arm, and covered her eyes with it; and then was gone.

Gone into the deepening night, and howling wind, and pelting rain; urging her way on towards the mist-enshrouded city, where the blurred lights gleamed; and with her black hair and disordered headgear fluttering round her reckless face.

CHAPTER XIV.

ANOTHER MOTHER AND DAUGHTER.

In an ugly and dark room, an old woman, ugly and dark too, sat listening to the wind and rain, and crouching over a meagre fire. More constant to the last-named occupation than the first, she never changed her attitude, unless, when any stray drops of rain fell hissing on the smouldering embers, to raise her head with an awakened attention to the whistling and pattering outside, and gradually to let it fall again lower and lower and lower as she sunk into a brooding state of thought, in which the noises of the night were as indistinctly regarded as is the monotonous rolling of a sea by one who sits in contemplation on its shore.

There was no light in the room save that which the fire afforded. Glaring sullenly from time to time like the eye of a fierce beast half asleep, it revealed no objects that needed to be jealous of a better display. A heap of rags, a heap of bones, a wretched bed, two or three mutilated chairs or stools, the black walls and blacker ceiling, were all its winking brightness shone upon. As the old woman, with a gigantic and distorted image of herself, thrown half upon the wall behind her, half

upon the roof above, sat bending over the few loose
bricks within which it was pent, on the damp hearth
of the chimney — for there was no stove — she
looked as if she were watching at some witch's
altar for a favorable token; and but that the movement of her chattering jaws and trembling chin was
too frequent and too fast for the slow flickering of
the fire, it would have seemed an illusion wrought
by the light, as it came and went, upon a face as
motionless as the form to which it belonged.

If Florence could have stood within the room,
and looked upon the original of the shadow thrown
upon the wall and roof, as it cowered thus over the
fire, a glance might have sufficed to recall the figure
of Good Mrs. Brown; notwithstanding that her
childish recollection of that terrible old woman was
as grotesque and exaggerated a presentment of the
truth, perhaps, as the shadow on the wall. But
Florence was not there to look on; and Good Mrs.
Brown remained unrecognized, and sat staring at
her fire, unobserved.

Attracted by a louder sputtering than usual, as
the rain came hissing down the chimney in a little
stream, the old woman raised her head impatiently,
to listen afresh. And this time she did not drop it
again; for there was a hand upon the door, and a
footstep in the room.

"Who's that?" she said, looking over her shoulder.

"One who brings you news," was the answer in a
woman's voice.

"News? Where from?"

"From abroad."

"From beyond seas?" cried the old woman, starting up.

"Ay, from beyond seas."

The old woman raked the fire together hurriedly, and going close to her visitor, who had entered and shut the door, and who now stood in the middle of the room, put her hand upon the drenched cloak, and turned the unresisting figure, so as to have it in the full light of the fire. She did not find what she had expected, whatever that might be; for she let the cloak go again, and uttered a querulous cry of disappointment and misery.

"What is the matter?" asked her visitor.

"Oho! Oho!" cried the old woman, turning her face upward, with a terrible howl.

"What is the matter?" asked the visitor again.

"It's not my gal!" cried the old woman, tossing up her arms, and clasping her hands above her head. "Where's my Alice? Where's my handsome daughter? They've been the death of her!"

"They've not been the death of her yet, if your name's Marwood," said the visitor.

"Have you seen my gal, then?" cried the old woman. "Has she wrote to me?"

"She said you couldn't read," returned the other.

"No more I can!" exclaimed the old woman, wringing her hands.

"Have you no light here?" said the other, looking round the room.

The old woman, mumbling and shaking her head, and muttering to herself about her handsome daughter, brought a candle from a cupboard in the corner, and thrusting it into the fire with a trembling hand, lighted it with some difficulty, and set it on the table. Its dirty wick burnt dimly at first, being choked in its own grease; and when the bleared eyes and failing sight of the old woman could distinguish anything by its light, her visitor was sitting with her arms folded, her eyes turned downwards, and a handkerchief she had worn upon her head lying on the table by her side.

"She sent to me by word of mouth, then, my gal, Alice?" mumbled the old woman after waiting for some moments. "What did she say?"

"Look," returned the visitor.

The old woman repeated the word in a scared, uncertain way; and shading her eyes, looked at the speaker, round the room, and at the speaker once again.

"Alice said, 'Look again, mother;'" and the speaker fixed her eyes upon her.

Again the old woman looked round the room, and at her visitor, and round the room once more. Hastily seizing the candle, and rising from her seat, she held it to the visitor's face, uttered a loud cry, set down the light, and fell upon her neck!

"It's my gal! It's my Alice! It's my handsome daughter, living and come back!" screamed the old woman, rocking herself to and fro upon the breast that coldly suffered her embrace. "It's my gal! It's my Alice! It's my handsome daughter living and come back!" she screamed again, dropping on the floor before her, clasping her knees, laying her head against them, and still rocking herself to and fro with every frantic demonstration of which her vitality was capable.

"Yes, mother," returned Alice, stooping forward for a moment, and kissing her, but endeavoring even in the act to disengage herself from her embrace. "I am here at last. Let go, mother; let go. Get up and sit in your chair. What good does this do ? "

" She's come back harder than she went ! " cried the mother, looking up in her face, and still holding to her knees. " She don't care for me ! after all these years, and all the wretched life I've led ! "

" Why, mother ! " said Alice, shaking her ragged skirts to detach the old woman from them, " there are two sides to that. There have been years for me as well as you, and there has been wretchedness for me as well as you. Get up, get up ! "

Her mother rose, and cried, and wrung her hands, and stood at a little distance gazing on her. Then she took the candle again, and going round her, surveyed her from head to foot, making a low moaning all the time. Then she put the candle down, resumed her chair, and beating her hands together to a kind of weary tune, and rolling herself from side to side, continued moaning and wailing to herself.

Alice got up, took off her wet cloak, and laid it aside. That done, she sat down as before, and with her arms folded, and her eyes gazing at the fire, remained silently listening with a contemptuous face to her old mother's inarticulate complainings.

" Did you expect to see me return as youthful as I went away, mother ? " she said at length, turning her eyes upon the old woman. " Did you think a foreign life, like mine, was good for good looks ? One would believe so to hear you ! "

" It ain't that ! " cried the mother. " *She* knows it ! "

" What is it, then ? " returned the daughter. " It

had best be something that don't last, mother, or my way out is easier than my way in."

"Hear that!" exclaimed the mother. "After all these years she threatens to desert me in the moment of her coming back again!"

"I tell you, mother, for the second time, there have been years for me as well as you," said Alice. "Come back harder? Of course I have come back harder. What else did you expect?"

"Harder to me! To her **own** dear mother!" cried the old woman.

"I don't know who began to harden me, if my own dear mother didn't," she returned, sitting with her folded arms, and knitted brows, and compressed lips, as if she were bent on excluding by force every softer feeling from her breast. "Listen, mother, to a word or two. If we understand each other now, we shall not fall out any more, perhaps. I went away a girl, and have come back a woman. I went away undutiful enough, and have come back no better, you may swear. But have you been very dutiful to me?"

"I!" cried the old woman. "To my own gal! A mother dutiful to her own child!"

"It sounds unnatural, don't it?" returned the daughter, looking coldly on her with her stern, regardless, hardy, beautiful face; "but I have thought of it sometimes, in the course of *my* lone years, till I have got used to it. I have heard some talk about duty, first and last; but it has always been of my duty to other people. I have wondered now and then — to pass away the time — whether no one ever owed any duty to me."

Her mother sat mowing, and mumbling, and

shaking her head, but whether angrily, or remorsefully, or in denial, or only in her physical infirmity, did not appear.

"There was a child called Alice Marwood," said the daughter with a laugh, and looking down at herself in terrible derision of herself, "born among poverty and neglect, and nursed in it. Nobody taught her, nobody stepped forward to help her, nobody cared for her."

"Nobody!" echoed the mother, pointing to herself, and striking her breast.

"The only care she knew," returned the daughter, "was to be beaten, and stinted, and abused sometimes: and she might have done better without that. She lived in homes like this, and in the streets, with a crowd of little wretches like herself; and yet she brought good looks out of this childhood. So much the worse for her. She had better have been hunted and worried to death for ugliness."

"Go on! go on!" exclaimed the mother.

"I am going on," returned the daughter. "There was a girl called Alice Marwood. She was handsome. She was taught too late, and taught all wrong. She was too well cared for, too well trained, too well helped on, too much looked after. You were very fond of her — you were better off then. What came to that girl comes to thousands every year. It was only ruin, and she was born to it."

"After all these years!" whined the old woman. "My gal begins with this."

"She'll soon have ended," said the daughter. "There was a criminal called Alice Marwood — a girl still, but deserted and an outcast. And she was tried, and she was sentenced. And Lord, how the gentlemen in the court talked about it! and how grave the judge was on her duty, and on her having perverted the gifts of nature — as if he didn't know better than anybody there that they had been made curses to her! — and how he preached about the strong arm of the Law — so very strong to save her, when she was an innocent and helpless little wretch! and how solemn and religious it all was! I have thought of that many times since, to be sure!"

She folded her arms tightly on her breast, and laughed in a tone that made the howl of the old woman musical.

"So Alice Marwood was transported, mother," she pursued, "and was sent to learn her duty where there was twenty times less duty, and more wickedness, and wrong, and infamy, than here. And Alice Marwood is come back a woman. Such a woman as she ought to be, after all this. In good time there will be more solemnity, and more fine talk, and more strong arm, most likely, and there will be an end of her; but the gentlemen needn't be afraid of being thrown out of work. There's crowds of little wretches, boy and girl, growing up in any of the streets they live in, that'll keep them to it till they've made their fortunes."

The old woman leaned her elbows on the table, and resting her face upon her two hands, made a show of being in great distress — or really was, perhaps.

"There! I have done, mother," said the daughter, with a motion of her head, as if in dismissal of the subject. "I have said enough. Don't let you and

I talk of being dutiful, whatever we do. Your childhood was like mine, I suppose. So much the worse for both of us. I don't want to blame you, or to defend myself; why should I? That's all over, long ago. But I am a woman — not a girl now — and you and I needn't make a show of our history, like the gentlemen in the court. *We* know all about it well enough."

Lost and degraded as she was, there was a beauty in her, both of face and form, which, even in its worst expression, could not but be recognized as such by any one regarding her with the least attention. As she subsided into silence, and her face, which had been harshly agitated, quieted down; while her dark eyes, fixed upon the fire, exchanged the reckless light that had animated them, for one that was softened by something like sorrow; there shone through all her wayworn misery and fatigue a ray of the departed radiance of the fallen angel.

Her mother, after watching her for some time without speaking, ventured to steal her withered hand a little nearer to her across the table; and finding that she permitted this, to touch her face, and smooth her hair. With the feeling, as it seemed, that the old woman was at least sincere in this show of interest, Alice made no movement to check her; so, advancing by degrees, she bound up her daughter's hair afresh, took off her wet shoes, if they deserved the name, spread something dry upon her shoulders, and hovered humbly about, muttering to herself, as she recognized her old features and expression more and more.

"You are very poor, mother, I see," said Alice, looking round, when she had sat thus for some time.

"Bitter poor, my deary," replied the old woman.

She admired her daughter, and was afraid of her. Perhaps her admiration, such as it was, had originated long ago, when she first found anything that was beautiful appearing in the midst of the squalid fight of her existence. Perhaps her fear was referable, in some sort, to the retrospect she had so lately heard. Be this as it might, she stood, submissively and deferentially, before her child, and inclined her head, as if in a pitiful entreaty to be spared any further reproach.

"How have you lived?"

"By begging, my deary."

"And pilfering, mother?"

"Sometimes, Ally — in a very small way. I am old and timid. I have taken trifles from children now and then, my deary, but not often. I have tramped about the country, pet, and I know what I know. I have watched."

"Watched?" returned the daughter, looking at her.

"I have hung about a family, my deary," said the mother, even more humbly and submissively than before.

"What family?"

"Hush, darling. Don't be angry with me; I did it for the love of you. In memory of my poor gal beyond seas." She put out her hand deprecatingly, and drawing it back again, laid it on her lips.

"Years ago, my deary," she pursued, glancing timidly at the attentive and stern face opposed to her, "I came across his little child by chance."

"Whose child?"

"Not his, Alice deary; don't look at me like that;

not his. How could it be his? You know he has none."

"Whose, then?" returned the daughter. "You said his."

"Hush, Ally; you frighten me, deary. Mr. Dombey's — only Mr. Dombey's. Since then, darling, I have seen them often. I have seen *him*."

In uttering this last word, the old woman shrunk and recoiled, as if with a sudden fear that her daughter would strike her. But though the daughter's face was fixed upon her, and expressed the most vehement passion, she remained still: except that she clenched her arms tighter and tighter within each other, on her bosom, as if to restrain them by that means from doing an injury to herself, or some one else, in the blind fury of the wrath that suddenly possessed her.

"Little he thought who I was!" said the old woman, shaking her clenched hand.

"And little he cared!" muttered her daughter between her teeth.

"But there we were," said the old woman, "face to face. I spoke to him, and he spoke to me. I sat and watched him as he went away down a long grove of trees; and, at every step he took, I cursed him soul and body."

"He will thrive in spite of that," returned the daughter disdainfully.

"Ay, he is thriving," said the mother.

She held her peace; for the face and form before her were unshaped by rage. It seemed as if the bosom would burst with the emotions that strove within it. The effort that constrained and held it pent up was no less formidable than the rage itself:

no less bespeaking the violent and dangerous character of the woman who made it. But it succeeded, and she asked, after a silence, —

"Is he married ?"

"No, deary," said the mother.

"Going to be ?"

"Not that I know of, deary. But his master and friend is married. Oh, we may give him joy! We may give 'em all joy!" cried the old woman, hugging herself with her lean arms in her exultation. "Nothing but joy to us will come of that marriage. Mind me!"

The daughter looked at her for an explanation.

"But you are wet and tired: hungry and thirsty," said the old woman, hobbling to the cupboard; "and there's little here, and little" — diving down into her pocket, and jingling a few halfpence on the table — "little here. Have you any money, Alice deary ?"

The covetous, sharp, eager face with which she asked the question and looked on, as her daughter took out of her bosom the little gift she had so lately received, told almost as much of the history of this parent and child as the child herself had told in words.

"Is that all ?" said the mother.

"I have no more. I should not have this, but for charity."

"But for charity, eh, deary ?" said the old woman, bending greedily over the table to look at the money, which she appeared distrustful of her daughter's still retaining in her hand, and gazing on. "Humph! six and six is twelve, and six eighteen — so — we must make the most of it. I'll go buy something to eat and drink."

With greater alacrity than might have been expected in one of her appearance — for age and misery seemed to have made her as decrepit as ugly — she began to occupy her trembling hands in tying an old bonnet on her head, and folding a torn shawl about herself : still eying the money in her daughter's hand with the same sharp desire.

"What joy is to come to us of this marriage, mother?" asked the daughter. "You have not told me that."

"The joy," she replied, attiring herself with fumbling fingers, "of no love at all, and much pride and hate, my deary. The joy of confusion and strife among 'em, proud as they are, and of danger — danger, Alice!"

"What danger?"

"I have seen what I have seen. I know what I know!" chuckled the mother. "Let some look to it. Let some be upon their guard. My gal may keep good company yet!"

Then, seeing that, in the wondering earnestness with which her daughter regarded her, her hand involuntarily closed upon the money, the old woman made more speed to secure it, and hurriedly added, "But I'll go buy something, I'll go buy something."

As she stood with her hand stretched out before her daughter, her daughter, glancing again at the money, put it to her lips before parting with it.

"What, Ally! Do you kiss it?" chuckled the old woman. "That's like me — I often do. Oh, it's so good to us!" squeezing her own tarnished halfpence up to her bag of a throat, "so good to us in everything but not coming in heaps!"

"I kiss it, mother," said the daughter, "or I did then — I don't know that I ever did before — for the giver's sake."

"The giver, eh, deary?" retorted the old woman, whose dimmed eyes glistened as she took it. "Ay! I'll kiss it for the giver's sake, too, when the giver can make it go farther. But I'll go spend it, deary. I'll be back directly."

"You seem to say you know a great deal, mother," said the daughter, following her to the door with her eyes. "You have grown very wise since we parted."

"Know!" croaked the old woman, coming back a step or two. "I know more than you think. I know more than _he_ thinks, deary, as I'll tell you by and by. I know all about him."

The daughter smiled incredulously.

"I know of his brother, Alice," said the old woman, stretching out her neck with a leer of malice absolutely frightful, "who might have been where you have been — for stealing money — and who lives with his sister, over yonder, by the north road out of London."

"Where?"

"By the north road out of London, deary. You shall see the house, if you like. It ain't much to boast of, genteel as his own is. No, no, no," cried the old woman, shaking her head and laughing; for her daughter had started up, "not now; it's too far off; it's by the milestone, where the stones are heaped; — to-morrow, deary, if it's fine, and you are in the humor. But I'll go spend —"

"Stop!" and the daughter flung herself upon her, with her former passion raging like a fire. "The sister is a fair-faced devil, with brown hair?"

The old woman, amazed and terrified, nodded her head.

"I see the shadow of him in her face! It's a red house, standing by itself. Before the door there is a small green porch."

Again the old woman nodded.

"In which I sat to-day! Give me back the money."

"Alice! Deary!"

"Give me back the money, or you'll be hurt."

She forced it from the old woman's hand as she spoke, and, utterly indifferent to her complainings and entreaties, threw on the garments she had taken off, and hurried out with headlong speed.

The mother followed, limping after her as she could, and expostulating with no more effect upon her than upon the wind and rain and darkness that encompassed them. Obdurate and fierce in her own purpose, and indifferent to all besides, the daughter defied the weather and the distance, as if she had known no travel or fatigue, and made for the house where she had been relieved. After some quarter of an hour's walking, the old woman, spent and out of breath, ventured to hold by her skirts; but she ventured no more, and they travelled on in silence through the wet and gloom. If the mother now and then uttered a word of complaint, she stifled it, lest her daughter should break away from her and leave her behind; and the daughter was dumb.

It was within an hour or so of midnight when they left the regular streets behind them, and

entered on the deeper gloom of that neutral ground
where the house was situated. The town lay in the
distance, lurid and lowering; the bleak wind howled
over the open space; all around was black, wild,
desolate.

"This is a fit place for me!" said the daughter,
stopping to look back. "I thought so, when I was
here before, to-day."

"Alice, my deary," cried the mother, pulling her
gently by the skirt. "Alice!"

"What now, mother?"

"Don't give the money back, my darling; please
don't. We can't afford it. We want supper, deary.
Money is money, whoever gives it. Say what you
will, but keep the money."

"See there!" was all the daughter's answer.
"That is the house I mean. Is that it?"

The old woman nodded in the affirmative; and a
few more paces brought them to the threshold.
There was the light of fire and candle in the room
where Alice had sat to dry her clothes; and, on her
knocking at the door, John Carker appeared from
that room.

He was surprised to see such visitors at such an
hour, and asked Alice what she wanted.

"I want your sister," she said. "The woman
who gave me money to-day."

At the sound of her raised voice Harriet came
out.

"Oh!" said Alice. "You are here! Do you
remember me?"

"Yes," she answered, wondering.

The face that had humbled itself before her
looked on her now with such invincible hatred and

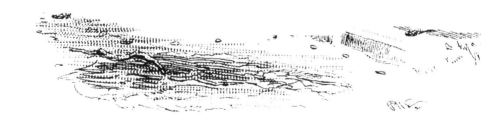

defiance; and the hand that had gently touched her arm was clenched with such a show of evil purpose, as if it would gladly strangle her; that she drew close to her brother for protection.

"That I could speak with you, and not know you! That I could come near you, and not feel what blood was running in your veins, by the tingling of my own!" said Alice with a menacing gesture.

"What do you mean? What have I done?"

"Done!" returned the other. "You have sat me by your fire; you have given me food and money; you have bestowed your compassion on me! You! whose name I spit upon!"

The old woman, with a malevolence that made her ugliness quite awful, shook her withered hand at the brother and sister in confirmation of her daughter, but plucked her by the skirts again, nevertheless, imploring her to keep the money.

"If I dropped a tear upon your hand, may it wither it up! If I spoke a gentle word in your hearing, may it deafen you! If I touched you with my lips, may the touch be poison to you! A curse upon this roof that gave me shelter! Sorrow and shame upon your head! Ruin upon all belonging to you!"

As she said the words, she threw the money down upon the ground, and spurned it with her foot.

"I tread it in the dust: I wouldn't take it if it paved my way to heaven! I wish the bleeding foot that brought me here to-day had rotted off, before it led me to your house!"

Harriet, pale and trembling, restrained her brother, and suffered her to go on uninterrupted.

"It was well that I should be pitied and forgiven by you, or any one of your name, in the first hour of my return! It was well that you should act the kind good lady to me! I'll thank you when I die; I'll pray for you, and all your race, you may be sure!"

With a fierce action of her hand, as if she sprinkled hatred on the ground, and with it devoted those who were standing there to destruction, she looked up once at the black sky, and strode out into the wild night.

The mother, who had plucked at her skirts again and again in vain, and had eyed the money lying on the threshold with an absorbing greed that seemed to concentrate her faculties upon it, would have prowled about until the house was dark, and then groped in the mire on the chance of repossessing herself of it. But the daughter drew her away, and they set forth straight, on their return to their dwelling; the old woman whimpering and bemoaning their loss upon the road, and fretfully bewailing, as openly as she dared, the undutiful conduct of her handsome girl in depriving her of a supper on the very first night of their reunion.

Supperless to bed she went, saving for a few coarse fragments; and those she sat mumbling and munching over a scrap of fire, long after her undutiful daughter lay asleep.

Were this miserable mother, and this miserable daughter, only the reduction to their lowest grade of certain social vices sometimes prevailing higher up? In this round world of many circles within circles, do we make a weary journey from the high grade to the low, to find at last that they lie close together, that the two extremes touch, and that our journey's end is but our starting-place? Allowing for great difference of stuff and texture, was the pattern of this woof repeated among gentle blood at all?

Say, Edith Dombey! And Cleopatra, best of mothers, let us have your testimony!

CHAPTER XV.

THE dark blot on the street is gone. Mr. Dombey's mansion, if it be a gap among the other houses any longer, is only so because it is not to be vied with in its brightness, and haughtily casts them off. The saying is, that home is home, be it never so homely. If it hold good in the opposite contingency, and home is home, be it never so stately, what an altar to the Household Gods is raised up here!

Lights are sparkling in the windows this evening, and the ruddy glow of fires is warm and bright upon the hangings and soft carpets, and the dinner waits to be served, and the dinner-table is handsomely set forth, though only for four persons, and the sideboard is cumbrous with plate. It is the first time that the house has been arranged for occupation since its late changes, and the happy pair are looked for every minute.

Only second to the wedding morning, in the interest and expectation it engenders among the household, is this evening of the coming home. Mrs. Perch is in the kitchen taking tea; and has made the tour of the establishment, and priced the silks and damasks by the yard, and exhausted every interjection in the dictionary, and out of it, expressive of admiration and wonder. The upholsterer's foreman, who has left his hat, with a pocket-handkerchief in it, both smelling strongly of varnish, under a chair in the hall, lurks about the house, gazing upward at the cornices, and downward at the carpets, and occasionally, in a silent transport of enjoyment, taking a rule out of his pocket, and skirmishingly measuring expensive objects, with unutterable feelings. Cook is in high spirits, and says, Give *her* a place where there's plenty of company (as she'll bet you sixpence there will be now), for she is of a lively disposition, and she always was from a child, and she don't mind who knows it; which sentiment elicits from the breast of Mrs. Perch a responsive murmur of support and approbation. All the housemaid hopes is, happiness for 'em — but marriage is a lottery, and the more she thinks about it, the more she feels the independence and the safety of a single life. Mr. Towlinson is saturnine and grim, and says that's his opinion too, and give him war besides, and down with the French — for this young man has a general impression that every foreigner is a Frenchman, and must be by the laws of nature.

At each new sound of wheels they all stop, whatever they are saying, and listen; and more than once there is a general starting up and a cry of "Here they are!" But here they are not yet; and cook begins to mourn over the dinner, which has been put back twice, and the upholsterer's foreman still goes lurking about the rooms, undisturbed in his blissful reverie.

Florence is ready to receive her father and her new mamma. Whether the emotions that are throbbing in her breast originate in pleasure or in pain she hardly knows. But the fluttering heart sends added color to her cheeks, and brightness to her eyes; and they say downstairs, drawing their heads together — for they always speak softly when they speak of her — how beautiful Miss Florence looks to-night, and what a sweet young lady she has grown, poor dear! A pause succeeds; and then cook, feeling, as president, that her sentiments are waited for, wonders whether — and there stops. The housemaid wonders too, and so does Mrs. Perch, who has the happy social faculty of always wondering when other people wonder, without being at all particular what she wonders at. Mr. Towlinson, who now descries an opportunity of bringing down the spirits of the ladies to his own level, says, Wait and see: he wishes some people were well out of this. Cook leads a sigh then, and a murmur of "Ah, it's a strange world, — it is indeed!" and, when it has gone round the table, adds persuasively, "But Miss Florence can't well be the worse for any change, Tom." Mr. Towlinson's rejoinder, pregnant with frightful meaning, is, "Oh, can't she, though!" and sensible that a mere man can scarcely be more prophetic, or improve upon that, he holds his peace.

Mrs. Skewton, prepared to greet her darling daughter and dear son-in-law with open arms, is appropriately attired for that purpose in a very youthful costume, with short sleeves. At present, however, her ripe charms are blooming in the shade of her own apartments, whence she has not emerged since she took possession of them a few hours ago, and where she is fast growing fretful, on account of the postponement of dinner. The maid who ought to

be a skeleton, but is in truth a buxom damsel, is, on
the other hand, in a most amiable state; considering
her quarterly stipend much safer than heretofore,
and foreseeing a great improvement in her board
and lodging.

Where are the happy pair for whom this brave
home is waiting? Do steam, tide, wind, and horses
all abate their speed, to linger on such happiness?
Does the swarm of loves and graces hovering about
them retard their progress by its numbers? Are
there so many flowers in their happy path, that
they can scarcely move along, without entanglement
in thornless roses and sweetest brier?

They are here at last! The noise of wheels is
heard, grows louder, and a carriage drives up to the
door! A thundering knock from the obnoxious foreigner anticipates the rush of Mr. Towlinson and
party to open it; and Mr. Dombey and his bride
alight, and walk in arm-and-arm.

"My sweetest Edith!" cries an agitated voice
upon the stairs. "My dearest Dombey!" and the
short sleeves wreathe themselves about the happy
couple in turn, and embrace them.

Florence had come down to the hall too, but did
not advance: reserving her timid welcome until
these nearer and dearer transports should subside.
But the eyes of Edith sought her out upon the
threshold; and, dismissing her sensitive parent
with a slight kiss on her cheek, she hurried on to
Florence and embraced her.

"How do you do, Florence?" said Mr. Dombey,
putting out his hand.

As Florence, trembling, raised it to her lips, she
met his glance. The look was cold and distant

enough, but it stirred her heart to think that she observed in it something more of interest than he had ever shown before. It even expressed a kind of faint surprise, and not a disagreeable surprise, at sight of her. She dared not raise her eyes to his any more; but she felt that he looked at her once again, and not less favorably. Oh! what a thrill of joy shot through her, awakened by even this intangible and baseless confirmation of her hope that she would learn to win him through her new and beautiful mamma!

"You will not be long dressing, Mrs. Dombey, I presume?" said Mr. Dombey.

"I shall be ready immediately."

"Let them send up dinner in a quarter of an hour."

With that Mr. Dombey stalked away to his own dressing-room, and Mrs. Dombey went upstairs to hers. Mrs. Skewton and Florence repaired to the drawing-room, where that excellent mother considered it incumbent on her to shed a few irrepressible tears, supposed to be forced from her by her daughter's felicity; and which she was still drying, very gingerly, with a laced corner of her pocket-handkerchief, when her son-in-law appeared.

"And how, my dearest Dombey, did you find that delightfullest of cities, Paris?" she asked, subduing her emotion.

"It was cold," returned Mr. Dombey.

"Gay as ever," said Mrs. Skewton, "of course."

"Not particularly. I thought it dull," said Mr. Dombey.

"Fie, my dearest Dombey!" archly; "dull!"

"It made that impression upon me, madam," said

Mr. Dombey with grave politeness. "I believe Mrs. Dombey found it dull too. She mentioned once or twice that she thought it so."

"Why, you naughty girl!" cried Mrs. Skewton, rallying her dear child, who now entered, "what dreadfully heretical things have you been saying about Paris?"

Edith raised her eyebrows with an air of weariness; and passing the folding doors, which were thrown open to display the suite of rooms in their new and handsome garniture, and barely glancing at them as she passed, sat down by Florence.

"My dear Dombey," said Mrs. Skewton, "how charmingly these people have carried out every idea that we hinted! They have made a perfect palace of the house, positively."

"It is handsome," said Mr. Dombey, looking round. "I directed that no expense should be spared; and all that money could do has been done, I believe."

"And what can it not do, dear Dombey?" observed Cleopatra.

"It is powerful, madam," said Mr. Dombey.

He looked in his solemn way towards his wife, but not a word said she.

"I hope, Mrs. Dombey," addressing her after a moment's silence, with especial distinctness, "that these alterations meet with your approval?"

"They are as handsome as they can be," she returned with haughty carelessness. "They should be so, of course. And I suppose they are."

An expression of scorn was habitual to the proud face, and seemed inseparable from it; but the contempt with which it received any appeal to admiration, respect, or consideration on the ground of his riches, no matter how slight or ordinary in itself, was a new and different expression, unequalled in intensity by any other of which it was capable. Whether Mr. Dombey, wrapped in his own greatness, was at all aware of this, or no, there had not been wanting opportunities already for his complete enlightenment; and at that moment it might have been effected by the one glance of the dark eye that lighted on him, after it had rapidly and scornfully surveyed the theme of his self-glorification. He might have read in that one glance that nothing that his wealth could do, though it were increased ten thousand fold, could win him, for its own sake, one look of softened recognition from the defiant woman linked to him, but arrayed with her whole soul against him. He might have read in that one glance that even for its sordid and mercenary influence upon herself she spurned it, while she claimed its utmost power as her right, her bargain — as the base and worthless recompense for which she had become his wife. He might have read in it that, ever baring her own head for the lightning of her own contempt and pride to strike, the most innocent allusion to the power of his riches degraded her anew, sunk her deeper in her own respect, and made the blight and waste within her more complete.

But dinner was announced, and Mr. Dombey led down Cleopatra; Edith and his daughter following. Sweeping past the gold and silver demonstration on the sideboard as if it were heaped-up dirt, and deigning to bestow no look upon the elegancies around her, she took her place at his board for the first time, and sat, like a statue, at the feast.

Mr. Dombey, being a good deal in the statue way himself, was well enough pleased to see his handsome wife immovable and proud and cold. Her deportment being always elegant and graceful, this as a general behavior was agreeable and congenial to him. Presiding, therefore, with his accustomed dignity, and not at all reflecting on his wife by any warmth or hilarity of his own, he performed his share of the honors of the table with a cool satisfaction; and the installation dinner, though not regarded downstairs as a great success, or very promising beginning, passed off, above, in a sufficiently polite, genteel, and frosty manner.

Soon after tea, Mrs. Skewton, who affected to be quite overcome and worn out by her emotions of happiness, arising in the contemplation of her dear child united to the man of her heart, but who, there is reason to suppose, found this family party somewhat dull, as she yawned for one hour continually behind her fan, retired to bed. Edith, also, silently withdrew, and came back no more. Thus, it happened that Florence, who had been upstairs to have some conversation with Diogenes, returning to the drawing-room with her little work-basket, found no one there but her father, who was walking to and fro in dreary magnificence.

"I beg your pardon. Shall I go away, papa?" said Florence faintly, hesitating at the door.

"No," returned Mr. Dombey, looking round over his shoulder; "you can come and go here, Florence, as you please. This is not my private room."

Florence entered, and sat down at a distant little table with her work; finding herself for the first time in her life — for the very first time within her memory from her infancy to that hour — alone with her father as his companion. She, his natural companion, his only child, who in her lonely life and grief had known the suffering of a breaking heart; who, in her rejected love, had never breathed his name to God at night, but with a tearful blessing, heavier on him than a curse; who had prayed to die young, so she might only die in his arms; who had, all through, repaid the agony of slight and coldness, and dislike, with patient unexacting love, excusing him, and pleading for him, like his better angel!

She trembled, and her eyes were dim. His figure seemed to grow in height and bulk before her as he paced the room: now it was all blurred and indistinct; now clear again, and plain; and now she seemed to think that this had happened, just the same, a multitude of years ago. She yearned towards him, and yet shrank from his approach. Unnatural emotion in a child, innocent of wrong! Unnatural the hand that had directed the sharp plough, which furrowed up her gentle nature for the sowing of its seeds!

Bent upon not distressing or offending him by her distress, Florence controlled herself, and sat quietly at her work. After a few more turns across and across the room, he left off pacing it; and withdrawing into a shadowy corner at some distance, where there was an easy-chair, covered his head with a handkerchief, and composed himself to sleep.

It was enough for Florence to sit there watching him; turning her eyes towards his chair from time to time; watching him with her thoughts, when her face was intent upon her work; and sorrowfully glad to think that he *could* sleep while she was there, and that he was not made restless by her strange and long-forbidden presence.

What would have been her thoughts if she had known that he was steadily regarding her; that the veil upon his face, by accident or by design, was so adjusted that his sight was free, and that it never wandered from her face an instant! That when she looked towards him, in the obscure dark corner, her speaking eyes, more earnest and pathetic in their voiceless speech than all the orators of all the world, and impeaching him more nearly in their mute address, met his, and did not know it! That when she bent her head again over her work, he drew his breath more easily, but with the same attention looked upon her still — upon her white brow and her falling hair and busy hands; and, once attracted, seemed to have no power to turn his eyes away!

And what were his thoughts meanwhile? With what emotions did he prolong the attentive gaze covertly directed on his unknown daughter? Was there reproach to him in the quiet figure and the mild eyes? Had he begun to feel her disregarded claims, and did they touch him home at last, and waken him to some sense of his cruel injustice?

There are yielding moments in the lives of the sternest and harshest men, though such men often keep their secret well. The sight of her in her beauty, almost changed into a woman without his knowledge, may have struck out some such moments even in his life of pride. Some passing thought that he had had a happy home within his reach — had had a household spirit bending at his feet —

had overlooked it in his stiff-necked, sullen arrogance, and wandered away and lost himself — may
have engendered them.   Some simple eloquence
distinctly heard, though only uttered in her eyes,
unconscious that he read them, as, "By the death-
beds I have tended, by the childhood I have suffered,
by our meeting in this dreary house at midnight, by
the cry wrung from me in the anguish of my heart,
O father, turn to me and seek a refuge in my love
before it is too late!" may have arrested them.
Meaner and lower thoughts, as that his dead boy
was now superseded by new ties, and he could forgive the having been supplanted in his affection,
may have occasioned them.   The mere association
of her as an ornament, with all the ornament and
pomp about him, may have been sufficient.   But, as
he looked, he softened to her more and more.   As
he looked, she became blended with the child he had
loved, and he could hardly separate the two.   As he
looked, he saw her for an instant by a clearer and
a brighter light, not bending over that child's pillow
as his rival — monstrous thought! — but as the
spirit of his home, and in the action tending himself no less, as he sat once more with his bowed-
down head upon his hand at the foot of the little
bed.   He felt inclined to speak to her, and call her
to him.   The words "Florence, come here!" were
rising to his lips — slowly and with difficulty, they
were so very strange — when they were checked
and stifled by a footstep on the stair.

It was his wife's.   She had exchanged her dinner
dress for a loose robe, and had unbound her hair,
which fell freely about her neck.   But this was not
the change in her that startled him.

"Florence dear," she said, "I have been looking for you everywhere."

As she sat down by the side of Florence, she stooped and kissed her hand. He hardly knew his wife. She was so changed. It was not merely that her smile was new to him — though that he had never seen; but her manner, the tone of her voice, the light of her eyes, the interest and confidence, and winning wish to please, expressed in all — this was not Edith.

"Softly, dear mamma. Papa is asleep."

It was Edith now. She looked towards the corner where was, and he knew that face and manner very well.

"I scarcely thought you could be here, Florence."

Again, how altered and how softened in an instant!

"I left here early," pursued Edith, "purposely to sit upstairs and talk with you. But, going to your room, I found my bird was flown, and I have been waiting there ever since, expecting its return."

If it had been a bird indeed, she could not have taken it more tenderly and gently to her breast than she did Florence.

"Come, dear!"

"Papa will not expect to find me, I suppose, when he wakes?" hesitated Florence.

"Do you think he will, Florence?" said Edith, looking full upon her.

Florence drooped her head, and rose, and put up her work-basket. Edith drew her hand through her arm, and they went out of the room like sisters. Her very step was different and new to him, Mr.

Dombey thought, as his eyes followed her to the door.

He sat in his shadowy corner so long, that the church clocks struck the hour three times before he moved that night. All that while his face was still intent upon the spot where Florence had been seated. The room grew darker as the candles waned and went out; but a darkness gathered on his face, exceeding any that the night could cast, and rested there.

Florence and Edith, seated before the fire in the remote room where little Paul had died, talked together for a long time. Diogenes, who was of the party, had at first objected to the admission of Edith, and, even in deference to his mistress's wish, had only permitted it under growling protest. But, emerging by little and little from the ante-room, whither he had retired in dudgeon, he soon appeared to comprehend that, with the most amiable intentions, he had made one of those mistakes which will occasionally arise in the best-regulated dogs' minds; as a friendly apology for which he stuck himself up on end between the two, in a very hot place in front of the fire, and sat panting at it, with his tongue out, and a most imbecile expression of countenance, listening to the conversation.

It turned, at first, on Florence's books and favorite pursuits, and on the manner in which she had beguiled the interval since the marriage. The last theme opened up to her a subject which lay very near her heart, and she said, with the tears starting to her eyes, —

"Oh, mamma! I have had a great sorrow since that day."

"You a great sorrow, Florence!"

"Yes. Poor Walter is drowned."

Florence spread her hands before her face, and wept with all her heart. Many as were the secret tears which Walter's fate had cost her, they flowed yet when she thought or spoke of him.

"But tell me, dear," said Edith, soothing her, "who was Walter? What was he to you?"

"He was my brother, mamma. After dear Paul died, we said we would be brother and sister. I had known him a long time — from a little child. He knew Paul, who liked him very much; Paul said, almost at the last, 'Take care of Walter, dear papa! I was fond of him!' Walter had been brought in to see him, and was there then — in this room."

"And *did* he take care of Walter?" inquired Edith sternly.

"Papa? He appointed him to go abroad. He was drowned in shipwreck on his voyage," said Florence, sobbing.

"Does he know that he is dead?" asked Edith.

"I cannot tell, mamma. I have no means of knowing. Dear mamma!" cried Florence, clinging to her as for help, and hiding her face upon her bosom, "I know that you have seen —"

"Stay! Stop, Florence!" Edith turned so pale, and spoke so earnestly, that Florence did not need her restraining hand upon her lips. "Tell me all about Walter first; let me understand this history all through."

Florence related it, and everything belonging to it, even down to the friendship of Mr. Toots, of whom she could hardly speak in her distress without

a tearful smile, although she was deeply grateful to
him.   When she had concluded her account, to the
whole of which Edith, holding her hand, listened
with close attention, and when a silence had succeeded, Edith said, —

"What is it that you know I have seen,
Florence ? "

"That I am not," said Florence, with the same
mute appeal, and the same quick concealment of
her face as before, "that I am not a favorite child,
mamma.   I never have been.   I have never known
how to be.   I have missed the way, and had no one
to show it to me.   Oh, let me learn from you how
to become dearer to papa!   Teach me! you, who
can so well!" and clinging closer to her, with some
broken, fervent words of gratitude and endearment,
Florence, relieved of her sad secret, wept long, but
not as painfully as of yore, within the encircling
arms of her new mother.

Pale, even to her lips, and with a face that strove
for composure until its proud beauty was as fixed as
death, Edith looked down upon the weeping girl,
and once kissed her.   Then gradually disengaging
herself, and putting Florence away, she said, stately
and quiet as a marble image, and in a voice that
deepened as she spoke, but had no other token of
emotion in it, —

"Florence, you do not know me!   Heaven forbid
that you should learn from me ! "

"Not learn from you ? " repeated Florence in
surprise.

"That I should teach you how to love, or be loved,
Heaven forbid!" said Edith.   "If you could teach
me, that were better ; but it is too late.   You are

dear to me, Florence. I did not think that anything could ever be so dear to me as you are in this little time."

She saw that Florence would have spoken here, so checked her with her hand and went on.

"I will be your true friend always. I will cherish you as much, if not as well, as any one in this world could. You may trust in me — I know it, and I say it, dear — with the whole confidence even of your pure heart. There are hosts of women whom he might have married, better and truer in all other respects than I am, Florence; but there is not one who could come here, his wife, whose heart could beat with greater truth to you than mine does."

"I know it, dear mamma!" cried Florence. "From that first most happy day I have known it."

"Most happy day!" Edith seemed to repeat the words involuntarily, and went on. "Though the merit is not mine, for I thought little of you until I saw you, let the undeserved reward be mine in your trust and love. And in this — in this, Florence; on the first night of my taking up my abode here; I am led on, as it is best I should be, to say it for the first and last time."

Florence, without knowing why, felt almost afraid to hear her proceed, but kept her eyes riveted on the beautiful face so fixed upon her own.

"Never seek to find in me," said Edith, laying her hand upon her breast, "what is not here. Never, if you can help it, Florence, fall off from me because it is *not* here. Little by little you will know me better, and the time will come when you will know

me as I know myself.   Then, be as lenient to me as
you can, and do not turn to bitterness the only
sweet remembrance I shall have."

The tears that were visible in her eyes, as she
kept them fixed on Florence, showed that the composed face was but as a handsome mask; but she
preserved it, and continued, —

"I *have* seen what you say, and know how true it
is.   But believe me — you will soon, if you cannot
now — there is no one on this earth less qualified to
set it right or help you, Florence, than I.   Never
ask me why, or speak to me about it, or of my husband more.   There should be, so far, a division and
a silence between us two, like the grave itself."

She sat for some time silent; Florence scarcely
venturing to breathe meanwhile, as dim and imperfect shadows of the truth, and all its daily consequences, chased each other through her terrified, yet
incredulous imagination.   Almost as soon as she
had ceased to speak, Edith's face began to subside
from its set composure to that quieter and more
relenting aspect which it usually wore when she and
Florence were alone together.   She shaded it, after
this change, with her hands; and when she arose,
and with an affectionate embrace bade Florence good-
night, went quickly, and without looking round.

But, when Florence was in bed, and the room was
dark except for the glow of the fire, Edith returned,
and saying that she could not sleep, and that her
dressing-room was lonely, drew a chair upon the
hearth, and watched the embers as they died away.
Florence watched them too from her bed, until they,
and the noble figure before them, crowned with its
flowing hair, and in its thoughtful eyes reflecting

back their light, became confused and indistinct, and finally were lost in slumber.

In her sleep, however, Florence could not lose an undefined impression of what had so recently passed. It formed the subject of her dreams, and haunted her; now in one shape, now in another; but always oppressively; and with a sense of fear. She dreamed of seeking her father in wildernesses, of following his track up fearful heights, and down into deep mines and caverns; of being charged with something that would release him from extraordinary suffering — she knew not what, or why — yet never being able to attain the goal and set him free. Then she saw him dead, upon that very bed, and in that very room, and knew that he had never loved her to the last, and fell upon his cold breast, passionately weeping. Then a prospect opened, and a river flowed, and a plaintive voice she knew cried, "It is running on, Floy! It has never stopped! You are moving with it!" And she saw him at a distance stretching out his arms towards her, while a figure, such as Walter's used to be, stood near him, awfully serene and still. In every vision Edith came and went, sometimes to her joy, sometimes to her sorrow, until they were alone upon the brink of a dark grave, and Edith pointing down, she looked and saw — what? — another Edith lying at the bottom.

In the terror of this dream, she cried out, and awoke, she thought. A soft voice seemed to whisper in her ear, "Florence, dear Florence, it is nothing but a dream!" and, stretching out her arms, she returned the caress of her new mamma, who then went out at the door in the light of the gray morn-

ing.   In a moment Florence sat up, wondering
whether this had really taken place or not; but she
was only certain that it was gray morning indeed,
and that the blackened ashes of the fire were on the
hearth, and that she was alone.

So passed the night on which the happy pair
came home.

CHAPTER XVI.

MANY succeeding days passed in like manner; except that there were numerous visits received and paid, and that Mrs. Skewton held little levees in her own apartments, at which Major Bagstock was a frequent attendant, and that Florence encountered no second look from her father, although she saw him every day. Nor had she much communication in words with her new mamma, who was imperions and proud to all the house but her — Florence could not but observe that — and who, although she always sent for her or went to her when she came home from visiting, and would always go into her room at night before retiring to rest, however late the hour, and never lost an opportunity of being with her, was often her silent and thoughtful companion for a long time together.

Florence, who had hoped for so much from this marriage, could not help sometimes comparing the bright house with the faded, dreary place out of which it had arisen, and wondering when, in any shape, it would begin to be a home; for that it was no home then for any one, though everything went on luxuriously and regularly, she had always a secret misgiving. Many an hour of sorrowful reflection by day and night, and many a tear of blighted hope, Florence bestowed upon the assurance her new mamma had given her so strongly, that there was no one on the earth more powerless than herself to teach her how to win her father's heart. And soon Florence began to think — resolved to think would be the truer phrase — that as no one knew so well how hopeless of being subdued or changed her father's coldness to her was, so she had given her this warning, and forbidden the subject in very compassion. Unselfish here, as in her every act and fancy, Florence preferred to bear the pain of this new wound, rather than encourage any faint foreshadowings of the truth as it concerned her father; tender of him, even in her wandering thoughts. As for his home, she hoped it would become a better one, when its state of novelty and transition should be over: and, for herself, thought little and lamented less.

If none of the new family were particularly at home in private, it was resolved that Mrs. Dombey at least should be at home in public without delay. A series of entertainments in celebration of the late nuptials, and in cultivation of society, were arranged chiefly by Mr. Dombey and Mrs. Skewton; and it was settled that the festive proceedings should commence by Mrs. Dombey's being at home upon a certain evening, and by Mr. and Mrs. Dombey's requesting the honor of the company of a great many incongruous people to dinner on the same day.

Accordingly, Mr. Dombey produced a list of sundry eastern magnates who were to be bidden to this feast on his behalf; to which Mrs. Skewton, acting for her dearest child, who was haughtily careless on the subject, subjoined a western list, comprising Cousin Feenix, not yet returned to Baden-Baden, greatly to the detriment of his personal estate; and a variety of moths of various degrees and ages, who had, at various times, fluttered round the light of her fair daughter, or herself, without any lasting injury to their wings. Florence was enrolled as a member of the dinner-party by Edith's command — elicited by a moment's doubt and hesitation on the part of Mrs. Skewton; and Florence, with a wondering heart, and with a quick instinctive sense of everything that grated on her father in the least, took her silent share in the proceedings of the day.

The proceedings commenced by Mr. Dombey, in a cravat of extraordinary height and stiffness, walking restlessly about the drawing-room until the hour appointed for dinner; punctual to which, an East India Director, of immense wealth, in a waistcoat apparently constructed in serviceable deal by some plain carpenter, but really engendered in the tailor's art, and composed of the material called nankeen, arrived, and was received by Mr. Dombey alone. The next stage of the proceedings was Mr. Dombey sending his compliments to Mrs. Dombey, with a correct statement of the time; and the next, the East India Director's falling prostrate, in a conversational point of view, and, as Mr. Dombey was not the man to pick him up, staring at the fire until rescue appeared in the person of Mrs. Skewton; whom the Director, as a pleasant start in life for the evening, mistook for Mrs. Dombey, and greeted with enthusiasm.

The next arrival was a Bank Director, reputed to

be able to buy up anything — human Nature generally, if he should take it in his head to influence the
Money Market in that direction — but who was a
wonderfully modest-spoken man, almost boastfully
so, and mentioned his "little place" at Kingston-
upon-Thames, and its just being barely equal to
giving Dombey a bed and a chop, if he would come
and visit it.   Ladies, he said, it was not for a man
who lived in his quiet way to take upon himself to
invite — but if Mrs. Skewton and her daughter, Mrs.
Dombey, should ever find themselves in that direction, and would do him the honor to look at a little
bit of a shrubbery they would find there, and a poor
little flower-bed or so, and a humble apology for a
pinery, and two or three little attempts of that sort
without any pretension, they would distinguish him
very much.   Carrying out his character, this gentleman was very plainly dressed, in a wisp of cambric
for a neckcloth, big shoes, a coat that was too loose
for him, and a pair of trousers that were too spare;
and mention being made of the Opera by Mrs.
Skewton, he said he very seldom went there, for
he couldn't afford it.   It seemed greatly to delight
and exhilarate him to say so; and he beamed on his
audience afterwards, with his hands in his pockets,
and excessive satisfaction twinkling in his eyes.

Now Mrs. Dombey appeared, beautiful and proud,
and as disdainful and defiant of them all as if the
bridal wreath upon her head had been a garland of
steel spikes put on to force concession from her
which she would die sooner than yield.   With her
was Florence.   When they entered together, the
shadow of the night of the return again darkened
Mr. Dombey's face.   But unobserved: for Florence

did not venture to raise her eyes to his, and Edith's indifference was too supreme to take the least heed of him.

The arrivals quickly became numerous. More Directors, Chairmen of public companies, elderly ladies carrying burdens on their heads for full dress, Cousin Feenix, Major Bagstock, friends of Mrs. Skewton, with the same bright bloom on their complexion, and very precious necklaces on very withered necks. Among these, a young lady of sixty-five, remarkably coolly dressed as to her back and shoulders, who spoke with an engaging lisp, and whose eyelids wouldn't keep up well, without a great deal of trouble on her part, and whose manners had that indefinable charm which so frequently attaches to the giddiness of youth. As the greater part of Mr. Dombey's list were disposed to be taciturn, and the greater part of Mrs. Dombey's list were disposed to be talkative, and there was no sympathy between them, Mrs. Dombey's list, by magnetic agreement, entered into a bond of union against Mr. Dombey's list, who, wandering about the rooms in a desolate manner, or seeking refuge in corners, entangled themselves with company coming in, and became barricaded behind sofas, and had doors opened smartly from without against their heads, and underwent every sort of discomfiture.

When dinner was announced, Mr. Dombey took down an old lady like a crimson velvet pincushion stuffed with bank notes, who might have been the identical old lady of Threadneedle Street, she was so rich, and looked so unaccommodating; Cousin Feenix took down Mrs. Dombey; Major Bagstock took down Mrs. Skewton; the young thing with the

shoulders was bestowed, as an extinguisher, upon
the East India Director; and the remaining ladies
were left on view in the drawing-room by the remaining gentlemen, until a forlorn hope volunteered
to conduct them downstairs, and those brave spirits
with their captives blocked up the dining-room door,
shutting out seven mild men in the stony-hearted
hall. When all the rest were got in and were
seated, one of these mild men still appeared, in
smiling confusion, totally destitute and unprovided
for, and, escorted by the butler, made the complete
circuit of the table twice before his chair could be
found, which it finally was, on Mrs. Dombey's left
hand; after which the mild man never held up his
head again.

Now the spacious dining-room, with the company seated round the glittering table, busy with
their glittering spoons, and knives and forks, and
plates, might have been taken for a grown-up
exposition of Tom Tiddler's ground, where children pick up gold and silver. Mr. Dombey, as
Tiddler, looked his character to admiration; and
the long plateau of precious metal frosted, sep-
arating him from Mrs. Dombey, whereon frosted
Cupids offered scentless flowers to each of them,
was allegorical to see.

Cousin Feenix was in great force, and looked
astonishingly young. But he was sometimes
thoughtless in his good humor — his memory occasionally wandering like his legs — and on this occasion he caused the company to shudder. It
happened thus. The young lady with the back,
who regarded Cousin Feenix with sentiments of
tenderness, had entrapped the East India Director

into leading her to the chair next him : in return for which good office, she immediately abandoned the Director, who, being shaded on the other side by a gloomy black velvet hat surmounting a bony and speechless female with a fan, yielded to a depression of spirits, and withdrew into himself. Cousin Feenix and the young lady were very lively and humorous, and the young lady laughed so much at something Cousin Feenix related to her, that Major Bagstock begged leave to inquire, on behalf of Mrs. Skewton (they were sitting opposite, a little lower down), whether that might not be considered public property.

"Why, upon my life," said Cousin Feenix, " there's nothing in it; it really is not worth repeating : in point of fact, it's merely an anecdote of Jack Adams. I dare say my friend Dombey " — for the general attention was concentrated on Cousin Feenix — " may remember Jack Adams, Jack Adams, not Joe ; that was his brother. Jack — little Jack — man with a cast in his eye, and a slight impediment in his speech — man who sat for somebody's borough. We used to call him in my parliamentary time W. P. Adams, in consequence of his being Warming Pan for a young fellow who was in his minority. Perhaps my friend Dombey may have known the man ? "

Mr. Dombey, who was as likely to have known Guy Fawkes, replied in the negative. But one of the seven mild men unexpectedly leaped into distinction by saying *he* had known him, and adding, — "Always wore Hessian boots ! "

"Exactly," said Cousin Feenix, bending forward to see the mild man, and smile encouragement at him down the table. "That was Jack. Joe wore —"

"Tops!" cried the mild man, rising in public estimation every instant.

" *Of* course," said Cousin Feenix, "you were intimate with 'em ? "

" I knew them both," said the mild man. With whom Mr. Dombey immediately took wine.

"Devilish good fellow, Jack!" said Cousin Feenix, again bending forward, and smiling.

"Excellent," returned the mild man, becoming bold on his success. "One of the best fellows I ever knew."

"No doubt you have heard the story ? " said Cousin Feenix.

"I shall know," replied the bold mild man, "when I have heard your Ludship tell it." With that, he leaned back in his chair and smiled at the ceiling, as knowing it by heart, and being already tickled.

"In point of fact, it's nothing of a story in itself," said Cousin Feenix, addressing the table with a smile, and a gay shake of his head, "and not worth a word of preface. But it's illustrative of the neatness of Jack's humor. The fact is, that Jack was invited down to a marriage — which I think took place in Barkshire ? "

"Shropshire," said the bold mild man, finding himself appealed to.

"Was it ? Well! In point of fact, it might have been in any shire," said Cousin Feenix. "So, my friend being invited down to this marriage in Anyshire," with a pleasant sense of the readiness of this joke, "goes. Just as some of us, having had the honor of being invited to the marriage of my lovely and accomplished relative with my friend Dombey, didn't require to be asked twice, and were devilish glad to be present on so interesting an occasion. —Goes — Jack goes. Now, this marriage was, in point of fact, the marriage of an uncommonly fine girl with a man for whom she didn't care a button, but whom she accepted on account of his property, which was immense. When Jack returned to town, after the nuptials, a man he knew, meeting him in the lobby of the House of Commons, says, 'Well, Jack, how are the ill-matched couple?' 'Ill-matched!' says Jack. 'Not at all. It's a perfectly fair and equal transaction. *She* is regularly bought, and you may take your oath *he* is as regularly sold!'"

In his full enjoyment of this culminating point of his story, the shudder which had gone all round the table like an electric spark, struck Cousin Feenix and he stopped. Not a smile, occasioned by the only general topic of conversation broached that day, appeared on any face. A profound silence ensued; and the wretched mild man, who had been as innocent of any real foreknowledge of the story as the child unborn, had the exquisite misery of reading in every eye that he was regarded as the prime mover of the mischief.

Mr. Dombey's face was not a changeful one, and, being cast in its mould of state that day, showed little other apprehension of the story, if any, than that which he expressed when he said solemnly, amidst the silence, that it was "Very good." There was a rapid glance from Edith towards Florence, but otherwise she remained, externally, impassive and unconscious.

Through the various stages of rich meats and wines, continual gold and silver, dainties of earth, air, fire, and water, heaped-up fruits, and that unnecessary article in Mr. Dombey's banquets — ice — the dinner slowly made its way; the later stages being achieved to the sonorous music of incessant double knocks, announcing the arrival of visitors, whose portion of the feast was limited to the smell thereof. When Mrs. Dombey rose, it was a sight to see her lord, with stiff throat, and erect head, hold the door open for the withdrawal of the ladies; and to see how she swept past him with his daughter on her arm.

Mr. Dombey was a grave sight, behind the decanters, in a state of dignity; and the East India Director was a forlorn sight, near the unoccupied end of the table, in a state of solitude; and the major was a military sight, relating stories of the Duke of York to six of the seven mild men (the ambitious one was utterly quenched); and the Bank Director was a lowly sight, making a plan of his little attempt at a pinery, with dessert knives, for a group of admirers; and Cousin Feenix was a thoughtful sight, as he smoothed his long wristbands and stealthily adjusted his wig. But all these sights were of short duration, being speedily broken up by coffee, and the desertion of the room.

There was a throng in the state rooms upstairs, increasing every minute; but still Mr. Dombey's list of visitors appeared to have some native impossibility of amalgamation with Mrs. Dombey's list, and no one could have doubted which was which. The single exception to this rule, perhaps, was Mr. Carker, who now smiled among the company, and

who, as he stood in the circle that was gathered about Mrs. Dombey — watchful of her, of them, his .chief, Cleopatra, and the major, Florence, and everything around — appeared at ease with both divisions of guests, and not marked as exclusively belonging to either.

Florence had a dread of him, which made his presence in the room a nightmare to her. She could not avoid the recollection of it, for her eyes were drawn towards him every now and then, by an attraction of dislike and distrust that she could not resist. Yet her thoughts were busy with other things; for as she sat apart — not unadmired or unsought, but in the gentleness of her quiet spirit — she felt how little part her father had in what was going on, and saw, with pain, how ill at ease he seemed to be, and how little regarded he was as he lingered about, near the door, for those visitors whom he wished to distinguish with particular attention, and took them up to introduce them to his wife, who received them with proud coldness, but showed no interest, or wish to please, and never, after the bare ceremony of reception, in consultation of his wishes, or in welcome of his friends, opened her lips. It was not the less perplexing or painful to Florence that she, who acted thus, treated her so kindly, and with such loving consideration, that it almost seemed an ungrateful return on her part even to know of what was passing before her eyes.

Happy Florence would have been, might she have ventured to bear her father company by so much as a look; and happy Florence was in little suspecting the main cause of his uneasiness. But afraid of seeming to know that he was placed at any disadvantage, lest he should be resentful of that knowledge; and divided between her impulse towards him, and her grateful affection for Edith; she scarcely dared to raise her eyes towards either. Anxious and unhappy for them both, the thought stole on her through the crowd, that it might have been better for them if this noise of tongues and tread of feet had never come there, — if the old dulness and decay had never been replaced by novelty and splendor, — if the neglected child had found no friend in Edith, but had lived her solitary life, unpitied and forgotten.

Mrs. Chick had some such thoughts too, but they were not so quietly developed in her mind. This good matron had been outraged, in the first instance, by not receiving an invitation to dinner. That blow partially recovered, she had gone to a vast expense to make such a figure before Mrs. Dombey at home as should dazzle the senses of that lady, and heap mortification, mountains high, on the head of Mrs. Skewton.

"But I am made," said Mrs. Chick to Mr. Chick, "of no more account than Florence. Who takes the smallest notice of me? No one!"

"No one, my dear," assented Mr. Chick, who was seated by the side of Mrs. Chick against the wall, and could console himself, even there, by softly whistling.

"Does it at all appear as if I was wanted here?" exclaimed Mrs. Chick with flashing eyes.

"No, my dear, I don't think it does," said Mr. Chick.

"Paul's mad!" said Mrs. Chick.

Mr. Chick whistled.

"Unless you are a monster, which I sometimes think you are," said Mrs. Chick with candor, "don't sit there humming tunes. How any one, with the most distant feelings of a man, can see that mother-in-law of Paul's, dressed as she is, going on like that with Major Bagstock, for whom, among other precious things, we are indebted to your Lucretia Tox —"

"*My* Lucretia Tox, my dear!" said Mr. Chick, astounded.

"Yes," retorted Mrs. Chick with great severity, "*your* Lucretia Tox. I say, how anybody can. see that mother-in-law of Paul's, and that haughty wife of Paul's, and those indecent old frights with their backs and shoulders, and, in short, this at home generally, and can hum" — on which word Mrs. Chick laid a scornful emphasis that made Mr. Chick start — "is, I thank Heaven, a mystery to me!"

Mr. Chick screwed his mouth into a form irreconcilable with humming or whistling, and looked very contemplative.

"But I hope I know what is due to myself," said Mrs. Chick, swelling with indignation, "though Paul has forgotten what is due to me. I am not going to sit here, a member of this family, to be taken no notice of. I am not the dirt under Mrs. Dombey's feet yet — not quite yet," said Mrs. Chick, as if she expected to become so about the day after to-morrow. "And I shall go. I will not say (whatever I may think) that this affair has been got up solely to degrade and insult me. I shall merely go. I shall not be missed!"

Mrs. Chick rose erect with these words, and took

the arm of Mr. Chick, who escorted her from the
room, after half an hour's shady sojourn there.
And it is due to her penetration to observe that she
certainly was not missed at all.

But she was not the only indignant guest; for
Mr. Dombey's list (still constantly in difficulties)
were, as a body, indignant with Mrs. Dombey's list,
for looking at them through eyeglasses, and audibly
wondering who all those people were; while Mrs.
Dombey's list complained of weariness, and the
young thing with the shoulders, deprived of the
attentions of that gay youth, Cousin Feenix (who
went away from the dinner-table), confidentially
alleged to thirty or forty friends that she was bored
to death. All the old ladies with the burdens on
their heads had greater or less cause of complaint
against Mrs. Dombey; and the Directors and Chairmen coincided in thinking that if Dombey must
marry, he had better have married somebody nearer
his own age, not quite so handsome, and a little
better off. The general opinion among this class of
gentlemen was, that it was a weak thing in Dombey,
and he'd live to repent it. Hardly anybody there,
except the mild men, stayed, or went away, without
considering himself or herself neglected and aggrieved by Mr. Dombey or Mrs. Dombey; and the
speechless female in the black velvet hat was found
to have been stricken mute, because the lady in the
crimson velvet had been handed down before her.
The nature even of the mild men got corrupted,
either from their curdling it with too much lemon-
ade, or from the general inoculation that prevailed;
and they made sarcastic jokes to one another, and
whispered disparagement on stairs and in by-places.

The general dissatisfaction and discomfort so diffused itself, that the assembled footmen in the hall were as well acquainted with it as the company above. Nay, the very linkmen outside got hold of it, and compared the party to a funeral out of mourning, with none of the company remembered in the will.

At last the guests were all gone, and the linkmen too; and the street, crowded so long with carriages, was clear; and the dying lights showed no one in the rooms but Mr. Dombey and Mr. Carker, who were talking together apart, and Mrs. Dombey and her mother: the former seated on an ottoman; the latter reclining in the Cleopatra attitude, awaiting the arrival of her maid. Mr. Dombey having finished his communication to Carker, the latter advanced obsequiously to take leave.

"I trust," he said, "that the fatigues of this delightful evening will not inconvenience Mrs. Dombey to-morrow."

"Mrs. Dombey," said Mr. Dombey, advancing, "has sufficiently spared herself fatigue to relieve you from any anxiety of that kind. I regret to say, Mrs. Dombey, that I could have wished you had fatigued yourself a little more on this occasion."

She looked at him with a supercilious glance, that it seemed not worth her while to protract, and turned away her eyes without speaking.

"I am sorry, madam," said Mr. Dombey, "that you should not have thought it your duty —"

She looked at him again.

"— Your duty, madam," pursued Mr. Dombey, "to have received my friends with a little more deference. Some of those whom you have been

pleased to slight to-night in a very marked manner,
Mrs. Dombey, confer a distinction upon you, I must
tell you, in any visit they pay you."

"Do you know that there is some one here?" she
returned, now looking at him steadily.

"No! Carker! I beg that you do not. I insist
that you do not," cried Mr. Dombey, stopping that
noiseless gentleman in his withdrawal. "Mr.
Carker, madam, as you know, possesses my confidence. He is as well acquainted as myself with
the subject on which I speak. I beg to tell you,
for your information, Mrs. Dombey, that I consider
these wealthy and important persons confer a distinction upon *me:*" and Mr. Dombey drew himself
up, as having now rendered them of the highest
possible importance.

"I ask you," she repeated, bending her disdainful
steady gaze upon him, "do you know that there is
some one here, sir?"

"I must entreat," said Mr. Carker, stepping forward, "I must beg, I must demand, to be released.
Slight and unimportant as this difference is —"

Mrs. Skewton, who had been intent upon her
daughter's face, took him up here.

"My sweetest Edith," she said, "and my dearest
Dombey, our excellent friend Mr. Carker, for so I
am sure I ought to mention him —"

Mr. Carker murmured, "Too much honor."

"— Has used the very words that were in my
mind, and that I have been dying, these ages, for an
opportunity of introducing. Slight and unimportant! My sweetest Edith, and my dearest Dombey,
do we not know that any difference between you
two — No, Flowers; not now."

Flowers was the maid, who, finding gentlemen present, retreated with precipitation.

"— That any difference between you two," resumed Mrs. Skewton, "with the heart you possess in common, and the excessively charming bond of feeling that there is between you, *must* be slight and unimportant? What words could better define the fact? None. Therefore I am glad to take this slight occasion — this trifling occasion that is so replete with Nature, and your individual characters, and all that — so truly calculated to bring the tears into a parent's eyes — to say that I attach no importance to them in the least, except as developing these minor elements of Soul; and that, unlike most mammas-in-law (that odious phrase, dear Dombey!) as they have been represented to me to exist in this I fear too artificial world, I never shall attempt to interpose between you at such a time, and never can much regret, after all, such little flashes of the torch of what's-his-name — not Cupid, but the other delightful creature."

There was a sharpness in the good mother's glance at both her children, as she spoke, that may have been expressive of a direct and well-considered purpose hidden between these rambling words. That purpose, providently to detach herself in the beginning from all the clankings of their chain that were to come, and to shelter herself with the fiction of her innocent belief in their mutual affection, and their adaptation to each other.

"I have pointed out to Mrs. Dombey," said Mr. Dombey in his most stately manner, "that in her conduct, thus early in our married life, to which I object, and which I request may be corrected.

Carker," with a nod of dismissal, "good-night to you!"

Mr. Carker bowed to the imperious form of the bride, whose sparkling eye was fixed upon her husband; and stopping at Cleopatra's couch on his way out, raised to his lips the hand she graciously extended to him, in lowly and admiring homage.

If his handsome wife had reproached him, or even changed countenance, or broken the silence in which she remained by one word, now that they were alone (for Cleopatra made off with all speed), Mr. Dombey would have been equal to some assertion of his case against her. But the intense, unutterable, withering scorn with which, after looking upon him, she dropped her eyes as if he were too worthless and indifferent to her to be challenged with a syllable — the ineffable disdain and haughtiness in which she sat before him — the cold, inflexible resolve with which her every feature seemed to bear him down, and put him by — he had no resource against; and he left her, with her whole overbearing beauty concentrated on despising him.

Was he coward enough to watch her, an hour afterwards, on the old well staircase, where he had once seen Florence in the moonlight, toiling up with Paul? Or was he in the dark by accident, when, looking up, he saw her coming, with a light, from the room where Florence lay, and marked again the face so changed, which *he* could not subdue?

But, it could never alter as his own did. It never, in its utmost pride and passion, knew the shadow that had fallen on his, in the dark corner, on the night of the return and often since; and which deepened on it now as he looked up.

CHAPTER XVII.

FLORENCE, Edith, and Mrs. Skewton were together next day, and the carriage was waiting at the door to take them out. For Cleopatra had her galley again now, and Withers, no longer the wan, stood upright in a pigeon-breasted jacket and military trousers, behind her wheel-less chair at dinner-time, and butted no more. The hair of Withers was radiant with pomatum in these days of down, and he wore kid gloves, and smelt of the water of Cologne.

They were assembled in Cleopatra's room. The Serpent of old Nile (not to mention her disrespectfully) was reposing on her sofa, sipping her morning chocolate at three o'clock in the afternoon, and Flowers the maid was fastening on her youthful cuffs and frills, and performing a kind of private coronation ceremony on her with a peach-colored velvet bonnet; the artificial roses in which nodded to uncommon advantage, as the palsy trifled with them like the breeze.

"I think I am a little nervous this morning, Flowers," said Mrs. Skewton. "My hand quite shakes."

"You were the life of the party last night, ma'am, you know," returned Flowers, "and you suffer for it to-day, you see."

Edith, who had beckoned Florence to the window, and was looking out, with her back turned on the toilet of her esteemed mother, suddenly withdrew from it, as if it had lightened.

"My darling child," cried Cleopatra languidly, "*you* are not nervous? Don't tell me, my dear Edith, that you, so enviably self-possessed, are beginning to be a martyr too, like your unfortunately constituted mother. Withers, some one at the door."

"Card, ma'am," said Withers, taking it towards Mrs. Dombey.

"I am going out," she said, without looking at it.

"My dear love," drawled Mrs. Skewton, "how very odd to send that message without seeing the name! Bring it here, Withers. Dear me, my love; Mr. Carker too! that very sensible person!"

"I am going out," repeated Edith in so imperious a tone, that Withers, going to the door, imperiously informed the servant who was waiting, "Mrs. Dombey is going out. Get along with you," and shut it on him.

But the servant came back after a short absence, and whispered to Withers again, who once more, and not very willingly, presented himself before Mrs. Dombey.

"If you please, ma'am, Mr. Carker sends his respectful compliments, and begs you would spare him one minute, if you could — for business, ma'am, if you please."

"Really, my love," said Mrs. Skewton in her

mildest manner; for her daughter's face was threatening; "if you would allow me to offer a word, I should recommend — "

"Show him this way," said Edith. As Withers disappeared to execute the command, she added, frowning on her mother, "As he comes at your recommendation, let him come to your room."

"May I — shall I go away?" asked Florence hurriedly.

Edith nodded yes, but, on her way to the door, Florence met the visitor coming in. With the same disagreeable mixture of familiarity and forbearance with which he had first addressed her, he addressed her now in his softest manner — hoped she was quite well — needed not to ask with such looks to anticipate the answer — had scarcely had the honor to know her last night, she was so greatly changed — and held the door open for her to pass out; with a secret sense of power in her shrinking from him, that all the deference and politeness of his manner could not quite conceal.

He then bowed himself for a moment over Mrs. Skewton's condescending hand, and lastly bowed to Edith. Coldly returning his salute without looking at him, and neither seating herself nor inviting him to be seated, she waited for him to speak.

Intrenched in her pride and power, and with all the obduracy of her spirit summoned about her, still her old conviction that she and her mother had been known by this man in their worst colors from their first acquaintance; that every degradation she had suffered in her own eyes was as plain to him as to herself; that he read her life as though it were a vile book, and fluttered the leaves before her in slight looks and tones of voice which no one else could detect; weakened and undermined her. Proudly as she opposed herself to him, with her commanding face exacting his humility, her disdainful lip repulsing him, her bosom angry at his intrusion, and the dark lashes of her eye sullenly veiling their light, that no ray of it might shine upon him — and submissively as he stood before her, with an entreating, injured manner, but with complete submission to her will — she knew, in her own soul, that the cases were reversed, and that the triumph and superiority were his, and that he knew it full well.

"I have presumed," said Mr. Carker, "to solicit an interview, and I have ventured to describe it as being one of business, because — "

"Perhaps you are charged by Mr. Dombey with some message of reproof," said Edith. "You possess Mr. Dombey's confidence in such an unusual degree, sir, that you would scarcely surprise me if that were your business."

"I have no message to the lady who sheds a lustre upon his name," said Mr. Carker. "But I entreat that lady, on my own behalf, to be just to a very humble claimant for justice at her hands — a mere dependent of Mr. Dombey's — which is a position of humility; and to reflect upon my perfect helplessness last night, and the impossibility of my avoiding the share that was forced upon me in a very painful occasion."

"My dearest Edith," hinted Cleopatra in a low voice, as she held her eyeglass aside, "really very charming of Mr. What's-his-name. And full of heart! "

"For I do," said Mr. Carker, appealing to Mrs. Skewton with a look of grateful deference, — "I do venture to call it a painful occasion, though merely because it was so to me, who had the misfortune to be present. So slight a difference, as between the principals — between those who love each other with disinterested devotion, and would make any sacrifice of self in such a cause — is nothing. As Mrs. Skewton herself expressed, with so much truth and feeling last night, it is nothing."

Edith could not look at him, but she said after a few moments, —

"And your business, sir — "

"Edith, my pet," said Mrs. Skewton, "all this time Mr. Carker is standing. My dear Mr. Carker, take a seat, I beg."

He offered no reply to the mother, but fixed his eyes on the proud daughter, as though he would only be bidden by her, and was resolved to be bidden by her. Edith, in spite of herself, sat down, and slightly motioned with her hand to him to be seated too. No action could be colder, haughtier, more insolent in its air of supremacy and disrespect, but she had struggled against even that concession ineffectually, and it was wrested from her. That was enough ! Mr. Carker sat down.

" May I be allowed, madam," said Carker, turning his white teeth on Mrs. Skewton like a light — " a lady of your excellent sense and quick feeling will give me credit for good reason, I am sure — to address what I have to say to Mrs. Dombey, and to leave her to impart it to you, who are her best and dearest friend — next to Mr. Dombey ? "

Mrs. Skewton would have retired, but Edith

stopped her. Edith would have stopped him too, and indignantly ordered him to speak openly, or not at all, but that he said, in a low voice — "Miss Florence — the young lady who has just left the room — "

Edith suffered him to proceed. She looked at him now. As he bent forward, to be nearer, with the utmost show of delicacy and respect, and with his teeth persuasively arrayed in a self-depreciating smile, she felt as if she could have struck him dead.

"Miss Florence's position," he began, "has been an unfortunate one. I have a difficulty in alluding to it to you, whose attachment to her father is naturally watchful and jealous of every word that applies to him." Always distinct and soft in speech, no language could describe the extent of his distinctness and softness when he said these words, or came to any others of a similar import. "But, as one who is devoted to Mr. Dombey in his different way, and whose life is passed in admiration of Mr. Dombey's character, may I say, without offence to your tenderness as a wife, that Miss Florence has unhappily been neglected — by her father? May I say by her father?"

Edith replied, "I know it."

"You know it!" said Mr. Carker, with a great appearance of relief. "It removes a mountain from my breast. May I hope you know how the neglect originated; in what an amiable phase of Mr. Dombey's pride — character, I mean?"

"You may pass that by, sir," she returned, "and come the sooner to the end of what you have to say."

"Indeed, I am sensible, madam," replied Carker, — "trust me, I am deeply sensible that Mr. Dombey can require no justification in anything to you. But, kindly judge of my breast by your own, and you will forgive my interest in him, if, in its excess, it goes at all astray."

What a stab to her proud heart to sit there, face to face with him, and have him tendering her false oath at the altar again and again for her acceptance, and pressing it upon her like the dregs of a sickening cup she could not own her loathing of, or turn away from! How shame, remorse, and passion raged within her, when, upright in her beauty before him, she knew that in her spirit she was down at his feet!

"Miss Florence," said Carker, "left to the care — if one may call it care — of servants and mercenary people, in every way her inferiors, necessarily wanted some guide and compass in her younger days, and, naturally, for want of them, has been indiscreet, and has in some degree forgotten her station. There was some folly about one Walter, a common lad, who is fortunately dead now: and some very undesirable association, I regret to say, with certain coasting sailors, of anything but good repute, and a runaway old bankrupt."

"I have heard the circumstances, sir," said Edith, flashing her disdainful glance upon him, "and I know that you pervert them. You may not know it; I hope so."

"Pardon me," said Mr. Carker, "I believe that nobody knows them so well as I. Your generous and ardent nature, madam — the same nature which is so nobly imperative in vindication of your beloved

and honored husband, and which has blessed him
as even his merits deserve — I must respect, defer
to, bow before.   But, as regards the circumstances,
which is, indeed, the business I presumed to solicit
your attention to, I can have no doubt, since in the
execution of my trust as Mr. Dombey's confidential
— I presume to say — friend, I have fully ascertained them.   In my execution of that trust; in
my deep concern, which you can so well understand,
for everything relating to him, intensified, if you
will (for I fear I labor under your displeasure), by
the lower motive of desire to prove my diligence,
and make myself the more acceptable; I have long
pursued these circumstances by myself and trust-
worthy instruments, and have innumerable and
most minute proofs."

She raised her eyes no higher than his mouth,
but she saw the means of mischief vaunted in every
tooth it contained.

"Pardon me, madam," he continued, "if, in my
perplexity, I presume to take counsel with you, and
to consult your pleasure.   I think I have observed
that you are greatly interested in Miss Florence?"

What was there in her he had not observed, and
did not know?   Humbled and yet maddened by the
thought, in every new presentment of it, however
faint, she pressed her teeth upon her quivering lip
to force composure on it, and distantly inclined her
head in reply.

"This interest, madam — so touching an evidence
of everything associated with Mr. Dombey being
dear to you — induces me to pause before I make
him acquainted with these circumstances, which, as
yet, he does not know.   It so far shakes me, if I

may make the confession, in my allegiance, that on the intimation of the least desire to that effect from you, I would suppress them."

Edith raised her head quickly, and, starting back, bent her dark glance upon him. He met it with his blandest and most deferential smile, and went on.

"You say that, as I describe them, they are perverted. I fear not — I fear not : but let us assume that they are. The uneasiness I have for some time felt on the subject arises in this : that the mere circumstance of such association, often repeated, on the part of Miss Florence, however innocently and confidingly, would be conclusive with Mr. Dombey, already predisposed against her, and would lead him to take some step (I know he has occasionally contemplated it) of separation and alienation of her from his home. Madam, bear with me, and remember my intercourse with Mr. Dombey, and my knowledge of him, and my reverence for him, almost from childhood, when I say that if he has a fault, it is a lofty stubbornness, rooted in that noble pride and sense of power which belong to him, and which we must all defer to ; which is not assailable like the obstinacy of other characters ; and which grows upon itself from day to day, and year to year."

She bent her glance upon him still ; but, look as steadfast as she would, her haughty nostrils dilated, and her breath came somewhat deeper, and her lip would slightly curl as he described that in his patron to which they must all bow down. He saw it ; and though his expression did not change, she knew he saw it.

"Even so slight an incident as last night's," he said, "if I might refer to it once more, would serve to illustrate my meaning better than a greater one. Dombey and Son know neither time, nor place, nor season, but bear them all down. But I rejoice in its occurrence, for it has opened the way for me to approach Mrs. Dombey with this subject to-day, even if it has entailed upon me the penalty of her temporary displeasure. Madam, in the midst of my uneasiness and apprehension on this subject, I was summoned by Mr. Dombey to Leamington. There I saw you. There I could not help knowing what relation you would shortly occupy towards him — to his enduring happiness and yours. There I resolved to await the time of your establishment at home here, and to do as I have now done. I have, at heart, no fear that I shall be wanting in my duty to Mr. Dombey if I bury what I know in your breast ; for where there is but one heart and mind between two persons — as in such a marriage — one almost represents the other. I can acquit my conscience therefore, almost equally, by confidence, on such a theme, in you or him. For the reasons I have mentioned, I would select you. May I aspire to the distinction of believing that my confidence is accepted, and that I am relieved from my responsibility ? "

He long remembered the look she gave him — who could see it, and forget it ? — and the struggle that ensued within her. At last she said, —

"I accept it, sir. You will please to consider this matter at an end, and that it goes no farther."

He bowed low and rose. She rose too, and he took leave with all humility. But Withers, meeting him on the stairs, stood amazed at the beauty of his teeth, and at his brilliant smile ; and, as he rode away upon his white-legged horse, the people took him for a dentist, such was the dazzling show he made. The people took *her*, when she rode out in her carriage presently, for a great lady, as happy as she was rich and fine. But, they had not seen her, just before, in her own room, with no one by; and they had not heard her utterance of the three words, "Oh, Florence, Florence!"

Mrs. Skewton, reposing on her sofa, and sipping her chocolate, had heard nothing but the low word business, for which she had a mortal aversion, insomuch that she had long banished it from her vocabulary, and had gone nigh, in a charming manner and with an immense amount of heart (to say nothing of soul), to ruin divers milliners and others in consequence. Therefore, Mrs. Skewton asked no questions, and showed no curiosity. Indeed, the peach-velvet bonnet gave her sufficient occupation out of doors: for, being perched on the back of her head, and the day being rather windy, it was frantic to escape from Mrs. Skewton's company, and would be coaxed into no sort of compromise. When the carriage was closed, and the wind shut out, the palsy played among the artificial roses again, like an almshouse full of superannuated zephyrs; and altogether Mrs. Skewton had enough to do, and got on but indifferently.

She got on no better towards night; for when Mrs. Dombey, in her dressing-room, had been dressed and waiting for her half an hour, and Mr. Dombey, in the drawing-room, had paraded himself into a state of solemn fretfulness (they were all three going out to dinner), Flowers the maid appeared with a pale face to Mrs. Dombey, saying, —

"If you please, ma'am, I beg your pardon, but I can't do nothing with missis!"

"What do you mean?" asked Edith.

"Well, ma'am," replied the frightened maid, "I hardly know. She's making faces!"

Edith hurried with her to her mother's room. Cleopatra was arrayed in full dress, with the diamonds, short sleeves, rouge, curls, teeth, and other juvenility all complete; but Paralysis was not to be deceived, had known her for the object of its errand, and had struck her at her glass, where she lay like a horrible doll that had tumbled down.

They took her to pieces in very shame, and put the little of her that was real on a bed. Doctors were sent for, and soon came. Powerful remedies were resorted to; opinions given that she would rally from this shock, but would not survive another; and there she lay speechless, and staring at the ceiling, for days: sometimes making inarticulate sounds in answer to such questions, as did she know who were present? and the like: sometimes giving no reply, either by sign or gesture, or in her unwinking eyes.

At length she began to recover consciousness, and in some degree the power of motion, though not yet of speech. One day the use of her right hand returned; and showing it to her maid, who was in attendance on her, and appearing very uneasy in her mind, she made signs for a pencil and some paper. This the maid immediately provided, thinking she was going to make a will, or write some last request; and Mrs. Dombey being from home, the maid awaited the result with solemn feelings.

After much painful scrawling and erasing, and

putting in of wrong characters, which seemed to tumble out of the pencil of their own accord, the old woman produced this document: —

"Rose-colored curtains."

The maid being perfectly transfixed, and with tolerable reason, Cleopatra amended the manuscript by adding two words more, when it stood thus : —

"Rose-colored curtains for doctors."

The maid now perceived remotely that she wished these articles to be provided for the better presentation of her complexion to the faculty; and as those in the house who knew her best had no doubt of the correctness of this opinion, which she was soon able to establish for herself, the rose-colored curtains were added to her bed, and she mended with increased rapidity from that hour. She was soon able to sit up, in curls and a laced cap and nightgown, and to have a little artificial bloom dropped into the hollow caverns of her cheeks.

It was a tremendous sight to see this old woman in her finery leering and mincing at Death, and playing off her youthful tricks upon him as if he had been the major; but an alteration in her mind that ensued on the paralytic stroke was fraught with as much matter for reflection, and was quite as ghastly.

Whether the weakening of her intellect made her more cunning and false than before, or whether it confused her between what she had assumed to be and what she really had been, or whether it had awakened any glimmering of remorse, which could neither struggle into light nor get back into total darkness, or whether, in the jumble of her faculties, a combination of these effects had been shaken up, which is perhaps the more likely supposition, the

result was this : — That she became hugely exact in
respect of Edith's affection and gratitude and attention to her; highly laudatory of herself as a most
inestimable parent; and very jealous of having any
rival in Edith's regard. Further, in place of remembering that compact made between them for an avoid-
ance of the subject, she constantly alluded to her
daughter's marriage as a proof of her being an in-
comparable mother ; and all this, with the weakness
and peevishness of such a state, always serving for
a sarcastic commentary on her levity and youthfulness.

"Where is Mrs. Dombey ? " she would say to her
maid.

" Gone out, ma'am.'"

"Gone out! Does she go out to shun her mamma,
Flowers ? "

"La bless you, no, ma'am. Mrs. Dombey has
only gone out for a ride with Miss Florence."

" Miss Florence! Who's Miss Florence ? Don't
tell me about Miss Florence. What's Miss Florence
to her, compared to me ? "

The apposite display of the diamonds, or the
peach-velvet bonnet (she sat in the bonnet to receive visitors, weeks before she could stir out of
doors), or the dressing of her up in some gaud or
other, usually stopped the tears that began to flow
hereabouts ; and she would remain in a complacent
state until Edith came to see her; when at a glance
of the proud face, she would relapse again.

"Well, I am sure, Edith!" she would cry, shaking her head.

" What is the matter, mother ? "

"Matter! I really don't know what *is* the mat-

ter. The world is coming to such an artificial and
ungrateful state, that I begin to think there's no
Heart — or anything of that sort — left in it, positively. Withers is more a child to me than you are.
He attends to me much more than my own daughter.
I almost wish I didn't look so young — and all that
kind of thing — and then perhaps I should be more
considered."

"What would you have, mother?"

"Oh, a great deal, Edith," impatiently.

"Is there anything you want that you have not?
It is your own fault if there be."

"My own fault!" beginning to whimper. "The
parent I have been to you, Edith : making you a
companion from your cradle! And when you neglect me, and have no more natural affection for me
than if I was a stranger — not a twentieth part of
the affection that you have for Florence — but I am
only your mother, and should corrupt *her* in a day!
— you reproach me with its being my own fault."

"Mother, mother, I reproach you with nothing.
Why will you always dwell on this?"

"Isn't it natural that I should dwell on this,
when I am all affection and sensitiveness, and am
wounded in the cruellest way, whenever you look
at me?"

"I do not mean to wound you, mother. Have you
no remembrance of what has been said between us?
Let the Past rest."

"Yes, rest! And let gratitude to me rest; and
let affection for me rest; and let *me* rest in my out-
of-the-way room, with no society and no attention,
while you find new relations to make much of, who
have no earthly claim upon you! Good gracious,

Edith, do you know what an elegant establishment you are at the head of ? "

"Yes. Hush!"

"And that gentlemanly creature, Dombey — do you know that you are married to him, Edith, and that you have a settlement, and a position, and a carriage, and I don't know what ? "

"Indeed I know it, mother; well."

"As you would have had with that delightful good soul — what did they call him ? — Granger — if he hadn't died. And who have you to thank for all this, Edith ? "

"You, mother; you."

"Then put your arms round my neck, and kiss me; and show me, Edith, that you know there never was a better mamma than I have been to you. And don't let me become a perfect fright with teasing and wearing myself at your ingratitude, or when I'm out again in society no soul will know me, not even that hateful animal, the major."

But sometimes, when Edith went nearer to her, and, bending down her stately head, put her cold cheek to hers, the mother would draw back as if she were afraid of her, and would fall into a fit of trembling, and cry out that there was a wandering in her wits. And sometimes she would entreat her, with humility, to sit down on the chair beside her bed, and would look at her (as she sat there brooding) with a face that even the rose-colored curtains could not make otherwise than scared and wild.

The rose-colored curtains blushed, in course of time, on Cleopatra's bodily recovery, and on her dress — more juvenile than ever, to repair the ravages of illness— and on the rouge, and on the teeth, and on the curls, and on the diamonds, and the short sleeves, and the whole wardrobe of the doll that had tumbled down before the mirror. They blushed, too, now and then, upon an indistinctness in her speech, which she turned off with a girlish giggle, and on an occasional failing in her memory, that had no rule in it, but came and went fantastically, as if in mockery of her fantastic self.

But they never blushed upon a change in the new manner of her thought and speech towards her daughter. And though that daughter often came within their influence, they never blushed upon her loveliness irradiated by a smile, or softened by the light of filial love, in its stern beauty.

CHAPTER XVIII.

THE forlorn Miss Tox, abandoned by her friend Louisa Chick, and bereft of Mr. Dombey's countenance — for no delicate pair of wedding cards, united by a silver thread, graced the chimney-glass in Princess's Place, or the harpsichord, or any of those little posts of display which Lucretia reserved for holiday occupation — became depressed in her spirits, and suffered much from melancholy. For a time the Bird Waltz was unheard in Princess's Place, the plants were neglected, and dust collected on the miniature of Miss Tox's ancestor with the powdered head and pigtail.

Miss Tox, however, was not of an age or of a disposition long to abandon herself to unavailing regrets. Only two notes of the harpsichord were dumb from disuse when the Bird Waltz again warbled and trilled in the crooked drawing-room; only one slip of geranium fell a victim to imperfect nursing, before she was gardening at her green baskets again, regularly every morning; the powdered-headed ancestor had not been under a cloud for more than six weeks, when Miss Tox breathed on his benignant visage, and polished him up with a piece of wash-leather.

Still, Miss Tox was lonely, and at a loss. Her attachments, however ludicrously shown, were real and strong; and she was, as she expressed it, "deeply hurt by the unmerited contumely she had met with from Louisa." But there was no such thing as anger in Miss Tox's composition. If she had ambled on through life, in her soft-spoken way, without any opinions, she had, at least, got so far without any harsh passions. The mere sight of Louisa Chick in the street one day, at a considerable distance, so overpowered her milky nature, that she was fain to seek immediate refuge in a pastrycook's, and there, in a musty little back-room usually devoted to the consumption of soups, and pervaded by an ox-tail atmosphere, relieve her feelings by weeping plentifully.

Against Mr. Dombey Miss Tox hardly felt that she had any reason of complaint. Her sense of that gentleman's magnificence was such that, once removed from him, she felt as if her distance always had been immeasurable, and as if he had greatly condescended in tolerating her at all. No wife could be too handsome or too stately for him, according to Miss Tox's sincere opinion. It was perfectly natural that, in looking for one, he should look high. Miss Tox with tears laid down this proposition, and fully admitted it twenty times a day. She never recalled the lofty manner in which Mr. Dombey had made her subservient to his convenience and caprices, and had graciously permitted her to be one of the nurses of his little son. She only thought, in her own words, "that she had passed a great many happy hours in that house, which she must ever remember with gratification, and that she could never cease to regard Mr. Dombey as one of the most impressive and dignified of men."

Cut off, however, from the implacable Louisa, and being shy of the major (whom she viewed with some distrust now), Miss Tox found it very irksome to know nothing of what was going on in Mr. Dombey's establishment. And, as she really had got into the habit of considering Dombey and Son as the pivot on which the world in general turned, she resolved, rather than be ignorant of intelligence which so strongly interested her, to cultivate her old acquaintance, Mrs. Richards, who, she knew, since her last memorable appearance before Mr. Dombey, was in the habit of sometimes holding communication with his servants. Perhaps Miss Tox, in seeking out the Toodle family, had the tender motive hidden in her breast of having somebody to whom she could talk about Mr. Dombey, no matter how humble that somebody might be.

At all events, towards the Toodle habitation Miss Tox directed her steps one evening, what time Mr. Toodle, cindery and swart, was refreshing himself with tea in the bosom of his family. Mr. Toodle had only three stages of existence. He was either taking refreshment in the bosom just mentioned, or he was tearing through the country at from twenty-five to fifty miles an hour, or he was sleeping after his fatigues. He was always in a whirlwind or a calm, and a peaceable, contented, easy-going man Mr. Toodle was in either state. He seemed to have made over all his own inheritance of fuming and fretting to the engines with which he was connected, which panted, and gasped, and chafed, and wore themselves out in a most unsparing manner, while Mr. Toodle led a mild and equable life.

"Polly, my gal," said Mr. Toodle, with a young Toodle on each knee, and two more making tea for him, and plenty more scattered about — Mr. Toodle was never out of children, but always kept a good supply on hand — "you ain't seen our Biler lately, have you ?"

"No," replied Polly, "but he's almost certain to look in to-night. It's his right evening, and he's very regular."

"I suppose," said Mr. Toodle, relishing his meal infinitely, "as our Biler is a-doin' now about as well as a boy *can* do, eh, Polly ?"

"Oh! he's a-doing beautiful!" responded Polly.

"He ain't got to be at all secret-like — has he, Polly ?" inquired Mr. Toodle.

"No!" said Mrs. Toodle plumply.

"I'm glad he ain't got to be at all secret-like, Polly," observed Mr. Toodle in his slow and measured way, and shovelling in his bread and butter with a clasp-knife, as if he were stoking himself, "because that don't look well; do it, Polly ?"

"Why, of course it don't, father. How can you ask ?"

"You see, my boys and gals," said Mr. Toodle, looking round upon his family, "wotever you're up to in a honest way, it's my opinion as you can't do better than be open. If you find yourselves in cuttings or in tunnels, don't you play no secret games. Keep your whistles going, and let's know where you are."

The rising Toodles set up a shrill murmur expressive of their resolution to profit by the paternal advice.

"But what makes you say this along of Rob,
father?" asked his wife anxiously.

"Polly, old 'ooman," said Mr. Toodle, "I don't
know as I said it particular along o' Rob, I'm sure.
I starts light with Rob only; I comes to a branch;
I takes on what I finds there; and a whole train of
ideas gets coupled on to him, afore I knows where
I am, or where they comes from. What a Junction
a man's thoughts is," said Mr. Toodle, "to be sure!"

This profound reflection Mr. Toodle washed down
with a pint mug of tea, and proceeded to solidify
with a great weight of bread and butter; charging
his young daughters, meanwhile, to keep plenty of
hot water in the pot, as he was uncommon dry, and
should take the indefinite quantity of "a sight of
mugs," before his thirst was appeased.

In satisfying himself, however, Mr. Toodle was
not regardless of the younger branches about him,
who, although they had made their own evening
repast, were on the lookout for irregular morsels,
as possessing a relish. These he distributed now
and then to the expectant circle, by holding out
great wedges of bread and butter, to be bitten at
by the family in lawful succession, and by serving
out small doses of tea in like manner with a spoon;
which snacks had such a relish in the mouths of
these young Toodles, that, after partaking of the
same, they performed private dances of ecstasy
among themselves, and stood on one leg apiece, and
hopped, and indulged in other saltatory tokens of
gladness. These vents for their excitement found,
they gradually closed about Mr. Toodle again, and
eyed him hard as he got through more bread and
butter and tea: affecting, however, to have no fur-

ther expectations of their own in reference to those viands, but to be conversing on foreign subjects, and whispering confidentially.

Mr. Toodle, in the midst of this family group, and setting an awful example to his children in the way of appetite, was conveying the two young Toodles on his knees to Birmingham by special engine, and was contemplating the rest over a barrier of bread and butter, when Rob the Grinder, in his sou'-wester hat and mourning slops, presented himself, and was received with a general rush of brothers and sisters.

"Well, mother!" said Rob, dutifully kissing her; "how are you, mother?"

"There's my boy!" cried Polly, giving him a hug, and a pat on the back. "Secret! Bless you, father, not he!"

This was intended for Mr. Toodle's private edification, but Rob the Grinder, whose withers were not unwrung, caught the words as they were spoken.

"What! father's been a-saying something more again me, has he?" cried the injured innocent. "Oh, what a hard thing it is that when a cove has once gone a little wrong, a cove's own father should be always a-throwing it in his face behind his back! It's enough," cried Rob, resorting to his coat-cuff in anguish of spirit, "to make a cove go and do something out of spite!"

"My poor boy!" cried Polly, "father didn't mean anything."

"If father didn't mean anything," blubbered the injured Grinder, "why did he go and say anything, mother? Nobody thinks half so bad of me as my own father does. What a unnatural thing! I wish somebody'd take and chop my head off. Father wouldn't mind doing it, I believe, and I'd much rather he did that than t'other."

At these desperate words all the young Toodles shrieked; a pathetic effect, which the Grinder improved by ironically adjuring them not to cry for him, for they ought to hate him, they ought, if they was good boys and girls; and this so touched the youngest Toodle but one, who was easily moved, that it touched him not only in his spirit, but in his wind too; making him so purple that Mr. Toodle, in consternation, carried him out to the water-butt, and would have put him under the tap, but for his being recovered by the sight of that instrument.

Matters having reached this point, Mr. Toodle explained, and the virtuous feelings of his son being thereby calmed, they shook hands, and harmony reigned again.

"Will you do as I do, Biler, my boy?" inquired his father, returning to his tea with new strength.

"No, thankee, father. Master and I had tea together."

"And how *is* master, Rob?" said Polly.

"Well, I don't know, mother; not much to boast on. There ain't no bisness done, you see. He don't know anything about it, the cap'en don't. There was a man come into the shop this very day, and says, 'I want a so-and-so,' he says — some hard name or another. 'A which?' says the cap'en. 'A so-and-so,' says the man. 'Brother,' says the cap'en, 'will you take a observation round the shop?' 'Well,' says the man, 'I've done it.' 'Do you see wot you want?' says the cap'en. 'No, I don't,' says the man. 'Do you know it wen you *do* see it?' says the cap'en. 'No, I don't,' says the

man. 'Why, then, I tell you wot, my lad,' says the cap'en, 'you'd better go back and ask wot it's like outside, for no more don't I!'"

"That ain't the way to make money, though, is it?" said Polly.

"Money, mother! He'll never make money. He has such ways as I never see. He ain't a bad master, though, I'll say that for him. But that ain't much to me, for I don't think I shall stop with him long."

"Not stop in your place, Rob!" cried his mother; while Mr. Toodle opened his eyes.

"Not in that place, p'raps," returned the Grinder with a wink. "I shouldn't wonder—friends at court, you know—but never *you* mind, mother, just now; I'm all right, that's all."

The indisputable proof afforded in these hints, and in the Grinder's mysterious manner, of his not being subject to that failing which Mr. Toodle had, by implication, attributed to him, might have led to a renewal of his wrongs, and of the sensation in the family, but for the opportune arrival of another visitor, who, to Polly's great surprise, appeared at the door, smiling patronage and friendship on all there.

"How do you do, Mrs. Richards?" said Miss Tox. "I have come to see you. May I come in?"

The cheery face of Mrs. Richards shone with a hospitable reply, and Miss Tox, accepting the proffered chair, and gracefully recognizing Mr. Toodle on her way to it, untied her bonnet strings, and said that, in the first place, she must beg the dear children, one and all, to come and kiss her.

The ill-starred youngest Toodle but one, who would appear, from the frequency of his domestic troubles, to have been born under an unlucky planet, was pre-

vented from performing his part in this general
salutation by having fixed the sou'-wester hat (with
which he had been previously trifling) deep on his
head, hind side before, and being unable to get it off
again; which accident presenting to his terrified
imagination a dismal picture of his passing the rest
of his days in darkness, and in hopeless seclusion
from his friends and family, caused him to struggle
with great violence, and to utter suffocating cries.
Being released, his face was discovered to be very
hot, and red, and damp; and Miss Tox took him on
her lap, much exhausted.

"You have almost forgotten me, sir, I dare say?"
said Miss Tox to Mr. Toodle.

"No, ma'am, no," said Toodle. "But we've all
on us got a little older since then."

"And how do you find yourself, sir?" inquired
Miss Tox blandly.

"Hearty, ma'am, thankee," replied Toodle. "How
do *you* find *your*self, ma'am? Do the rheumaticks
keep off pretty well, ma'am? We must all expect
to grow into 'em as we gets on."

"Thank you," said Miss Tox. "I have not felt
any inconvenience from that disorder yet."

"You're wery fortunate, ma'am," returned Mr.
Toodle. "Many people at your time of life, ma'am,
is martyrs to it. There was my mother —" But
catching his wife's eye here, Mr. Toodle judiciously
buried the rest in another mug of tea.

"You never mean to say, Mrs. Richards," cried
Miss Tox, looking at Rob, "that that is your —"

"Eldest, ma'am," said Polly. "Yes, indeed, it is.
That's the little fellow, ma'am, that was the innocent
cause of so much."

"This here, ma'am," said Toodle, "is him with the short legs — and they was," said Mr. Toodle, with a touch of poetry in his tone, "unusual short for leathers — as Mr. Dombey made a Grinder on."

The recollection almost overpowered Miss Tox. The subject of it had a peculiar interest for her directly. She asked him to shake hands, and congratulated his mother on his frank, ingenuous face. Rob, overhearing her, called up a look to justify the eulogium, but it was hardly the right look.

"And now, Mrs. Richards," said Miss Tox, — "and you too, sir," addressing Toodle, — "I'll tell you, plainly and truly, what I have come here for. You may be aware, Mrs. Richards — and possibly you may be aware too, sir — that a little distance has interposed itself between me and some of my friends, and that where I used to visit a good deal I do not visit now."

Polly, who, with a woman's tact, understood this at once, expressed as much in a little look. Mr. Toodle, who had not the faintest idea what Miss Tox was talking about, expressed that, also, in a stare.

"Of course," said Miss Tox, "how our little coolness has arisen is of no moment, and does not require to be discussed. It is sufficient for me to say that I have the greatest possible respect for, and interest in, Mr. Dombey;" Miss Tox's voice faltered; "and everything that relates to him."

Mr. Toodle, enlightened, shook his head, and said he had heerd it said, and, for his own part, he did think, as Mr. Dombey was a difficult subject.

"Pray don't say so, sir, if you please," returned Miss Tox. "Let me entreat you not to say so, sir, either now, or at any future time. Such observations cannot but be very painful to me; and to a gentleman, whose mind is constituted as I am quite sure yours is, can afford no permanent satisfaction."

Mr. Toodle, who had not entertained the least doubt of offering a remark that would be received with acquiescence, was greatly confounded.

"All that I wish to say, Mrs. Richards," resumed Miss Tox, — "and I address myself to you too, sir, — is this. That any intelligence of the proceedings of the family, of the welfare of the family, of the health of the family, that reaches you, will be always most acceptable to me. That I shall be always very glad to chat with Mrs. Richards about the family, and about old times. And as Mrs. Richards and I never had the least difference (though I could wish now that we had been better acquainted, but I have no one but myself to blame for that), I hope she will not object to our being very good friends now, and to my coming backwards and forwards here when I like, without being a stranger. Now, I really hope, Mrs. Richards," said Miss Tox earnestly, "that you will take this as I mean it, like a good-humored creature as you always were."

Polly was gratified, and showed it. Mr. Toodle didn't know whether he was gratified or not, and preserved a stolid calmness.

"You see, Mrs. Richards," said Miss Tox — "and I hope you see too, sir — there are many little ways in which I can be slightly useful to you, if you will make no stranger of me; and in which I shall be delighted to be so. For instance, I can teach your children something. I shall bring a few little books if you'll allow me, and some work, and

of an evening, now and then, they'll learn — dear
me, they'll learn a great deal, I trust, and be a
credit to their teacher."

Mr. Toodle, who had a great respect for learn-
ing, jerked his head approvingly at his wife, and
moistened his hands with dawning satisfaction.

"Then, not being a stranger, I shall be in nobody's way," said Miss Tox, "and everything will
go on just as if I were not here. Mrs. Richards will
do her mending, or her ironing, or her nursing,
whatever it is, without minding me: and you'll
smoke your pipe, too, if you're so disposed, sir,
won't you?"

"Thankee, mum," said Mr. Toodle. "Yes; I'll
take my bit of backer."

"Very good of you to say so, sir," rejoined Miss
Tox, "and I really do assure you now, unfeignedly,
that it will be a great comfort to me, and that whatever good I may be fortunate enough to do the
children, you will more than pay back to me, if
you'll enter into this little bargain comfortably, and
easily, and good-naturedly, without another word
about it."

The bargain was ratified on the spot; and Miss
Tox found herself so much at home already, that
without delay she instituted a preliminary examination of the children all round — which Mr. Toodle
much admired — and booked their ages, names, and
acquirements on a piece of paper. This ceremony,
and a little attendant gossip, prolonged the time
until after their usual hour of going to bed, and
detained Miss Tox at the Toodle fireside until it
was too late for her to walk home alone. The
gallant Grinder, however, being still there, politely

offered to attend her to her own door; and as it
was something to Miss Tox to be seen home by a
youth whom Mr. Dombey had first inducted into
those manly garments which are rarely mentioned
by name, she very readily accepted the proposal.

After shaking hands with Mr. Toodle and Polly,
and kissing all the children, Miss Tox left the
house, therefore, with unlimited popularity, and
carrying away with her so light a heart that it
might have given Mrs. Chick offence if that good
lady could have weighed it.

Rob the Grinder, in his modesty, would have
walked behind, but Miss Tox desired him to keep
beside her, for conversational purposes; and, as she
afterwards expressed it to his mother, " drew him
out " upon the road.

He drew out so bright, and clear, and shining,
that Miss Tox was charmed with him. The more
Miss Tox drew him out, the finer he came — like
wire. There never was a better or more promising
youth — a more affectionate, steady, prudent, sober,
honest, meek, candid young man — than Rob drew
out that night.

"I am quite glad," said Miss Tox, arrived at her
own door, "to know you. I hope you'll consider
me your friend, and that you'll come and see me as
often as you like. Do you keep a money-box ? "

" Yes, ma'am," returned Rob; "I'm saving up
against I've got enough to put in the bank, ma'am."

"Very laudable indeed," said Miss Tox. "I'm
glad to hear it. Put this half-crown into it, if you
please."

" Oh, thank you, ma'am," replied Rob, " but
really I couldn't think of depriving you."

"I commend your independent spirit," said Miss Tox, "but it's no deprivation, I assure you. I shall be offended if you don't take' it, as a mark of my good-will. Good-night, Robin."

"Good-night, ma'am," said Rob, "and thank you!"

Who ran sniggering off to get change, and tossed it away with the pieman. But they never taught honor at the Grinders' School, where the system that prevailed was particularly strong in the engendering of hypocrisy. Insomuch that many of the friends and masters of past Grinders said, If this were what came of education for the common people, let us have none. Some more rationally said, Let us have a better one. But, the governing powers of the Grinders' Company were always ready for *them*, by picking out a few boys who had turned out well, in spite of the system, and roundly asserting that they could have only turned out well because of it. Which settled the business of those objectors out of hand, and established the glory of the Grinders' Institution.

CHAPTER XIX.

TIME, sure of foot and strong of will, had so pressed onward, that the year enjoined by the old instrument-maker, as the term during which his friend should refrain from opening the sealed packet accompanying the letter he had left for him, was now nearly expired, and Captain Cuttle began to look at it of an evening with feelings of mystery and uneasiness.

The captain, in his honor, would as soon have thought of opening the parcel one hour before the expiration of the term as he would have thought of opening himself, to study his own anatomy. He merely brought it out, at a certain stage of his first evening pipe, laid it on the table, and sat gazing at the outside of it, through the smoke, in silent gravity, for two or three hours at a spell. Sometimes, when he had contemplated it thus for a pretty long while, the captain would hitch his chair, by degrees, farther and farther off, as if to get beyond the range of its fascination; but, if this were his design, he never succeeded: for even when he was brought up by the parlor wall, the packet still attracted him; or if his eyes, in thoughtful wandering, roved to the ceiling or the fire, its image immediately followed, and posted itself conspicuously among the coals, or took up an advantageous position on the whitewash.

In respect of Heart's Delight, the captain's parental regard and admiration knew no change. But, since his last interview with Mr. Carker, Captain Cuttle had come to entertain doubts whether his former intervention in behalf of that young lady and his dear boy Wal'r had proved altogether so favorable as he could have wished, and as he at the time believed. The captain was troubled with a serious misgiving that he had done more harm than good, in short; and in his remorse and modesty, he made the best atonement he could think of, by putting himself out of the way of doing any harm to any one, and, as it were, throwing himself overboard for a dangerous person.

Self-buried, therefore, among the instruments, the captain never went near Mr. Dombey's house, or reported himself in any way to Florence or Miss Nipper. He even severed himself from Mr. Perch, on the occasion of his next visit, by dryly informing that gentleman that he thanked him for his company, but had cut himself adrift from all such acquaintance, as he didn't know what magazine he mightn't blow up, without meaning of it. In this self-imposed retirement the captain passed whole days and weeks without interchanging a word with any one but Rob the Grinder, whom he esteemed as a pattern of disinterested attachment and fidelity. In this retirement, the captain, gazing at the packet of an evening, would sit smoking, and thinking of

Florence and poor Walter, until they both seemed to his homely fancy to be dead, and to have passed away into eternal youth, the beautiful and innocent children of his first remembrance.

The captain did not, however, in his musings, neglect his own improvement, or the mental culture of Rob the Grinder. That young man was generally required to read out of some book to the captain for one hour every evening; and, as the captain implicitly believed that all books were true, he accumulated, by this means, many remarkable facts. On Sunday nights the captain always read for himself, before going to bed, a certain Divine Sermon once delivered on a Mount; and although he was accustomed to quote the text, without book, after his own manner, he appeared to read it with as reverent an understanding of its heavenly spirit as if he had got it all by heart in Greek, and had been able to write any number of fierce theological disquisitions on its every phrase.

Rob the Grinder, whose reverence for the inspired writings, under the admirable system of the Grinders' School, had been developed by a perpetual bruising of his intellectual shins against all the proper names of all the tribes of Judah, and by the monotonous repetition of hard verses, especially by way of punishment, and by the parading of him at six years old in leather breeches three times a Sunday, very high up, in a very hot church, with a great organ buzzing against his drowsy head, like an exceedingly busy bee — Rob the Grinder made a mighty show of being edified when the captain ceased to read, and generally yawned and nodded while the reading was in progress. The latter fact being never so much as suspected by the good captain.

Captain Cuttle, also, as a man of business, took to keeping books. In these he entered observations on the weather, and on the currents of the wagons and other vehicles: which he observed, in that quarter, to set westward in the morning and during the greater part of the day, and eastward towards the evening. Two or three stragglers appearing in one week, who "spoke him" — so the captain entered it — on the subject of spectacles, and who, without positively purchasing, said they would look in again, the captain decided that the business was improving, and made an entry in the day-book to that effect; the wind then blowing (which he first recorded) pretty fresh, west and by north; having changed in the night.

One of the captain's chief difficulties was Mr. Toots, who called frequently, and who, without saying much, seemed to have an idea that the little back-parlor was an eligible room to chuckle in, as he would sit and avail himself of its accommodations in that regard by the half-hour together, without at all advancing in intimacy with the captain. The captain, rendered cautious by his late experience, was unable quite to satisfy his mind whether Mr. Toots was the mild subject he appeared to be, or was a profoundly artful and dissimulating hypocrite. His frequent reference to Miss Dombey was suspicious; but the captain had a secret kindness for Mr. Toots's apparent reliance on him, and forbore to decide against him for the present; merely eying him with a sagacity not to be described, whenever he approached the subject that was nearest to his heart.

"Captain Gills," blurted out Mr. Toots one day all at once, as his manner was, "do you think you could think favorably of that proposition of mine, and give me the pleasure of your acquaintance?"

"Why, I'll tell you what it is, my lad," replied the captain, who had at length concluded on a course of action; "I've been turning that there over."

"Captain Gills, it's very kind of you," retorted Mr. Toots. "I'm much obliged to you. Upon my word and honor, Captain Gills, it would be a charity to give me the pleasure of your acquaintance. It really would."

"You see, brother," argued the captain slowly, "I don't know you."

"But you never *can* know me, Captain Gills," replied Mr. Toots, steadfast to his point, "if you don't give me the pleasure of your acquaintance."

The captain seemed struck by the originality and power of this remark, and looked at Mr. Toots as if he thought there was a great deal more in him than he had expected.

"Well said, my lad," observed the captain, nodding his head thoughtfully; "and true. Now, lookee here. You've made some observations to me, which gives me to understand as you admire a certain sweet creetur. Hey?"

"Captain Gills," said Mr. Toots, gesticulating violently with the hand in which he held his hat, "admiration is not the word. Upon my honor, you have no conception what my feelings are. If I could be dyed black, and made Miss Dombey's slave, I should consider it a compliment. If, at the sacrifice of all my property, I could get transmigrated into Miss Dombey's dog — I — I really think I should never leave off wagging my tail. I should be so perfectly happy, Captain Gills!"

Mr. Toots said it with watery eyes, and pressed his hat against his bosom with deep emotion.

"My lad," returned the captain, moved to compassion, "if you're in arnest — "

"Captain Gills," cried Mr. Toots, "I'm in such a state of mind, and am so dreadfully in earnest, that if I could swear to it upon a hot piece of iron, or a live coal, or melted lead, or burning sealing-wax, or anything of that sort, I should be glad to hurt myself, as a relief to my feelings." And Mr. Toots looked hurriedly about the room, as if for some sufficiently painful means of accomplishing his dread purpose.

The captain pushed his glazed hat back upon his head, stroked his face down with his heavy hand — making his nose more mottled in the process — and planting himself before Mr. Toots, and hooking him by the lapel of his coat, addressed him in these words, while Mr. Toots looked up into his face with much attention and some wonder.

"If you're in arnest, you see, my lad," said the captain, "you're a object of clemency, and clemency is the brightest jewel in the crown of a Briton's head, for which you'll overhaul the constitution, as laid down in Rule Britannia, and, when found, *that* is the charter as them garden angels was a-singing of, so many times over. Stand by! This here proposal o' yourn takes me a little aback. And why? Because I holds my own only, you understand, in these here waters, and haven't got no consort, and maybe don't wish for none. Steady! You

hailed me first, along of a certain young lady as
you was chartered by. Now, if you and me is to
keep one another's company at all, that there young
creetur's name must never be named or referred to.
I don't know what harm mayn't have been done by
naming of it too free afore now, and thereby I
brings up short. D'ye make me out pretty clear,
brother ? "

"Well, you'll excuse me, Captain Gills," replied
Mr. Toots, "if I don't quite follow you sometimes.
But upon my word I — It's a hard thing, Captain
Gills, not to be able to mention Miss Dombey. I
really have got such a dreadful load here " — Mr.
Toots pathetically touched his shirt-front with both
hands — "that I feel, night and day, exactly as if
somebody was sitting upon me."

"Them," said the captain, "is the terms I offer.
If they're hard upon you, brother, as mayhap they
are, give 'em a wide berth, sheer off, and part company cheerily !"

"Captain Gills," returned Mr. Toots, "I hardly
know how it is, but after what you told me when I
came here for the first time, I — I feel that I'd
rather think about Miss Dombey in your society
than talk about her in almost anybody else's.
Therefore, Captain Gills, if you'll give me the
pleasure of your acquaintance, I shall be very
happy to accept it on your own conditions. I wish
to be honorable, Captain Gills," said Mr. Toots,
holding back his extended hand for a moment, "and
therefore I am obliged to say that I *can not* help
thinking about Miss Dombey. It's impossible for
me to make a promise not to think about her."

"My lad," said the captain, whose opinion of Mr.

Toots was much improved by this candid avowal, "a man's thoughts is like the wind, and nobody can't answer for 'em for certain, any length of time together. Is it a treaty as to words?"

"As to words, Captain Gills," returned Mr. Toots, "I think I can bind myself."

Mr. Toots gave Captain Cuttle his hand upon it, then and there; and the captain, with a pleasant and gracious show of condescension, bestowed his acquaintance upon him formally. Mr. Toots seemed much relieved and gladdened by the acquisition, and chuckled rapturously during the remainder of his visit. The captain, for his part, was not ill pleased to occupy that position of patronage, and was exceedingly well satisfied by his own prudence and foresight.

But rich as Captain Cuttle was in the latter quality, he received a surprise that same evening from a no less ingenuous and simple youth than Rob the Grinder. That artless lad, drinking tea at the same table, and bending meekly over his cup and saucer, having taken sidelong observations of his master for some time, who was reading the newspaper with great difficulty, but much dignity, through his glasses, broke silence by saying, —

"Oh! I beg your pardon, captain, but you mayn't be in want of any pigeons, may you, sir?"

"No, my lad," replied the captain.

"Because I was wishing to dispose of mine, captain," said Rob.

"Ay, ay?" cried the captain, lifting up his bushy eyebrows a little.

"Yes; I'm going, captain, if you please," said Rob.

"Going! Where are you going?" asked the captain, looking round at him over the glasses.

"What! didn't you know that I was going to leave you, captain?" asked Rob with a sneaking smile.

The captain put down the paper, took off his spectacles, and brought his eyes to bear on the deserter.

"Oh, yes, captain, I am going to give you warning. I thought you'd have known that beforehand, perhaps," said Rob, rubbing his hands, and getting up. "If you could be so good as provide yourself soon, captain, it would be a great convenience to me. You couldn't provide yourself by to-morrow morning, I am afraid, captain; could you, do you think?"

"And you're a-going to desert your colors, are you, my lad?" said the captain, after a long examination of his face.

"Oh, it's very hard upon a cove, captain," cried the tender Rob, injured and indignant in a moment, "that he can't give lawful warning, without being frowned at in that way, and called a deserter. You haven't any right to call a poor cove names, captain. It ain't because I'm a servant, and you're a master, that you're to go and libel me. What wrong have I done? Come, captain, let me know what my crime is, will you?"

The stricken Grinder wept, and put his coat-cuff in his eye.

"Come, captain," cried the injured youth, "give my crime a name! What have I been and done? Have I stolen any of the property? Have I set the house afire? If I have, why don't you give me in charge, and try it? But to take away the character of a lad that's been a good servant to you, because he can't afford to stand in his own light for your good, what a injury it is, and what a bad return for faithful service! This is the way young coves is spiled and drove wrong. I wonder at you. captain, I do."

All of which the Grinder howled forth in a lachrymose whine, and backing carefully towards the door.

"And so you've got another berth, have you, my lad?" said the captain, eying him intently.

"Yes, captain, since you put it in that shape, I *have* got another berth," cried Rob, backing more and more; "a better berth than I've got here, and one where I don't so much as want your good word, captain, which is fort'nate for me, after all the dirt you've throw'd at me, because I'm poor, and can't afford to stand in my own light for your good. Yes, I *have* got another berth; and if it wasn't for leaving you unprovided, captain, I'd go to it now, sooner than I'd take them names from you, because I'm poor, and can't afford to stand in my own light for your good. Why do you reproach me for being poor, and not standing in my own light for your good, captain? How can you so demean yourself?"

"Look ye here, my boy," replied the peaceful captain. "Don't you pay out no more of them words."

"Well, then, don't you pay in no more of your words, captain," retorted the roused innocent, getting louder in his whine, and backing into the shop. "I'd sooner you took my blood than my character."

"Because," pursued the captain calmly, "you have heerd, maybe, of such a thing as a rope's end."

"Oh, have I, though, captain?" cried the taunting Grinder. "No, I haven't. I never heerd of any such a article!"

"Well," said the captain, "it's my belief as you'll know more about it pretty soon, if you don't keep a bright lookout. I can read your signals, my lad. You may go."

"Oh! I may go at once, may I, captain?" cried Rob, exulting in his success. "But mind! *I* never asked to go at once, captain. You are not to take away my character again, because you send me off of your own accord. And you're not to stop any of my wages, captain!"

His employer settled the last point by producing the tin canister, and telling the Grinder's money out in full upon the table. Rob, snivelling and sobbing, and grievously wounded in his feelings, took up the pieces one by one, with a sob and a snivel for each, and tied them up separately in knots in his pocket-handkerchief; then he ascended to the roof of the house, and filled his hat and pockets with pigeons; then, came down to his bed under the counter and made up his bundle, snivelling and sobbing louder, as if he were cut to the heart by old associations; then he whined, "Good-night, captain; I leave you without malice!" and then, going out upon the doorstep, pulled the little Midshipman's nose as a parting indignity, and went away down the street grinning triumph.

The captain, left to himself, resumed his perusal of the news as if nothing unusual or unexpected had taken place, and went reading on with the greatest assiduity. But never a word did Captain Cuttle understand, though he read a vast number, for Rob the Grinder was scampering up one column and down another all through the newspaper.

It is doubtful whether the worthy captain had ever felt himself quite abandoned until now; but now, old Sol Gills, Walter, and Heart's Delight were lost to him indeed, and now Mr. Carker deceived and jeered him cruelly. They were all represented in the false Rob, to whom he had held forth many a time on the recollections that were warm within him; he had believed in the false Rob, and had been glad to believe in him; he had made a companion of him, as the last of the old ship's company; he had taken the command of the little Midshipman with him at his right hand; he had meant to do his duty by him, and had felt almost as kindly towards the boy as if they had been shipwrecked and cast upon a desert place together. And now that the false Rob had brought distrust, treachery, and meanness into the very parlor, which was a kind of sacred place, Captain Cuttle felt as if the parlor might have gone down next, and not surprised him much by its sinking, or given him any very great concern.

Therefore Captain Cuttle read the newspaper with profound attention and no comprehension, and therefore Captain Cuttle said nothing whatever about Rob to himself, or admitted to himself that he was thinking about him, or would recognize in the most distant manner that Rob had anything to do with his feeling as lonely as Robinson Crusoe.

In the same composed, business-like way the captain stepped over to Leadenhall Market in the dusk,

and effected an arrangement with a private watch-
man on duty there, to come and put up and take
down the shutters of the Wooden Midshipman every
night and morning.   He then called in at the eat-
ing-house to diminish by one-half the daily rations
theretofore supplied to the Midshipman, and at the
public-house to stop the traitor's beer.   "My young
man," said the captain, in explanation to the young
lady at the bar, "my young man having bettered
himself, miss."   Lastly, the captain resolved to take
possession of the bed under the counter, and to turn
in there o' nights instead of upstairs, as sole guardian of the property.

From this bed Captain Cuttle daily rose thence-
forth, and clapped on his glazed hat at six o'clock
in the morning, with the solitary air of Crusoe
finishing his toilet with his goatskin cap ; and although his fears of a visitation from the savage tribe,
MacStinger, were somewhat cooled, as similar apprehensions on the part of that lone mariner used to be
by the lapse of a long interval without any symptoms of the cannibals, he still observed a regular
routine of defensive operations, and never encountered a bonnet without previous survey from his
castle of retreat.   In the meantime (during which
he received no call from Mr. Toots, who wrote to
say he was out of town) his own voice began to
have a strange sound in his ears : and he acquired
such habits of profound meditation from much polishing and stowing away of the stock, and from
much sitting behind the counter reading, or looking
out of window, that the red rim made on his forehead by the hard glazed hat sometimes ached again
with excess of reflection.

The year being now expired, Captain Cuttle deemed it expedient to open the packet; but as he had always designed doing this in the presence of Rob the Grinder, who had brought it to him, and as he had an idea that it would be regular and ship-shape to open it in the presence of somebody, he was sadly put to it for want of a witness. In this difficulty, he hailed one day with unusual delight the announcement in the Shipping Intelligence of the arrival of the Cautious Clara, Captain John Bunsby, from a coasting voyage; and to that phil-osopher immediately despatched a letter by post, enjoining inviolable secrecy as to his place of resi-dence, and requesting to be favored with an early visit in the evening season.

Bunsby, who was one of those sages who act upon conviction, took some days to get the conviction thoroughly into his mind, that he had received a letter to this effect. But, when he had grappled with the fact and mastered it, he promptly sent his boy with the message, " He's a-coming to-night." Who, being instructed to deliver those words and disappear, fulfilled his mission like a tarry spirit charged with a mysterious warning.

The captain, well pleased to receive it, made prep-aration of pipes and rum and water, and awaited his visitor in the back-parlor. At the hour of eight, a deep lowing, as of a nautical bull, outside the shop-door, succeeded by the knocking of a stick on the panel, announced to the listening ear of Captain Cuttle that Bunsby was alongside; whom he in-stantly admitted, shaggy and loose, and with his stolid mahogany visage, as usual, appearing to have no consciousness of anything before it, but to be attentively observing something that was taking place in quite another part of the world.

"Bunsby," said the captain, grasping him by the hand, "what cheer, my lad, what cheer?"

"Shipmet," replied the voice within Bunsby, unaccompanied by any sign on the part of the commander himself, "hearty, hearty."

"Bunsby!" said the captain, rendering irrepressible homage to his genius, "here you are! a man as can give an opinion as is brighter than di'monds — and give me the lad with the tarry trousers as shines to me like di'monds bright, for which you'll overhaul the Stanfell's Budget, and when found make a note. Here you are, a man as gave an opinion in this here very place, that has come true, every letter on it," which the captain sincerely believed.

"Ay, ay!" growled Bunsby.

"Every letter," said the captain.

"For why?" growled Bunsby, looking at his friend for the first time. "Which way? If so, why not? Therefore."

With these oracular words — they seemed almost to make the captain giddy; they launched him upon such a sea of speculation and conjecture — the sage submitted to be helped off with his pilot coat, and accompanied his friend into the back-parlor, where his hand presently alighted on the rum-bottle, from which he brewed a stiff glass of grog; and presently afterwards on a pipe, which he filled, lighted, and began to smoke.

Captain Cuttle, imitating his visitor in the matter of these particulars, though the rapt and imperturbable manner of the great commander was far above his powers, sat in the opposite corner of the fireside, observing him respectfully, and as if he waited for some encouragement or expression of curiosity on Bunsby's part which should lead him to his own affairs. But as the mahogany philosopher gave no evidence of being sentient of anything but warmth and tobacco, except once, when, taking his pipe from his lips to make room for his glass, he incidentally remarked, with exceeding gruffness, that his name was Jack Bunsby — a declaration that presented but small opening for conversation — the captain, bespeaking his attention in a short complimentary exordium, narrated the whole history of Uncle Sol's departure, with the change it had produced in his own life and fortunes; and concluded by placing the packet on the table.

After a long pause Mr. Bunsby nodded his head.

" Open ? " said the captain.

Bunsby nodded again.

The captain accordingly broke the seal, and disclosed to view two folded papers, of which he severally read the indorsements, thus: " Last Will and Testament of Solomon Gills." " Letter for Ned Cuttle."

Bunsby, with his eye on the coast of Greenland, seemed to listen for the contents. The captain therefore hemmed to clear his throat, and read the letter aloud.

" ' My dear Ned Cuttle. When I left home for the West Indies — ' "

Here the captain stopped, and looked hard at Bunsby, who looked fixedly at the coast of Greenland.

" ' — In forlorn search of intelligence of my dear

boy, I knew that, if you were acquainted with my
design, you would thwart it, or accompany me; and
therefore I kept it secret. If you ever read this
letter, Ned, I am likely to be dead. You will easily
forgive an old friend's folly then, and will feel for
the restlessness and uncertainty in which he wandered away on such a wild voyage. So no more of
that. I have little hope that my poor boy will ever
read these words, or gladden your eyes with the sight
of his frank face any more.' No, no; no more," said
Captain Cuttle, sorrowfully meditating; "no more.
There he lays, all his days — "

Mr. Bunsby, who had a musical ear, suddenly bel-
lowed, "In the Bays of Biscay, O!" which so affected
the good captain, as an appropriate tribute to departed worth, that he shook him by the hand in
acknowledgment, and was fain to wipe his eyes.

"Well, well!" said the captain with a sigh, as the
lament of Bunsby ceased to ring and vibrate in the
skylight. "Affliction sore, long time he bore, and
let us overhaul the wollume, and there find it."

"Physicians," observed Bunsby, "was in vain."

"Ay, ay, to be sure," said the captain; "what's
the good o' *them* in two or three hundred fathom
o' water?" Then, returning to the letter, he read
on: — " 'But if he should be by when it is opened;'"
the captain involuntarily looked round, and shook
his head; "'or should know of it at any other
time;'" the captain shook his head again; "'my
blessing on him! In case the accompanying paper
is not legally written, it matters very little, for
there is no one interested but you and he, and my
plain wish is, that if he is living he should have
what little there may be, and if (as I fear) other-

wise, that you should have it, Ned. You will respect my wish, I know. God bless you for it, and for all your friendliness, besides, to SOLOMON GILLS.' Bunsby!" said the captain, appealing to him solemnly, "what do you make of this? There you sit, a man as has had his head broke from infancy up'ards, and has got a new opinion into it at every seam as has been opened. Now, what do you make o' this?"

"If so be," returned Bunsby with unusual promptitude, "as he's dead, my opinion is he won't come back no more. If so be as he's alive, my opinion is he will. Do I say he will? No. Why not? Because the bearings of this obserwation lays in the application on it."

"Bunsby!" said Captain Cuttle, who would seem to have estimated the value of his distinguished friend's opinions in proportion to the immensity of the difficulty he experienced in making anything out of them; "Bunsby," said the captain, quite confounded by admiration, "you carry a weight of mind easy, as would swamp one of my tonnage soon. But, in regard o' this here will, I don't mean to take no steps towards the property — Lord forbid! — except to keep it for a more rightful owner; and I hope yet as the rightful owner, Sol Gills, is living and'll come back, strange as it is that he ain't forwarded no despatches. Now, what is your opinion, Bunsby, as to stowing of these here papers away again, and marking outside as they was opened, such a day, in presence of John Bunsby and Ed'ard Cuttle?"

Bunsby, descrying no objection, on the coast of Greenland or elsewhere, to this proposal, it was

carried into execution; and that great man, bringing
his eye into the present for a moment, affixed his
sign-manual to the cover, totally abstaining, with
characteristic modesty, from the use of capital letters.   Captain Cuttle, having attached his own left-
handed signature, and locked up the packet in the
iron safe, entreated his guest to mix another glass
and smoke another pipe; and doing the like himself,
fell a-musing over the fire on the possible fortunes
of the poor old instrument-maker.

And now a surprise occurred, so overwhelming and
terrific that Captain Cuttle, unsupported by the
presence of Bunsby, must have sunk beneath it, and
been a lost man from that fatal hour.

How the captain, even in the satisfaction of admit-
ting such a guest, could have only shut the door and
not locked it, of which negligence he was undoubtedly guilty, is one of those questions that must for
ever remain mere points of speculation, or vague
charges against destiny.   But, by that unlocked
door, at this quiet moment, did the fell MacStinger
dash into the parlor, bringing Alexander MacStinger
in her parental arms, and confusion and vengeance
(not to mention Juliana MacStinger, and the sweet
child's brother, Charles MacStinger, popularly known
about the scenes of his youthful sports as Chowley)
in her train.   She came so swiftly and so silently,
like a rushing air from the neighborhood of the
East India Docks, that Captain Cuttle found himself in the very act of sitting looking at her, before
the calm face with which he had been meditating
changed to one of horror and dismay.

But, the moment Captain Cuttle understood the
full extent of his misfortune, self-preservation dic-

tated an attempt at flight. Darting at the little door which opened from the parlor on the steep little range of cellar steps, the captain made a rush, head foremost, at the latter, like a man indifferent to bruises and contusions, who only sought to hide himself in the bowels of the earth. In this gallant effort he would probably have succeeded, but for the affectionate dispositions of Juliana and Chowley, who, pinning him by the legs — one of those dear children holding on to each — claimed him as their friend, with lamentable cries. In the meantime, Mrs. MacStinger, who never entered upon any action of importance without previously inverting Alexander MacStinger, to bring him within the range of a brisk battery of slaps, and then sitting him down to cool as the reader first beheld him, performed that solemn rite, as if on this occasion it were a sacrifice to the Furies; and having deposited the victim on the floor, made at the captain with a strength of purpose that appeared to threaten scratches to the interposing Bunsby.

The cries of the two elder MacStingers, and the wailing of young Alexander, who may be said to have passed a piebald childhood, forasmuch as he was black in the face during one-half of that fairy period of existence, combined to make this visitation the more awful. But when silence reigned again, and the captain, in a violent perspiration, stood meekly looking at Mrs. MacStinger, its terrors were at their height.

"Oh, Cap'en Cuttle, Cap'en Cuttle!" said Mrs. MacStinger, making her chin rigid, and shaking it in unison with what, but for the weakness of her sex, might be described as her fist. "Oh, Cap'en

Cuttle, Cap'en Cuttle, do you dare to look me in the face, and not be struck down in the herth ? "

The captain, who looked anything but daring, feebly muttered, " Stand by ! "

" Oh, I was a weak and trusting fool when I took you under *my* roof, Cap'en Cuttle, I was ! " cried Mrs. MacStinger. " To think of the benefits I've showered on that man, and the way in which I brought my children up to love and *h*onor him as if he was a father to 'em, when there ain't a 'ouse-keeper, no, nor a lodger in our street, don't know that I lost money by that man, and by his guzzlings and his muzzlings " — Mrs. MacStinger used the last word for the joint sake of alliteration and aggrava-tion, rather than for the expression of any idea — "and when they cried out one and all, shame upon him for putting upon an industrious woman, up early and late for the good of her young family, and keeping her poor place so clean that a individual might have ate his dinner, yes, and his tea too, if he was so disposed, off any one of the floors or stairs, in spite of all his guzzlings *and* his muzzlings, such was the care and pains bestowed upon him ! "

Mrs. MacStinger stopped to fetch her breath ; and her face flushed with triumph in this second happy introduction of Captain Cuttle's muzzlings.

" And he runs awa-a-a-ay ! " cried Mrs. MacStinger, with a lengthening out of the last syllable that made the unfortunate captain regard himself as the mean-est of men ; " and keeps away a twelvemonth ! From a woman ! Sitch is his conscience ! He hasn't the courage to meet her hi-i-i-igh ; " long syllable again ; " but steals away like a felion. Why, if that baby of mine," said Mrs. MacStinger with sudden rapidity, "was to offer to go and steal away, I'd do my duty as a mother by him, till he was covered with wales!"

The young Alexander, interpreting this into a positive promise, to be shortly redeemed, tumbled over with fear and grief, and lay upon the floor. exhibiting the soles of his shoes, and making such a deafening outcry, that Mrs. MacStinger found it necessary to take him up in her arms, where she quieted him, ever and anon, as he broke out again, by a shake that seemed enough to loosen his teeth.

"A pretty sort of a man is Cap'en Cuttle," said Mrs. MacStinger, with a sharp stress on the first syllable of the captain's name, "to take on for — and to lose sleep for, and to faint along of — and to think dead forsooth — and to go up and down the blessed town like a madwoman, asking questions after! Oh, a pretty sort of a man! Ha, ha, ha, ha! He's worth all that trouble and distress of mind, and much more. *That's* nothing, bless you! Ha, ha, ha, ha! Cap'en Cuttle," said Mrs. MacStinger, with severe reaction in her voice and manner, "I wish to know if you're a-coming home?"

The frightened captain looked into his hat, as if he saw nothing for it but to put it on, and give himself up.

"Cap'en Cuttle," repeated Mrs. MacStinger in the same determined manner, "I wish to know if you're a-coming home, sir?"

The captain seemed quite ready to go, but faintly suggested something to the effect of "not making so much nise about it."

"Ay, ay, ay!" said Bunsby in a soothing tone. "Awast, my lass, awast!"

"And who may YOU be, if you please?" retorted Mrs. MacStinger with chaste loftiness. "Did you ever lodge at Number Nine, Brig Place, sir? My memory may be bad, but not with me, I think. There was a Mrs. Jollson lived at Number Nine before me, and perhaps you're mistaking me for her. That is my only ways of accounting for your familiarity, sir."

"Come, come, my lass, awast, awast!" said Bunsby.

Captain Cuttle could hardly believe it, even of this great man, though he saw it done with his waking eyes; but Bunsby, advancing boldly, put his shaggy blue arm round Mrs. MacStinger, and so softened her by his magic way of doing it, and by these few words — he said no more — that she melted into tears after looking upon him for a few moments, and observed that a child might conquer her now, she was so low in her courage.

Speechless and utterly amazed, the captain saw him gradually persuade this inexorable woman into the shop, return for rum and water and a candle, take them to her, and pacify her without appearing to utter one word. Presently he looked in with his pilot coat on, and said, "Cuttle, I'm a-going to act as convoy home;" and Captain Cuttle, more to his confusion than if he had been put in irons himself for safe transport to Brig Place, saw the family pacifically filing off, with Mrs. MacStinger at their head. He had scarcely time to take down his canister, and stealthily convey some money into the hands of Juliana MacStinger, his former favorite, and Chowley, who had the claim upon him that he was naturally of a maritime build, before the Midshipman was abandoned by them all ; and Bunsby, whispering that he'd carry on smart, and hail Ned Cuttle again before he went aboard, shut the door upon himself, as the last member of the party.

Some uneasy ideas that he must be walking in his sleep, or that he had been troubled with phantoms, and not a family of flesh and blood, beset the captain at first, when he went back to the little parlor, and found himself alone. Illimitable faith in, and immeasurable admiration of, the commander of the Cautious Clara, succeeded, and threw the captain into a wondering trance.

Still, as time wore on, and Bunsby failed to reappear, the captain began to entertain uncomfortable doubts of another kind. Whether Bunsby had been artfully decoyed to Brig Place, and was there detained in safe custody as hostage for his friend ; in which case it would become the captain, as a man of honor, to release him by the sacrifice of his own liberty. Whether he had been attacked and defeated by Mrs. MacStinger, and was ashamed to show himself after his discomfiture. Whether Mrs. MacStinger, thinking better of it, in the uncertainty of her temper, had turned back to board the Midshipman again, and Bunsby, pretending to conduct her by a short cut, was endeavoring to lose the family amid the wilds and savage places of the city. Above all, what it would behoove him, Captain Cuttle, to do, in case of his hearing no move, either of the MacStingers or of Bunsby, which, in these wonderful and unforeseen conjunctions of events, might possibly happen.

He debated all this until he was tired ; and still no Bunsby. He made up his bed under the counter, all ready for turning in; still no Bunsby. At length, when the captain had given him up, for that night, at least, and had begun to undress, the sound of approaching wheels was heard, and, stopping at the door, was succeeded by Bunsby's hail.

The captain trembled to think that Mrs. Mac-Stinger was not to be got rid of and had been brought back in a coach.

But no. Bunsby was accompanied by nothing but a large box, which he hauled into the shop with his own hands, and as soon as he had hauled in, sat upon. Captain Cuttle knew it for the chest he had left at Mrs. MacStinger's house, and looking, candle in hand, at Bunsby more attentively, believed that he was three sheets in the wind, or, in plain words, drunk. It was difficult, however, to be sure of this; the commander having no trace of expression in his face when sober.

"Cuttle," said the commander, getting off the chest, and opening the lid, "are these here your traps?"

Captain Cuttle looked in and identified his property.

"Done pretty taut and trim, hey, shipmet?" said Bunsby.

The grateful and bewildered captain grasped him by the hand, and was launching into a reply expressive of his astonished feelings, when Bunsby disengaged himself by a jerk of his wrist, and seemed to make an effort to wink with his revolving eye, the only effect of which attempt, in his condition, was nearly to overbalance him. He then abruptly opened the door, and shot away to rejoin the Cautious Clara with all speed — supposed to be his invariable custom, whenever he considered he had made a point.

As it was not his humor to be often sought, Captain Cuttle decided not to go or send to him next day, or until he should make his gracious pleasure known in such wise, or, failing that, until some little time should have elapsed. The captain, therefore, renewed his solitary life next morning, and thought profoundly, many mornings, noons, and nights, of old Sol Gills, and Bunsby's sentiments concerning him, and the hopes there were of his return. Much of such thinking strengthened Captain Cuttle's hopes; and he humored them and himself by watching for the instrument-maker at the door, as he ventured to do now, in his strange liberty — and setting his chair in its place, and arranging the little parlor as it used to be, in case he should come home unexpectedly. He likewise, in his thoughtfulness, took down a certain little miniature of Walter as a schoolboy from its accustomed nail, lest it should shock the old man on his return. The captain had his presentiments, too, sometimes, that he would come on such a day; and one particular Sunday, even ordered a double allowance of dinner, he was so sanguine. But come old Solomon did not. And still the neighbors noticed how the seafaring man in the glazed hat stood at the shop-door of an evening, looking up and down the street.

CHAPTER XX.

DOMESTIC RELATIONS.

It was not in the nature of things that a man of Mr. Dombey's mood, opposed to such a spirit as he had raised against himself, should be softened in the imperious asperity of his temper; or that the cold, hard armor of pride, in which he lived encased, should be made more flexible by constant collision with haughty scorn and defiance. It is the curse of such a nature — it is a main part of the heavy retribution on itself it bears within itself — that while deference and concession swell its evil qualities, and are the food it grows upon, resistance, and a questioning of its exacting claims, foster it too, no less. The evil that is in it finds equally its means of growth and propagation in opposites. It draws support and life from sweets and bitters: bowed down before, or unacknowledged, it still enslaves the breast in which it has its throne; and, worshipped or rejected, is as hard a master as the Devil in dark fables.

Towards his first wife, Mr. Dombey, in his cold and lofty arrogance, had borne himself like the removed being he almost conceived himself to be. He had been "Mr. Dombey" with her when she

first saw him, and he was "Mr. Dombey" when she
died. He had asserted his greatness during their
whole married life, and she had meekly recognized
it. He had kept his distant seat of state on the top
of his throne, and she her humble station on its
lowest step; and much good it had done him, so to
live in solitary bondage to his one idea. He had
imagined that the proud character of his second
wife would have been added to his own — would
have merged into it, and exalted his greatness. He
had pictured himself haughtier than ever, with
Edith's haughtiness subservient to his. He had
never entertained the possibility of its arraying
itself against him. And now, when he found it
rising in his path at every step and turn of his
daily life, fixing its cold, defiant, and contemptuous
face upon him, this pride of his, instead of withering, or hanging down its head beneath the shock,
put forth new shoots, became more concentrated and
intense, more gloomy, sullen, irksome, and unyielding, than it had ever been before.

Who wears such armor, too, bears with him ever
another heavy retribution. It is of proof against
conciliation, love, and confidence; against all gentle
sympathy from without, all trust, all tenderness, all
soft emotion; but, to deep stabs in the self-love, it
is as vulnerable as the bare breast to steel; and such
tormenting festers rankle there as follow on no other
wounds, no, though dealt with the mailed hand of
pride itself, on weaker pride, disarmed and thrown
down.

Such wounds were his. He felt them sharply, in
the solitude of his old rooms; whither he now began
often to retire again, and pass long solitary hours.

It seemed his fate to be ever proud and powerful;
ever humbled and powerless where he would be
most strong. Who seemed fated to work out that
doom ?

Who ? Who was it who could win his wife as she
had won his boy ? Who was it who had shown him
that new victory, as he sat in the dark corner ? Who
was it whose least word did what his utmost means
could not ? Who was it who, unaided by his love,
regard, or notice, thrived and grew beautiful when
those so aided died ? Who could it be, but the
same child at whom he had often glanced uneasily
in her motherless infancy, with a kind of dread lest
he might come to hate her; and of whom his foreboding was fulfilled, for he DID hate her in his
heart ?

Yes, and he would have it hatred, and he made it
hatred, though some sparkles of the light in which
she had appeared before him, on the memorable
night of his return home with his bride, occasionally
hung about her still. He knew now that she was
beautiful; he did not dispute that she was graceful
and winning, and that in the bright dawn of her
womanhood she had come upon him, a surprise.
But he turned even this against her. In his sullen
and unwholesome brooding, the unhappy man, with
a dull perception of his alienation from all hearts,
and a vague yearning for what he had all his life
repelled, made a distorted picture of his rights and
wrongs, and justified himself with it against her.
The worthier she promised to be of him, the greater
claim he was disposed to antedate upon her duty
and submission. When had she ever shown him
duty and submission ? Did she grace his life — or.

Edith's? Had her attractions been manifested first to him — or Edith? Why, he and she had never been, from her birth, like father and child! They had always been estranged. She had crossed him every way and everywhere. She was leagued against him now. Her very beauty softened natures that were obdurate to him, and insulted him with an unnatural triumph.

It may have been that in all this there were mutterings of an awakened feeling in his breast, however selfishly aroused by his position of disadvantage, in comparison with what she might have made his life. But he silenced the distant thunder with the rolling of his sea of pride. He would bear nothing but his pride. And in his pride, a heap of inconsistency, and misery, and self-inflicted torment, he hated her.

To the moody, stubborn, sullen demon that possessed him, his wife opposed her different pride in its full force. They never could have led a happy life together; but nothing could have made it more unhappy than the wilful and determined warfare of such elements. His pride was set upon maintaining his magnificent supremacy, and forcing recognition of it from her. She would have been racked to death, and turned but her haughty glance of calm, inflexible disdain upon him to the last. Such recognition from Edith! He little knew through what a storm and struggle she had been driven onward to the crowning honor of his hand. He little knew how much she thought she had conceded when she suffered him to call her wife.

Mr. Dombey was resolved to show her that he was supreme. There must be no will but his. Proud he desired that she should be, but she must be proud for, not against him. As he sat alone, hardening, he would often hear her go out and come home, treading the round of London life with no more heed of his liking or disliking, pleasure or displeasure, than if he had been her groom. Her cold, supreme indifference — his own unquestioned attribute usurped — stung him more than any other kind of treatment could have done; and he determined to bend her to his magnificent and stately will.

He had been long communing with these thoughts, when one night he sought her in her own apartment, after he had heard her return home late. She was alone, in her brilliant dress, and had but that moment come from her mother's room. Her face was melancholy and pensive when he came upon her; but it marked him at the door; for, glancing at the mirror before it, he saw immediately, as in a picture-frame, the knitted brow and darkened beauty that he knew so well.

"Mrs. Dombey," he said, entering, "I must beg leave to have a few words with you."

"To-morrow," she replied.

"There is no time like the present, madam," he returned. "You mistake your position. I am used to choose my own times; not to have them chosen for me. I think you scarcely understand who and what I am, Mrs. Dombey."

"I think," she answered, "that I understand you very well."

She looked upon him as she said so, and folding her white arms, sparkling with gold and gems, upon her swelling breast, turned away her eyes.

If she had been less handsome, and less stately in her cold composure, she might not have had the power of impressing him with the sense of disadvantage that penetrated through his utmost pride. But she had the power, and he felt it keenly. He glanced round the room: saw how the splendid means of personal adornment, and the luxuries of dress, were scattered here and there, and disregarded; not in mere caprice and carelessness (or so he thought), but in a steadfast, haughty disregard of costly things: and felt it more and more. Chaplets of flowers, plumes of feathers, jewels, laces, silks and satins; look where he would, he saw riches despised, poured out, and made of no account. The very diamonds — a marriage gift — that rose and fell impatiently upon her bosom, seemed to pant to break the chain that clasped them round her neck, and roll down on the floor where she might tread upon them.

He felt his disadvantage, and he showed it. Solemn and strange among this wealth of color and voluptuous glitter, strange and constrained towards its haughty mistress, whose repellent beauty it repeated, and presented all around him, as in so many fragments of a mirror, he was conscious of embarrassment and awkwardness. Nothing that ministered to her disdainful self-possession could fail to gall him. Galled and irritated with himself, he sat down, and went on in no improved humor, —

"Mrs. Dombey, it is very necessary that there should be some understanding arrived at between us. Your conduct does not please me, madam."

She merely glanced at him again, and again averted her eyes; but she might have spoken for an hour, and expressed less.

"I repeat, Mrs. Dombey, does not please me. I

have already taken occasion to request that it may be corrected. I now insist upon it."

"You chose a fitting occasion for your first re-monstrance, sir, and you adopt a fitting manner and a fitting word for your second. *You* insist! To *me!*"

"Madam," said Mr. Dombey with his most offensive air of state, "I have made you my wife. You bear my name. You are associated with my position and my reputation. I will not say that the world in general may be disposed to think you honored by that association; but I will say that I am accustomed to 'insist' to my connections and dependents."

"Which may you be pleased to consider me?" she asked.

"Possibly I may think that my wife should partake — or does partake, and cannot help herself — of both characters, Mrs. Dombey."

She bent her eyes upon him steadily, and set her trembling lips. He saw her bosom throb, and saw her face flush and turn white. All this he could know, and did: but he could not know that one word was whispering in the deep recesses of her heart, to keep her quiet; and that the word was Florence.

Blind idiot, rushing to a precipice! He thought she stood in awe of *him!*

"You are too expensive, madam," said Mr. Dombey. "You are extravagant. You waste a great deal of money — or what would be a great deal in the pockets of most gentlemen — in cultivating a kind of society that is useless to me, and, indeed, that upon the whole is disagreeable to me.

I have to insist upon a total change in all these respects. I know that, in the novelty of possessing a tithe of such means as fortune has placed at your disposal, ladies are apt to run into a sudden extreme. There has been more than enough of that extreme. I beg that Mrs. Granger's very different experiences may now come to the instruction of Mrs. Dombey."

Still the fixed look, the trembling lips, the throbbing breast, the face now crimson and now white; and still the deep whisper Florence, Florence, speaking to her in the beating of her heart.

His insolence of self-importance dilated as he saw this alteration in her. Swollen no less by her past scorn of him, and his so recent feeling of disadvantage, than by her present submission (as he took it to be), it became too mighty for his breast, and burst all bounds. Why, who could long resist his lofty will and pleasure? He had resolved to conquer her, and look here!

"You will further please, madam," said Mr. Dombey in a tone of sovereign command, "to understand distinctly, that I am to be deferred to and obeyed. That I must have a positive show and confession of deference before the world, madam. I am used to this. I require it as my right. In short, I will have it. I consider it no unreasonable return for the worldly advancement that has befallen you; and I believe nobody will be surprised, either at its being required from you, or at your making it. — To me — to me!" he added with emphasis.

No word from her. No change in her. Her eyes upon him.

"I have learnt from your mother, Mrs. Dombey," said Mr. Dombey with magisterial importance, "what no doubt you know, namely, that Brighton is recommended for her health. Mr. Carker has been so good — "

She changed suddenly. Her face and bosom glowed as if the red light of an angry sunset had been flung upon them. Not unobservant of the change, and putting his own interpretation upon it, Mr. Dombey resumed, —

"Mr. Carker has been so good as to go down and secure a house there for a time. On the return of the establishment to London, I shall take such steps for its better management as I consider necessary. One of these will be the engagement, at Brighton (if it is to be effected), of a very respectable reduced person there, a Mrs. Pipchin, formerly employed in a situation of trust in my family, to act as house-keeper. An establishment like this, presided over but nominally, Mrs. Dombey, requires a competent head."

She had changed her attitude before he arrived at these words, and now sat — still looking at him fixedly — turning a bracelet round and round upon her arm; not winding it about with a light, womanly touch, but pressing and dragging it over the smooth skin, until the white limb showed a bar of red.

"I observed," said Mr. Dombey — "and this concludes what I deem it necessary to say to you at present, Mrs. Dombey — I observed a moment ago, madam, that my allusion to Mr. Carker was received in a peculiar manner. On the occasion of my happening to point out to you, before that confidential agent, the objection I had to your mode of receiving my visitors, you were pleased to object to his presence. You will have to get the better of that objection, madam, and to accustom yourself to it, very probably, on many similar occasions; unless you adopt the remedy which is in your own hands, of giving me no cause of complaint. Mr. Carker," said Mr. Dombey, who, after the emotion he had just seen, set great store by this means of reducing his proud wife, and who was perhaps sufficiently willing to exhibit his power to that gentleman in a new and triumphant aspect, " Mr. Carker being in my confidence, Mrs. Dombey, may very well be in yours to such an extent. I hope, Mrs. Dombey," he continued after a few moments, during which, in his increasing haughtiness, he had improved on his idea, " I may not find it necessary ever to intrust Mr. Carker with any message of objection or remonstrance to you; but as it would be derogatory to my position and reputation to be frequently holding trivial disputes with a lady upon whom I have conferred the highest distinction that it is in my power to bestow, I shall not scruple to avail myself of his services if I see occasion."

" And now," he thought, rising in his moral magnificence, and rising a stiffer and more impenetrable man than ever, "she knows me and my resolution."

The hand that had so pressed the bracelet was laid heavily upon her breast, but she looked at him still with an unaltered face, and said in a low voice, —

" Wait! For God's sake! I must speak to you."

Why did she not, and what was the inward struggle that rendered her incapable of doing so for minutes, while, in the strong constraint she put upon her face, it was as fixed as any statue's — looking upon him with neither yielding nor unyielding, liking nor hatred, pride nor humility: nothing but a searching gaze?

"Did I ever tempt you to seek my hand? Did I ever use any art to win you? Was I ever more conciliating to you, when you pursued me, than I have been since our marriage? Was I ever other to you than I am?"

"It is wholly unnecessary, madam," said Mr. Dombey, "to enter upon such discussions."

"Did you think I loved you? Did you know I did not? Did you ever care, man! for my heart, or propose to yourself to win the worthless thing? Was there any poor pretence of any in our bargain? Upon your side, or on mine?"

"These questions," said Mr. Dombey, "are all wide of the purpose, madam."

She moved between him and the door to prevent his going away, and, drawing her majestic figure to its height, looked steadily upon him still.

"You answer each of them. You answer me before I speak, I see. How can you help it; you who know the miserable truth as well as I? Now, tell me. If I loved you to devotion, could I do more than render up my whole will and being to you, as you have just demanded? If my heart were pure and all untried, and you its idol, could you ask more? could you have more?"

"Possibly not, madam," he returned coolly.

"You know how different I am. You see me looking on you now, and you can read the warmth of passion for you that is breathing in my face."

Not a curl of the proud lip, not a flash of the dark eye, nothing but the same intent and searching look, accompanied these words. "You know my general history. You have spoken of my mother. Do you think you can degrade, or bend or break, *me* to submission and obedience ? "

Mr. Dombey smiled, as he might have smiled at an inquiry whether he thought he could raise ten thousand pounds.

"If there is anything unusual here," she said, with a slight motion of her hand before her brow, which did not for a moment flinch from its immovable and otherwise expressionless gaze, "as I know there are unusual feelings here," raising the hand she pressed upon her bosom, and heavily returning it, "consider that there is no common meaning in the appeal I am going to make you. Yes, for I am going" — she said it as in prompt reply to something in his face — "to appeal to you."

Mr. Dombey, with a slightly condescending bend of his chin that rustled and crackled his stiff cravat, sat down on a sofa that was near him, to hear the appeal.

"If you can believe that I am of such a nature now," — he fancied he saw tears glistening in her eyes, and he thought, complacently, that he had forced them from her, though none fell on her cheek, and she regarded him as steadily as ever, — "as would make what I now say almost incredible to myself, said to any man who had become my husband, but, above all, said to you, you may, perhaps, attach the greater weight to it. In the dark end to which we are tending, and may come, we shall not involve ourselves alone (that might not be much), but others."

Others! He knew at whom that word pointed, and frowned heavily.

"I speak to you for the sake of others. Also your own sake; and for mine. Since our marriage you have been arrogant to me; and I have repaid you in kind. You have shown to me and every one around us, every day and hour, that you think I am graced and distinguished by your alliance. I do not think so, and have shown that too. It seems you do not understand, or (so far as your power can go) intend that each of us shall take a separate course; and you expect from me, instead, a homage you will never have."

Although her face was still the same, there was emphatic confirmation of this "Never" in the very breath she drew.

"I feel no tenderness towards you; that you know. You would care nothing for it, if I did or could. I know as well that you feel none towards me. But we are linked together; and in the knot that ties us, as I have said, others are bound up. We must both die; we are both connected with the dead already, each by a little child. Let us forbear."

Mr. Dombey took a long respiration, as if he would have said, Oh! was *this* all?

"There is no wealth," she went on, turning paler as she watched him, while her eyes grew yet more lustrous in their earnestness, "that could buy these words of me, and the meaning that belongs to them. Once cast away as idle breath, no wealth or power can bring them back. I mean them; I have weighed them; and I will be true to what I undertake. If you will promise to forbear on your part, I will promise to forbear on mine. We are a most unhappy pair, in whom, from different causes, every sentiment that blesses marriage, or justifies it, is rooted out; but in the course of time, some friendship, or some fitness for each other, may arise between us. I will try to hope so, if you will make the endeavor too; and I will look forward to a better and a happier use of age than I have made of youth or prime."

Throughout she had spoken in a low, plain voice, that neither rose nor fell; ceasing, she dropped the hand with which she had enforced herself to be so passionless and distinct, but not the eyes with which she had so steadfastly observed him.

"Madam," said Mr. Dombey with his utmost dignity, "I cannot entertain any proposal of this extraordinary nature."

She looked at him yet, without the least change.

"I cannot," said Mr. Dombey, rising as he spoke, "consent to temporize or treat with you, Mrs. Dombey, upon a subject as to which you are in possession of my opinions and expectations. I have stated my *ultimatum*, madam, and have only to request your very serious attention to it."

To see the face change to its old expression, deepened in intensity! To see the eyes droop as from some mean and odious object! To see the lighting of the haughty brow! To see scorn, anger, indignation, and abhorrence starting into light, and the pale blank earnestness vanish like a mist! He could not choose but look, although he looked to his dismay.

"Go, sir!" she said, pointing with an imperious hand towards the door. "Our first and last confidence is at an end. Nothing can make us stranger to each other than we are henceforth."

"I shall take my rightful course, madam," said Mr. Dombey, "undeterred, you may be sure, by any general declamation."

She turned her back upon him, and, without reply, sat down before her glass.

"I place my reliance on your improved sense of duty, and more correct feeling, and better reflection, madam," said Mr. Dombey.

She answered not one word. He saw no more expression of any heed of him, in the mirror, than if he had been an unseen spider on the wall, or beetle on the floor, or rather, than if he had been the one or other, seen and crushed when she last turned from him, and forgotten among the ignominious and dead vermin of the ground.

He looked back, as he went out at the door, upon the well-lighted and luxurious room, the beautiful and glittering objects everywhere displayed, the shape of Edith in its rich dress seated before her glass, and the face of Edith as the glass presented it to him; and he betook himself to his old chamber of cogitation, carrying away with him a vivid picture in his mind of all these things, and a rambling and unaccountable speculation (such as sometimes comes into a man's head) how they would all look when he saw them next.

For the rest, Mr. Dombey was very taciturn, and very dignified, and very confident of carrying out his purpose; and remained so.

He did not design accompanying the family to Brighton; but he graciously informed Cleopatra at breakfast, on the morning of departure, which arrived a day or two afterwards, that he might be expected down soon. There was no time to be lost in getting Cleopatra to any place recommended as being salutary; for, indeed, she seemed upon the wane, and turning of the earth earthy.

Without having undergone any decided second attack of her malady, the old woman seemed to have crawled backward in her recovery from the first. She was more lean and shrunken, more uncertain in her imbecility, and made stranger confusions in her mind and memory. Among other symptoms of this last affliction, she fell into the habit of confounding the names of her two sons-in-law, the living and the deceased; and in general called Mr. Dombey either "Grangeby," or "Domber," or indifferently both.

But she was youthful, very youthful, still; and in her youthfulness she appeared at breakfast, before going away, in a new bonnet, made express, and a travelling robe that was embroidered and braided like an old baby's. It was not easy to put her into a flyaway bonnet now, or to keep the bonnet in its place on the back of her poor nodding head, when it was got on. In this instance, it had not only the extraneous effect of being always on one side, but of being perpetually tapped on the crown by Flowers the maid, who attended in the background during breakfast to perform that duty.

"Now, my dearest Grangeby," said Mrs. Skewton, "you must posively prom," she cut some of her words short, and cut out others altogether, "come down very soon."

"I said just now, madam," returned Mr. Dombey loudly and laboriously, "that I am coming in a day or two."

"Bless you, Domber!"

Here the major, who was come to take leave of the ladies, and who was staring through his apoplectic eyes at Mrs. Skewton's face, with the disinterested composure of an immortal being, said, —

"Begad, ma'am, you don't ask old Joe to come!"

"Sterious wretch, who's he?" lisped Cleopatra. But a tap on the bonnet from Flowers seeming to jog her memory, she added, "Oh! You mean yourself, you naughty creature!"

"Devilish queer, sir," whispered the major to Mr. Dombey. "Bad case. Never *did* wrap up enough;" the major being buttoned to the chin. "Why, who should J. B. mean by Joe, but old Joe Bagstock — Joseph — your slave — Joe, ma'am? Here! Here's the man! Here are the Bagstock bellows, ma'am!" cried the major, striking himself a sounding blow on the chest.

"My dearest Edith — Grangeby — it's most trordinry thing," said Cleopatra pettishly, "that Major —"

"Bagstock! J. B.!" cried the major, seeing that she faltered for his name.

"Well, it don't matter," said Cleopatra. "Edith, my love, you know I never could remember names — what was it? oh! — most trordinry thing that so many people want come down see me. I'm not going for long. I'm coming back. Surely they can wait till I come back!"

Cleopatra looked all round the table as she said it, and appeared very uneasy.

"I won't have visitors — really don't want visitors," she said; "little repose — and all that sort of thing — is what I quire. No odious brutes must proach me till I've shaken off this numbness;" and, in a grisly resumption of her coquettish ways, she made a dab at the major with her fan, but over-set Mr. Dombey's breakfast-cup instead, which was in quite a different direction.

Then she called for Withers, and charged him to see particularly that word was left about some trivial alterations in her room, which must be all made before she came back, and which must be set about immediately, as there was no saying how soon she might come back; for she had a great many engagements, and all sorts of people to call upon. Withers received these directions with becoming deference, and gave his guarantee for their execution; but when he withdrew a pace or two behind her it appeared as if he couldn't help look-ing strangely at the major, who couldn't help look-ing strangely at Mr. Dombey, who couldn't help looking strangely at Cleopatra, who couldn't help nodding her bonnet over one eye, and rattling her knife and fork upon her plate in using them as if she were playing castanets.

Edith alone never lifted her eyes to any face at the table, and never seemed dismayed by anything her mother said or did. She listened to her dis-jointed talk, or at least turned her head towards her when addressed; replied in a few low words when necessary; and sometimes stopped her when she was rambling, or brought her thoughts back with a monosyllable to the point from which they had strayed. The mother, however unsteady in other things, was constant in this — that she was always observant of her. She would look at the beautiful face, in its marble stillness and severity, now with a kind of fearful admiration; now in a giggling, foolish effort to move it to a smile; now with capricious tears and jealous shakings of her head, as imagining herself neglected by it; always with an attraction towards it, that never fluctuated like her other ideas, but had constant possession of her. From Edith she would sometimes look at Florence, and back again at Edith, in a manner that was wild enough; and sometimes she would try to look elsewhere, as if. to escape from her daughter's face; but back to it she seemed forced to come, although it never sought hers unless sought, or troubled her with one single glance.

The breakfast concluded, Mrs. Skewton, affecting to lean girlishly upon the major's arm, but heavily supported on the other side by Flowers the maid, and propped up behind by Withers the page, was conducted to the carriage, which was to take her, Florence, and Edith to Brighton.

"And is Joseph absolutely banished?" said the major, thrusting in his purple face over the steps. "Damme, ma'am, is Cleopatra so hard-hearted as to forbid her faithful Antony Bagstock to approach the presence?"

"Go along!" said Cleopatra; "I can't bear you. You shall see me when I come back, if you are very good."

"Tell Joseph he may live in hope, ma'am," said the major; "or he'll die in despair."

Cleopatra shuddered and leaned back. "Edith, my dear," she said. "Tell him — "

"What?"

"Such dreadful words," said Cleopatra. "He uses such dreadful words!"

Edith signed to him to retire, gave the word to go on, and left the objectionable major to Mr. Dombey. To whom he returned whistling.

"I'll tell you what, sir," said the major, with his hands behind him, and his legs very wide asunder, "a fair friend of ours has removed to Queer Street."

"What do you mean, major?" inquired Mr. Dombey.

"I mean to say, Dombey," returned the major, "that you'll soon be an orphan-in-law."

Mr. Dombey appeared to relish this waggish description of himself so very little that the major wound up with the horse's cough as an expression of gravity.

"Damme, sir," said the major, "there is no use in disguising a fact. Joe is blunt, sir. That's his nature. If you take old Josh at all, you take him as you find him; and a de-vilish rusty, old rasper, of a close-toothed, J. B. file you *do* find him. Dombey," said the major, "your wife's mother is on the move, sir."

"I fear," returned Mr. Dombey with much philosophy, "that Mrs. Skewton is shaken."

"Shaken, Dombey!" said the major. "Smashed!"

"Change, however," pursued Mr. Dombey, "and attention may do much yet."

"Don't believe it, sir," returned the major. "Damme, sir, she never wrapped up enough. If a man don't wrap up," said the major, taking in another button of his buff waistcoat, "he has nothing to fall back upon. But some people *will* die. They *will* do it. Damme, they *will*. They're obstinate. I tell you what, Dombey, it may not be ornamental; it may not be refined; it may be rough and tough; but a little of the genuine old English Bagstock stamina, sir, would do all the good in the world to the human breed."

After imparting this precious piece of information, the major, who was certainly true blue, whatever other endowments he may have possessed or wanted, coming within the "genuine old English" classification, which has never been exactly ascertained, took his lobster eyes and his apoplexy to the club, and choked there all day.

Cleopatra, at one time fretful, at another selfcomplacent, sometimes awake, sometimes asleep, at all times juvenile, reached Brighton the same night, fell to pieces as usual, and was put away in bed; where a gloomy fancy might have pictured a more potent skeleton than the maid who should have been one, watching at the rose-colored curtains, which were carried down to shed their bloom upon her.

It was settled in high council of medical authority that she should take a carriage airing every day, and that it was important she should get out every day and walk if she could. Edith was ready to attend her — always ready to attend her, with the same mechanical attention and immovable beauty — and they drove out alone; for Edith had an uneasiness in the presence of Florence, now that her mother was worse, and told Florence, with a kiss, that she would rather they two went alone.

Mrs. Skewton, on one particular day, was in the irresolute, exacting, jealous temper that had developed itself on her recovery from her first attack. After sitting silent in the carriage watching Edith for some time, she took her hand and kissed it passionately. The hand was neither given nor withdrawn, but simply yielded to her raising of it, and being released, dropped down again, almost as if it were insensible. At this she began to whimper and moan, and say what a mother she had been, and how she was forgotten! This she continued to do at capricious intervals, even when they had alighted; when she herself was halting along with the joint support of Withers and a stick, and Edith was walking by her side, and the carriage slowly following at a little distance.

It was a bleak, lowering, windy day, and they were out upon the Downs, with nothing but a bare sweep of land between them and the sky. The mother, with a querulous satisfaction in the monotony of her complaint, was still repeating it in a low voice from time to time, and the proud form of her daughter moved beside her slowly, when there came advancing over a dark ridge before them two other figures, which in the distance were so like an exaggerated imitation of their own, that Edith stopped.

Almost as she stopped, the two figures stopped; and that one which to Edith's thinking was like a distorted shadow of her mother, spoke to the other earnestly, and with a pointing hand towards them. That one seemed inclined to turn back, but the other, in which Edith recognized enough that was like herself to strike her with an unusual feeling, not quite free from fear, came on; and then they came on together.

The greater part of this observation she made while walking towards them, for her stoppage had been momentary. Nearer observation showed her that they were poorly dressed, as wanderers about the country; that the younger woman carried knitted work or some such goods for sale; and that the old one toiled on empty-handed.

And yet, however far removed she was in dress, in dignity, in beauty, Edith could not but compare the younger woman with herself still. It may have been that she saw upon her face some traces which she knew were lingering in her own soul, if not yet written on that index; but, as the woman came on, returning her gaze, fixing her shining eyes upon her, undoubtedly presenting something of her own air and stature, and appearing to reciprocate her own thoughts, she felt a chill creep over her, as if the day were darkening, and the wind were colder.

They had now come up. The old woman holding out her hand importunately stopped to beg of Mrs. Skewton. The younger one stopped too, and she and Edith looked in one another's eyes.

"What is it that you have to sell?" said Edith.

"Only this," returned the woman, holding out her wares without looking at them. "I sold myself long ago."

"My lady, don't believe her," croaked the old woman to Mrs. Skewton; "don't believe what she says. She loves to talk like that. She's my handsome and undutiful daughter. She gives me nothing but reproaches, my lady, for all I have done for her. Look at her now, my lady, how she turns upon her poor old mother with her looks."

As Mrs. Skewton drew her purse out with a trembling hand, and eagerly fumbled for some money, which the other old woman greedily watched for —

their heads all but touching in their hurry and decrepitude — Edith interposed, —

"I have seen you," addressing the old woman, "before."

"Yes, my lady," with a courtesy. "Down in Warwickshire. The morning among the trees. When you wouldn't give me nothing. But the gentleman, *he* give me something! Oh, bless him, bless him!" mumbled the old woman, holding up her skinny hand, and grinning frightfully at her daughter.

"It's of no use attempting to stay me, Edith!" said Mrs. Skewton, angrily anticipating an objection from her. "You know nothing about it. I won't be dissuaded. I am sure this is an excellent woman, and a good mother."

"Yes, my lady, yes," chattered the old woman, holding out her avaricious hand. "Thankee, my lady. Lord bless you, my lady. Sixpence more, my pretty lady, as a good mother yourself."

"And treated undutifully enough, too, my good old creature, sometimes, I assure you," said Mrs. Skewton, whimpering. "There! shake hands with me. You're a very good old creature — full of what's-his-name — and all that. You're all affection and et cetera, ain't you?"

"Oh, yes, my lady!"

"Yes, I'm sure you are; and so's that gentlemanly creature Grangeby. I must really shake hands with you again. And now you can go, you know; and I hope," addressing the daughter, "that you'll show more gratitude, and natural what's-its-name, and all the rest of it — but I never *did* remember names — for there never was a better mother than the good old creature's been to you. Come, Edith!"

As the ruin of Cleopatra trotted off whimpering, and wiping its eyes with a gingerly remembrance of rouge in their neighborhood, the old woman hobbled another way, mumbling and counting her money. Not one word more, nor one other gesture, had been exchanged between Edith and the younger woman, but neither had removed her eyes from the other for a moment. They had remained confronted until now, when Edith, as awakening from a dream, passed slowly on.

"You're a handsome woman," muttered her shadow, looking after her; "but good looks won't save us. And you're a proud woman; but pride won't save us. We had need to know each other when we meet again!"